THE
GOOD
DOCTOR

BOOKS BY JESSICA PAYNE

Make Me Disappear
The Lucky One

THE
GOOD
DOCTOR

JESSICA PAYNE

bookouture

Published by Bookouture in 2023

An imprint of Storyfire Ltd.
Carmelite House
50 Victoria Embankment
London EC4Y 0DZ

www.bookouture.com

ISBN: 978-1-83790-257-6
eBook ISBN: 978-1-83790-256-9

To Annie, who I think would have thoroughly enjoyed this book. Miss you, friend.

CONTENT NOTE

This book contains mention of fatal illness and physician-assisted suicide. If these are potentially sensitive topics for you, please read with care.

PROLOGUE

Now

I never thought I'd get a second chance at happily ever after.

Not after what I did, and to someone I loved, no less. I don't deserve this. But if I'm lucky enough to get a do-over, I'll take it.

I walk down an empty hall, my footsteps echoing back at me. Reminding me of how my happily ever after dissolved last time. Or rather, was viciously torn apart. That memory beats in time with my heart.

A reminder.

A warning.

This time, things will be different. Because Elton is different. Elton is *good* and kind and handsome and... the list goes on. What happened before would never happen with him. He's not perfect, but he's pretty damn close. I wrap my arms around myself, smiling as I think of him, of us.

I stop in front of a steel door marked 307.

This storage facility is like every other—gray concrete walls, scuffed corners, a dark elevator, a borrowed dolly with a wobbling wheel. It's my last time coming here. We don't need a storage unit anymore—we have an entire house. Three bedrooms and two baths, a kitchen and dining room, a *basement...*

Excitement bolts through me, just thinking of it. After so long on the road, Elton and I are settling down. Getting married. I've said yes to the job of my dreams.

I reach for the lock, and it's cold in my hand. The key fits in and it opens with a satisfying click.

Behind this rolltop front sits everything I own—everything *we* own. Because we are a *we* now. An *us.* I even changed my last name early, so I didn't have to go through the hassle of getting a new license a month after starting the new job. Elton liked that—*Look, we're already Mr. and Mrs. Woods!*

Even though it's everything we own, the unit—one of their smallest—is only half-full. Stacks of boxes from our lives before we started travel nursing. Old chipped plates, a pan or two, winter-weather gear we didn't need in Southern California. I study it. Maybe we should just donate it all to charity. Start new. After years of travel nursing and saving money, we can afford it.

"You beat me here." Elton's voice comes from behind me, and I jump.

"Geez. Give a girl warning, would you?"

"Sorry." He grins and leans in, pressing his lips to mine. I expect it to be a quick smooch so we can get to loading boxes on the dolly. He's driving the moving van to Oregon on his own, six weeks ahead of me. But no. His hand snakes around my waist, pulling me close, pressing me against his warm body. His other hand gently cradles my head, urging me closer. Our breath meshes, and for a moment, we become one—breath heavy, crushed together, hearts pounding furiously.

"Elton—" I break away with a laugh.

But he maneuvers me inside the unit. Pulls down the rolltop door, shutting out the world.

"Elton," I say in a warning tone, raising a finger to wag playfully at him. "We're in a *storage* unit."

"I know." He grins, that mischievous grin, and runs a hand through his sandy hair, advancing on me. I take a step away, but he follows, and a second later, I'm pressed against a wardrobe box. "We've never done it in a storage unit."

I laugh, giving in. Storage unit it is.

Elton kisses me again. This time, I reciprocate, yanking at his shirt, pressing my mouth to his flesh, losing myself in him. In *us*.

Yes, this time will be different. We have the perfect house waiting for us in Portland. We have the perfect jobs lined up at the hospital there. And we have each other—the perfect match for our happily ever after.

This time will be perfect.

ONE

CHLOE

Now

This hospital is like all the others—bright fluorescent hallways that hide the shadows, decorated with overly cheery abstract art. You'd never guess that through the double doors a patient is taking their last breath. That in the basement sits a morgue with a dozen bodies waiting to go to the funeral home. Or that like me, a hundred providers populate the hospital, trying our damndest to keep people alive.

Mostly, we run off caffeine. The empty to-go thermos banging around in my bag is proof of my own addiction, but I reach for it and take a swig, anyway, hoping for those final sweet droplets of coffee and cream to hit my tongue. I come up empty —staring at the double-insulated mug and sighing in disgust.

I knew I should have gotten the next size up. Four more ounces can feel lifesaving on days like today, running off a few hours of sleep after a cross-country move. Hopefully, there's coffee at hospital orientation. Hopefully *good* coffee, the sort catered by a local coffee shop instead of the drivel served up by the cafeteria. I turn a corner, squeaking away in my new leather clogs, my gift to myself for graduating my nurse practitioner program and getting this job.

A door at the end of the hall is open wide, a printed-out sign proclaiming *Hospital Orientation—Providers Only*. I stop in front of it. *Providers* only. I exhale, a thrill of excitement replacing the high of caffeine. After ten years as a nurse, I'm a provider now. A fully certified nurse practitioner, trained in the ways to help people stay alive and live better. I can take my own patients, write prescriptions, do everything a doctor can short of performing surgery.

I twist the shiny rock on my ring finger and feel something inside me settle.

It's not just a new job. It's a new *life*. And I can't wait for it to start.

I straighten my shoulders and enter the room, looking around at the other white-coat-wearing men and women. Like me, they smile, anticipation in their eyes. Happy to be here—to have a new job helping people.

"Welcome." A woman with thick glasses and a name tag that says *Gabriella, Human Resources* beckons me forward. "Name?"

"Chloe Woods." I give her a smile and wait as she gathers several forms, shuffling them inside a bright folder with the hospital's logo on the front.

"Feel free to take any seat. We'll get started in just a minute." She hands over the folder, I accept it with a nod of thanks, and I turn to face my future coworkers. An empty table waits in one corner, and I meander that way, taking it all in, wanting to remember this moment.

But then I see a familiar form.

My fingers brush the table, letting the folder slide from my fingertips. I blink across the room, sure I'm just imagining things. My inner demons trying to trick me—*You thought you'd be happy? You don't deserve it, not after what you did.*

I stare, mouth gaping open. For a second, I thought I saw—

I go still, not accepting what's right in front of me. *Who* is right in front of me. It's not possible. He should be in Seattle, not here, in Portland. Not here, where I'm finally about to start my new life with my fiancé.

I'm partially hidden behind a small group of nurse practitioners, gossiping about their previous jobs. I wipe my suddenly sweat-soaked palms over my pants and remind myself to breathe. He's poised across the hospital meeting room, one hand tucked casually into a pocket, the other gesturing as he debates something with a nurse in gray scrubs. His back is to me, but I swear it's him—the broad shoulders, the way he tilts his head as the other man speaks.

I shift to one side, giving me a better view, and my heart rate spikes, pulse sounding in my ears. Sweat breaks out along the back of my neck.

He laughs, and that strong jawline, that flash of perfect teeth are unmistakable.

Jameson Smith, MD.

Ex-husband.

The reason I fled Seattle and started over.

And the love of my life.

No. After what we did, he isn't allowed to be the love of my life.

I grasp for the nearest chair and take a seat to steady my weak knees. It's impossible that he'd be here—I'm just tired. It must be someone who looks like him. It's the Pacific Northwest mountaineer look—the untrimmed beard, the hair a little shaggy, the broad shoulders because, of course, this person rock climbs or backpacks or chops wood for the fun of it, like every other man who thinks the Pacific Northwest means you need to look like a lumberjack. Just like I wear beanies and hoodies and drink coffee like it's going out of style, he just has the *look*.

Medical staff surround me, but in this moment, they fade

away. Become the background noise of what is akin to a slow-motion code blue, as I think I might pass out from shock.

I see it coming—the shifting of the black leather loafers. The moment where he freezes, catching sight of me. Like the time hiking in Montana when I turned a corner and came face-to-face with a mountain lion.

Fight or flight.

I duck my head. Maybe he didn't see my face.

He is the man I hate.

The man I love. *Loved.* Past tense. He'd all but destroyed me, my ability to trust, my ability to love. To trust myself enough to allow myself to *be* loved.

I'm a different person now. I'm strong, I'm capable, I'm worthy of love. I squeeze my eyes shut and repeat the mantra to myself.

When I open my eyes, I gaze down at my new employee folder to look anywhere but at him—yes, it's definitely him—and try to think, *think* how the hell this could have happened. The last time I saw Jameson was three years ago in Arizona. Right after I called him out for everything he did, yanked off my wedding ring, left it in a hotel room, and disappeared from his life.

We haven't spoken since. Haven't shared so much as an email or phone call. I made it clear what he'd done—what *we'd* done—was far too traumatic for me to ever speak to him again.

It's a physical sensation when his gaze lands on me, like something's hit me, knocked the air from my lungs. Solemn deep brown eyes, filled first with confusion, then widening in shock, then—

I gulp and turn away, avoiding the tumble of emotions that cross that handsome face.

Anger. Violence. A reminder of what happened three years ago.

He starts my way, slow even footsteps. Like that damn

mountain lion, stalking me like prey. My stomach flops, the coffee threatening to come back up. What I wouldn't give for an antiemetic right now, anything to calm the churning in my gut.

I open my mouth for a breath—but it comes out as a gasp, my skin itching with the desire to get up and run from this room. To find Elton, and say, *You know what, never mind—let's go back to traveling the world. This settling down thing is silly.* I press my palms to the table, push back my chair, as though I'll do exactly that.

But I can't. Elton and I are doing the *thing*—we left our old jobs behind, moved cross-country, bought a house, took on a mortgage, picked out furniture, planned a wedding—*everything.* The point being, I can't just leave this room. I can't quit this job. We're finally going to get married. Be a family.

And the worst part is, I can't do anything about Jameson. Because I'm just as guilty as he is.

TWO

CHLOE

Now

"Chloe."

Jameson's voice comes out smooth, like he's addressing a respected coworker and not his ex-wife.

It takes me too long to reply, my mind rebelling at the reality he's here—*right here in front of me.* I rack my brain for an appropriate response.

"Jameson" is what I manage. All I can do is stare, unbelieving. I thought I'd never see him again. We divorced almost immediately. My lawyer contacted his, forms were signed digitally, and we were granted a divorce. I'd expected an argument. A refusal. His lack of fight was just more proof of what he'd done, his guilty conscience, releasing me.

Until now.

His face is the same—the picture of calm. There's even a hint of a smile, though it lacks humor, more that he forced his lips to curve up in order to appear polite. Anyone else in the room might not realize he's pretending. But I once thought we were soulmates. I can read him easily enough—the tension in the clench of his jaw, the way the skin around his eyes creases, a finger tapping slowly on the table. It unnerves me. Makes me take slow, deep breaths to stay calm.

He can't hurt me here, now. We're in a hospital meeting room, surrounded by others. A flush of heat fills me, gives me courage. I'm safe for the time being, though my sympathetic nervous system clearly thinks otherwise—I'm shaking like a leaf.

His smile falters, and he drops into the seat next to mine, our shoulders brushing. I fight not to jerk back like he's scalded me. I don't want to be that woman anymore—the one who was afraid to speak up. I'm older now, I've worked all over the country, I earned my freaking doctorate to do this job. I have a right to be here.

I exhale. I just wish he wasn't here with me.

"You work here?" I ask.

"It would seem so." His voice carries an edge.

I press my lips together. "I thought you were in Seattle."

"It was time for a change of scenery."

It makes sense he'd move—that's what his sort does. It makes it harder to be caught. But to Portland, where I am? What cruel joke of the world is this?

"Oh, you've met Dr. Smith. Excellent." A woman's overly cheerful voice interrupts us. I jerk my head up to see her, a manager type with a short blonde bob and a bright smile. She adjusts her cardigan and extends a hand. "I'm Debra. You interviewed with me. And this is Dr. Smith. You'll be working primarily with him."

My mouth opens, but there are no words. Beside me, Jameson's hands curl into fists, and I know he's thinking the same thing I am—*how the hell did this happen?*

"Looks like you'll be fast friends." Debra chuckles. "Just remember, Dr. Smith, Chloe graduated her program recently, so be sure to teach her everything you know. I'm so glad you have a new nurse practitioner to work with. It's been almost two months of you on your own."

Her words penetrate but don't quite make sense. "Excuse me?" I say.

Debra just smiles. "You'll work great together."

Realization dawns, stealing what little breath I have left. Not only are we in the same city—at the same hospital—we're working together. He's the doctor I'll be working with, sharing patients, covering shifts for one another, assisting one another with procedures.

It's a coincidence. But I don't believe in coincidences. I should have picked a different specialty—anything besides critical care, *our* specialty—but it's where my passion was from day one. I just never thought I'd come face-to-face with him or, worse, have to work with him.

He waits until Debra moves on to the next staff member. He turns to me, waits until I meet his gaze, and murmurs in a low voice, "We have a lot to talk about."

My stomach bottoms out, wanting to know, but also afraid to hear whatever it is he plans to discuss.

"O-okay." I can't think of anything better to say.

"Okay?" he repeats, sarcasm raising his voice a notch. "It's not okay, Chloe. You left me. We were married and in love and had a whole life planned, and you just *left*."

It hadn't been quite that simple. Nor is he wrong. That young, naïve woman buried deep inside me wants to explain. But the part of me that's grown up and has seen the world rebels against the idea that I owe him an explanation. I think back to the letter I left. The *reason* I left.

"I didn't know you would be here," I say. It's meant to reassure him—*see, I have no intention of telling everyone what you do with your spare time! It's fine!*

He frowns as though offended. "But I am here. And so are you. You owe me answers, Chloe."

Anger makes its way through the fear. "I don't owe you anything."

He leans closer and looks right at me, anger flashing in his eyes. "Don't you?"

The door at the front of the room slaps shut, a familiar form stepping in. It's at that moment Jameson looks down and notices the ring on my hand. He follows my relieved gaze to Elton, and his jaw works. He no doubt recognizes him.

"Who is that?" But he asks like he already knows the answer.

"My fiancé."

"That guy?" he asks with a sneer. "You left me for that guy?"

"It wasn't like that." Excuses rush to the tip of my tongue, but Jameson is on his feet already.

"We need to talk more. But not here. Not now." He pauses, leaning close to whisper, "Just remember our vows."

Heat builds at my neck, my face. I struggle to understand what he's getting at. "Our vows?"

That faint, humorless smile. "Till death do we part."

I pull back and look at him, the implication in his words leaving me cold.

It's a threat.

He strides away, disappears out the door before I can speak, before Elton has a chance to realize who he is. When Elton spots me, his cyan-blue eyes light up, dimple flickering as he smiles, and he comes across the room to wrap an arm around me, press a kiss to my temple.

"How's your first day going?" he asks.

I look at him and lie, because like Jameson said, not here, not now.

"Perfect." The irony in that one word makes my heart trip.

A ripple of anxiety rushes through me. My perfect new start dissolves right before my eyes. I look up at Elton and wish I could tell him everything. But I can't. Because then he would leave me. No one who saves lives for a living could love me after what I've done.

THREE

CHLOE

Now

"I've only got five minutes, but I wanted to come see you."
Elton's eyes crinkle with his wide, dimpled smile. This close, the
dusting of freckles over his cheeks stand out, remnants of our
time in sunny California. He presses another kiss to my temple
and squeezes my hand. "I found the empty call rooms." He says
it in a suggestive voice, and usually I'd play along. Tease back.
But today, I can't. When I don't respond, he continues, "I know
you'll love it here. The coffee shop is incredible, too."

"Okay, I'll check it out." My words come out flat.

Elton's cheer dissipates in a second. "What's wrong?" He
sits beside me—right where Jameson was mere seconds ago. The
whiplash in their personalities—Jameson all dark and angry and
threatening, with Elton's sunny cheerfulness—makes me shake
my head. It's possible this is all a dream, and I'm still tucked
safely into our new bed, under our down comforter that smells
faintly of lavender, and the molded memory-foam pillows that
feel like heaven...

"Chloe. *Chloe.*"

I look at him. Whatever he sees on my face makes his eyes go wide.

"What happened?" His voice lowers to a whisper. He glances around, as though the boogeyman is waiting, and he somehow missed him.

Except Jameson is the boogeyman, and Jameson already left. Slid out of the room like a snake before Elton had a chance to notice.

I hesitate. I can't tell Elton everything. But I have to tell him this much. "Jameson is here."

Elton cocks his head. "Jameson who?"

"Who do you think?" I snap. The pen in my hand flexes beneath my sweaty hand, and I return it to the table before I break it. "Sorry." I sigh. "Jameson. My ex-husband. He's here, at this hospital. I'm supposed to work with him."

Elton's mouth gapes open like he can't quite find the words. "Wait, what? I thought he was in Seattle."

"He's here."

Elton is silent, and I search his face for his reaction—his *real* reaction, not the one he's trying to summon to put a positive spin on things, to be optimistic, to be the kindhearted, caring fiancé he is. I squirm in my seat. Elton is the most important person in my world—I don't want Jameson's appearance to screw anything up. We have a life we're starting together. A wedding we're a mere two months away from.

"I've been here over a month and haven't seen him." Elton stares into the distance a moment. "But I've been doing orientation training in classrooms. Not on the unit. So I wouldn't have seen him, I guess." He swallows. "Okay, well..." We look at one another, and I know we're both thinking the same thing—we can't afford for me to quit this job. It took months to get an interview, much less hired. We just signed a mortgage. Bought a new car. Neither of which we can afford on his income alone.

The squeal of the hospital phone on Elton's hip interrupts.

"I have to go. We'll talk tonight, okay?"

And he disappears too, leaving me alone and wondering how we're going to handle this.

* * *

Today was supposed to be a good day. The sort of day that kicks off the best part of your life—the part where you have the job you've worked hard to achieve and paid a small fortune in student loans to have. And then I'd go home to my shiny new house with my handsome, loving fiancé and we'd talk about how happy we were over a nice meal of pasta and wine. Maybe we'd even talk about starting a family. Having kids. Adopting a golden retriever, like the one I had growing up.

The things I'd wanted since my parents died. The thing I'd dreamed of. The dream Jameson had stolen from me but was finally within my grasp again.

Orientation ends, and I escape the hospital to tuck myself into my new Lexus for the drive home. This morning, which feels like years ago, I'd savored the Pacific Northwest air. The smell of pines, that clean *mountain* scent, that probably I was only imagining here in downtown Portland, but it felt like home. I don't pause to smell the air. I slam the door and lock it. Grip the steering wheel like I'm holding on for dear life.

My pulse pounds. A dull ache forms behind my eyes, a tension headache coming on. I try to come up with an explanation of how I just happened to end up in the same hospital as Jameson. It's true that the medical world is a small one—even in travel nursing, I'd run into some of the same people repeatedly. Hell, Elton and I met again months after I left Seattle when we happened to be assigned to a San Diego hospital together. But *this*, this is something else entirely.

I used a recruiter at first when we decided to come to Portland—Maggy somebody. She'd gotten me a few interviews, but none of them led to employment. This job hadn't come through her, though. It came through LinkedIn, someone who worked for the hospital itself, in HR, inviting me to apply. Recruiting through LinkedIn isn't uncommon—I get a few invitations a month. But the invite that led to this job was different. Maybe too good to be true, now that I think about it: the position I was looking for in the city I was hoping to live.

Another coincidence.

I tap my fingers over the steering wheel, but the name of the hospital recruiter doesn't come to me. I'll have to find the original message. Anyway, I'd applied, and two weeks later interviewed. And here I am.

Working with Jameson.

At first, I'd kept an eye on him from afar—googling him occasionally, checking his social media from an account under a different name. But it had been a while since I'd done that. And he rarely posted, rarely was in the spotlight.

I try to envision the three of us working on a hospital unit together. Me, the fiancé, the ex-husband. It's like a bad joke with no punchline. But at least Elton will be there—I won't be trapped alone with Jameson.

Then again, maybe that's not such a good thing. Elton doesn't know who Jameson really is—what he's done. I've never told him, because if I did, he'd want to do something about it. And if we do something about Jameson, Jameson will undoubtedly drag me down with him. If my part in it came out, Elton would never speak to me again. I'd lose everything.

We're nurses. Our job is to save people.

My phone buzzes as I come to a stoplight, and I groan, sure it's Elton again. He's been texting me all day. I know he means well but I need him to stop telling me that *it's okay* and *we'll figure something out*. He doesn't know the half of it.

But when I pick up the phone, it's not him. It's a phone number, no contact info attached. But I know who it is—I'd know that number anywhere. It's Jameson.

Jameson: *We need to talk.*

FOUR

JAMESON

Now

He had hidden in the stairwell and watched her walk down the hall. She had the same long dark hair, the same willowy form with steps like a dancer who'd just stepped off stage. He'd waited until she'd gone round the corner, then strode after her, hands in pockets, head down, like he was merely walking to get a coffee or check on a patient on the other side of the hospital.

He'd trailed behind as she tried to find her way from the new employee orientation to the elevators. He followed down the steps as she took the elevator from the fifth floor to the ground floor. When she'd tried to sort out how to get back to the parking garage—she'd gotten off a floor too early—he listened as she politely asked someone for directions. "Excuse me. I'm sorry, but I'm new. How do I get to the provider parking lot?"

A man had answered. A man who, like himself, saw she was not just another woman in scrubs. Not just another nurse— nurse practitioner now—but some ethereal creature capable of great beauty and great destruction, in equal parts.

Now, at home, Jameson pressed his forehead against the

glass of his condo, eyes squeezed shut, remembering every moment. The man—Jameson's own resident, who he knew had a girlfriend or wife or something—had flirted. Then offered to show her the way.

Jameson had ground his teeth, tightened his fists. Emotions surged through him, emotions that were a total mindfuck.

He loved her.

He despised her.

He watched as she got in a fancy new car, so unlike the old clunky one she'd loved for the years they were together. She drove away. And he felt relief and the ache of loss in equal measures as he all but collapsed to the cold concrete ground of the parking garage.

He couldn't be sure when he'd fallen in love with her. Only that he had, and it was a precarious kind of love—the obsessive kind that digs deep into your soul, that affects your every decision and, maybe, your health. The sort that leads to bad decisions.

Like the bad decision he was contemplating now.

She'd zoomed off to god knows where—except he *did* know where, he did—a little cul-de-sac just a few miles from downtown. In the opposite direction of his steel box of a condo, but close, regardless.

He could go there.

He could observe her interaction with her *fiancé*. His face puckered at the word. At the thought of Chloe with another man. But to what end? Unless he intended to do something, what was the point?

He needed a plan.

But instead, Jameson stood at a floor-to-ceiling window that faced glowing downtown Portland, reds and greens and yellows reflected in the shimmering, slow-moving Willamette River. His fists clenched, as though that would keep him from leaping into action. Into chasing after her.

He hadn't eaten all day. Had only drank coffee, to get himself through rounds, and now bourbon, to numb the revolving emotions—seething anger, pathetic helplessness, longing he thought he'd left behind when he'd so fully immersed himself in his work, when he'd left their home and moved to Portland—

But no. It was still there. *She* was still there, that flame he couldn't set down for her, flickering like one of those damn trick birthday candles you can't blow out no matter how hard you try.

His phone pinged—a familiar ping, his sister reaching out to him. Jameson pulled the phone from his pocket long enough to read the message—*I thought we were meeting for dinner? Where are you?*—then tucked it back away.

He'd forgotten Laura. But she'd forgive him. She always did.

He pulled away from the view and returned to the kitchen to refresh his drink. And if he was being honest with himself, to keep himself from going after Chloe. If he drank enough, he wouldn't drive. He couldn't risk losing his license, it would mean losing everything that mattered to him now.

Somehow, darkness had fallen while he stood there, contemplating going to her home, contemplating the past. Debating the present. Being all too aware how dangerous he and Chloe might be to one another in this circumstance.

The bourbon in hand, Jameson retreated to his office, sitting in front of a desk too wide for one person, opening up a laptop too small for someone his size. He pecked at keys, logging in to the hospital system, and skimmed his list of patients.

He saw the sickest ones. The ones in danger of dying at any moment. That's how ICUs were—the patients who needed constant care, who without it, might tumble into the abyss that was death. And he was in charge of them—the IV drips of life-sustaining medication, the settings on ventilators that delivered

oxygen to their lungs, balloon pumps that kept a heart func-
tioning well enough to get a patient to surgery.

He literally had lives in his hands at all times. It was a big
responsibility.

His phone was eternally turned up to full volume, so he'd
never miss a call that might mean a patient was on the verge of
death. After she left Seattle, his work became his life. His
passion. His reason for living.

But before she left? She was his reason.

Which meant there was a solid year where he existed in a
gray space. Neither living nor dead. He couldn't let her in
again. And now, it felt like she was a beacon, mere miles away,
calling out to him. Pulling him to her, but not with any good
intention.

This was strictly a working relationship—it *had* to be.

For more than one reason, she could be the death of him.

FIVE

CHLOE

Now

The Lexus fits neatly beside the Honda Elton and I shared these past years. When we got to Portland, we needed a second car, and he'd urged me to pick out whatever I wanted, volunteering to keep the older car himself.

At the time it seemed fun and exciting. I'd never had a new car before. It was sleek and shiny with a fancy keyless entry fob. It even *smelled* good, and I'd sat inside on the plush leather seats for a solid half hour, just taking it all in.

But now, in the dimness of the garage filled with moving boxes, Jameson's text message taunting me from where my phone sits in the passenger's seat, I'd give anything to be back in those moments from *before*. Back when it was Elton and me on the road—before we had the house, the engagement ring, the new jobs. Life was good. But I'd wanted more. A home. A family.

I cast an uneasy glance toward the phone. The garage door grinds shut behind me, enclosing me in darkness, and I sit in the car, running my fingers over the smooth leather of the steering wheel. Elton will have heard the garage door—will know I'm home and wonder why I'm sitting out here in the dark. I'm not a little girl, and I shouldn't hide. But I wish I could.

Silencing my phone, I shove it in my bag, where I can pretend it and Jameson's text don't exist. At least for a little while.

The doorknob twists beneath my hand, and I step into the kitchen. I paste a smile on my face, ready to greet my fiancé, to pretend I'm okay. But he's not there. A sparkling quartz countertop, shiny stainless steel, and no Elton. Though he has opened a bottle of wine—red—and the cork sits sideways on the counter, red wine dripping from it. It makes me think of blood—blood sprayed across a wall, which reminds me of Jameson—and I grab a paper towel to wipe it away. Light floods in from the rear windows. It should be cheerful, airy, what with the tall ceilings and brick fireplace and smattering of new furniture. Instead, it feels too big, like I'm all alone here.

"Elton?" I call his name up the stairwell, where the bedrooms are, but there's only silence.

A glance at the clock tells me it's 4:52 p.m.—a little earlier than I expected to be home. Maybe he's out on a run. Or grabbing dinner. Though we've sworn we're going domestic, we still get takeout more nights than not.

With Elton nowhere to be seen, I sift through a stack of moving boxes until I find the one labeled *Wineglasses*. If ever there was a night I needed a drink, it's tonight. I pour a glass half-full, then tip in a little more. With a long exhale, I settle into the only piece of furniture not covered in boxes, the brand-new deep red leather couch we bought. *An investment*, Elton said, when I gawked at the price tag. Now, another reason I can't escape Portland General Hospital and Jameson.

Speaking of, that text. I take a long sip of my wine, pull my phone from my bag, and read it again.

We need to talk.

It implies a need for action—for me to reply and say *Okay, about what?* Or *Okay, when?* My fingers move over the screen, hesitantly typing out one response, then the other, then deleting both.

What do I say? Or maybe I don't say anything. I mean, I'm not at work. I'm not *on the clock*, so to say. He's not my husband anymore. Despite what he said I don't *owe* him anything. My wineglass rests at my lips as I mull it over, taking one slow sip after another. We'll have to talk eventually. I mean, we'll be *working* together. *Tomorrow.*

And the words he'd whispered—*till death do we part.*

They leave my stomach tied in knots.

Nervous energy forces me to do *something*, and I pace the room, staring out floor-to-ceiling back windows that look out over a green space behind our house. It had been a perk to buying the home—a huge place our future children could play. A dog could run. But now, I notice the tall, broad maple trees. The low-lying bushes. A series of boulders. Places someone could hide, could watch us through these big windows.

God, I'm paranoid. This all started as something happy—I wanted to move back to the Pacific Northwest, and Elton agreed. We bought this big house where we would get married and start a family. I imagined all the mornings we'd drink coffee together as we got ready for work. Or how we'd take turns cooking dinner while the other poured wine and talked. I dreamed of the day I'd take a pregnancy test and it would read positive, the way he'd light up when I told him. When we toured the house virtually, I'd even picked out which room would be our baby's nursery, and with flushed cheeks, told Elton. He'd grinned and said, "I think you're right, Chloe. That would be the perfect room for our baby."

But the appearance of Jameson has me thinking all the dark thoughts, like when I spend too much time listening to true crime podcasts.

I go back to the couch, log in to LinkedIn, and search my messages for the one I got that led to me applying for the job in the first place. It takes a few minutes, but it pops up—from just over two months ago.

Dear Chloe Woods,
    We have an exciting opportunity for you to consider in Portland, Oregon! A city that sits in the shadow of Mount Hood and along the Willamette River. A rich art scene and—

I scroll past the details all recruiting messages include, trying to convince someone how much they'll love any given city or small town. At the end a name signs off:

Zoey Constance, HR Department, Portland General Hospital

It seems legit. I've received LinkedIn messages like this since I got my RN license. Though with having just graduated, this was the first I'd received to come work as a nurse practitioner. I'd jumped on it, desperate for a job. Now, I can't help but question it, how convenient it was I'd been contacted about a job in Portland—a city I both had wanted to live in *and* Jameson happened to already be working in.

I set down my phone and blow out a breath. Maybe we can find a way to keep the house while I look for another job. Maybe I could call our travel recruiter and do one last travel assignment while I do yet another job search. We'd have to push back the wedding, another expense I need this job for, but maybe—

A creak comes from behind me, and I whip around.

"Whoa. You okay?"

Elton steps into the kitchen, tool bag in one hand, still dressed in scrubs. I didn't hear him come in—didn't hear a door open or close.

"Where have you been?" My voice comes out too loud,

demanding. Adrenaline sizzles in my veins as I try to catch my breath.

He cocks his head but doesn't comment. "In the basement. I don't think it will be too hard to finish. We could probably turn it into another bedroom and a family room if we wanted to." He sets the tool bag on the counter, eyes the wine bottle, the glass in my hand. "You just get home?"

I nod, looking over at the phone that lies face up. An urge to flip it over hits me—like I should hide Jameson's text from him. The sensation makes me go hot with guilt, and I turn, take another gulp of wine. I just don't want Elton to worry. That's all. Texting with an ex-husband would make anyone paranoid.

"So." Elton grabs the wine bottle and the second glass.

"So." I take a seat at the dining room table. My gaze flickers over his bag of tools. I've always loved how handy he is. That he can fix something without calling someone for help. He was excited to have his own house to work on, his own projects to improve the place. I don't want to take that away from him.

Elton picks up his wineglass. I know what comes next, and it has me sweating, wishing I'd poured more wine, wondering if I go upstairs and go to bed early, I'll wake up, and this will have all been a dream.

"Your ex is in Portland. At Portland General. This job has you working *with* him." His words are casual, like it's no big deal, and I half want to hug him for that, half want to shake him —it *is* a big deal. But, of course, he doesn't understand the degree to which it's a big deal. *Why* it's a big deal. And I can't tell him.

"Yeah."

He settles across from me at the oak table, another new purchase, wine bottle in one hand. We don't usually drink wine —we've always been more beer or bourbon people—but it's all part of growing up, I guess. Or something like that. Along with ugly towels, his mother gifted us a table runner and half a dozen wines she dubbed "lovely" and "fragrant". To me, they all just smelled like wine.

"And you didn't know?"

It takes me a second to realize what he's asking—or maybe, accusing. My back goes rigid, and I look up at him, searching his blue gaze, the lines of his freckled face, the way his jaw sets. He's not mad. Just—*asking*. There's a vulnerability there that digs at me, makes my chest hurt.

"Of course not." The last thing in the world I want him to think is that I brought us here—near Jameson—on purpose. I figured with a two-to-three-hour drive between Portland and Seattle, we'd never see each other. Though both cities are in the Pacific Northwest, they are practically islands unto themselves. Entirely different cultures, save the rain and coffee addiction.

"I shouldn't have asked that. I'm sorry." Elton gives me an apologetic smile. "It's just... You never really told me what happened. One minute you two were the hospital's sweethearts, married and in love, and..." His voice trails off as he furrows his brow. "The next, you were in San Diego. Alone."

My phone vibrates in my pocket, and I clutch at it, try to stop the buzzing as Elton is distracted pouring himself a glass of wine that, again, looks like blood.

God, what is wrong with me?

I shut my eyes to close out the vision—the *memory*.

When Elton realizes I don't plan on commenting on his last statement he continues. "So, what do we do? It took you months to get this job. We need the money."

"I don't know." I look up, and he's watching me with expressive eyes, full of concern. I can't help but think we should have picked anywhere but here. It was me who wanted to come back to the Pacific Northwest—wanted to see mountains in the distance and catch the scent of pine on the wind, relax into the culture that deems dressing up to be overrated and coffee worth its weight in gold.

Stupid, immature things. But once, it felt like home. And with no family left to speak of, I'd hoped it would feel like home again, but this time, with Elton.

So we'd moved here. We'd spent a small fortune on a house, twice as much as we would have in the Midwest or the south, both perfectly good places to live. Because I'd wanted to.

Elton nudges his chair closer and presses a hand to my forearm. "Did he hurt you, Chloe? You're usually an open book, but you won't talk about him. About why you left."

I pause, wineglass halfway to my mouth. "No, of course not."

But that isn't the whole truth.

My phone buzzes again. I swear I turned the vibrate mode off, but apparently, I only silenced the ringer.

"I'll be right back." I set my wineglass down. "Bathroom."

I disappear down the hall and lock myself in our first-floor half bath, full of blue wallpaper with bright yellow daisies and lights so bright I have to squint to not be blinded. I splash cold water on my face and look into the mirror. I should just never go back to the hospital. Never step foot there again. I got a sign-on bonus, but it hasn't paid out yet. I can call the recruiter, explain the situation.

But what if there isn't another job? This felt like a lucky break. Or... I pause. A setup.

But what if we go months with me unemployed and aren't able to pay the mortgage? What if we lose everything? There is no telling how long I'd go without finding another job.

Another buzz. I curse, pull my phone out, and stare at three more texts from Jameson.

Jameson: *We need to talk. Now.*

Jameson: *Chloe, don't do anything rash.*

And last, and most unsettling:

Jameson: *Whatever you do, don't quit this job.*

Air leaves my lungs, and I sink to the ground.

Maybe he means it as a concerned coworker. A physician who wants what's best for the new nurse practitioner who's supposed to work with him. But I don't think so. When I hear Jameson's words in my head, they don't come out full of worry for my career's well-being. No, they come out harsh and dark and full of threat. *Don't quit this job.*

I fill in the rest in my head: *Or else.*

* * *

When I make it back to the kitchen, Elton is dishing food from to-go containers.

"I ordered out. Dinner's ready." He offers me a plate full of Greek salad, falafel, and pita bread.

Back at the table, Elton wastes no time launching right back in. "So, job stuff." He pauses. "I'll support you either way. We can figure out the money thing. We have a little in savings. I'll bet my parents would even give us a loan, and I'm happy to ask. You don't have to work with him. It's whatever *you* feel comfortable with."

I pause, a piece of pita halfway to my mouth. *I'll find a job somewhere else. I'll do online teaching. I'll run advanced life support care courses until I get another hospital job—*

All things that run through my mind.

But Jameson's words are in my head. The awareness of what he's capable of. And somewhere in there, the fact that just yesterday, I was excited for this job. For being a nurse practitioner in the hospital, taking my own patients, being in charge of their care. That this was supposed to be the start of our happily ever after, and that it pisses me off that Jameson—the person who screwed this up for me last time—is here, screwing it up all over again.

I take a bite of pita. It tastes dry in my mouth, but I chew anyway. The biggest problem is that staying is dangerous. But at this point, leaving is, too. If I'm supposed to work for Jameson, I have no doubt he has access to my hospital HR records—so he'll know where I live, even if I quit. We're not in a position to sell the house. And I won't leave Elton. I couldn't if I wanted to. I love him.

I swallow the pita and wash it down with wine.

"I'll stay," I say. "For now."

SIX

CHLOE

Now

We crawl into bed two hours later. Elton reaches for the bedside table, retrieves a biography about some famous runner. I reach for my own book but find myself hesitating as I stare at the cover. It's a thriller, my favorite genre. But it's also dark and twisty, and suddenly reminiscent of my own situation. I throw back the covers.

"Be right back."

Downstairs, I dig through boxes until I find something lighter—something that maybe will settle my mind and let me sleep. A romcom with a happy ending. The sort of thing that never happens in real life.

"You okay?" Elton asks as I tuck in beside him. He rolls over, reaches out, brushes a strand of hair behind my ear.

I close my eyes and bask in the attention. His hand moves, cups my face, and I lean into it.

"You worried?" His voice comes out a whisper, soft and comforting.

"A little. Nervous."

"Well..." Elton's voice trails off.

He's a fixer. The sort that if you tell him your problem, he'll come up with a solution. And right now, there is no solution. Not a good one, anyway, not one *he* can control.

I open my eyes and smile. "Just about the new job."

He searches my face. Whatever he sees there must reassure him.

"I was nervous, too. On my first day."

I snort. "We're travel nurses. This is what we do." We've worked in over a dozen hospitals over the past years, short assignments to fill staffing needs. Which means we've started at new jobs just as many times.

"It's different when it's permanent," he says.

"Yeah. I guess so."

"You want to make a good impression. I mean, we could work at this hospital until retirement."

Our eyes meet. He's right. We've settled in. Settled down.

"I'm really happy here. I feel like this place is right for us." Elton moves closer, wrapping an arm around my hips, pulling me to him. I shut my eyes, breathe in his scent. When he kisses me, I kiss him back.

After a second, he presses his forehead to mine.

"Are you happy here?"

I flick my eyes open, hearing the faintest hint of concern in his voice. "Yes. I love Portland. It reminds me of where I grew up. Like a small town, even though it's a city."

"And are you happy with me?"

I search his gaze, trying to understand where this is coming from.

"Of course, Elton. I love you."

"Good." He rolls on top of me, hands roaming lower.

For a second, I resist—sex is the last thing on my mind. The job, the hospital, *Jameson's* sudden appearance in my life—or me in his—is at the forefront. But sex is a big part of how Elton and I have always connected and communicated. How we've played. And in this moment, I can disconnect from everything else. I can turn off my worries and be here and now with him.

I reach for his shirt. His pants. Feel the hardness of him through fabric and find my brain shutting off, my mind letting go, as I lose myself in my fiancé.

Life isn't perfect.

But maybe this is good enough. Elton knew I was stressed, knew I was worried. And he's helping me forget about all of it.

At least for tonight.

SEVEN

CHLOE

Then

I'd been warned: nurses eat their young.

My nursing instructors told me a dozen times in nursing school, but being me, I thought things were different now. That since my sole goal was to help people, I'd somehow escape the passive-aggressive culture around new nurses.

I was wrong.

Twelve nurses filled the nurses' station, twelve computers at the ready. Twelve spots for a nurse to sit, all filled with men and women in an assortment of scrubs, stethoscopes hung around necks, coffee cups gripped in hands or empty nearby. But there were only eleven chairs, because the chair I should be using served as a footrest for the charge nurse. Her dark blue scrubs bulged as she leaned forward, fingers flying over the keyboard, the click-clacks a constant background with so many nurses charting.

"Excuse me." I edged up to her desk and flashed her a tentative smile. I'd hoped we'd become friends, or at least friendly. I took a breath to infuse my voice with confidence and asked, "Do you mind if I grab that?"

"Huh?" Helen made the single syllable nasally, looked up from the computer screen slowly as though we didn't all have more patients than we could handle. I shifted my weight, eager to get to work; I was already behind and it wasn't even lunchtime. *Temporary staffing shortage due to a surge in patients,* hospital management assured us.

But it wasn't temporary. Two months in, and we were still understaffed and taking too many patients. I half wanted to quit —the pressure of keeping people alive got to me some nights. Made me go to the corner store and buy a bottle of whatever cheap wine was on sale and finish it myself. Not that I ever actually did. But I feared my student loans too much to dream of leaving. I couldn't give up on my degree that fast. And I wouldn't disappoint my brother, Nathan, either. He was so proud to tell his buddies, "My little sister is a nurse!"

"Do you mind if I grab this chair? I need to chart my patients' vital signs." I gestured to the chairless computer station. I'd scribbled temperatures and blood pressures and heart rates on a piece of paper, folded up in my pocket. But it didn't count unless it was charted—if it wasn't charted, it never happened, according to the unit manager who hired me.

"You're young, why don't you just stand? My feet hurt." She turned back to her monitor, the conversation over. I opened my mouth to tell her how ridiculous that was—but her mouth set in a line, and I wilted. It had taken several months to get hired after graduation. I couldn't afford to lose my job.

And I won't, I assured myself. But Helen was the charge nurse, so technically my boss, and apparently her feet hurt. I sighed and turned away. The desk was too low to stand at. Maybe I could kneel? I crouched down in front of the computer, ignoring the side-eye another nurse gave me—probably glad Helen had someone new to pick on—and swiped my badge to log in.

My cheeks burned as I pecked in numbers and filled in blanks for my patient assessment—*lungs clear, heart sounds normal, regular rhythm*—trying to focus on the screen in front of me, wondering how a person became like Helen. I would certainly never treat anyone that way, especially not someone new, someone who wanted to *help* people for god's sake. This is what I got for trying to get my life together, plan a future, all that bullshit my brother lectured me on. Not that he was wrong —I knew he was right—but it was so much easier to float along in life, waiting tables and making cappuccinos. People were nicer, too.

I logged out, eyes burning with unshed tears—*how could she think it was okay to treat me this way?*—but before I could step from the nursing station, broad shoulders and blue scrubs blocked my path. *Navy* blue scrubs, the color all the doctors wore.

"Oh, sorry—" I tried to weave around him, not even glancing up, but a chair stood in the way, his big hand on its back. It was enough to make me stop. Look up.

"I saw you needed a chair." A warm smile. Dark eyes. Mahogany hair a little long and scruffy. "I have patient consults, so I won't be using mine."

"Dr. Smith—"

"Jameson, please. And you're Chloe, right? Good to meet you." He rolled the chair around me, shoved it right in front of my computer. "I'm in office 102. Mind putting it back at the end of your shift? Thanks." He gave me one last bright smile, a friendly wink—and before I could so much as murmur "thank you," strode down the hall, greeting one of the janitors by name.

I stared after Dr. Smith—*Jameson*, ignoring a sigh of disgust from Helen. I settled into the chair—comfy and smelling faintly of him, warm and spicy—to finish my charting. Maybe this nursing thing would work out after all.

* * *

The next day, my last of four twelve-hour shifts in a row, Jameson sat alone in the cafeteria, tucked into a corner booth. He wore those same blue scrubs, but today, his eyes weren't lit up. He didn't smile. He picked at a chicken Caesar salad, frowned at his laptop, and as I approached, his whole body heaved with a sigh. After I'd taken command of his chair— which was much more comfy than those allocated for the nursing staff—Helen managed to get on her sore feet and wander over.

"Watch out for that one," she'd said, a knowing look in her eyes. "He's Dr. Death."

"Dr. Death?" It wasn't the first time I'd heard the name, but it was my first opportunity to get an explanation.

But she just nodded sagely and wandered off. I still hadn't sorted out what that meant, but I could at least say thank you.

"Hi," I said.

He looked up, ran a hand over his face as though wiping away whatever was troubling him.

"Chloe. Nice to see you." He summoned a smile, and my heart fluttered.

It occurred to me I had no idea how he knew my name. Which made me feel special for about two seconds, until I remembered I wore an employee badge, and my name was in eighteen-point font right on my chest. I chewed my lip, trying to get my thoughts in order.

"Uh, you, too. I just wanted to say thank you. For yesterday."

Our gazes met, something softening in his. He used a toe to nudge out a chair.

"Want to sit? I was going to grab coffee. Can I get you one?"

I glanced at the clock on the wall. I was only on a fifteen-minute break, but I did want to sit with him. I did want coffee. Something about his kindness, his cool calm, the fact he even spoke to me—an experienced physician to a brand-new nurse—made me want to say yes. So I nodded. Took the seat. I couldn't help noticing the email on his computer: *Rise in Patient Deaths—Task Force Forming.* I held back a snort—of course patient deaths were on the rise. That's what happened when there weren't enough nurses to care for the patients.

A second later, Jameson appeared with coffee, creamer, and sugar packets.

"How's your day going?" He settled in the chair across from me, closing the laptop lid, pushing the salad away. He cleared the space until it was only our coffee cups and our hands between us. For a moment, I had a vision of our hands interlacing. The hospital cafeteria fell away as the space became intimate.

I forced my breath steady and shook away the idea. Clutched my hands around the paper coffee cup so they didn't tremble.

"It's going okay. I'm pretty new, so—still getting the hang of things. We've had a lot of patients lately." I glanced up at him, for just a second, trying to puzzle out why he was being nice to me. People in general were not *nice*—they had goals, and if you stood in the way, you got stomped on. I learned that in the years I spent in foster care. And yet I kept trying. Hadn't I learned?

He nodded, never looking away, giving me his full attention. I'd heard more than one patient talk about how much they liked him—and I could see why. He really listened. Unlike the men I'd been on dates with from the various dating apps.

Not that this was a date. It wasn't.

"We have had a lot of patients. A lot of very sick ones."

I nodded, sat awkwardly for a moment. "Well, thank you for yesterday."

"Yesterday?" His brows lifted. "Oh, the chair." He waved a hand, shook his head. "Grab it anytime. I'm rarely in my office. Helen is a good nurse, but she—" He started to say something. Stopped himself with a wry smile, met my eyes again with a conspiratorial look. "Well, I won't say it out loud. Not here, anyway. I would suggest—if you don't mind me suggesting—" He actually stopped. Waited for me to respond.

"Go ahead." I sat up, eager for any advice, especially from him.

"Don't let her bully you. The second you push back, she'll stop. She does this to all the new nurses."

Frustration built inside me.

"But why?" Wariness forgotten, I leaned forward. "Why treat people like that? I'm working my ass off, trying to do my job without killing anyone, why would she—" I caught myself. Let out a sigh. "Sorry, I just... I just don't understand. I'm finally trying to get my life together, and I got this job, and all I want to do is help people."

"Hey." He reached out. Touched two fingers to the top of my hand, and they were warm, and I couldn't help looking up, staring right at him. "It's not your fault," he said. "It's how she was treated way back when. How she thinks it's done. So don't let her do it."

I wanted to say *it's not that easy* or maybe *you don't understand—you're a doctor.*

But the way he looked at me, I thought, maybe it could be that easy. Maybe he was right. I decided I liked him.

The way he smiled at me, I suspected he liked me, too. Someone this kind, this concerned with another person's well-being—the rumors of Dr. Death—whatever that meant? They had to be just that—rumors.

EIGHT

CHLOE

Now

"Chloe! Chloe Woods!"

My name echoes down the hospital hall and my heart goes double-time. But it's not Jameson—it's a woman. I ignore my sweating palms, the way my smile trembles, and turn to greet her.

"Oh, Debra. Hi." Around us, nurses in scrubs shuffle by. Bright fluorescent lighting keeps it from being obvious if it's day or night, which is reasonable as the hospital never sleeps.

The manager from orientation hurries up to me, an extra-large cup of coffee gripped in her hand. She gives me a bright, overly whitened smile. "Good morning. I was hoping to ask you a favor."

"Oh." I stare at her, wide-eyed. It's not quite 6:30 a.m. I'm here early, because it's my first real day, and also because I've already been awake for two hours, stomach swimming with the knowledge I'll be working in the same office as my ex-husband. "Sure."

I can't keep the hesitation from my voice, but not because

I'm opposed to favors. More because despite my declaration to Elton that I'll give working with Jameson a shot, it still feels like a theoretical—like if I survive today, I'd be back tomorrow, and I can't guarantee that.

"Great. Well, I know from your resume you have experience in a mortality reduction task force."

I swallow, wondering where she's going with this. What a mortality reduction task force means. Dread grows inside me as I wait for her to continue.

"We need a provider just to sit in. To serve as an adviser. Would you be interested?"

This cannot be happening.

Not today.

Not again.

I bite back an immediate "no."

This was one part of travel nursing I loved—we were never anywhere long enough to be pulled in on teams or task forces or whatever the new term for them was. We were temporary, fulfilling a staffing need, then gone in the wind to our next assignment. Nothing was permanent. Less responsibility. There was no address Jameson could follow should he ever want to track me down. It felt safer, freer.

"Sure," I say, because from Debra's expression, that's what she expects me to say. Then I remember the email, the one that led to me applying to this job. "Oh, hey, where is Zoey Constance's office? She's the one who invited me to apply. I'd like to thank her."

Debra blinks at me. "Pardon?"

"Zoey? Zoey Constance? She's in HR."

Debra shakes her head. "I'm afraid we don't have a Zoey Constance. You must be mistaken. My dog is named Zoey, I'd remember that name!" She smiles. "Anyway, I'm so glad you'll help out."

"Of course," I say. Then something occurs to me, something

I maybe should have asked before. "Hey, Debra, where did the last person in my position move to? Why did they leave?"

"Oh, she—" Debra blinks, clearly taken by surprise. "Well, that's private, of course." She smiles, but it lacks the luster her previous smiles have had—and then she's calling, "Have a wonderful first day," and rushing off. I stand there, my heart heavy, but my curiosity piqued.

There's only a single reason these task forces form. Because people are dying. Furthermore, Zoey Constance doesn't work in HR at Portland General Hospital.

Which means someone else emailed me, inviting me to work here. And I think I know who that someone is. What I don't know is why he brought me here.

I also want to know why his last nurse practitioner left. If she ran before it was too late, just like I did.

* * *

Eventually, I make it upstairs to a unit I walked through yesterday, eyes peeled for Jameson. It looks different now, lights dimmed in a nod to the fact it's an hour at which patients are sleeping. Blond wood paneling, white trim, the ever-present nurse's station, this one a square, patient rooms wrapped around it in a U-shape.

My heart pounding in my ears, I pass through the unit, shoulders back. Nurses and respiratory therapists look up, give me a quick once-over—I'm a new face. A new name. Their gazes land on my badge—*Chloe Woods, ARNP*—and their expressions turn assessing. Wondering if I'll be any good to work with. If I can be trusted. If I'll listen when they tell me something's wrong with their patient, or if I'll blow them off.

I'm the former, always, but not every provider is. After working as a nurse for years, I understand their caution, and I give them a compassionate smile to show them I'm on their side.

I walk down the lonely hall to where Jameson's office is. On my tour, Debra waved her hand and said, "The office you'll share with Dr. Smith is in no man's land, down that way." Now, it seems it's an abandoned section of the hospital. Sure, there are other offices, but there are no nameplates, no whiteboards with *out of office* scribbled on them. Just an empty hall, oddly far from the unit. "They rebuilt the ICU two years ago, but left the offices where they were," she explained.

Now, I feel like I'm walking into enemy territory. Deserted enemy territory, where if I scream, no one will hear me.

Which is ridiculous. I shake my head and force my body forward. But before I can go far, footsteps behind me make me spin.

Jameson. Towering over me. Too close. I stumble backward.

"Oh good, you're here."

He clutches two paper coffee cups, and he thrusts one my way. "Mocha, right?" And as soon as I accept it, he keeps walking. He palms a ring of keys and unlocks the office door, goes inside, and I'm left in the hall, my chest seizing with nerves.

I raise my free hand to my collarbone, my neck, feel my pulse pounding away, and remember to breathe.

"You coming?" His voice echoes down the hall. "We have work to do."

My legs move on their own accord. The mocha in my hand might be a peace offering, but I don't want to accept anything from him, and as I pause at the doorframe, I search the office for a trash can to dump it in.

But Jameson is there. Jameson, watching me with his striking brown eyes that always pulled me in, made it hard to look away. Today, I meet those eyes and feel... What do I feel? I tamp down an emotion I can't identify, some combination of shock this is happening and annoyance he got me a damn mocha. Not to mention, paranoia at being alone with him this far from anyone else.

"You're here early." His words come out terse. "This is the office." He waves a hand. "There's room for you over there." A second laptop sits on a counter that wraps around the room. A second chair, albeit a rickety one that will definitely not work if I end up staying longer than a week. Books line a shelf above the desk, and there's that same obnoxious bright lighting in this room, too. "I have a consult in five minutes. Then we have rounds starting at seven."

"That's early for rounds."

"Yes. I like to get them done immediately." Jameson turns his back on me to focus on his computer. It allows me a moment to observe him—to see nothing has changed, other than maybe the creases at the corners of his eyes are a bit deeper, and his hair has a hint of gray here and there. It does nothing to take away from his classic good looks.

The corner space is mine, and I set my bag and purse down. The mocha is still in my hand. I don't know what to do with it, so I decide to set it on the desk and leave it there until I can dispose of it without him witnessing me doing so.

I debate how to proceed, how to act around him.

The last time we spent any real time together, we were married. Yesterday, we were enemies. I sink into the nearest chair and stare at his back, thinking about Debra's ask. Half of me is trying to figure out how we'll have a working relationship. The other half of me thinks it's ridiculous to even consider it, given what I know. I can't *work* with him.

"What's the consult?" I ask, since apparently, we're getting straight to business.

"DNR." The three letters roll off his tongue.

Do not resuscitate. Basically, there are times when a patient is sick enough or old enough that they choose to not be resuscitated if they "code"—if their heart stops beating properly or their blood pressure tanks. If their body tries to die. There are in-betweens, too. Normal, healthy people are "full code," but some people will choose to be a "partial code," meaning they're okay with getting lifesaving medications, but maybe don't want chest compressions should their heart stop beating properly.

"Someone who wants to be a DNR?" I ask.

"Someone who should be a DNR," he replies. He doesn't move, still slouched over the laptop. So, probably someone very sick who wouldn't recover well or at all if they were coded. Who might prefer to be allowed to die.

"I can do that."

Jameson does a quarter turn, eyes me over his shoulder. "You can do that?"

"Why wouldn't I? You want to talk to him about why he should be a DNR, right? Suggest he consider it? Let him know his options so he can make a decision?"

Jameson gives me a stiff nod.

"Okay. Who's the patient?"

Jameson spins all the way around, giving me his attention, and it's just like yesterday—I can feel it. A physical sensation like a blanket draped over my body. Once, I loved that feeling. That level of focus and attention from him. Today, I try to not think about it too hard. To listen as he tells me about George, a long-term patient of his who has been coded three times and each time comes back a little worse off for it.

"He's in his late eighties. Shocking he's survived this long with the heart failure he has. But he just keeps going." Jameson tells me a little more about him—that his wife passed away three years ago, that he spends more time in the hospital than out of it.

"So why now? What's the change that makes you think he should be a DNR?" I look up from my notes.

"He had another heart attack, had another stent placed. He won't do well if it happens again."

I finish writing my notes and stand. "Okay. I'll go do this and be back for rounds."

"Thanks." He nods and continues typing away at his computer.

Out in the hall I can breathe again. I don't know what I expected—but this isn't it. I expected anger. Maybe threats. A continuation of yesterday's terse conversation in the conference room. Maybe that was coming. Maybe he is as busy as he seems, and he hasn't had time for that yet. I'm still his ex-wife. Still the person who knows what he's capable of.

Or maybe that's it—he knows that I know he's dangerous. So far, I'm doing exactly what he's said to do. I didn't quit my job. I came in today. I accepted the mocha and sat with him in his office. Maybe, he thinks I'm afraid of him.

I start back toward the unit, rereading my notes on George.

He's not wrong.

NINE

CHLOE

Then

Borrowing his chair became habit—or maybe an excuse to go in his office. To soak him in, to pretend I belonged there. I learned his whispered nickname, Dr. Death, was because he was one of three local physicians who believed in physician-assisted suicide, something I learned about in nursing school. The idea was when a patient was so sick they had no quality of life—often bed-bound and in constant, agonizing pain—they should have the choice to end their life with dignity. It was legal in Washington State, and Jameson helped them with it. I respected him for that—it couldn't be easy to help someone die, but he did it anyway.

He also traveled a lot—hiking in Alaska, skydiving in Montana, one adventure after another. It was on one such day, when I was sure he was out of town, that I opened his door only to have it swing wide and his handsome face appear, dark brows raised in curiosity.

"Oh, it's you." He smiled. "Come in. I'm just finishing something, one sec."

My face flushed hot, like I'd been caught doing something naughty. I was under the impression he was still in Missouri, exploring cave systems.

"It's okay. I don't want to interrupt. I thought you were still on vacation."

He blinked, as if making sense of my words. "Vacation, right. It got cut short. Let me just finish this real fast. Let's talk."

I shuffled in, standing awkwardly. I looked anywhere but at him. My gaze landed on a family photo—one of several. Sparkling white snow in the background. Jameson, his arm thrown over a woman who had to be his sister—they shared the same big brown eyes. Beside them, his parents, at retirement age. They all wore Patagonia ski jackets, each in a different color, and smiled with straight white teeth. A picture-perfect family. Every time I looked at that photo, my gut filled with longing—if my own parents hadn't died in a car crash when I was twelve, would we have a photo like that somewhere? Maybe over the mantel of our childhood home, a brick bungalow with a wood-burning fireplace that sold just three months after their death. I'd never know. A lost possibility. A childhood wrenched away.

Someday, I'd have my own family. I'd meet someone who would be my happily ever after, and I'd never be alone again. My brother had tried hard—but he was only a few years older, so I was stuck in the foster system until he was eighteen. And now we were close, talking and texting nearly every day.

But it wasn't the same as belonging, having someone you loved, who chose to love you in return. Someday, I wanted to have a family, a husband. My parents had a relationship like none other—still holding hands, still whispering and giggling after fifteen years of marriage. Dancing in the living room. In some twisted way, it was almost right that they died together. I couldn't imagine one surviving without the other.

Someday, I would have that person in my life. I'd wake up

beside him and snuggle into his warm body instead of waking up alone, chilly in my own twin-size bed. We'd share everything, and for once, I'd feel whole. Complete.

Jameson's voice jolted me from my thoughts.

"Anyway, I'm glad you're here. I wanted to ask you something." He waved a hand toward a second chair, and I obediently sat, smiling through my nerves.

Perhaps a code would be called, or my nurse phone could ring, signaling a patient needed something. Not that I wanted to escape Jameson—I didn't. But I wanted to escape what felt like being caught red-handed.

We'd had lunch together a time or two, always by accident. I'd grab a salad, and he'd swoop in and ask if I had time to discuss a patient, or I'd be at the coffee bar, and he'd insist on paying and we'd go on a slow walk around the hospital, debating the merits of this or that. He wanted to know what I thought about the new unit manager, or the recent change in policy. What my opinion was and why. His gentle questions made me feel important, like he cared. That feeling, after a decade of being alone, and before that, passed unwanted from one foster home to another, was addicting.

Today, he typed a final line or two, then spun in his chair.

"I did some checking around." He braced his hands on his knees. His hair was a mess without hair gel, curlier than I realized. He gazed at me with intense, dark eyes, and I found myself gazing back. Outside the office, a pair of voices echoed down the hall, and he shoved the door shut.

Suddenly, we were alone.

"Checking around?" My voice came out soft and faint.

"Yes." His brow furrowed. "I hope I'm not being presumptuous, but I don't think this is one-sided. Is it?"

He looked at me expectantly.

Is what? I didn't say that out loud. I just stared at him, hoping he'd go on. The photos of his family looked on as I waited, and I couldn't help sparing them another glance—he was so lucky to have a family like that.

"Okay, good." He nodded to himself, but again, I didn't follow. "There is no hospital policy against it, so that being the case, my understanding is you get off work at seven tonight. I'm not opposed to going out like this." He gestured at what I presumed were our scrubs. My mind raced, trying to keep up. "But I understand if you'd prefer to get changed. So, bearing that in mind, would you do me the honor of going to dinner with me tonight?"

"Dinner?" My voice came out too high, almost a squeak.

His mouth curved into a gentle smile.

"Dinner. Maybe dessert afterward, too. I have a sweet tooth, and I think you do, too, given your mochas."

"You're asking me to dinner, like a—"

Jameson chuckled and rolled his chair closer.

"A date. You, Chloe, are amazing. I can talk to you about anything, everything. I'd love to spend more time with you. So, I'm doing the reasonable thing and proposing we go out."

My jaw might have hit the floor, but I gathered myself. Forced my brain to work again. This was an awful idea. An incredible, awful idea. I liked that we were friendly. That I could come snoop around his office and pretend I knew him. Bask in the illusion of having a family like his. What if this ended in disaster? It would all come crashing down. He was a doctor; I was a nurse, working on the same unit. I might lose my job if it went sideways.

Then again—what if it became real? What if we went on this date and I liked it, and he liked it, and we became more than sort of friends, and—

A shudder ran through me. Did I dare dream of a future? The photos of his family, how close they looked, how happy— was this my chance? A chance at a partner? A *family*?

It was safer to say no. To maintain this friendship, which was better than the nothing I'd had before.

"Please? Will you go out with me, Chloe?"

I couldn't resist his eyes—the hopeful smile that told me this could be something. That he *wanted* it to be something. I decided it was a risk worth taking. "Yes."

* * *

Somehow, I made it through the rest of my shift. Every time Jameson walked by, I shared a smile with him—we had a secret, just the two of us, an excitement boiling just beneath the surface. And when he came to check on my patients, he brushed a hand casually over my shoulder sending electricity through my whole body. I was about to burst.

On my break, I found the nearest stairwell and dialed my brother.

"Hey, what's up?" In the background, the crack of a baseball hitting a bat. Masculine cheers, someone laughing, the baseball season in full swing.

"You at practice?" I asked. He played minor league baseball but had been called up twice to play with the major league team.

"Kind of. I'm done, but the guys are screwing around." The click of a door, and the background noise disappeared. "You okay? You don't usually call this early."

I leaned against the stair railing and shut my eyes. I felt like I was in high school all over again. "I have a date."

"Oh yeah? Tell me more." I could hear the smile in his voice.

His enthusiasm buoyed me along. "He's a doctor at the hospital. His name is Jameson."

Nathan whistled. "Damn, sis."

"I really like him. He's kind and handsome and—" I stopped short. "I'm nervous. I haven't been on a date in years. Help me."

Nathan chuckled. "You're gonna be fine. Just be yourself."

"What if it's awkward, though?"

"Is it awkward at the hospital?"

"No," I murmured. "It's... easy."

"Well, it'll be easy tonight, too, then."

I hoped he was right.

* * *

That night, we met at Bartholomew's, a swanky new glass-and-steel restaurant on a corner in Seattle.

"Wine? Drinks?" Jameson met my gaze across the table, bottomless brown eyes locking on mine and holding me there long enough it became intimate.

"Sure. I mean, yes, please." I had answered too fast. Then, too passively. I was messing this up already, and we only just sat down. I was out of practice. I hadn't had time to date during nursing school, or much desire. I'd focused on the moment. One day at a time. The basic rule of survival.

"Which do you prefer?" Jameson held out a stiff menu that was the drinks list—wine down one column, cocktails down the other.

"Oh, I'm not—" I halted my words. Accepted the menu. Took a long look, then pointed to a drink at random. "Old fashioned."

His lips turned up, as though he knew I'd chosen something I'd heard of in a movie. "Two, please," he said as the waiter approached. "Templeton, if you've got it."

The waiter took it down on a paper pad and murmured something about the specials. I barely heard it, between sneaking looks across the table at Jameson sans scrubs. He'd pulled on a black button-up with black dress pants. With his styled dark hair, he looked like he'd just rolled off Hollywood Boulevard and was ready for his next role. But of course, his next role wasn't starring in a movie. It was saving lives.

When Jameson turned back to me, he leaned in and murmured, "Can I tell you a secret?"

I tried not to swallow my tongue. Not trusting words, I nodded.

He pressed fingertips on top of my hand, as though this were a very serious matter.

"I'm nervous." He let out a little chuckle with his confession, cheeks going pink. "I'm never nervous. But you... you make me nervous."

"Me?"

"You."

Warmth filled me. I made Jameson Smith nervous? Confidence surged through me.

"Want to know my secret?"

"Of course." He raised an eyebrow, offered a devious smile.

"I'm nervous, too."

We both laughed, and seconds later, a bartender delivered our drinks.

"Cheers." Jameson raised his glass, and we clinked. "To going on dates with people who make us nervous."

TEN

CHLOE

Now

My first task as a nurse practitioner is to ask someone if they want to be allowed to die. George, a man with a white beard reminiscent of Santa Claus, listens as I talk to him about his options.

I pull up a chair and sit close, meeting his gaze.

"I'm Chloe Woods, a nurse practitioner working with Dr. Smith. He wanted me to come talk to you about your options moving forward."

A gleam comes to George's vivid blue eyes—a knowing. "Yeah. I figured someone would want to. Miracle I've survived this long." He straightens the teal quilt with the hospital logo over his lap. "I just had my eighty-eighth birthday. Can you believe that?" He chuckles. "Didn't think I'd see sixty, much less eighty-eight."

I smile. "Happy belated birthday. Did you do anything fun?"

"Oh, yes." He nods. "My wife always made me pumpkin cheesecake. She passed a few years back." He blinks rapidly and looks away, as though the mention of her is too much. "But... my daughter found the recipe. She made it for me. Delicious. Grandkids came, too. It was a good time."

"That sounds great." I take a settling breath—I've always found it difficult to discuss death with patients. It's a part of life, and I know that. I've witnessed that, dozens of times. But it's one thing to know it—it's another thing to confront someone head-on with their own mortality.

"It was. Anyway, what were you saying?"

"Well, we took a look at your chart. Your vital signs. What's going on with your heart. Dr. Smith believes it's unlikely you would survive if you had another event." I pause, realizing my wording is vague. "Another heart attack, or if you were to code here in hospital. Or, if you did survive—he's concerned about your quality of life afterward." I examine his face, measuring his reaction.

George watches me a beat, those clear blue eyes thoughtful. "And what do you think?"

I pause, considering everything I know about him. His age alone would usually incline me to have this conversation, but especially coupled with his heart issues and other health concerns.

"I agree with Dr. Smith. I think it's a good time to have this conversation so that you are in control of what happens next."

He nods slowly. "I understand. My golfing buddy had to call 911 at home last year. He lives in a home now. Never gets out of bed. Can barely talk. Last time I went to see him—" George clears his throat, sits up. "Didn't even recognize me. Had drool dripping down his lip. That's not for me." He shakes his head. "I'd rather be with Betty, anyway."

"Your wife?"

Another nod. "She's in Heaven, waiting for me."

"I'll bet she is."

"So, what do I need to do then?"

"Well, you have options." I take the papers I brought in with me and show them to him. "Right now, you're what we call a 'full code,' meaning that if something were to happen, we'd do everything in our power to get you back. That's on one end. At the other end is DNR—do not resuscitate. It means we'd do nothing—we would keep you comfortable, but not stop the dying process. But you don't have to pick one or the other. There are lots of in-betweens." I go through the details with him and ask if he has any questions. "You can think about it, too. You don't have to do anything right now. But we wanted to have the conversation so that you can make your own choices."

"I appreciate that." George sighs. "Well, like I said. I miss my Betty. You got a pen?"

I give him one and watch as he chooses "DNR" and signs his name below. I sign as a witness.

"You can also change your mind at any time. If tonight you want to decide differently, just let your nurse know. I'll come back and we can fill out a new form."

"Thank you, Chloe. But I won't change my mind. I miss Betty something terrible. And I don't want to end up drooling all over myself." He gives me a kind smile. "Now if you'll excuse me, I'm going to eat my breakfast."

I take my leave of his room, stopping to inform the nurse of his change in code status, then head back toward the office. I'm relieved George was easy to talk to—some patients are defensive, which is understandable, even if my goal is to make sure they are aware of their options. My tension rachets back up, approaching the office. Approaching Jameson. The door is shut, and I knock gently, not quite feeling as though I belong.

"Jameson?" No answer, and I go right in. He's gone, which gives me a chance for a proper look around.

Jameson's desk space includes a small collection of coffee mugs, in varying degrees of fullness. A photo of him and his family in front of what might be the French Alps, a vast moun-

tainous background behind windburned smiling faces, all
wearing thick coats and ski pants. His parents look the same.
His sister does, too, though I suppose only a few years have
passed. I stare at the photo a second longer, wondering where I
packed my own family photos. I'd like to show them to Elton—
to maybe frame them, so our eventual children know what their
grandparents looked like.

I glance at the computer screen next. He hasn't been gone
long—the computer has yet to go to sleep. George's chart is
pulled up, which I've already seen, but I'm curious what else he
has open. I reach for the mouse and click through his internet
tabs—the Littmann stethoscopes website, a drug reference
guide, and Google Maps.

It appears he's shopping for a new stethoscope—a black one
with the capability to record anything he listens to. I can't help
but wonder if he wants to record his patients' hearts as they stop
beating. It's a dark, twisted thought, but I think it, nonetheless.
The drug reference website shows a search for lansoprazole, a
medicine to fight acid reflux. Hardly damning. I navigate to the
last tab next.

The air leaves my lungs in a single whoosh.

It's my neighborhood. My address. My *house,* down to the
red brick front and the Japanese maple.

I glance back toward the office door. It's still shut tight, but
he could be back at any moment. I gaze at the image of the
house—taken in fall, the leaves a fiery orange and red—before
tabbing back through the programs he has opened so they are in
the order where I found them.

So he's checking out my house, where I live. What does that
mean?

Maybe, nothing. I work for him. He has access to my
employee files. But then why pull it up on a map? It might be
mild curiosity, wondering how well Elton and I are doing. Or
far darker, far worse. I stare at the screen, contemplating what

to do—tell Elton? Confront him? Call up a security company and ask them to come install a system ASAP?

I don't know. Technically, he hasn't done anything. Yet.

I bite my lip and step away from the computer. A stack of notebooks sits in one corner, all spiral bound and college ruled, the sort that go on sale every fall. I take a notebook at random from the pile. Scrawled across the front in black marker is 2020. The year the pandemic hit hard. The year I left Jameson.

I take a half step back, sink into the nearest chair, which happens to be Jameson's. I'm about to flip it open—to see what notes he's taken—but the latch to the door clicks, and the door starts to swing open. In a panic, I shove it in the satchel near my feet, and look up, hoping Jameson doesn't notice.

But it's not Jameson.

"Holy shit." The woman's hand flies to her mouth, and her eyes—familiar brown eyes, because she shares them with her fraternal twin—go wide. "It's you."

My mouth opens, but no words come out. Panic zings through me. Another familiar face in this hospital. But one that has much reason to hate me as Jameson does.

"It's *you*," she says again, as though still grappling with the idea. She reaches up, runs a hand through her dark hair, taking me in. And then her face hardens into anger. "What are you doing here?" Laura Smith—Jameson's sister—snaps. "Let me guess, you're back for money."

"Laura. Hi," I manage, but her piercing gaze tells me this will not be a happy reunion. "No. I don't want money."

She pulls back, glances at Jameson's computer as though it somehow embodies him. Her arms cross over her chest. "Are you two back together?"

"No, no..." I raise my hands and wince. "I'm sorry, Laura, we're not—no. That's not what this is."

Her eyebrows shoot up. She goes still. "Then what is this?"

"I'm working here. We're... working together."

"Oh." She puts one hand on her hip and purses her lips. She takes me in, an eyebrow rising when she notices the engagement ring on my left ring finger. Then her smile turns cruel. "Well, that must make things... interesting."

Taking in that smile, her narrowed eyes, the anger radiating through her stiff body, I can't help but wonder if she had something to do with me ending up here.

I'm about to ask—because what have I got to lose, she already hates my guts—but Jameson edges in around her.

"Shit," he mutters, taking in the two of us. "Laura, not now." He looks at me. "Did George consent?"

"Yes. I just need to change his status in the computer."

"If not now, then when?" Laura interrupts. She stands a little straighter, reminding me of a dangerous predatory animal —a lioness or maybe a rattlesnake—readying before it strikes.

"Later," Jameson says. "We have work to do."

Laura levels another look my way. I want to stand up for myself, but with the two of them here, I'm outnumbered. And, from what little she knows, she has every right to be mad—in her mind, I took off on her brother. Maybe it's a good thing she's mad, maybe that means she *doesn't* know what he's up to, what we did. Because if she did, she'd take my side. Probably.

Laura wears a white jacket, like all the other physicians. Her name is scrawled in italics—*Laura Smith, MD*. Below that, the hospital name. So she came to Portland, too; she's not just visiting.

"Work," Jameson repeats, shooing his sister out of the office.

"Wait." It's a bad idea, but I have to do *something*. We're going to be working together for the foreseeable future—better to get this conversation over with. "Laura, can we talk? Later?"

She scrutinizes me, eyes still flashing with anger. "Yes. In fact, I insist. Tomorrow, after work. Wine place across the street." From her pocket, she produces a card and flicks it my way. It hits the ground before I can grab it, but she's turned on her heel and stalked off before I can lean down to get it.

Another enemy to make nice with. Just perfect.

I pick up the card.

Laura Smith, MD

Head of Cardiology

A phone number and email address below that. I pocket the card. I got a new phone, a new number, when I walked out. I left her in the past, just like I had Jameson.

He takes his seat and turns his back on me. Just like before. Frustration overtakes fear—what the hell are we doing here? Pretending everything from yesterday, from before, never happened?

"I'm not quitting," I say.

Jameson turns his chair so we're facing one another. "That's good."

That's good? Good because it means I have a job? Because it's good for my health? I can't decipher his tone. The hair on my arms goes on end, and I fight the desire to cross my arms, my legs, to take a defensive posture.

My gaze drops to my bag, where I shoved the notebook. He can't see it, not unless he gets close.

"Thanks for handling everything with George. Would you mind grabbing us more coffee? Then we can get started."

It takes me too long to respond, silence filling the space between us before I jolt to action.

"Coffee?"

"Yeah. I know it's not your job, but—I figure we could both use caffeine." He holds out cash. "Should cover it. I'll grab it next time. I just have one more thing to take care of before rounds."

I hesitate, like it's a trap. But I'm not drinking the mocha he got me, and I'm craving caffeine.

"Okay." Our eyes meet as I get to my feet and reach for the

cash, almost excited to take a breather from his presence. Our fingers touch as he hands it to me, and it makes me want to pause. Want to really look at him and understand what's behind his gaze. But he looks away, and my face heats; I imagined it. Some remnant from the past. There's nothing between us but secrets and threats.

I hurry from the office, down the hall, toward where the coffee shop is. My chest loosens, and I take a deep breath.

I've ordered coffee and carried it halfway back when overhead, the speaker turns on, and a woman booms, "Code blue, Room 808. Repeat, code blue, Room 808."

George's room.

I bite back a curse and sprint up the stairwell. Suspicion spikes my heart rate, makes me consider dumping the coffees as I run, but that might make someone slip and fall, get hurt. I have a feeling I know exactly what little thing Jameson needed to *take care* of.

And once again, he's drawn me in, made me a part of it.

ELEVEN

CHLOE

Then

At work, we tried not to be too obvious. Rumors were already flying about the nurse and doc who ate lunch together, grabbed coffee, went for a quick walk when the unit was quiet.

It was on my next-to-last shift after three twelve-hour shifts in a row—just enough time in between to eat and sleep and maybe shower if I was feeling ambitious. I wiped at my eyes, resisting the urge for another cup of coffee. I slung my bag over one shoulder, counting the moments until collapsing into bed—maybe into Jameson's bed, if he invited me over. It was early days, still. Invites hoped for, not assumed.

I walked down the hall, searching for him. "Have you seen Dr. Smith?" I asked the night-shift nurse who'd replaced me, a traveler named Ethan or Elton. I couldn't remember which.

"He's in with 304." He nodded at the door, slanted open a few inches.

I'd taken care of that patient all day, a lovely woman not an inch over five foot, who was admitted following her collapsing on the treadmill at the local YMCA. Her tests were clear, and she was being held overnight out of caution, particularly because she was the mother of one of the attending physicians.

I knocked softly at the door, adjusting my bag. I didn't want to interrupt if they were in the middle of an important conversation. A moment passed with silence, so I stepped in, peered around the privacy curtain. A dim room greeted me. I could barely make out Jameson's form leaning over the bed, doing something.

My brows drew together. My hand gripped the curtain a little tighter.

"Jameson?"

He jolted and stood upright, swinging around.

"What are you doing here?" He stepped away from the patient, closer to me, blocking her from view. I'd never felt anything but safe and warm in his presence, but I flinched. His eyes widened at my reaction. "Sorry. You just startled me. You okay?"

I stared at him, then beyond him into the dark room, and nodded.

"I was just going to say goodbye. See when you were getting off." Again, I couldn't help but peer around him for Ms. McCoy. A blanket hid her form, though. It had been such a busy day, my eyesight almost blurred, trying to see her. "Everything okay in here?"

"Just updating the patient." Jameson gave one glance behind him, then motioned me out the door. "Have a good night, Ms. McCoy."

She didn't respond that I could hear, but she was soft-spoken.

In the bright hallway, the world snapped into focus. Jameson, his white jacket, gentle smile. That flutter of confusion, discomfort, floated away at the sight of his handsome face. He glanced around then sneaked a peck on my forehead. "I'll be off in an hour."

"Oh, okay." My voice came out deflated. I didn't want to wait another hour to leave.

"Here, why don't you..." Jameson reached out, took my cool hand in his warm one. My skin tingled with his touch. "I've been meaning to give you this."

Something cool and hard fell into my hand.

"Let yourself in. I'll come join you when I'm done."

Our eyes met. In my hand rested a key to his condo.

Holy crap, he gave me a key.

"See you soon." Another peck, warm lips briefly on my skin. Then he strode to the next patient room and disappeared inside, leaving me with the chunk of metal that represented so much. It was a small gesture that meant more than just about anything else he'd ever done. I'd never been given entrance to a man's home before when he wasn't there. I stared after him, warm and awake, and having completely forgotten the interaction with Ms. McCoy.

Until, that is, the next day when I walked in with a giant cup of coffee, a smile on my face, high on early love, ready to take report. But when I set my things down and glanced in to check on Ms. McCoy, I found an empty patient room, cords dangling from the monitor, a splatter of blood staining the wall.

"It was an accident." The voice came from behind me, weary, grief-stricken.

"What do you mean?" I turned to find the same night-shift nurse. *Elton* read his name tag. Not Ethan. He rubbed at his face.

"She was confused. Ripped out her lines. Including the arterial line."

That explained the spray of blood. That's what arteries did when they were cut open, when a line was yanked out—they sprayed. Fast. A person could bleed out in minutes.

But his explanation didn't make sense. Ms. McCoy hadn't been confused at all. A patient could *become* confused, but that took at least a week or two, usually alone in a room staring at a blank wall—ICU psychosis—not a couple days with plenty of visitors.

Coldness settled in my belly. My hands trembled, and I set down my coffee so I wouldn't drop it. She was dead. Gone.

"The alarm went off, but we thought it was nothing. It took us a minute or two to get there, and by then—" His shoulders slumped. "Not sure we could have saved her anyway. Her blood pressure tanked. We coded her and gave her a ton of fluid, but the blood took like seven minutes to get up here, and it was just too long..."

I nodded numbly. Took the nearest chair and stared into the room. I was still a new nurse, and it was my first patient death. Though I hadn't been caring for her at the time, so maybe it didn't count. But it felt like it counted.

"Where's Ms. McCoy?" Jameson came up behind me, and the nurse repeated what he'd told me.

Suddenly, I wasn't looking at an empty patient room. I was looking at a dark room, Jameson twisting around, like he'd done something wrong. Hurrying to leave. Distracting me.

Doctor Death.

No. I rolled my eyes at myself. That was grief talking.

"So she was confused? She was okay last night. All day yesterday, right?" Jameson glanced my way for confirmation, and I nodded. We'd carried on a full conversation, she'd passed her neuro check with no difficulty, and she'd complained about the upcoming election.

Sorrow etched Jameson's face as I looked to him, like he'd tell me what to do—how to handle my first patient death.

But here, he was a doctor, and I was a nurse, and he had important things to do. Like see patients.

"Damn." Jameson stared into her room, anguished that Ms.

McCoy had passed—like he'd personally failed her. But he hadn't done anything wrong.

I moved closer, wrapped my arms around him, gave him a hug.

"It's not your fault. Sometimes things just happen."

TWELVE

CHLOE

Then

We continued dating—sneaking kisses in hospital hallways—going for elaborate dinners with cocktails and dessert. We were magnets, drawn together.

Or maybe lightning, seemingly coming from nowhere, and it was like our whole world lit up in an instant. Jameson's home became our home. We shared secret smiles at work and met in abandoned stairwells to share five minutes whenever we could.

With Jameson, I felt the first inkling of home I'd felt since my parents' car careened over a cliff. Day by day, two strangers became two lovers. The Dr. Death rumor mill took a break as they saw a softer side to him. And soon, we became the hospital's sweethearts, to boot.

We had dinner together nearly every night, but something was different this evening. The way he'd asked me to meet him —like it wasn't just another Friday meal together. Like it was significant. This time, I was afraid.

I texted Nathan.

Chloe: *Jameson said he wants to talk about something important tonight.*

It took Nathan a whole two minutes to reply.

Nathan: *He's going to propose.*

Excitement dashed through me, but then I remembered how he hadn't looked at me when he'd asked me to come over tonight. How he looked anywhere *but* me. Not the behavior of a man about to ask someone to spend the rest of her life with him.

Chloe: *I don't think so.*

I couldn't bring myself to text out what I was thinking: *God, what if he's going to break up with me?*

Or I was a complete idiot, and he had a girlfriend somewhere else. A girlfriend who'd found out about me.

I furiously typed a message out to Nathan detailing my fears. In my head, I added the part I couldn't say to anyone—*I'll be alone. Completely alone.*

In response, Nathan sent an eye-roll emoji and *Chill. From everything you've said he adores you.*

I read his message three times before I let myself breathe. He did adore me. Nathan was right. I was jumping to the worst-case scenario, the one where I would be alone again, the world screwing me over.

At that moment, a text came through from Jameson: *Dinner requests? Love you, xoxo*

Men who were about to break up with their girlfriends didn't send texts like this. Didn't do it over homemade meals at home. I exhaled.

Well, if it wasn't that, what could it be? I hadn't the slightest idea. And I would have guessed wrong, anyway. I would have never predicted what he was about to tell me.

* * *

When I arrived at his place, the smell of garlic and rosemary filled the air.

"Salmon fettuccine," Jameson called, peeking into the foyer from the kitchen, fixing me with a smile.

He's not breaking up with you, I reminded myself. "That sounds great."

"Drink?" he asked.

"Please."

Moments later we were seated at the eat-in bar, old fashioneds in our hands, facing one another. Jameson wore a button-up shirt, and he played with the top button, fixing it, undoing it. Just like he did with pens at work. I grasped his hand, held it in mine, halting the nervous behavior. That's all it took—his dark gaze bore into mine, and he sighed out. I could practically feel the tension radiating off him.

"What is it?" I asked.

Jameson looked back at the kitchen, like maybe the food would need attention and save him from saying whatever it was he needed to tell me. Then he looked back at me. His dark eyes searching mine.

Whatever this was, it was big.

My stomach bottomed out. What could be so horrible he was this scared? This nervous? I couldn't think of anything.

"I'm going to share with you something I haven't told anyone besides my sister. I think you need to know. Because we're getting serious."

"Okay."

"Do you believe in what I do?" he asked.

"What do you mean?" I clutched my glass and took a tiny sip, tempted to down the whole thing in one gulp.

"My work. Helping sick people be able to choose when and where they die."

I frowned, not understanding. "Of course. I've seen dozens of patients take months to die in the ICU, sedated and in pain. It's awful. It's like we're torturing them. We should never force a patient to choose death, but if it's what they want—especially if they're terminal..."

He nodded, staring at the floor. Jameson pressed his lips together. Exhaled. I waited, the silence between us growing big, ominous. I expected the worst—my heart already hurt with it, whatever it was. My hands clenched into fists as I waited, wishing he'd spit it out already.

"I travel to states where physician-assisted suicide is not legal. Not often, but... sometimes." He looked at me then, a hardness in his gaze I only saw at work, when he was busy saving a life or diagnosing a patient or talking a family member into better care for their loved one. "That's what I'm doing. Not rafting or hiking or—" He waved a hand. "The other things I say. I travel to where it's illegal, and I help people die the way they want to."

"You're..." I take a breath. I'd known he performed physician-assisted suicide in Washington State. He didn't talk much about it, but everyone knew. I assumed it was how the nickname Dr. Death got started.

"We're getting serious," Jameson repeated. "You're basically living here. I wanted you to know. No secrets between us."

Jameson waited for me to say something. To react. I had to think about it. To consider how I felt about him traveling out of state, risking everything. But he wasn't doing it for his own gain —he was doing it because he believed people had the right to choose when they died when they were terminally ill. When they were actively in pain and suffering and there was no light at the end of the tunnel.

I reached out, took his hand in mine. The nurse part of me didn't love that he was doing this, knew that it could get him in trouble. But I also knew how much he cared about people. How much he hated to see them in pain, and I knew this came from a place of caring.

I also knew lots of people on death's doorstep purposefully overdosed all by themselves—a horrible, painful end that sometimes they got wrong. Sometimes they survived and were in worse shape for it. Jameson was alleviating pain. Ending suffering. And I couldn't help the other twinge, that bit of me that relished he considered me so important that he had to—no, *wanted to*—share this with me. That I was special to him.

"I'm glad you're helping people," I said. "And thank you for telling me."

THIRTEEN

JAMESON

Now

He waited until she left the office on a supposed coffee run to exhale. To shake his head and try to figure out what the hell was wrong with him.

Chloe Woods.

Jameson stared at her name on the screen. It didn't fit quite right. She'd outright refused to become Chloe Smith—preferring instead to keep her maiden name, and he'd never argued, even though he'd dreamed of the two of them, of their eventual children, all having the same last name. He would have even taken hers, so they could match—the Smith Family, the Darling Family, he didn't care which way it went.

But *Chloe Woods*... and she'd changed it before she'd even married Elton. Jesus. He'd heard of women doing that so they could have the same name on their honeymoon and get their new passports in time, that sort of bullshit. But it didn't seem like Chloe. Not the Chloe he knew.

He took a long drink of his coffee, which was not actually empty, and wiped his mouth on his sleeve. His watch read 7:07

a.m., which meant he was seven minutes late for rounds, but he needed a moment to himself to clear his head.

He thought for a solid year that she'd come back to him.

Jameson backspaced, and this time typed *Elton Woods*. His basic information popped right up on the hospital database—*ICU nurse, 13 years' experience*. His photo accompanied it. They'd met before, working in Seattle, but he hadn't stayed long enough for Jameson to ever properly know him. A traveler, they called his sort.

For the briefest moment, Jameson considered Chloe had an affair with Elton back in Seattle—but no. It wasn't possible. They spent every waking moment together when they weren't at work, and some of those, too, were spent together. Jameson leaned back in the office chair, pondered how the hell he'd ended up in this situation.

He didn't have long to ponder, though. The small gray hospital phone rang on his hip.

"Hello?"

"Your patient in 808 is crashing."

"Be right there." He cursed at the timing—not twenty minutes after George agreed to be a DNR. This wasn't good.

He rushed down the hall, through a set of double doors, and into the medical ICU. Room 808 was a corner room, and nurses and doctors alike stepped out of the way as he hurried to get there.

Inside the room, the curtains were drawn, making it dim. A single light illuminated enough that Jameson could make out a tired face, a body covered up to his chin in white linen blankets, his patient—George was his name—apparently asleep on the bed.

But George was not asleep.

George was dead.

And Jameson had missed being here for his last moments.

"You should have called me earlier." Jameson's attention

turned to the nurse in the corner who stood wringing her hands. She was new, and young, and probably she'd never seen a dead person before. Jameson pressed his lips together, drawing them into a line. He looked at George again. At the nurse, who refused to meet his eyes. At the monitor, which showed a flatline—the sign of a heart that ceased beating.

Because it was what had to be done, Jameson yanked the stethoscope from around his neck. He put it on, pressed the bell to George's chest, and upon hearing no beat, pulled it off. A glance at the clock.

"Time of death, 7:19 a.m." He turned on his heel to leave the room, but another nurse stood in the shadows, blocking the way. "Excuse me," he began gruffly, then pulled to a stop. "Chloe."

She looked at him. At George's body. A tremor ran through Jameson, watching her. Wondering what she saw, what she thought...

"He's dead?" she asked, a tendril of something in her voice —anger? Grief?

He nodded stiffly. "Yes."

They stepped from the room, and she picked up two cups and handed him one. He took one last look back at Room 808, shook his head, trying to push past the feelings inside of him— he should have been there for George's death, should have gotten there before he'd taken his last breath. Instead, he'd merely pressed a stethoscope to his chest and declared him gone to this world.

"The timing," she said.

"I know."

"We *just* signed the papers—" Her voice went thin, like she might cry.

"Yes. You saved him from an awful death."

She didn't say anything, but when he glanced at her, she was watching him, and it made him shiver. She knew how he felt before *he* did for much of their marriage. She'd say he was easy to read—something he'd tried to remedy in the ensuing months, years. He didn't want to be easy to read. Didn't want people to know how he felt, what he might be thinking.

"I don't like missing a patient's death," he said, then realized he was providing an excuse for his terse behavior.

She nodded, crossed her arms. Matched him pace for pace, and for a second, it was like the old days, when she'd take her fifteen-minute breaks to join him for coffee, or he'd find her during lunch and bring her favorite cookie from the bakery across the street. An urge to swing an arm over her shoulders hit him—to pull her close, comfort her, like back then. He resisted it. He was *angry* with her. Furious, really. But furious wouldn't serve him here and now. He had to tuck it away.

All the same, Jameson didn't want to talk about George, even with her. It reminded him too much of when they'd pour bourbon and sit on their condo patio, staring out across the Puget Sound, talking shop. She'd always been smart. Smart enough, he'd tell her, she could have been a doctor. She'd reply, *All nurses are smart enough to be doctors. We just enjoy having a life outside of work*, or some variation on that. And she was right. Not that nurses weren't workaholics, too, but most of them had better work-life balance than he did.

He couldn't help he was obsessed with what he did, though. He helped people in a way no one else could.

FOURTEEN

CHLOE

Then

After six months on the unit, I met with the nurse manager to review my performance at work.

"You're doing great." She flashed me a bright smile. "I'd like to invite you to join a task force. It's good to be involved in affecting change in the hospital, and it'll look great on your resume." She slid a printout my way. "We have a team on reducing infection rates, another that works on unit policies. Oh, and there's a new one—" She pulled the paper back and scribbled it by hand at the bottom of the list. "We've had a rise in patient deaths in recent months. We're investigating the cause. Dr. Smith swears it's because we have sicker patients, and he's probably right, but we have to look into it."

My gaze shifted to the scribbled add-on. "I'll do that one," I said. "It sounds important."

It also sounded like an opportunity to work with Jameson, which was always a plus. Last month he'd asked me to move in with him. We were becoming inseparable, and for the first time in years, I felt calm, happy, like life was going exactly how it was supposed to. Nathan teased me every time we spoke on the phone. "You married yet?" he'd ask, and I'd tell him to knock it off, secretly wondering if that was in my future with Jameson.

A week later, I joined the Mortality Reduction Task Force for its first meeting.

"We need someone to gather information on all the patients who have died on the unit in the past six months."

I raised my hand, volunteering. Jameson was not on the actual task force, but he was sitting in as an adviser and representative of the other doctors. Our eyes met across the room, and he winked at me, like he was proud I was doing something to help the patients on our unit.

The real work started a week later, as I came in for an extra shift, when I'd sit in a small office and research patients. I came prepared with my usual mocha, a warm sweater for the unit that was always too cold, and earbuds to listen to music. My role included looking up patient charts for every patient who had passed away in the past year. I was to catalog who worked on their case, their cause of death, any incidents leading up to their death, and other bits of information. It wasn't as exciting as working on the unit, but Jameson was there, and I was getting paid overtime.

I went back and forth between the electronic charting software and a hospital-issued laptop, where I entered data as I looked it up. Patient medical record number, day and time of death, reported cause of death, autopsy results, their care team, and more. The work was tedious, but by the end of the day, I'd made it through the first two months of the six-month period we planned to catalog, looking for patterns.

Only one had emerged.

I drained my mocha, heart palpitating in my chest. This couldn't be right—I'd somehow screwed up. I gazed at the numbers, reopened three patient charts to make sure I'd recorded everything correctly. I scrolled the rows and columns of the spreadsheet, double-checking I hadn't skipped a row or double-assigned anything.

Everything was right. Which wasn't possible.

Eighty-seven percent of the patients who had died were Jameson's patients.

It was the only pattern I could find. I pushed back from the desk and stared at the screen, not believing what was right in front of me, racking my brain for where the error might be.

I grabbed the empty coffee cup and hastily left the office. My thoughts spun out. Jameson was a *good* doctor, one of the kindest I'd ever met. He took great pride in caring for his patients, took meticulous notes and never hesitated to consult another specialty when needed. At night, we'd share drinks and he'd talk over a difficult patient, how he was trying to figure out the best care for them. It didn't make sense that such a high percentage of the death rate was for his patients—though, now that I thought of it, he did take care of the sickest patients on the unit.

Around me, nurses whisked by, meds held in their hands as they hurried to give them on time. A surgical team in white jackets and chests puffed out with self-importance stood blocking the hall, making everyone else, including me, skirt around them as they talked about a new golf course in town.

Jameson was nowhere.

I veered off my course for his office and instead found the nearest staircase, where I wandered down three flights to the cafe. I needed time to think.

"Sixteen-ounce mocha," I murmured. "Extra shot, please."

I paid and stepped aside to lean on the nearest wall. It was cool to the touch, which made me realize how hot I was—scared and concerned for what this might mean for Jameson. For his career.

Getting a coffee was nothing more than putting off the

inevitable. I had to tell him, to warn him before the unit manager found out and approached him with it.

I took the elevator back up, shuffling past the surgical team as they crowded onto it before I could step off.

Turning a corner, I came up short.

Jameson stood right in front of me, his laptop under one arm, a coffee in the other.

"Hey, I was just looking for you." He smiled, leaned in, inhaled against my skin, and pressed a kiss to my jaw. "Missed you. Do you have time for a quick break?"

"I—um—yes, of course."

He grinned. "Great. Come on." Jameson led the way to his office.

"You look upset." He frowned as we sat down, facing one another. "Everything okay?"

"I'm just..." I hesitated and took a long swig of my mocha to buy myself time. "It's hard. Reading about people who died for hours on end."

"Yes, it must be." Jameson rolled his chair closer, pressed a hand to my knee. "Remember, we're doing our best. For every one patient who dies, ten or twenty more go home to their families."

"I know." I took a breath and looked down at my lap. I had to tell him. *I had to.* "I'm worried, though."

"About?" He tilted his head, dark eyes searching my face, empathy turning his face soft, attentive.

I lowered my voice. "Jameson, a lot of the patients who died are yours. I've only made it through two months, and it's more than half. A lot more than half."

His face did something then—all expression falling away. A look I'd never seen before. He brushed a hair from his face and eventually summoned a faint smile.

"Well, I'm not surprised. I do take care of the sickest patients. And you said you've only made it two months." He shrugged. "It might be a sampling error. It will probably average out with the other providers once you have more than a two-month spread of time."

I processed his words. It was a small sample—two months' worth of patients. Any provider's numbers could skew in that amount of time. And he took the sickest patients, too.

I could breathe again. He was right. It was just a coincidence.

FIFTEEN

JAMESON

Now

Laura waited a whole hour before messaging him.

> Laura: *You're working with Chloe? What the hell?*

He didn't have time to discuss it now—but he *did* want to discuss it.

> Jameson: *Lunch. In my office.*

It wouldn't be hard to get rid of Chloe for a short while—the way she watched him, shied away from his touch, bit her lip every time he shut the office door. He was relieved she'd listened when he told her not to leave. Still couldn't believe he'd gone off and actually said *till death do we part* yesterday.

Even if he had meant it.

A lash of anger rolled through him. She'd tricked him three years ago. Sent him on an errand and left a note and her ring and likely gone to the airport. He'd followed. But he was too late. By the time he arrived at their condo, she was long gone. He'd called and emailed—begged and threatened and acted in a most ungentlemanly manner.

That, he didn't regret.

That, she deserved.

But now, he needed her to stay if he was going to keep the truth hidden.

And he needed Laura's help with that.

* * *

Laura appeared in the doorway like a vampire—out of nowhere, silent, eyes still slit with annoyance.

"Come in."

"Where is she?" Laura asked.

"Not here. Now come in. Let's talk."

Laura sighed and stepped in but refused to sit. She perched on the edge of the extra desk—no, *Chloe's* desk—and bounced her foot.

"Lunch?" she asked.

Jameson sighed. "Such a woman. Always wants food first."

"Hey, you invited me."

He handed over a sandwich rolled in foil.

"Now why am I here?" Laura took a giant bite and chewed. "Damn it, Jameson. I hate mayo."

"I told them no mayo." He shrugged. "Anyway, I need you to be nice to Chloe."

She snorted. "No way. She fucked you over. Fucked you up. And now she's back, fucking with you all over again. What does she want? You back?"

"She's engaged."

"That doesn't mean she doesn't want you back."

Jameson considered a beat, then shook his head. "Listen, just be nice to her."

"Why would I do that?" A spot of mustard appeared on her lip, and Jameson held out a napkin.

"Because." He raised his brows at her. "I think she's here for a reason. And I'm going to stop her. But first, I need her to trust me. So be nice, okay?"

Laura tilted her head and reached for the can of soda Jameson got for himself. She popped the top and took a long drink.

"So I'm being nice to ultimately screw her over?"

He nodded. "Yes. Think of it as the perfect revenge."

Laura thought it over. "I do like revenge."

"Good. So it's settled. You'll be nice."

"I can't be too nice. That would be suspicious."

Jameson fought a strong desire to grind his teeth. "Listen, you don't have to be her best friend, but could you—"

"I got it." Laura waved a hand at him, wrapped up the rest of the sandwich. "Gotta go. Remember, next time no mayo."

SIXTEEN

CHLOE

Now

After patient rounds and doing assessments in the ICU, I excuse myself for lunch, nearly melting in relief when Jameson doesn't try to go with me. But I don't go to the cafeteria. Instead, I wander through the halls and stairwells, searching for the rooftop healing garden, as promised at hospital orientation. I assumed there would be a well-established path there, signs and arrows pointing the way, as there is for the cafeteria, radiology, the various ICUs, and every other spot in the hospital. But no. It's like a hidden oasis. Or at least, I hope it is.

It takes ten minutes of wrong turns and walking in circles to find the right stairwell. My phone buzzes in my pocket, but I ignore it. It's not the hospital phone, so it can't be urgent, and after arriving seconds after George's death, then working several hours in Jameson's presence, I need a second to myself.

A heavy door stands at the end of the hall, and I shove it open, only to be greeted with a gust of summery wind—it's only sixty or seventy, but the breeze carries a hint of heat, like the Pacific Northwest is trying to warm up in time for summer.

Sunshine hits my face as I take the last step to the roof, and I close my eyes for a second, just breathing.

When I open them, I gasp. I'd imagined a couple of rickety tables with a shrub or two. Instead, brilliant green hedges line the space, tiny pink flowers erupting from them. Small Japanese maples twist and turn, their leaves a tantalizing crimson red. Pots and raised beds are sprinkled throughout, growing flowers in every color. And sprinkled here and there are small, tile-top iron tables with matching chairs. The whole space is lined with small stones, creating pathways throughout the greenery.

I take a tentative step forward, surprised to find I have the rooftop to myself. If I were a nurse, I'd eat lunch up here every day—then again, as long as it took me to get up here, maybe that's not an option with a strict half-hour lunch. I have a little more freedom as a provider.

Though working beside Jameson feels anything but.

I chew my lip and gaze out over the hospital campus. It's a clear day, and in the distance I can see Mount Hood. I pull my phone out to snap a photo to send to Elton—*Let's go here!* I'm already imagining I'll text him. It was one of the things we wanted to do back in the Pacific Northwest, check out all the mountains. Mount St. Helens is close, too, as well as the caves.

"Caves?" he'd gasped, with almost childlike excitement when I told him. A smile comes to my lips thinking of it.

"Yes, caves," I'd said. "Just remember it's a volcano."

That hadn't stifled his excitement, though. If anything, it made him more eager to check it out.

I take the photo and send it to him, then realize my phone buzzing was Elton sending me a text.

Elton: *Where are you?*

Right as I start to type out a message in response, he sends another.

Elton: *You texted me you were going to lunch, but you're not in the cafeteria. You're not in your office. Jameson's not there, either, and neither of you are on the unit.*

Another breeze flutters over the rooftop, carrying the scent of the flowers with it. It should relax me, should remind me there are good things in this world. But I read Elton's message a second time, trying to understand what he's getting at.

And then it hits me.

He's jealous. He's wondering if... I squint and read the message again. He's wondering if I'm with Jameson somewhere.

He's never been jealous before. Never had a reason to. And it's *Jameson*—why would he think I'd go anywhere with him?

Chloe: *I'm on the roof of the hospital—at the garden. What's wrong?*I hit send.

Elton: *Alone?*

Chloe: *Yes? Did you get the photo I sent you?*

Three dots appear, then disappear. Elton typing, maybe hesitating. I stand and cross my arms, walking around the garden, taking it all in. A small vegetable garden grows in a corner. Only tiny green tendrils have come up yet, but there are labels handwritten—*tomatoes, green beans, squash*. It's cozy. The sort of thing that a grieving family member could come up and appreciate, forget their loved one's problems for just a few minutes.

A glance at my watch tells me I've been up here for fifteen minutes already. It hasn't felt that long. With the breeze, the flowers, the break from white walls and incessantly beeping monitors, I almost feel like myself again.

Almost.

I turn to head back to the doorway, but my phone vibrates.

Elton: *I'm coming up.*

Annoyance surges through me. I'd be happy to see Elton, but not because he's trying to keep tabs on me.

Chloe: *Meet me in the cafeteria? I'm headed down.*

I leave the garden with one last look—I'll be back for sure, if only to get away from Jameson. The stairwell is dimmer than I recall, and I descend it carefully. At the bottom is another hall, concrete floors and white-washed walls. I hesitate. Did I come from the left or right? Or maybe, straight? Three halls come together here at the base of the stairs. Looking at them in turn, they're all identical.

My skin prickles as I choose the one to the left—surely, that's the right direction to the elevators that lead to the cafeteria. Though it could also be straight ahead. This hospital is over a hundred years old, several buildings combined over the years as it has grown. My footsteps echo over the concrete floor. I follow the hall as it turns right, then twists left. I expect an intersection, preferably one with signs, but as I take one more turn, it leads only to one place—another stairwell leading up to the roof.

A chill seeps through me, as I realize I'm lost. I turn on my heel and go back the way I came. When I arrive at the initial intersection of halls, I take the one to my left. Surely, that's it. But this hall is like a maze, with more hallways. A few doors, too, though when I work up the courage to knock on one— maybe someone inside can give me directions—no one answers. When I try the handle, it's locked.

Elton texts again.

Elton: *Where are you??*

I breathe out and stuff my phone away. I need to focus on getting out of here.

I turn back the way I came again, sure this means I just need to go back to the base of the stairs, take that third hall. But I walk for several minutes without finding it.

A tendril of panic snakes through me, up into my throat where it seems to squeeze. No. *No,* I will not panic.

Another text. I'm sure it's Elton, but when I grab my phone, it's Jameson.

Jameson: *You lost?*

My heart palpitates in my chest. That tendril of fear grips my chest, my throat, a little tighter.

Suddenly, footsteps boom down the hall, moving fast.

Not my footsteps.

I scurry behind another turn, press my body against the cold, bare wall, and hold my breath.

It's Jameson. It has to be.

The footsteps go silent.

Is he on the other side of this wall, waiting for me to make the first move? I wait one minute, then two, then three. My chest heaves with fast breaths, my armpits soaked with nervous sweat. Surely, he's smarter than this. Right?

It's my phone vibrating that breaks the spell. I grab at it, fumbling, trying to silence it. But it slips from my hand and hits the ground hard—hard enough to break something. I stop breathing, waiting for those footsteps to pound my way again.

But they don't.

Whoever it was is gone. I kneel, picking up the phone. The screen has a tiny crack at the edge, but that's all. Another message waits.

Jameson: *Tick-tock.*

I bite back the cry working its way up from my throat and turn, hurrying down the hall. I don't know if it goes to the cafeteria, but it has to lead *somewhere,* somewhere other people are. Somewhere I'll be safe.

I find a stairwell and grab the rail, taking the steps as fast as I can. It's on the second landing I hear it—the echo of footsteps, again. When I glance up through the concrete stairwell, there's a shadow—a shadow of someone hurrying down the stairs after me.

Or maybe they're just using *the stairs.*

Or maybe not.

I dash down the next set as fast as I can. The next door leading to a floor has a window, and through it I can see someone clad in scrubs. I burst through the door, catching a nurse bewildered.

"Where's the cafeteria?" I ask.

She stares at me, pushing dark bangs back. In her hand is a to-go container, and she points down the hall.

"Thank you," I say.

I don't look back again. Don't look to see who might be creeping up behind me. I feel like a child, escaping the boogeyman in the dark.

I hurry down the now-carpeted hallway. Those same abstract paintings are almost a comfort because they mean I'm in the main part of the hospital. With people. Where I'm safe. Where Jameson can't get me.

"Babe?" Elton's voice breaks through the murmur of staff crowding into the cafeteria. I look up. He stands there, watching me with wide concerned eyes. "You look like you've been..." He pauses, seems to think through his words. "Working out?" He blinks fast, nostrils flaring, and I realize it's suspicion in his voice.

"I got lost," I say. "The hallways—they're um..." I almost tell him the truth. Almost tell him someone was behind me. "Creepy," I end with.

Elton tilts his head, taking me in, and a soft empathetic smile breaks through.

"Yeah. They're sketchy, right? My first day here, they took us all around the hospital—through the old wings, too. They're about to do a bunch of renovation, so they cleared those areas out. I'll bet that's where you got lost. It's like a ghost town. Creepy." Elton opens his arms and pulls me into his chest. It's not exactly professional, but I bury my face in his neck, breathing in his scent. He gives me a squeeze. "Well, you're safe now."

"I know," I murmur. I wish I could stay here, in his arms, forever.

"Babe? You okay?"

I nod. "Just a little stressed. First day and all. And getting lost." I pull back enough to look him in the eye. To lose myself in his baby blues for just a second or two. His boyish grin appears.

"So, you gonna show me the rooftop garden sometime?"

"Yes," I say. "It was amazing. And deserted."

"Deserted, huh?" He leans in, and from the tone of his voice, I can tell he's about to suggest something dirty.

I laugh and pull away. "We're at work!"

"So? Never stopped us before."

I smile at him, and he reaches out, offers his hand. "Come on, let's grab a quick lunch. What do you say?"

"Sounds good."

I let Elton lead me away, toward the salad bar, but can't help one last glance backward.

My body stiffens. Jameson stands twenty feet away, at the edge of a hall, watching us.

SEVENTEEN

CHLOE

Then

The following week, I finished researching the six months of patients.

Sitting in that tiny narrow office, it was like reliving the week prior—staring at the screen, unbelieving.

Jameson wasn't wrong, his percentage had decreased. But only to sixty-seven percent. Two-thirds of the patients who'd died on the unit were patients he cared for. But that wasn't the only pattern. Many of them also had referrals in with cardiology, though most sick patients did. Plenty had comorbidities, complicating their health status. All of them were over the age of sixty-five—in other words, considered geriatric.

I chewed on the end of my pen. After three cups of coffee, I switched to water, and reached out for the reusable bottle, draining it in a single gulp. My gaze shifted to the clock on the wall. I had to meet Jameson for dinner in twenty minutes. I blew out a breath, chest tight at the thought of sharing this most recent discovery with him. He hadn't been upset before, but the way his face went stoic—so lacking emotion—scared me.

It reminded me of foster parents, a moment before they got mad. Or when a social worker came for a check-in, and they pretended everything was just fine. I didn't like that side of Jameson, not when usually he was the kind, empathetic man who wasn't afraid to hug a patient or offer comforting words to an upset nurse.

I would wait to turn in the spreadsheet to my manager until tomorrow. That would give me time to tell Jameson, so he could prepare. I slid the laptop into my bag and left the room, switching off the light. The nurse's station was in the midst of a rare quiet moment—half a dozen of them with their chairs swiveled, in an oblong circle, chatting to one another.

"Hey, Chloe. What are you doing here?" Helen's brow furrowed. "Since when do you work night shift?"

"I'm just here doing some things for the task force." I patted my bag, where the laptop nestled next to my water bottle and wallet. "Waiting for Jameson."

"Well, have a seat." A fellow nurse rolled a chair my way, and I settled into it. "We're talking about the Seahawks. Think they'll win the Super Bowl?"

I snorted. "Are they going to the Super Bowl?"

Groans sounded around me. I didn't understand the fascination with football, but the majority of the nurses I worked with did.

"Since you don't watch football, want to swap shifts so I can watch the game with my boyfriend?" Lisa, a petite nurse who'd been hired just after me, flashed me a hopeful smile.

"I'd be happy to."

Her eyes lit up, and she dove for the scheduling book next to the unit secretary. The other nurses kept talking about football—getting tickets to the game and how expensive they were—while I scanned the unit for Jameson.

"I'll be right back." I left my bag leaned against my chair and wandered the unit toward Jameson's office. But when I knocked and peeked my head in, the room was dark, empty. I rounded the corner, checking the backside of the unit, when I saw him. He stood, arms crossed, staring through the narrow window meant to give the nurse a glimpse into a patient room when they needed watching.

"Jameson?"

He jerked and turned my way, face coloring.

"What are you doing?" I asked.

He pressed his lips together and shook his head. "Mr. Jenkins. I don't think he'll make it through the night." I came closer, pressed a hand to his shoulder, and peered through the window to see a sleeping patient. A monitor overhead showed the patient's heart tracings blipping equally, his heart rate at eighty beats per minute, a normal blood pressure in the bottom right corner of the screen.

"He seems okay." I looked again. I hadn't actually taken care of Mr. Jenkins, but everything seemed normal—good vital signs. He rested comfortably, breathing on his own with only a nasal cannula to give him a little extra oxygen.

"Yeah. You're right. I'm just..." Jameson shrugged and shoved his hands in his pockets. "Worried, I guess." He looked at me. "You ready?"

"Yep."

"Okay. I need ten minutes, and I'll be good to go. Could you grab my coat from my office and lock up?" He offered me a set of keys.

We went in opposite directions and met back at the nurses' station a few minutes later. The circle of nurses had dispersed, preparing to give report to night shift. I tucked Jameson's keys into my bag, but something felt off—too light. Empty.

I put the bag on a table and opened it wide, realizing what was missing: the computer. The computer with all the patient mortality numbers on it. I looked up, scanning the surrounding desks, but not a single laptop was in sight.

"Has anyone seen a laptop?" I asked the scattered nurses. A chorus of "no." Maybe I'd forgotten it in the room. I swore I'd packed it up in my bag, but maybe it was still on the desk. I pulled the bag over one shoulder and strode off in that direction, heart in my throat—I couldn't lose a hospital-issued laptop. Especially not one that had all the data I'd spent the past week collecting. Hours of my life, on a document on that laptop. Information that would help us reduce deaths on the unit, that could literally save a life.

But the office was dark, empty desks, no laptop in sight.

"Chloe." Jameson stood back by the nurses' station, pulling his jacket on. "Ready?"

"My laptop is missing. The one I'm using to collect data for the task force."

"Missing? Where did you have it last?"

"Here. In my bag." I pulled the bag open again, showing it to him. "I swear I put it in here. But now it's gone." I filled him in on where I searched, how I'd left my bag when I went to look for him. It was nothing out of the ordinary—nurses tucked purses into drawers, left their pricey stethoscopes on the counter, and I regularly left my backpack tucked beneath a computer desk at the nurses' station—I hadn't thought twice about leaving my bag there, especially with the unit so quiet, a group of nurses I knew and trusted circled round.

"It's your personal laptop?" Lisa asked, handing me the form to switch shifts for the Super Bowl.

"No, the hospital one. It's gray with the hospital logo on it."

She frowned, sticking out her bottom lip. "I'm staying for another four hours. I'll keep an eye out. I can't imagine someone stole it. Maybe they grabbed it by mistake."

Her words were meant to be comforting, but there had been no mistake—whoever took it would have had to enter the nurses' station. Would have had to reach into my bag and pull it out. Would have gone unnoticed by the staff.

Which meant it was a nurse or a doctor who'd taken it.

* * *

My next shift came the following morning. I drove in alone, in the dark, because in winter the sun didn't rise until late. Jameson had taken off on another "adventure," this one to Hawaii, where euthanasia was legal, but it was nearly impossible to find a provider who would do it.

I walked onto the unit with my giant coffee mug to utter chaos: Helen running from the medicine room to the back corner with an IV bag in hand, two respiratory therapists wheeling a bright red code cart to the same room, and overhead, the squeal of the hospital operator announcing, "Code blue, code blue."

I dropped my things and didn't bother clocking in, instead sprinting to the room—Mr. Jenkins' room—to see if I could help. Adrenaline spiked the scene, half a dozen people in scrubs talking at once and a big beefy doc who worked night shift going to work on Mr. Jenkins' chest, applying compressions at the necessary one hundred per minute.

"Code cart is here," a respiratory therapist called out. Helen turned to grab the sticky palm-sized pads to apply to his chest. I raced for the code cart, pulling out the medicine drawer, reaching for syringes and epinephrine, drawing up two dosages in case we needed them.

"It's not a shockable rhythm," someone called. "Continue compressions. Epinephrine, one dose—"

And so the code went for twenty minutes in a whirlwind of activity as we tried to save Mr. Jenkins' life.

Twenty minutes later, the doctor called it.

My heart sank as the flatline crossed the monitor, as the body that was no longer a person lay cold and still. As Mr. Jenkins' time of death was called.

Report was quiet after that. I scribbled notes on my two patients from the night nurse, trying to pay attention, because this was important—*so important*—but I wanted to text Jameson. He wouldn't get the message, he'd be on his plane right now, but I wanted to tell him he was right. That something was wrong with Mr. Jenkins, that he had died.

But how had he known?

I mulled that over as I studied my patients' list of meds. Sometimes, my nursing instructors had told my class, you *just had a feeling*. A gut feeling you had to trust—if you thought something was wrong, they'd said, then something probably was. They'd rehashed examples from their own years working in a hospital, when they'd saved the life of a new mother, a perfectly healthy woman who'd just given birth, but one of them *just had a feeling*. So she'd checked on the patient every half hour, and sure enough, that night, the woman hemorrhaged. Only the nurse's quick reaction and constant monitoring saved her life.

When I had a free moment, I ducked into my manager's office and shared that the laptop had gone missing the day before—taken right out of my bag. I expected her to be mad, to tell me I'd have to pay for it. But instead, she furrowed her brow, looked thoughtful. "That's unfortunate. It's almost like someone doesn't want us to look into this. Or maybe," she added, "we simply have a computer thief on our hands."

"What do you mean?" I asked.

"I put Marie in charge of screening the six months prior to what you're screening. So we had something to compare your numbers to. Her laptop was taken last night in the five minutes it took her to use the restroom."

"That's so strange."

"I know." She looked down at her work phone. "Thanks for letting me know," she said, effectively dismissing me. "I'll get in touch about how to proceed."

I left her office, loitering in the hall, because something felt wrong. Off. What kind of nurse or doctor, the main people who had access to our locked unit, would steal a computer with that sort of information on it? Information that could help someone?

The only thing I could think of was someone who didn't *want* to help patients. Who didn't want to decrease the death rate. But that didn't make any sense. We were here to save lives.

My manager's words echoed in my head: *It's almost like someone doesn't want us to look into this.*

I took my lunch break around three that afternoon and called Jameson. The unit buzzed with activity, so I took my phone downstairs to the cafeteria and found a quiet nook. Three o'clock was late for lunch, but not if you were a nurse on a busy unit—sometimes, you missed lunch altogether. So I cobbled together a coffee and a pretzel from the cafe and relished the twenty minutes I'd have uninterrupted by my nurse phone's incessant ringing.

It took two tries before Jameson answered. I chewed a large bite of soft salty pretzel, as his voice came over the line. First, a whoop, like Nathan made the time I saw him hit a home run, then laughter. Scuffling in the background.

I frowned, trying to sort out what was happening.

"Jameson?"

"Sorry, babe. I'm on the beach trying out surfing."

"Surfing?" I set my pretzel down, not sure if I was more shocked he was playing in the water or that he'd called me *babe*. "I thought you were—" I cleared my throat. "Working."

That's what he'd said—that he was headed to Honolulu to assist with a cancer patient who was suffering. That they'd reached out to him through private channels and asked for help. *Begged* for it, really. He'd said all this in the reserved tones he used when discussing what he did when he wasn't at the hospital. Helping people who otherwise wouldn't have help as they ended their lives.

"How did things go?" I asked vaguely, not wanting to say it out loud—*how did the death go? Did they die okay?* I cringed at the thought.

Wind through the phone made it hard to hear his next words—but they came fast, excited. Maybe he didn't hear my question. Maybe he thought I said something else—why would he sound excited? It gnawed at me, left me wondering what he was thinking. At the hospital when a patient died, he got quiet —often tucked himself into his office. But he sounded positively happy.

Maybe that was a good thing. I mean, it had to wear on him, helping people die. And he was visiting Hawaii—a place that, compared to the Seattle winter with its dreary rain, sounded positively dreamlike.

But still, he told me he was going to spend the morning helping someone let go of this life and move on to the next. And given the time the flight took, it couldn't have been more than a couple hours prior. Long enough that it was surprising he was already at the beach, already trying surfing or whatever he was talking about.

"The waves are huge," he continued. "But I stood up twice!"

I bit my lip. I wanted to tell him about the laptops being stolen. And about Mr. Jenkins, how he was right about something being wrong, how he'd made it through the night, but not past morning report.

Instead, I said, "Well, have fun," and hung up, mixed emotions swirling through me. Maybe it was just the high of Hawaii. I'd never been, but people talked about it like it was heaven on earth.

Later that day, he texted.

Jameson: *Sorry about the noise at the beach. It's amazing here. You need to come with me next time. We can get a little hut on the beach and have the most romantic weekend, just the two of us.*

I read the text while sitting behind a mobile computer station in a patient room. The patient had just come back from open-heart surgery, and was intubated, a machine breathing for him. Half a dozen IV bags hung from an IV pole, tubing running various medications into his body, keeping his blood pressure stable as his body recovered. Our environments couldn't have been more different. I looked from the patient—still stable—to my phone.

Another text.

Jameson: *Miss you. Love you.*

I read the words, the warmth of relief soaking through me. The dichotomy of emotions settling.

I probably would have been excited to be on the beach, too. And maybe, it was his way of coping with death. After seeing so much, he probably needed a coping mechanism. I couldn't fault him for that.

EIGHTEEN

CHLOE

Then

Jameson got home two nights later, announced by the jangling of the front door. I greeted him with a smile as he bustled in, long dark overcoat sprinkled with snow.

"You're home early."

"I couldn't wait to see you." He shut the door, yanked his scarf off, and strode toward me, pulling me into his grasp.

"Good trip?" I hugged him back, the chill of the winter night clinging to him, making him smell of pine and snow.

"The best." He pulled back enough so we could meet eyes, and what I saw in his tore my thoughts away from the fact he'd just helped someone die in Hawaii.

"You seem really happy," I said.

He grinned, nodded, and worked off his coat, letting it fall to the ground in a way uncharacteristic to the man I knew.

"What's going on?"

Jameson dropped to one knee, and I stared. What the hell was he doing?

"Hawaii was amazing. All I thought about the whole time was you—how much you'd love it."

"Okay..." I shifted, trying to understand where he was going with this. Why he'd crouched down—to tie his shoe, maybe?

"I booked us tickets for tomorrow."

My eyes went wide. "What?"

"And for Laura and Nathan, too."

A beat of silence.

"Tickets?" I asked.

"To Hawaii." He grasped my hand, pressed a kiss to it.

"I don't understand. I have work. *You* have work. And Nathan's in the off-season, but doesn't Laura have—"

"Chloe, let's elope."

Suddenly, I lost track of what I was going to say. What I was thinking. My mind went blank, utterly blank, as I tried to make sense of what he was proposing—I mean, he was *proposing*.

A box appeared in his hand. He flipped it open. Sparkles caught the light, twinkled like a dozen stars. A pearl surrounded by small diamonds. It took me a second to realize what I was looking at—a ring. An engagement ring.

A sense of weightlessness came over me, like this moment couldn't be real, like I might float away and wake up tomorrow morning. Jameson would still be in Hawaii, and I'd have the day off work, and I'd go in and restart the research for the task force...

But I didn't float away. The world didn't collapse in on itself as my eyes flicked open to stare at the ceiling to the blaring of an alarm clock. Instead, I stared at Jameson, at an engagement ring, the words *let's elope* repeating in my ears.

And then it made sense—why he was so happy. He'd known he was going to propose.

This meant something else, too. That I would have my happily ever after. That we'd get married, and we'd be a family, and have kids, and they would have grandparents... In a moment, I imagined Christmas morning. Not waking up alone or volunteering to work an extra shift, because I had nothing better to do and no one to spend it with. No. I'd be at home. With Jameson. With our family. Together.

* * *

Four days later, we got married on a beach in Hawaii.

My brother, Nathan, and his sister, Laura, were our only guests. We held hands as the sun set behind us. Jameson stared down into my eyes, unblinking, until a tear rolled down his cheek, and he laughed, wiped it away.

"I give you today, I give you tomorrow... I promise to give you the best of myself." We repeat the words, one by one. "I promise to be your partner, your equal... to celebrate the good times and stand by you for the hard times. Completely and forever, till death do we part."

We kissed, we hugged, Laura took photo after photo, and we took selfies of the four of us, laughing as we all splashed into the warm ocean in our wedding attire.

It was the best night of my life.

I cringed, thinking that—god, why did people always say their wedding day was the best night of their life? There were so many other amazing moments. But caught up in Jameson's eyes, his arms, knowing I'd get him for the rest of our lives, I understood it. Having Nathan and Laura here with us only made it better. Like a true family.

Finally.

I was so happy, I'd forgotten everything else.

NINETEEN

CHLOE

Now

The house is eerily quiet as I enter through the garage door. Elton's car isn't there, waiting, but sometimes he parks on the road.

"Elton?" No response, and disappointment flickers in my gut. He'd told me at lunch he might get off early, so it's possible he headed to the gym or is out on a run, two of his favorite activities. I don't usually mind—having a fit husband is nothing to complain about. But Elton is more home than this house is, and I'm ready to feel at home after my first day working beside Jameson. After volunteering to consent a patient to be DNR status, and less than an hour later, him dying. Finding Jameson in his room. Being stalked through abandoned hallways of the hospital, though now that I'm home, it almost feels like a dream—maybe no one was behind me. Maybe it was my own echo of footsteps, or maybe it was another provider, on their way through the hospital.

My body quakes with a shiver. I'm glad this day is over.

I set my bag down on the kitchen counter and sigh at the

piles of boxes in every corner. The goal is to be unpacked before the wedding. The wedding less than two months away. But this business with Jameson makes me want to repack the boxes. To call the movers and have them return, load the truck, take them —anywhere.

George's face flashes in my head as I fish my phone out of my bag. A stronger person would stick around just for the patients. Apparently, I'm too selfish for that. I value my life, my freedom, my future with Elton. I check for a message from him, but there's nothing—likely, he's working until 7 p.m. after all, which gives me a couple hours to myself. Maybe not a bad thing. I can shower and cook a real meal, maybe make this place feel a little more like home.

Before I can put my phone away, a text comes through.

Jameson: *Did you go through my stuff?*

I freeze. The three dots appear, indicating he's still typing.

Jameson: *I want it back, Chloe. Now.*

My stomach flip-flops, and I consider lying. The journal is in my bag, five feet away on the counter. The one labeled 2020. The one I've yet to go through, that I stashed in my bag when Laura came in. My heart does something funny, that I'll bet would look scary if I were hooked up to a heart monitor. How did he even notice? There was a whole stack. Unless he spends a lot of time flipping through them. Unless maybe, he suspected I'd go through his stuff.

I pace around the living room, taking in our new home. The sparse furniture, the big picture windows and back patio and green space. This place that is ours. It all felt so solid, so sure, just yesterday.

I don't know what to say to Jameson, so I set my phone

down and step away, like if I distance myself from it, I can pretend I haven't seen his message. Nervous energy leaves me with the need to do something, anything. I turn on the stove to preheat. I'll make something for dinner—homemade pizza or lasagna or... casserole. Couples make casserole, right?

I leave my phone and grab my bag to hurry up the stairs, still thinking over Jameson's texts. I'll deny it. He left his office unlocked earlier—anyone could have grabbed it. Or he could have misplaced it. The Jameson I knew wasn't particularly organized. My heart speeds along in my chest as I come up with different excuses, but none of them are right.

What would I say if I *hadn't* taken it and he asked?

Or better, I'll return it tonight. I'll put it somewhere in his office, and tomorrow he'll find it and think he just set it in the wrong place.

Upstairs, I turn the shower on, ready to wash away the residue of the hospital. Hopefully the warm water will let me relax a little.

The shower hisses, and I strip. As the water heats up, I slide the purloined notebook in question from my bag. I flip it open and adjust my glasses to peer down at it. His handwriting is a typical physician's—nearly impossible to read—but I've learned his writing enough to make out most of it.

Somewhere in the house, a door shuts, just loud enough it's audible through the hall and stairwell. I tense and drop the notebook back into my bag. I don't want Elton to see this. To know about any of it.

"Elton?" I call.

No answer. I frown and reach for the shower knob to turn it off, but another sound echoes through the hall—a door slamming. I jump, an instant flush of adrenaline hitting my body.

"Hello?"

Still no answer. Elton would have climbed the stairs by now to give me a boyish grin and ask if he can join me in the shower.

He at least would have called back, "It's me" or "I'm home, babe."

Instead, there is only silence.

A beige towel hangs just so from where Elton placed it— "his and hers," he'd said proudly, and indeed, our initials are embroidered on them in crimson. Another gift from his mother.

I wrap it around my naked body, my hands shaking, then spend three whole seconds trying to determine the best action. Yell for help? Crawl out the window? Maybe it is Elton, and he came in the front instead of through the garage—maybe he didn't see my car, didn't hear me call to him.

But I called twice. Loudly.

We're in a new house, though. Maybe the sound didn't carry. Maybe he still has earbuds in.

I clutch the bathroom door, ease it open. Tiptoe out the bedroom door. Every movement is stiff with tension. Underfoot, the tile becomes carpet, dampening my steps. I flash back to being trapped in the hallway this afternoon, afraid to move, to make a peep. Sweat breaks out along my neckline. It's a little like someone is after me. No, it's *exactly* like that. I pass through the hall to the staircase and stop to listen.

Silence.

I count to ten.

More silence. Well, not silence. I can hear my heart, pounding against my rib cage.

Elton would have called out to me by now. Would have come to find me.

Of course, it's entirely possible the wind blew a door shut. We cracked windows in every room to let the house air out.

Just as I'm about to conclude I'm paranoid, a floorboard creaks downstairs. I go still. Try to even stop my own breathing. A *whoosh*, like a window opens, or maybe the back sliding door.

I step backward, as fast as I can while remaining silent, rush to the bedroom, shut the door, lock it, and—and nothing.

My phone is downstairs.

We don't have a landline.

I'm trapped. I steel myself and rush for a place to hide.

* * *

Exactly seventeen seconds later—I know because I'm huddled in the closet, counting—the garage door grinds to life. Distant whistling tells me it's Elton—he grew up spending his summers helping his grandparents with their farm in rural Nebraska and picked up the habit. He's told me they would all whistle tunes back and forth, make them up, copy familiar songs—it was *their thing*, he'd say. After losing my own family young, it sounded like something out of a movie. Too cute. Too good to be true.

Almost like Elton, except he's real. He's mine.

And now, the whistling tells me he's home. I jump to my feet, hand on the closet door, ready to race down the stairs and wrap myself around him in relief. But then I realize he might be in danger, and I move even faster. It's not until I nearly run into him on the staircase that I remember I'm naked, wrapped in a towel.

"Whoa. Chloe." His voice deepens a notch, and he grins. "Okay, I like this game. Gimme a sec, I'll join you in the shower." His hands land on my shoulders, smooth down my arms to my hips.

But someone was in the house. Someone besides him.

"I thought—" I glance over his shoulder, but the landing is empty. No one in the living room, either. I pull away and flit down the stairs to check the kitchen, dining room, and den. I even check the two closets.

"Babe, what's wrong?" Elton has taken a few steps down the stairs, his brow creased in a frown, realizing I'm not in the middle of seducing him. "Why are you naked?"

I close the last closet. My gaze lands on the back sliding

door, which lets out onto a stone and brick patio. I know I locked it this morning. And I was just down here, looking out at the patio. But now, it's unlocked and cracked open.

I hurry past Elton to my phone. There's a waiting message from Jameson from twenty minutes ago.

Return it to me now, or you'll regret it.

TWENTY

CHLOE

Then

"We're holding off on pursuing the mortality reduction program right now." My manager gave me a tight smile. "Sorry. We've had a quick rise in central line infections, and we know those can be prevented, so we'll focus on that first. I'll be in touch when we're ready to start again."

I nodded stiffly, wondering why the hell an ICU couldn't focus on more than one thing at a time. Especially when there was clearly an issue. The laptops may have gone missing, but I'd reported the basics—yes, there was an increase in deaths, and yes, it was substantial. So I'd left out the details—who could blame me? He was my *husband*. I spun the ring on my finger as I stepped away to return to my patient assignment.

It had been a whole three weeks since we eloped, and while it was long enough that everyone at work now knew, it was still strange being a *wife*.

Since my parents died, I'd wanted a family. Nathan was wonderful—an incredible older brother who did as much as he could. But now I was an adult, and he had his own passions—

baseball, mostly—and it was time for me to have my life. And now, I did. That gnawing desire for partnership, fulfilled.

I smiled at the thought, pulled my phone out, texted Jameson.

Chloe: *I love you.*

He was in Kansas, supposedly touring local breweries with a medical school friend.

Jameson: *Love you, too. Did you know Kansas is* not *flat?*

I chuckle, tuck my phone away, and do a quick check of both my patients—one of them intubated, two days post-op but not recovering well. The other came in for an arterial thrombosis and needed monitoring until it resolved. I checked their vitals, made sure they had no meds due before my end-of-shift report, and cleaned up their rooms, tossing plastic water cups and straightening the linen.

Another message came through, this one from Nathan.

Nathan: *You busy?*

I typed out a reply.

Chloe: *At work.*

Nathan: *I'll call later.*

I studied the message—it wasn't his usual—and went about finishing my shift.

At home, I ordered takeout.

Home. I loved that, and I loved that I shared a home with Jameson. Our home really felt like home, too. Dark, reclaimed wood. An overstuffed couch in dark gray, with throw pillows and blankets in fall colors. Sconce lighting that left everything with a soft edge that felt relaxing. There was a television, but it was tucked within the confines of an antique cabinet, with doors that opened wide on the rare occasion we used it. I opened those doors tonight, inhaling the sweet scent of the wood, and settled on the couch with pizza, a rare glass of wine, and Netflix.

After three twelve-hour shifts in a row, I was ready to kick back. I slouched down, took a bite of thin crust loaded with veggies and sausage, and flicked through the season's biggest hits before coming to one that looked like the newest replacement for *Grey's Anatomy*. Except it wasn't the typical medical drama —*based on a true story* scrolled across the bottom of the screen. The doctor was too handsome, with a devilish smile like he knew something no one else did. Meanwhile, three nurses stood in the background, arms crossed.

Medical Killers, the title read. *When doctors and nurses kill. Based on real-life cases.*

I paused on the show, thinking about how the death rate had jumped so suddenly in our unit that a task force was formed to deal with it. How odd it was that the task force had ground to a halt. How a month ago those laptops had vanished, and how at the time, I could only assume someone who didn't want the issue looked into had stolen them.

I could have continued scrolling—I'd certainly had enough medical stuff for the day, the week, the month—but something made me select it. The intro rolled, and I drank my wine, ate my pizza, curled into a ball beneath a quilt Jameson's own grand-mother had made him. I watched as the drama unfolded.

My phone buzzed, but I ignored it, drawn in by the show. The basic idea was that a doctor noticed one nurse who had patients dying more often than others.

It was a forty-five-minute reenactment, and at the end,

when someone caught the nurse injecting medication into a patient's IV—medication that was an overdose of what would already be in their body, making it hard to prove on autopsy—it flashed to a court scene. Testimony. The real nurse instead of the actor, speaking into the microphone, "I do what no one else has the guts to. I'm an angel of mercy. I don't force people who are ready to die to undergo painful treatments. I don't keep people alive for my own selfish reasons. I *help* them, more than anyone else ever has."

I reached for the remote to pause it—something about her words made me lose my taste for the wine, made the pizza in my stomach gurgle uncomfortably. While she was a far cry from a physician who helped a patient who had *chosen* their time to go, she clearly thought what she was doing was akin to what Jameson did. But before I could hit pause, a new screen flashed up and a voice-over began, reading off the text.

How to recognize a medical serial killer:
- *majority of cases take place in a hospital setting*
- *attention-seeking behavior*
- *odd behavior after a patient death or seeming "happy"*
- *disciplinary record*
- *thrill seeker*
- *tendency to predict when a patient will die*
- *frequently moving hospitals*
- *insulin poisoning the most common method*

The voice-over then added, "Perhaps the most difficult part about identifying a medical serial killer is that no nurse or physician or medical worker wants to believe a peer would do such a thing—would *kill* instead of save lives. These people go undetected for years, even decades, and yet when they're finally caught and their coworkers and even family members questioned, they're rarely surprised. The most common response we heard in interviews was something akin to 'I should have known. It's so obvious thinking back on it.'"

The words ran through my mind. *No nurse or physician or medical worker wants to believe a peer would do such a thing.* I squeezed my eyes shut and breathed. When I flicked them back open, I focused on the bulleted points, particularly *odd behavior after a patient death or seeming "happy."* And then the *tendency to predict when a patient will die.*

Jameson had acted odd on that phone call in Hawaii —*happy*—but I shushed the thought. I knew he wasn't a killer, and he'd just decided to propose to me. He was in *Hawaii.* Anyone would have been thrilled to be in Hawaii, and death was hardly new to him. My face burned with shame that I'd even thought of him. And yet, hadn't he predicted Mr. Jenkins' death?

Ugh. I stood up, disgusted with myself.

Of course he had. He was a skilled physician.

But what about Ms. McCoy? He'd been so odd around her that night, and then—

No, no, no.

I'd had too much to drink. Was exhausted. Was weirded out by the task force being shut down. I'd married Jameson. I wouldn't have married someone I thought was a killer. If anything, he was the most kind and sensitive man I'd known. He put himself at risk, his license as a doctor at risk, to help people.

Jameson was nothing like the nurse who considered herself to be an angel of mercy. Sure, a lot of what she said sounded similar to Jameson's explanation of why physician-assisted suicide should be legal, but they were entirely different things. One was murder. The other was a patient making a decision at the end of their life—choosing to die peacefully instead of living in agony for another month or two or six.

My phone went off again, and this time I picked up, only to find I'd missed several calls from Nathan. I turned the TV off, cleared my plate and wineglass, and perched at the kitchen table, calling him back.

"Hey, sis." His voice sounded thick, gravelly. Like maybe he'd been drinking, too.

"You okay?"

Silence. My heart kicked up a notch, going on high alert. This wasn't like him.

"Nathan? What's going on? Are you okay?"

"No. Not really."

"Tell me." I pressed the phone closer to my ear. It was a girl problem, probably. Someone had broken his heart. Or maybe, he'd been traded to a different team and had to move.

"They think something's wrong with me." His voice cracked.

"Wrong with you?"

"Remember how my shoulder was bugging me? And then my knee? And how my hands kept cramping up at practice?"

I thought back. He had mentioned his shoulder was being weird, but I hadn't thought much of it—he played baseball for a living. Athletes dealt with injuries all the time.

"I've been dropping things. And exhausted. And—" He sighed. "I'll get to the point. They don't know what's wrong. First, they thought I was having mini-strokes. Then something about a.... neuron thing? Now they want to do this electro-something-thing-or-other test. And some sort of nerve test, too."

The words were familiar to me, of course. Between prereqs and nursing school, I learned a lot about the body. But it was gibberish, all the same. Because I was getting his version of what he heard. Not the actual medical terms.

Cold panic filled me at the idea of something like *mini-strokes* in my relatively young brother.

"What do they think it might be?" I asked.

"Something called ama— Crap, hold on. They gave me a handout. I can't remember how to say it." A second later, papers rustle. "Amyotrophic lateral sclerosis." He sounded the words out, like a kid learning to read.

I all but stopped breathing.

"ALS?" I asked. "Lou Gehrig's disease?"

"Yeah. They said that was the other name for it. It's named after a baseball player. Wait, does that mean... Is playing baseball—"

"No." I swallowed, pressed my face into my hand, forced myself to take a slow steadying breath. This was bad. Very, very bad. "He's just a famous person who had it. It has nothing to do with you playing baseball."

"Oh, okay. Well, they said—"

I tuned him out, the symptoms falling into place.

And the diagnosis.

If he had ALS, that meant Nathan was going to die. It would be a slow painful death, his body slowly betraying him. It explained the cramping, the pain, the way his hands were shaking. It explained him dropping things and being tired, too.

"When are they doing the tests?" I heard myself say.

"Tomorrow," he replied.

I almost pulled the phone away to text Jameson—to say, *Come home now, please. I need you.*

But instead, I listened to Nathan's frantic rambling, trying to make sense of it. Somewhere along the way, I realized he didn't get it. He didn't understand.

There was no cure if that's what he had. No hope. No real treatment.

Only death awaited him.

TWENTY-ONE

CHLOE

Now

Elton stares at me expectantly. "Chloe?"

"I must have forgotten to lock the back door. I heard you come in and—" I pull my face into something resembling a smile, hoping he can't hear the roar of blood through my ears, the pounding of my heart in my chest.

Someone was here. In our house.

My gaze lands on my phone and panic spikes through me.

I think of our house, pulled up on Google Maps in Jameson's office. His threatening words, the texts. It screams Jameson.

I hadn't answered that last text, demanding I return the journal, or I'd regret it. I'd flitted around the living room and started dinner, gone upstairs, and...

That was enough time for him to get here from the hospital. To find a way inside and start looking for the journal. But would he do that? Maybe.

"Oh, well—I brought dinner. Sorry, I didn't know you wanted to cook." Elton holds up a paper bag, full to the brim with something delicious smelling—curry, I think. "Want to finish showering, and I'll get things ready?"

I want to stay right here beside him. Where I feel safe, at home. Where I can see him with my own eyes and know he's safe, too. But I won't be able to relax until I'm out of my scrubs and have washed off the day—being around sick patients, in a hospital that looks sterile but is anything but. Being around Jameson, who, now that I think about it, I swear I can smell. I take a step toward the back door he left open, sniffing the air—a warm, earthy scent. Jameson's scent.

Because he was here?

Or because we worked side by side in a tiny office?

"You okay?" Elton looks up from the brown paper bag, face creased with concern.

"Sure." I lean in, kiss him, say, "Thanks for grabbing dinner." *Must act normal.*

Elton steps closer. I let him close his arms around me. Feel his warmth, the solid comfort that is him. His hands slide down my sides, pulling my hips flush against him. I look up to see a teasing smirk, *that smirk*, the one that reminds me we haven't christened the kitchen table. The kitchen counter. Our old ritual, when we moved into a new place.

But I'm not in the mood. Not now.

My gaze slides back to the unlocked patio door. Jameson had what—not realized I was home? Thought he'd find the journal or look through my things or—I stand on tiptoe and kiss Elton again. Gently pull away and murmur, "Rain check. I'll be right back."

His smile flickers with disappointment, but he releases me. Goes back to pulling food cartons from the bag.

I'm halfway up the stairs when it hits me. Jameson only left because Elton arrived home. If Elton had been five minutes later, would this have all gone very differently?

I know what Jameson is capable of. I know the threats he's quietly lobbed my way.

I go back down the stairs, snatch up my phone, and type as I stride back to the bathroom.

Chloe: *Where are you?*

I send it to Jameson, and in seconds, there's a read receipt.

Jameson: *The hospital. Where's my journal?*

He's lying. I have no doubt.

I bite my lip. Huff out a breath. Consider demanding a photo as proof, but that would only make me sound paranoid. And put him on high alert. I set my phone down, remove my glasses, turn on the shower and step into it. I let the hot water soak my hair, my shoulders, my body. It scalds, and I bask in it.

My bag still sits on the bathroom floor, and I finish showering, step out and dry off, then make myself as comfortable as possible perched on the edge of the soaking tub.

I crack the door open and listen—Elton's still whistling, and in the background, there are tinny voices, like he's listening to a podcast. Occupied. I wipe my hands once more, making sure they're totally dry, clean my glasses of steam and put them back on, then pull out the notebook labeled 2020. I watched Jameson write in these notebooks when I lived with him, but he said they were private—contained patient information, and so were confidential.

But that's not how it works, at least not when you work for a big corporation of a hospital. Notes on patients are taken in the electronic medical record—not in spiral notebooks. I flip the first page open.

A name—*Mildred McCoy*. Her name makes my breath catch. I knew her. Not well, but well enough to remember her all these years later. And to remember the spray of blood across the wall the morning after she unexpectedly died. Jameson has listed out basic stats on the blue-lined notebook paper—demographics, her medical condition. He's added details like *enjoyed swimming and quilting.*

Below that, he's pasted in a cutout from the newspaper's obituary section: Mildred McCoy's obituary, complete with a black-and-white portrait of her, gray hair curled up on top of her head, a kind smile across her face. Making her suddenly very real. I remember she was soft-spoken, kind. I remember being newly in love with Jameson and trying to comfort him in the wake of her death.

I turn the page once, twice, three times, and it's more of the same. Patients who conveniently could have been at death's door. Many of whose names I recognize. Patients who no one would take notice of if they suddenly died.

About a third of the way through, it ends, and blank notebook pages continue. I flip back and count them—twenty-six... what would I even call these? Biographies? In all, *twenty-six.*

Downstairs, Elton calls, "Babe, you about ready? I'm starving."

"Be down in a sec," I call back.

I slowly close the notebook, having come to only one conclusion.

I've found a list of patients of his who are dead. Presumably, the other notebooks contain the same thing, ordered by year. It reminds me of one thing:

The way a serial killer keeps souvenirs of his victims to remember them by.

TWENTY-TWO

CHLOE

Then

Nathan was diagnosed with amyotrophic lateral sclerosis, or ALS, two weeks later.

Neurological disease.

Muscle weakness, stiffness. Progressive loss of function.

Unknown cause.

Death, most often in three to five years.

Death, by painful, panicking respiratory failure.

"And how do you treat it?" Nathan had asked. I'd flown in to attend the appointment with him. He sat in his plastic chair, hands clasped on his lap, leaning forward. Like he was getting instructions from a coach, not hearing a fatal diagnosis from a physician.

I reached out, took his hand. Tried to listen as the doctor listed off several medicines that would slow Nathan's decline.

"And that will make me better?" Nathan asked.

My chest clenched up. He still didn't get it. Nathan didn't understand the reality: there was no cure.

"No." The doctor's face curved into something resembling a

gentle smile, but there was nothing to smile about, and she knew it. She crossed her legs, tilted her head, pressed her lips together. "Nathan, there is no cure. It's important you understand that. The medications may slow the onset of symptoms. May give you more time. But the prognosis is three to five years on average. Ten percent of patients may live up to a decade, but —" Her gaze slid to me, then back to him. "Given how quickly your symptoms have come on, how quickly they've worsened— I may be wrong, and I have been before. Everyone is different. But I think you will likely progress faster than slower."

We both sat there, stunned.

Over the phone Jameson cleared his throat and asked, "So, Dr. Shelly, in your best estimation, how much time does Nathan have?"

She pursed her lips, like she'd hoped to avoid this question. She stared at the phone, then focused back on Nathan. "I'm sorry to say, Nathan, I would guess that without nutritional support and respiratory support, you have less than a year. With it, maybe two. Maybe."

More silence.

Then Nathan asks, "Respiratory support?"

"She means a ventilator," I say. "Like at the hospital."

"We can consider noninvasive ventilation," Dr. Shelly says. "At least to start with."

Nathan turned, his eyes wide. In mere seconds, his entire life had flipped upside down—from minor league baseball player looking at spending a season with the pros to being given a year to live. My own breath failed me, my own heart squeezed tight in panic. I couldn't imagine what was going through his head.

All I could think was *Nathan's going to die.*

Back at home two days later, Jameson brought me a drink— a strong one. He built a fire in the fireplace, stuffed it with newspaper, lit it, and sat beside me, one arm draped over my shoulders.

"We will get through this," he murmured, "together."

I stared at the growing flames. I'd asked Nathan to come stay with us—to let us help him. But he'd refused. He wanted to be where it felt like home to him, and that was Arizona.

He'd been dating a woman from there, and he wanted to stay close to her, too. So there would be lots of flying back and forth. Lots of visits. I might have to go stay with him near the end.

"How did he seem?" Jameson asked.

"Shocked. Even before we met with his doctor. Especially after."

"Understandable." Jameson exhaled. "Listen. We can talk about this later, but I want to mention it."

I looked up at him, met his eyes, that same warm intensity as usual.

"If there comes a time when he's done—when he wants to be done—I will help." He said the words softly, simply. It took me a second to realize what he meant.

"Oh," I said.

He meant if Nathan wanted to die, he would help him. Half of me was horrified, my stomach writhing at the thought of Nathan dying, period; the other half of me felt grateful in a way that made me want to collapse with grief, cry until there were no tears left. A heaviness descended over my chest, my shoulders, my whole body. Jameson was offering a great kindness.

A great, horrible kindness.

TWENTY-THREE

CHLOE

Then

I marked the passing months by Nathan—how he was feeling, how he was doing. It wasn't good. Like his doctor said he likely would, his disease process advanced fast, faster than normal. "It happens sometimes," she'd said.

And in the meantime, Nathan wouldn't let me visit more than once a month.

"Live your life," he'd say. "Stop coming here to watch me die."

He didn't want help and he didn't want pity. I shared with him what Jameson offered, to which he stoically nodded, but said nothing.

So, I tried to do what he said—I tried to keep living. In a way, it's all I could do. Faced with my brother's imminent death, I wanted to appreciate every moment. Soak in every day, and live it to the fullest. Jameson and I traveled. We trained for and ran a 5K together over the holiday, and signed up for a half marathon that summer. We collected books and furniture everywhere we went, making his condo "ours."

Life was as good as it could be, all things considered.

But I couldn't shake the feeling something was wrong. The high death rate at the hospital hung in the back of my mind. That medical serial killer show, which popped up every time we turned Netflix on, weighed on my conscience. Like I was missing something.

On a Wednesday morning, Jameson came around with the pharmacist, respiratory therapist, and charge nurse for rounds. My patients were up, so I grabbed the little cards I took notes on and reeled off the basics.

"Mr. Chad Silver is a seventy-two-year-old male in for a triple bypass. He had surgery two days ago and was extubated the same day. However, we haven't had much luck stabilizing his blood pressure, and he's still requiring a combination of dopamine and milrinone—" I continued through the report, listing off his other medications, his history, his wife's questions.

When I looked up from my cards, the pharmacist murmured, "Let's try weaning the dopamine today. I'll adjust his regular meds and see if that helps stabilize his blood pressure."

The respiratory therapist gave her own report: "He's looking good. I turned off the nasal cannula this morning, and O2 is sitting around ninety-eight percent."

All eyes turned to Jameson. He stroked his jaw, where he'd nicked himself shaving that morning, wincing as he ran a finger over the spot and pulled his hand away. "I don't know," Jameson murmured. "I'm worried about him. His pressure should have stabilized by now."

Silence followed.

"We can maintain the dopamine if you think—"

"No, it's fine," Jameson interrupted the pharmacist. "Just concerned. I have a feeling. Probably nothing." He met my gaze, gave me a tight smile, and the group moved on to the next patient. I didn't think anything of it.

Until the next morning, when I found Mr. Silver's room empty because his body had been sent to the morgue.

* * *

A week later, I was home on a Saturday, doing chores and catching up on laundry while Jameson worked a weekend shift. I'd looked into Mr. Silver's death—the autopsy showed heart failure, the most common cause of death after coronary artery bypass. It was a general diagnosis that more or less meant nothing. But in my head, it was another patient of Jameson's who'd died. The surgeon took responsibility—came on the unit in his blue scrubs and white jacket and assured Jameson there was nothing he could have done differently.

But I'd be lying if I told you I didn't wonder.

Today, I'd pushed it from my mind. My husband was a kind, ethical man. The sort who fought for patients to make their own decisions about death, which was more than a lot of doctors could say. He was the man I'd fallen in love with—*my* person, the only one who would still be there for me when Nathan lost his battle with ALS. My only family.

When I sat down, two baskets of laundry in front of me, I picked that same show.

Medical Killers.

The episode began, this one about a doctor who'd killed more than twenty of her patients over ten years before being caught.

"Likely, dozens more," the narrator shared. "But only twenty-two were confirmed."

I fished my favorite jeans from the laundry basket, folding them carefully and setting them to one side. I worked steadily, matching socks and sorting Jameson's shirts from my own, matching scrub tops to scrub bottoms, listening as the show droned on.

I moved on to the second basket, listening as Mary Dugan, doctor serial killer extraordinaire, killed several patients using insulin.

"She was caught only when a nurse noticed so many of her patients were dying. But it took six months before the nurse could get management to take her seriously. In the process, she nearly lost her job. In the end, lab testing not usually performed showed patients having extraordinarily high levels of insulin in their bodies."

I looked up from the laundry, thinking about our own patients. Many of them were recovering from open-heart surgery, a surgery significant enough that the body's stress hormones kicked into overdrive, decreasing the body's sensitivity to its naturally occurring insulin—which meant we gave patients insulin for days at a time post-op to keep their blood sugar controlled. It wouldn't be hard for someone to kick up their dosing for an hour or two, or even inject them with extra insulin. Though that wouldn't lead to heart failure, which is what many of our patients died of.

Jameson texted me right then: *Thai for dinner? I can pick up on my way home. Movie night?* He follows up with a kissing emoji.

Sure, I texted back. He knew what to order for me from our favorite Thai restaurant. A smile came to my mouth, thinking of it—that bond we shared. I exhaled, and piled up the laundry into the baskets.

Usually, I only put away my laundry, leaving Jameson's in a basket on the bed. He did the same when it was his turn to do laundry, but last week, he'd taken the time to put mine away for me—which I greatly appreciated after a long shift. So after I'd tucked my own clothes into my dresser, I reached for his basket. His underwear and socks went up top, jeans on the bottom. In between was a drawer for scrubs and another drawer for miscellaneous—shorts and shirts, anything that didn't go elsewhere.

But as I reached for the last pile of clothes, four sets of scrubs in varying shades of blue, I realized the jumbled mess that was his scrub drawer wouldn't hold more.

Your dresser is a mess, I texted him, shaking my head. But I set the scrubs aside and pulled the pile of older scrubs out. Half of them I'd never even seen him wear, so I began separating the piles into ones he would want to keep and ones he could consider donating.

But as I reached for them, my hand closed around something hard—several somethings hard, actually. Using both hands, I reached in, gathering the pile of whatever it was, and placed it gently on the bedspread. It was wrapped in a scrub top, and I folded back the layers until a dozen tiny vials sat before me.

Vials of medicine.

My hand flew to my mouth, recognizing the names printed on the labels—*propofol, rocuronium, midazolam, fentanyl, human insulin.*

They were controlled substances. Medicines he couldn't legally just have sitting around. Drugs that sedated and paralyzed. And the insulin—I couldn't imagine why anyone would have insulin if they weren't diabetic. Unless... My mind flashed to the episode I'd just watched.

They were all drugs that could kill someone.

I spun out excuses—these were for his out-of-state patients. The patients he illegally, but in my opinion ethically, helped die a peaceful death. But no—he said he always used their own medication for that. Pain medicine or anxiety medicine, usually a combination of both. It had to look like the patient had overdosed themselves. And he never mentioned using insulin. That didn't seem right at all.

A sweat broke out on the back of my neck. My body flushed cold with fear.

Okay, then maybe Washington-based deaths. It was legal

here. But no, again. Physician-assisted suicide required a prescription. The patient or someone close to them picked that prescription up. They self-administered it while the physician stood by. It was voluntary, their *choice*, every step of the way.

Well, maybe—yes, maybe he had these just like I'd taken a handful of things from the hospital for an at-home first aid kit. A syringe without a needle for cleaning a wound, some gauze, some tape—

But no. Those were basic supplies.

These were *medications* used only in a controlled setting like a hospital.

Deadly medications if not given carefully.

I couldn't think of a single good reason Jameson would have any of them.

I left the pile of vials on the bed, still swaddled in the scrub top. I didn't want to touch them. Though it was ridiculous, because I wasn't about to call the cops—at least not yet. But I didn't want my fingerprints on them, either.

I wandered the house, thoughts racing. My hands were clammy, my breath came in short pants. I didn't want to think too hard about what I'd found. About what it might mean. But then my gaze landed on the television—the episode list for *Medical Killers* pulled up alongside the show's logo.

Again, I let the thought in, let myself consider the possibility.

Was Jameson killing people?

I grabbed my phone, wiped my palms on my pants, and typed out a message slowly.

Chloe: *We need to talk. Please come straight home.*

TWENTY-FOUR

CHLOE

Now

Elton is downstairs, looking back and forth between two bottles of wine. He's swapped his scrubs for a white T-shirt and gray sweatpants, and I walk over to rub his back, attempting some semblance of normalcy.

"What ya doing?"

He points at the bottles. "White or red with curry?"

"Red, I think?" I shrug. "Whichever sounds better."

"That's not how it works, certain wines match with certain foods." He gives me a grin. "I'll ask the internet."

I help him carry the to-go containers to our table. I go back for the wine—he chose the red—and set my phone face down on the counter. I want twenty minutes with my fiancé, no one interrupting.

"Wine?" He holds up the bottle.

"Just a little. I have to run back into work for a few minutes. I forgot to write a note." I glance up, toward the windows at the back of the house. It's golden hour edging toward sunset, the sky a brilliant pink and orange, turning trees and boulders into silhouettes. Silhouettes that *move...*

I stop breathing and gape at where I swear something shifted, or took a step, or maybe scurried away.

Elton splashes half a glass worth of wine in my glass and slides it my way, not noticing my alarm.

"One sec." I step around my chair and go to the back window where the sliding door was open when I came downstairs. Where someone escaped before I caught them. Are they still out there, watching us now?

"What is it?" Elton comes up beside me, runs his hand down my back. "I'll bet there are coyotes out there." I glance at him, and he's grinning.

"Coyotes?" I look again, but now, it's just a pretty sky. Trees sway ever so slightly in the breeze. Probably, I'm paranoid after hearing someone down here.

But can you blame me?

We pull away from the windows and find our seats at the table.

"So, I didn't ask at lunch. How was working with Jameson?"

I shrug. "Oh, it was fine. We were so busy there wasn't time for it to be weird." There was time, however, for George to die minutes after signing a DNR. For Jameson's sister to show up and shoot lasers from her eyes at me. For him to follow me *here.*

I hesitate, realizing I've just lied to Elton. That's not like me. Not like us. Guilt makes me lower my eyes, avoid his gaze. "How about you?"

"They asked if I want to train to be a charge nurse." His eyes shine with pride. "I've always thought I'd be a good charge nurse."

"You really would be." He has great leadership skills and loves teaching and helping other nurses. It's right up his alley.

I reach for my wineglass and feel a tingle at the back of my neck.

That notorious tingle I read about in books and roll my eyes at thinking *that's not real*—but I feel it now, and when Elton goes to the sink to pour himself a glass of water, I whip around, taking in the backyard again. The extensive field beyond it. We're in this bright house lit up, on display, for anyone who might wander back there.

"Relax." Elton is suddenly there, his smile warm, loving. His hand skims over mine. "Just the wildlife. Birds, raccoons. Maybe a stray cat will come to the back door and beg for milk." He chuckles. "Just be careful, it might be a bobcat here in Oregon."

I nod, cheeks flushed with embarrassment. It's one thing to be paranoid. It's another for Elton to notice it. "Tell me more about your day," I say.

He considers then says, "Oh, apparently at this hospital you don't have to float to different units. They said I don't have to float to the neuro ICU if I don't want to."

"That's good." At some point, Elton had trained in a neuro ICU, and some hospitals expected him to float to the unit and work there when they were short-staffed—a unit he despised thanks to the frequently confused patients. According to him, he preferred a patient he could talk to and form a rapport with.

"Shoot, forgot napkins." He rises from the table again and crosses into the kitchen to search for them. I could get up and help him—I should—but I stay glued to my chair, still processing everything that happened today. That Jameson's issued multiple threats. That Zoey Constance doesn't seem to exist, but somehow invited me to apply to this job, *here,* where Jameson is.

And then, he came in our house. In our *home.*

Elton's found the napkins and is folding two of them into neat triangles like his mother does. Giving this simple thing the utmost attention because he wants to do it right—do it right for us, with me.

Maybe I do know why I lied. I don't want Elton to worry,

don't want him to suggest we change what I'm doing. Because I don't want to quit this job. I don't want to leave. A day ago I was over the moon to be in Portland, to be starting a new phase of life with Elton.

Something stirs inside me. Something I felt a hint of before, when everything fell apart with Jameson—when I realized what he was up to.

Rage.

Jameson randomly shows up in my life again. A fluke. Maybe karma, for what I allowed to happen. More likely, Jameson brought me here for some reason.

Whether he meant to or not, giving me a second opportunity.

It was a chance that just this morning, I didn't want. The only reason I'd gone to the hospital was because he'd threatened me—*don't quit this job.*

But the reason I'm going back tonight is entirely different. Jameson doesn't get to do this. Doesn't get to destroy my life or threaten my future with Elton. Doesn't get to come into our house and leave me looking around corners, hiding in closets, then rushing downstairs because Elton might be in danger, too.

He already betrayed me and left me more alone than before. I've finally found my happily ever after. I'm not going to let him take that away from me. I don't know how I'll do it. How I'll manage it without going down with him. But I have to find a way to trap him and prove what he's done.

TWENTY-FIVE

CHLOE

Then

Jameson tried calling three times, but all I could manage was to stare at the phone, at the photo of him that popped up, grinning on our wedding day. I hugged myself, trying not to think too hard, so the panic wouldn't take over.

A text came through.

Jameson: *I'll be home as soon as I can, but I'm admitting a new patient. Are you okay?*

Chloe: *No.*

I hit send and hoped it made him sweat, made him worry. The anxiety crawling through my chest made it hard to breathe. What the hell was he up to?

I forced myself to sit down at the table with my laptop. To think rationally.

This was *Jameson*. Why would he have these meds?

Or—I took a slow breath and met my gaze in the reflection

of the dark monitor screen—why did I *think* he might have them?

Medical Killers flickered in my mind, but I couldn't believe it. I just couldn't. Not when I saw how kind he was with patients. When I'd sat down to dinner with him countless times to have him rehash a patient's care with me, asking my opinion on if we were missing anything or should try something different. Not when the man in question was the only person other than my own brother who loved me.

What felt like hours later, the front door opened, closed. Deadbolt thrown. The whisking of a jacket removed, hung on a hook, and the pad of footsteps over the hardwood. Jameson's concerned face came around the corner. His eyes were wide, and he looked me up and down, as though expecting me to be injured.

"Are you okay?" He didn't wait for a response, coming close, wrapping his arms around me. His warmth, his scent engulfed me, a little sweaty from a long shift at the hospital. He pulled up a chair, gaze never leaving my face. "What happened? Is it Nathan?"

Being near him dashed the anger and courage I'd built up. I opened my mouth, trying to summon how mad I'd been in that first moment I'd laid eyes on the vials, but it escaped me. I was still mad, *so damn mad*, and scared—so, so scared. But he was right here in front of me. Jameson reached for my hand, clasped it.

"It's okay. We'll get through it, whatever it is. Just tell me." He scooted closer and pressed a hand to my knee. "Chloe? Talk to me."

But I couldn't. I couldn't form the words. Couldn't bear to look up and meet his eyes. If I found out the truth, and the truth was awful, then this would be over. I'd have to turn him in. He'd be taken away from me, our life. He'd go to prison, probably forever. This condo would be sold. Our family, our home, would disappear in the wink of an eye.

I'd be alone again.

I had to do or say something. He'd raced home, thanks to my text message. He knew something was wrong.

Holding his hand, I led him back toward the bedroom. I didn't say a word. It was somehow easier this way, even as fear bubbled up inside me and made it hard to take a proper breath. We stepped close to the bed, and I pointed at the collection of vials. I looked up, trying to read his expression.

Jameson stared at the vials a long moment, brow furrowing. His gaze shifted to me.

"Where did these come from?" he asked.

"Where did they—" I glanced down at them. "What do you mean? That's what I want to know. They were in your dresser."

The furrow deepened. His hand released mine, and he leaned over the bed, peering at them.

"Midazolam, propofol, rocuronium, fentanyl, insulin." He whispered the names of the drugs out loud. "Is this a joke?" He swung his head to look at me, face blank with confusion.

My insides did something funny then—twisted—half of me infuriated he was pretending to be clueless; half of me wanting to believe him. It would be so easy to believe him.

"Who else has been in our home, Jameson?"

Silence grew between us, thicker with every passing second.

"The maid," he said. "She was here this past week."

"The maid? Seriously? You said Matilda has worked for you for years, you think she'd do this?" My voice grew as my anger did. As I got more and more mad that he would do this—steal drugs, hide them in our home, then lie to me about it. That he would risk our relationship over this. Risk his license, his ability to practice medicine. What would make him do something so idiotic?

The only people who did things like this were drug addicts,

people so addicted to a high, they couldn't help themselves. But even that didn't explain the insulin. The fucking insulin featured in the show about medical serial killers.

"Why do you have these?" I asked again.

"These aren't mine. You have to believe me."

I shook my head, started to step away. But he grabbed my arm, yanked me close, forced me to look him in the eye. "Chloe, listen—"

My arm burned with his grip, and my breath caught, realizing how much bigger he was than me, something I'd never had to think about before. How much *stronger* he was.

Fear fluttered in my belly. In the same moment, his eyes grew large.

"Shit." He let me go, stepped back, hands up. "I'm sorry, Chloe. I'm sorry. I didn't mean to hurt you. Are you okay?"

"No. I'm not okay." The words flew from my mouth, surprising even me. "My husband has medications in his dresser drawer. Ones that could get us both in trouble. *Arrested.* We could lose our licenses." My mind caught up with my words—silenced me from adding the rest: *Too many of your patients are dying. You predict deaths.* I swallow those words. Keep them from escaping my mouth. I turn, hot tears running down my face, sniffling so I can get a breath.

Jameson didn't say anything for a long moment. When he finally spoke, he merely said, "I'm sorry, Chloe. I wish I had an answer for you. That I could say I stole them or am holding them for someone or—or *anything.* But I don't know how they got in my dresser. If it helps—" A humorless half laugh escapes him, or maybe a hiccupped sob. "At least two of these have to be refrigerated. Which means they aren't good anymore, can't be used. If they were mine, wouldn't I have put them in the refrigerator?"

I considered his words. I knew insulin always had to be pulled from the refrigerated part of our medication room. I didn't know about the others, and sometimes different preparations were shelf stable at room temperature. I was a nurse not a pharmacist. Of course, it didn't necessarily mean the drug didn't work—it just didn't work the way it was intended. Maybe the insulin would still kill someone. Maybe the rocuronium would still paralyze them to the extent their lungs stopped working, stopped supplying oxygen to their body, letting them die a slow, agonizing death.

My breath huffed out in a sigh.

"I don't know. This doesn't make sense. Who else would put them here?" I asked.

"I don't know." Jameson exhaled. "I have no idea. But I'm telling you the truth. They're not mine."

My phone rang from the other room, yanking my attention away from Jameson.

"Don't answer it." He reached for me again, but let his hand fall flat, afraid to touch me after grabbing me roughly. "Please stay here with me."

I hesitated. Jameson was afraid. A sight I'd never seen. His hands crossed over his chest, like he was holding himself. He watched me like he couldn't look away. The pull I felt toward him—toward this man I loved—caused physical pain as I denied myself what I wanted, to go to him. To wrap my arms around him. To tell him I believed him.

I didn't know what to think.

My phone went silent.

Jameson started to say something, but the ringing started up again.

"I have to get it. It might be Nathan." I left the room before he could react.

I picked up my phone. The screen read *Nathan*, complete with a picture of him in a baseball hat, grinning against the Arizona sunshine.

"Hello?" I said.

"Hey, sis." His voice sounded weak, distant.

"Hey. How are you?"

A long sigh. "Not good. I know this is the last thing you want to hear. But it's time. Can you and Jameson come?"

I blinked, reality coming back into focus.

What he meant was that he was ready to die.

TWENTY-SIX

CHLOE

Then

The next morning, Jameson set a plate of scrambled eggs and toast in front of me.

"Please eat," he said. His voice came out soft, pleading. Not at all like him. It strummed the cords of my heart, made them vibrate, wanting to cling to him. We hadn't touched since he grabbed me the night before. I'd slept on the couch, not because he wouldn't, but because I couldn't stand to curl up in the bed we shared, smell his earthy pine scent on the pillow next to mine.

But now, looking at him in soft morning light, I couldn't help myself. I reached out and grasped his hand as he set down a cup of coffee beside my plate. I needed him now more than ever. I'd imagined this day before—packing a bag, going through airport security, getting on a flight, knowing that when we returned, my brother would be dead. That this time next week, we'd have attended a funeral or be in the midst of planning one. That after this, everything changed.

"I'm scared," I said. "My parents died. And now he's dying.

And we—" I blinked back a fresh onslaught of tears. I couldn't say what I meant—*we aren't doing so well, either*—so I said, "I don't know what's going on, Jameson."

"Chloe." Jameson pressed a hand over mine and pulled out the nearest chair, scooting close until our knees touched. He wrapped me in his arms, pressed me to his chest, and kissed my forehead. "I know. I know you're scared. But I'm here. I'll never leave you alone. I promise."

"But the drugs—"

His body heaved a heavy sigh. Not one of frustration, but of grief. I clung tighter to him.

"I don't know, Chloe. That's the honest-to-god truth. It scares the shit out of me. It means someone was in our house. It means someone—" He stops short. "It means someone is trying to make it look like I'm up to something. Or that I stole drugs. Or... *something*. I don't know."

It felt like something out of a movie. Like an impossibility. But crazy things happened all the time. I listened to enough podcasts, watched enough shows, to know that.

"You have to trust me." Jameson unwrapped my arms from him and took my hands in his. "Do you trust me?"

I looked down at our hands, clasped together. Our wedding rings. I thought of the day he gave me his chair, and how he asked me out so sweetly, after looking into if the hospital even allowed staff to date one another. I thought about how he was so honest that he told me he was doing something that while ethical, was illegal. How much power he'd given me in sharing that part of himself with me. And how now, he was the only person who could do this thing for my brother—this thing Nathan had begged me for last night.

I exhaled and made a decision. "Yes, I trust you."

TWENTY-SEVEN

CHLOE

Now

I don't drive straight to the hospital. Instead, I wait for Elton to disappear upstairs after dinner and do my own web search, finding a single local listing for one Jameson Smith.

"I'll be back in a while," I call up to Elton.

His footsteps patter through the hall, and he appears at the top of the stairs.

"Be careful." He blows me a kiss. "I'll get some unpacking done while you're gone."

I get in my car and hop on the interstate, winding down a riverfront road to a four-floor building overlooking the Willamette River. Jameson's place. The Portland version of his Seattle condo. Typical.

He said he was at the hospital. According to the white pages, he lives on the fourth floor, which is utterly dark right now. I park the car and stare up at it, wishing I could invade his territory the way he's invaded mine. Wishing I could go upstairs and do something, I don't know what, to make him wonder if he's safe.

My fingers drum over the steering wheel as I debate what to do next. My gaze flicks back to the condo, and I find myself wondering not only what is hidden behind those walls, but what the walls *look* like. If he still insists on covering hardwood with rugs, because he doesn't like his feet to be cold. If he has the same favorite loveseat in heather gray, and if he still has any of the furniture we collected on our meandering road trips.

Elton texts.

Elton: *You doing okay? When do you think you'll be home?*

My stomach flutters. I'm not where I told him I'd be and he's checking in. He can't know where I am, can he? I take a quick glance around. There's no one—just other cars in the lot, empty and dark.

I shake my head and type back a message.

Chloe: *All good. Home ASAP.*

I'm paranoid. That's it.

Beside me lies the 2020 notebook. Deaths cataloged. I take a moment to flip it open, to use my phone to take photos of every page, pausing on the faces that look familiar. Patients I spoke to or cared for. More lives Jameson destroyed.

Maybe I'll be that better person after all.

* * *

It's nearly nine and night shift is in full swing as I step off the elevator and onto our floor. I hurry through the unit, eyes down, hoping to not attract attention. But I can't help stopping short when I see it.

A steel cart sits in the hall, a sheet draped over it.

It's meant to look unobtrusive, the sort of thing patients and families will look past, but I know what it is, have seen it dozens of times before—it's the cart designed to carry bodies down to the morgue. Its presence means someone else has died.

My pulse ticks a little faster—it's an ICU, people die here all the time—but Jameson has been here, supposedly all day and evening.

Except for when he was in my house, of course.

I stride over to the nurses' station, flip back the cover on the patient book, skim the list until I find one that's been crossed off. Declared dead, so far as the charge nurse is concerned.

Debra Schilling, female, fifty-seven, atrial fibrillation.

Atrial fibrillation is when the heart is in an erratic beat, but it's rarely deadly by itself. Especially at fifty-seven. In fact, it's easily treated, and many people wander around for days or weeks in what we call "A-fib" before they realize there's a problem.

"What happened here?" I ask the nearest nurse. He's a man with a mop of dark hair, thick-rimmed glasses. He comes close, peers down at it.

"No idea. Happened before I started my shift." He grabs his stethoscope off the nearest counter and disappears into a room. No other nurses are around to ask. The name stands out to me— looks familiar, but I can't think from where.

I let the book fall shut and head for the office, eyes lingering over the cart. My hand is on the office door when it hits me.

Debra Schilling. The hospital administrator in charge of forming the task force to reduce patient deaths in the hospital.

TWENTY-EIGHT

CHLOE

Then

Nathan chose to die that Saturday.

I woke early, before the sun, blinking into the dark hotel room. Jameson lay asleep beside me. I still wasn't entirely sure what I thought, how I felt. But he was my husband, and I did love him. Trusted him. Mostly.

Or maybe, I felt like I had no choice. He would help Nathan. And he would be there when there was no one else left. I *wanted* him to be there. My Jameson, who'd always been so sweet. So caring. Who I'd built a life with this past year.

I scrubbed at my eyes and checked my phone—just after 3 a.m. My mind buzzed, a mental countdown to the hours, minutes, seconds my brother had left in his life.

We'd been to see him the night before—watched as he wheezed, trying to take full breaths, as he choked down one last dinner. A nurse had come by and injected a medication that was supposed to slow the advancement of ALS—studies had shown that it worked for many patients. But not him. He had a

PICC line, a type of central venous access that looked more or less like an IV but was semipermanent. She cleaned the site, applied a new dressing to it, and gave him the medication.

"So glad you have visitors," she said on her way out.

Meanwhile, all I could think of was how unfair it was he was sick. That the medication hadn't worked for him. That the dose she'd just given would be entirely ineffectual because he would die in the morning.

His apartment was worse than I expected. His kitchen, once full of protein powder and fresh fruit and healthy snacks, was instead filled with Ensure shakes, applesauce, thickener that helped him swallow liquids without choking on them.

And I hated that.

I pulled myself out of bed and tiptoed to the bathroom, carefully shutting the door before I flicked on the light. My pale face stared back at me, and I began the process of making shitty hotel coffee—a paper cup beneath the Keurig knockoff. Water. Press the button. The hiss of steam as the water heated. I sat on the closed toilet lid and focused on breathing. This was Nathan's last morning.

God, I had to stop thinking like that. I had to stop glancing at my phone and counting how many hours of life he had left. It was torture. He *chose* this. A dignified death. It was one thing I could help him with.

Jameson woke around 5 a.m. We shuffled to the elevator still in pajamas and rode it down to the hot breakfast the hotel's advertisements bragged about. Jameson held my hand. Kept a hand on my shoulder. Pulled our chairs closer together when we finally sat down with plates of mediocre food.

"How you doing?" he murmured.

"Shitty," I replied.

Our eyes met, a moment of understanding.

"I know," he said.

I leaned my head on his shoulder, grateful I didn't have to explain or defend, that he didn't even try to comfort a thing that could not be comforted. Sometimes, I felt like I didn't deserve him. And right now, I was so grateful to have him by my side. He could have left when I confronted him about the vials of medication. If they really weren't his—if something was going on, if someone put them there—I'd assumed he was guilty. And he hadn't left. In fact, he'd apologized. Stayed when I turned around and asked for his help with Nathan. And on this Saturday morning, in a hotel lobby at a table that wobbled as we drank OJ and ate powdered scrambled eggs, he just wanted to be there for me.

"Thank you," I said.

"For what?"

"Just being you."

* * *

It had to look like a suicide.

When we arrived at Nathan's apartment, Jameson surveyed his meds and began crushing pills.

He looked up, pill grinder in hand. "Why don't you spend some time with him? You don't need to watch me do this."

He was right. I was here to be with Nathan—not to assist Jameson.

Sun filtered in through the blinds, illuminating the kitchen in bright Arizona sunshine. A beautiful day to die. Which wasn't fair—that today of all days was a gorgeous Arizona day. But maybe that was better. I went to Nathan's room and helped him into a wheelchair. We went out to the back patio, and I positioned him where the sunshine hit his face.

He tossed back his head, sandy hair glinting in the light, and soaked in the last bit of sunshine he'd ever have. I opened my mouth to beg him to wait—just a little longer. Another day. Another week. Even a few hours.

Instead, I said, "I love you, Nathan."

His lips curled in a smile. He did not open his eyes, but he reached out a trembling hand, and I took it.

"You're sure?" I asked.

"I'm sure," he said. Finally, he opened his eyes. He looked at me, searching my gaze. "It's okay, Chloe. I want this. I need this. Don't be sad for me. I had a great life. I got to play baseball. I got to have you as a sister. It's all I ever wanted. And now, I get to go be with Mom and Dad."

My throat closed up with grief, but I bit back a sob. Summoned a tearful smile.

Jameson stood at the doorway, and I knew what that meant. He wouldn't interrupt the moment, but it meant he was ready. He'd ground up the right pills, mixed them with a bottle of apple juice we'd brought over.

"I'm ready." Nathan's voice came out stronger than I'd heard it in a long time. He gave my hand a squeeze and let it fall by his side. "Let's do this."

We helped him get comfortable in bed. Jameson helped as he opened the pill bottles to make it look like he'd taken them himself.

I perched on the edge of his bed, one hand on his leg. It felt as though I were miles away, floating in a dream, and this couldn't be real. It wasn't *possible* that my brother, my healthy, strong, big brother, my only surviving family, was about to die.

"Can you leave, Chloe? Just for a minute, while I take the meds? Please."

I blinked, processing the request.

"You want me to go?"

"You can come right back in." Nathan tried to smile. "I just don't want you to see this. Okay?"

I managed a nod. Jameson stroked his hand across my shoulders. "I'll come get you in a minute."

"Okay."

I walked down the hall, back to the kitchen, numb. The apartment was still, silent. Lifeless, even though I knew they were in the bedroom, the door shut tight. Out back, on the patio, the spot where we'd sat just half an hour ago now looked forlorn, empty chairs and the open spot where I'd wheeled his wheelchair. The last time we'd sit around a table again.

Guilt hit hard. I should have come to visit more often. Yes, I was in nursing school, and then in a new job, but I worked three twelve-hour shifts a week. That meant four days off, and I'd only come to visit after I'd learned of his diagnosis. Of course, Nathan was busy, too. With baseball, and often out of town for his games or spring training. But still. We should have spent more time together.

Now, we were out of time.

A bump down the hall made me spin—but no Jameson. The bedroom door was still shut. It was taking a while. Or maybe, waiting for my brother to take the meds that would kill him, maybe that just felt like it lasted a long time. That was probably it.

I exhaled and wished for something—anything—to make this easier. But nothing would help. I just needed to be grateful Jameson was here to help. That no matter what, he'd be there for me.

Another sound, but this one like something or someone had fallen, a series of thumps, followed by a strangled grunt.

I didn't hesitate. I rushed back down the hall, to the door, but it went silent again. My breath came up short, my hand ready on the knob. I came to a stop.

Nathan asked me to leave for this part. I didn't want to burst in. It was his last request, the last thing he'd asked of me. And I trusted Jameson.

Right?

A gurgling sound, followed by coughing. My stomach swam, nerves in overdrive as my body hummed with panic, and I couldn't stop myself—I cracked open the door.

And gasped.

Jameson, on his knees on the bed, one arm wrapped around Nathan's head, tipping it back. The other held a large oral syringe, and he pushed the end in, forcing the liquid down Nathan's throat as he fought against him. Nathan's hands pawed at Jameson's grip, his head wrenched back and forth, trying—

Trying to stop him.

I burst through the door. "What are you doing?"

I didn't know the ins and outs of physician-assisted suicide. But I did know it had to be voluntary. The patient had to be in control at all moments. They had to take the medication themselves, had to *choose* in that moment to do it.

"You can't be in here." Jameson pointed at the door. "Go."

Nathan coughed again, spitting up what looked like his ground up meds.

"Chloe!" Jameson released Nathan and wrapped a rough hand around my arm, wrangling me from the room. When I pulled back, trying to get to Nathan, he lifted me easily. His arms were iron bars around my body, forcing me back into the hall. When he set me down, I shoved him as hard as I could, and he stumbled back into the wall.

"What the fuck are you doing?" he gasped.

I tried to dart around him, to get to Nathan, but he blocked me.

Jameson scowled. "I'm helping your brother. Don't make this harder for him."

"No, you're—" I racked my mind, replaying what I'd seen. His arm around Nathan. A syringe—not the cup he'd taken in there for Nathan to drink from, but a *syringe*, with which he was forcing Nathan to swallow the medicine. "Did he change his mind?" I asked.

"Stay here." Jameson shoved a finger in my face. His eyes turned dark as warning flashed in them. "I'll come get you."

He went back in and shut the door. I heard the click of the lock.

Anger welled up inside me, and a sob tore from my throat. I smacked my hands against the door, tried the doorknob, and only stopped short of trying to kick it in. I couldn't tell what was happening—if it was what Nathan wanted. Or if...

No, no, no.

I sank to the ground, palms pressed to my eyes as tears ran down my face. Nathan's panicked expression, his eyes wide, his hands grasping to get Jameson off him. It wasn't right. That's not how physician-assisted suicide worked, not ever. How many times had Jameson explained the patient was always in control? That even when he did the illegal ones, he wasn't actually doing anything other than providing the patient with courage, guidance.

But that's not what I just saw.

When Jameson eventually came to the door to let me in, I managed to not yell. To not scream. I went to Nathan's bedside, held his hand, and looked into his eyes until they shut.

"He's asleep now. It will take a little longer until he passes," Jameson said.

On the bedside table laid the syringe, the inside coated thick with the sludge that was juice and ground up medications. It was too late for Nathan—I knew he had little time left, even without us coming here today. I also knew Jameson wouldn't let me call for help. Wouldn't let me dial 911 and beg them to rush Narcan to Nathan's bedside. An urge inside me wanted to get him help, because what happened here wasn't voluntary. It was forced. But I wouldn't do that to Nathan. It hadn't happened the way it should have, the peaceful death he thought it would be. But it was done, and I wouldn't torture him by bringing him back to misery.

So I sat with my brother as he took his final breath, the last gasp of life leaving a body. The soul escaping. And then I stared down at the shell that had once been my brother.

I had tried to help him. But really, I'd only helped kill him.

TWENTY-NINE

CHLOE

Then

When Jameson told me we had to leave Nathan's house, I didn't argue. I gathered my things, and we left everything exactly as we found it and went to the hotel room.

I waited until we were back. Until he'd slouched on the bed, as though he were exhausted by Nathan's death. He lifted his gaze to meet mine, that gentle innocent look in his eyes I'd always believed.

That was a lie.

"I know what you are," I said. "I know what you do."

He cocked his head. "Excuse me?"

"You kill people. You've killed patients. There's no way this is all a coincidence." The heat built inside me, finally saying the words that had been on the tip of my tongue for weeks. That I denied. That I made excuses for, accepted his rationales for. "I first wondered with Ms. McCoy. No, *wondered* isn't the right word. I *thought* it was strange, but you're you—kind and rational and you always do the right thing. Then your patients' death rate was so high. Even once I did the whole six months, it was so much higher than the other doctors."

Jameson stood quickly, body vibrating with an energy that reminded me of the moment he yanked me out of Nathan's room. I retreated, raising a hand.

"Don't get near me, or I'll scream."

"Chloe—" He held his hands up, helpless. "What are you talking about?"

"And then the laptop was stolen. *Two* laptops."

"You think I did that?" His eyes widened. "That's insane."

"Right. I'm insane because I picked up on what you were doing. I'll bet it's insane, too, that I think you had something to do with the task force being shut down." I'd never let myself truly think about that, but the words rolled off my tongue easily.

He squeezed his eyes shut in what looked like an admission of guilt. "I didn't say to shut it down. I just said that we *know* we have a higher rate of central line infections, that that was something we could *do* something about to reduce deaths immediately."

I struggled to find the right words. I'd expected him to deny that, too. But he hadn't—he'd told me I was right. Suddenly, I couldn't control it anymore.

"You kill people." The words came out low, scathing. "You predict deaths. You're happy after you help them die. The drugs. I found the drugs. And you lied about that, too." My breath came out in angry huffs. "God damn it, Jameson. You're a *doctor*. What's the travel stuff you do? Combining business and pleasure?"

He opened his mouth to reply, but I cut him off.

"I watched this show on Netflix about medical serial killers. You know what they said? That people often see it but refuse to believe it. That after the fact—when the doctor is found guilty—they say something like *I should have known*. And you know what? I should have. Instead, I let you"—I raised my hands to make quotations—"'*help*' Nathan. And I came in, and I found him in a headlock. You put my dying brother in a headlock. You put what was supposed to be a glass of medicine in a syringe and forced it down his throat. Did he change his mind? Hesitate? Ask for one more hour? Five more minutes?" My voice grew louder with each accusation, my insides boiling with anger.

"No. Chloe, just listen—"

Someone knocked on the wall—three, heavy blows. "Quiet!" a man's voice shouted from the next-door room.

But I wouldn't be quiet. Not anymore.

"I'm leaving."

"Chloe—" He reached out to touch my shoulder.

"Don't touch me." I yanked back, smacked his hand away. "I still have bruises from when you grabbed me earlier." I held up an arm, let him see his fingerprints—from when I found the vials, from today, the fresh marks an angry pink.

"I'm sorry, but Chloe, just listen." He got close, too close, dark eyes round with something—panic, fear, frustration? I couldn't tell. I didn't care.

"Leave me alone." I grabbed my bag, began shoving my belongings in it.

"Stop." This time he moved in front of the door, blocking it. "I won't let you walk out of here."

I eyed him, realizing my mistake. I treated this moment like he was Jameson—not a killer. I should have waited until I wasn't trapped in a hotel room with him. Adrenaline raced through me, and I glanced back toward the window. We weren't on the first floor. It was a bad idea. But if he was dangerous—

"Don't even think about it."

Jameson grabbed me before I could stop him, crushing me to his chest. Panic took the angry heat and made me go ice cold. Fear streaked through me. My body shook, no longer really listening to his words, but trying to figure out how to get free of him.

"Chloe, just stop. *Think.* This is grief. You know I'm not a killer."

"Let me go!" I raised my voice, wrenching my shoulders in his grip. He squeezed me tighter, pressed his lips to my head, bracing my body against his so I couldn't fight.

"Chloe, listen to me. I had to help your brother die—"

"No, you didn't! You're not supposed to do that!" And I raised my knee, aiming desperately for his groin. Somehow, I hit it, and he groaned, deep and long, but didn't release me.

"God damn it, Chloe." A muted growl of rage. "What do you think is going to happen? You'll run home and tell everyone you think I'm a killer. You'll tell them about Nathan. And you know what? We'll both end up in prison. You'll go down with me. What do you think about that? You'll destroy us. Everything we've built. And you'll end up being called a murderer right along with me."

His threat hung in the air. I stopped fighting. Stopped struggling against him. Finally, he released me and stepped back. We stared at one another, his words echoing through my mind.

What he'd done slowly sank in.

We weren't a family. No, we were something else, something much darker.

Jameson was killing people, and I'd let him make me an accomplice.

We barely spoke.

Jameson suggested we go for a walk, that I take a shower. He tried to rub my back, to hold me. I said no to everything.

Grief for my brother made my limbs heavy. I felt suffocated, like I couldn't take a real breath. I imagined his home health nurse finding him, realizing he'd committed suicide. The phone call we would inevitably get. That I'd have to lie through. But cutting through all that was the awareness of what Jameson had done. How he'd poisoned us, the one thing in my life I thought was something real, something true. He ruined *us*. The family the two of us created. The home I'd found in our relationship. Our dream of a future, together.

So now, I waited. Jameson watched television, the volume on low. He paced the room, and watched me, expressionless. Like he didn't know what to do with me. The weight of his gaze made me want to squirm. Want to get out before he decided I was more trouble than I was worth.

Eventually, Jameson came and sat on the edge of the bed, the mattress dipping with his weight. "How about a drink?" I opened my eyes to see the last bit of sun shining scarlet and orange through the hotel curtains. "I could go to the liquor store. We could make old fashioneds, toast to Nathan."

I forced myself to wait a beat. To pretend to think about it. I rolled over, met his eyes, tamped down the fury coursing through my veins.

"Okay," I said. "A drink would be good."

Relief relaxed his features.

"Okay. I'll be back."

"Hey, Jameson?"

"Yeah?" He paused at the hotel door, wallet and car keys in hand.

"Can you try to find Arizona Gold? It was Nathan's favorite bourbon."

"Okay, sure. I'll look. Arizona Gold." He gave me a tight smile and let the door slap shut behind him. Hopefully, he'd look at least a couple places for Arizona Gold—a bourbon that so far as I knew, didn't exist. Hopefully, that would buy me enough time.

I lay unmoving on the bed for two solid minutes, then

climbed out and went to the window. Jameson's tall form strode across the parking lot to our rental car.

I didn't waste a second. I pulled out my phone and requested an Uber—the hotel was close to the airport, so they'd be here in five minutes. I grabbed my bag, swung it over one shoulder, and yanked the ring off my finger.

I hesitated, then grabbed a hotel notepad and wrote him a goodbye note.

> *Jameson—I can't look at you. Can't be around you. Can't handle what we did. Don't try to contact me. I'll have a lawyer get ahold of you. Please don't fight the divorce. This is what I want. Go along with it, and no one will know what happened here.*

I stopped just short of writing the real reasons, because I didn't want to give him motive to come after me, to try to hurt me: *You're a murderer. I don't forgive you. I hate you. If I could tell everyone what you've done, I would.*

What I wrote would make him think I'd keep his secret. And I would because I had no other choice.

I left the note. I left my ring.

And I left Jameson.

THIRTY

CHLOE

Now

Jameson has done it again.

Found a patient who could die, and no one would take notice. Sure, Debra was young compared to the other patients on the unit—but she had a heart condition. These things happen. I look up from the patient list to see the unit secretary staring at me. She's in her sixties, with curly red hair.

"Good evening, who are you?" she asks.

"New nurse practitioner."

"Oh." Her eyes widen, mouth forming an O, and she looks like someone's kicked her puppy. It's a strange reaction, but I'm in a hurry. I turn on my heel and leave the unit, not thinking much of it until I'm walking the maze of halls to the cafe. But her face plays in my mind. All I'd said was that I'm the new nurse practitioner. Has she heard things about me? But what? I just started.

Of course, it might not be about me. It might be about who I replaced, and why she left. At hospital orientation, Debra said Jameson had been on his own for almost two months. But what about before that? Why had the previous nurse practitioner left? I should have said something to the secretary—should have asked her why the reaction. The moment's passed, though. I shift impatiently, waiting in line.

I need coffee to deal with this shit.

When it's my turn to order, I don't do my usual "Hi, how are you tonight?" My mind is too bogged down by Debra's death. By how much my world has changed in the past day.

"Mocha," I say. "Sixteen ounce." A beat passes as the barista enters it in her computer. "Wait, can I—I'll have an Americano instead. Extra shot."

She nods, pecks at the screen, and turns it so I can use my phone to pay.

Even my traditional mocha has been marred by Jameson.

I accept the too strong, hot coffee, and let its bitterness fill me as I find a staircase and climb the three floors. My pocket buzzes with a text from Elton, but it's just a photo—our upstairs bathroom, soap dish and toothbrush holder unpacked and in place. He's step-by-step putting our lives together.

Meanwhile, I feel like I'm tearing it apart. I exhale. I can't screw this up. I can't let Jameson hurt us, our life. I can't let him take me down with him.

The office door is locked, but I have a key now, and I insert it, twist, slide through and set my stuff on the desk. I relock it from the inside and pause to survey the room. It's different— scattered. Jameson, I presume, has gone through every book on the shelves. Flipped through each of his notebooks, which are now in disarray. The cabinet over his desk is left cracked open, and a pile of protein bars litters one corner, drug guides and books on euthanasia in the other.

I slide the notebook from my bag and place it at the bottom of the stack. He'll probably know I put it back. But maybe this will introduce the slightest bit of doubt that somehow, he missed it. It would work on me. But Jameson is more confident than I ever was.

His computer is logged out, so I grab the waiting laptop on my side of the office and type in my username, my password. The computer slowly connects to the network. Debra seemed healthy as could be this morning, running down the hall to catch me. It's hard to believe she's dead. I wonder if she had a family—children? Grandchildren? Or just her dog Zoey?

I click to find her patient chart and go straight for the notes, where the attending physician would write up what happened that they believed led to her death. Of course, the note is by none other than Dr. Jameson Smith.

> *Ms. Schilling was admitted for atrial fibrillation and low blood pressure. Cardioversion was scheduled for nine tomorrow morning. However, at approximately 5 p.m., she suffered a fall in her room, reportedly hitting her head on the toilet when she fell. The nurse was at the patient's side when I arrived, but Ms. Schilling had no pulse and was unresponsive. A code blue was called—*

My heart sinks. The note continues another paragraph, giving the image of a tragic accident.

Jameson is dangerous. I've known that. It's one reason I never stopped running, stopped moving. I'm still not sure why it seemed like a good idea now. Maybe because he'd never shown up. Never messaged or called or emailed or sent a letter. I'd assumed he'd moved on. But here we are. Debra will be just another entry in Jameson's latest notebook.

I'm about to exit out of the charting software. I've returned the notebook and finished snooping, and I'm ready to go home to Elton. But then I recall my desire to know more about whoever filled this position before me. Whoever the mystery woman is, she'd be a good person to talk to. I want to know why she left—if she, too, realized something wasn't quite right. Maybe together we can find a way to corner Jameson. And why the unit secretary seemed weirded out by my presence.

I find George's chart. Jameson mentioned he'd been admitted to the hospital multiple times over the past year. I press a finger to the mouse pad, slide it until I've scrolled down to notes from nine months ago. And that's when I see a name appear with the same initials title I use—*ARNP*, or advanced registered nurse practitioner.

Cassandra Valencia, ARNP.

I stare at her name, wondering who she is. I should be able to look her up in the hospital directory if her entry hasn't been deleted yet. I open the window and type her name in, and instantly, a profile pops up. Basic information—her name, how long she's been practicing (eight years), her specialty in the ICU. At the bottom is her email address.

I can email her. Who knows if she still has access to her email, but she might. Or, if she moved to a different hospital in the same system, one across town or in a nearby city, she would keep the same email address. I copy it then open another window, navigating to our hospital email page.

But something's not right. I squint at the screen because it's already logged in. But I've never checked my email from this laptop—only from home, and I set it up on my cell phone, too. A series of emails—dozens, it seems, as I scroll down, all unopened. Mostly, hospital-wide reminders: an upcoming blood drive, a new parking policy. Guilt flits through me, as I realize I'm in someone else's email. I should log out. Should delete their browser history and log in using my own credentials.

I navigate to a dropdown menu, and hover the mouse over *Log Out*. But before I click, my gaze lands on the name at the top—the owner of this email address.

Cassandra Valencia.

My head buzzes at the coincidence—but actually, it's not a coincidence. She filled this role before me. Sat at this desk. I have her old computer. She never logged out of her email, or had auto-log-in enabled, and so here I am.

My heart speeds, sweat breaking out along my neck. I don't know why, exactly—she quit her job, left. Why should I care that I'm logged in to her email by accident, or that she clearly hasn't checked it in a long time? That's what happens when you move from one job to another. Probably, in another week or two, her account will be closed out. Shut off. Cease to exist as the hospital won't want to pay for an email account that's not being used.

But I can't force myself to close the window. To log out or navigate away. My hands are shaking as I do something I know is wrong—I click through her file folders. I want to know more about her. Maybe there's forwarding information here some-where, or maybe on her signature block she's included a cell phone number—*yes*, a way I could contact her.

My body goes still when I scroll further and see the next file folder name.

Mortality Reduction Task Force. I click. Inside are a dozen emails exchanged with none other than Debra Schilling.

I select the top one—the most recent one. It's dated back in mid-May, nearly two months ago. A couple weeks before I received the job offer. So probably, right before she left. I read the email, heart ticking faster with every word. Fear spiraling through me, paralyzing me, as I read it a second time, because I don't want to believe I'm caught in a nightmare.

Debra, we need to talk. I'm being followed. He was in my house, I'm sure of it. I know you want to wait for more evidence. I get it. But I'm in danger. Either we go to the police or I'm done. I'm afraid he's going to hurt me.

Cassandra Valencia, ARNP

Debra hadn't wanted to talk about the previous nurse practitioner. For *privacy* reasons. Or was it to keep her safe? Not
wanting to tell me where she'd gone or a way to contact her.

I exhale a slow breath.

Cassandra found out—the *he* she mentions is obviously
Jameson, and she discovered what Jameson was doing. He was
following her. Just like he followed me. Just like when I thought
I saw movement out behind the house. I had felt watched
because I *was* being watched.

I swallow. She knew what he was doing, told Debra, was
ready to report it to the police. Debra knew, and now Debra is
dead. Cassandra is... well, gone. She probably hightailed it out
of here. I can't blame her. And here I am, knowingly entering
the hornet's nest.

This does not bode well for me. For my own safety.

I speed through the rest of the emails in case there's something more incriminating on Jameson, but the rest is all business
for the task force. And no phone number or alternate email for
Cassandra. Part of me feels relieved someone else figured it out,
too. Realized what Jameson was up to, planned on doing something about it. Then Debra had enlisted my help, knowing I
would be working with him—hoping, perhaps, I'd figure out
what Cassandra had. That I'd help her. But now, it's too late.

I drop my face into my hands, groaning. I need to leave. Go
home and drink something stronger than coffee. I close out the
email and delete my browser history. Take one last look around
the office. Short of stealing another notebook, there's nothing I
can do here. And it's too late to do anything for Debra. I stand
to go, but the metallic click of a key in the lock makes me freeze.

The door opens and Jameson steps inside.

THIRTY-ONE

JAMESON

Now

Jameson entered his office, schooling his features.

She shouldn't be here this late. In fact, he'd watched as she left the hospital. Made certain she'd headed home.

"Why are you still here?" she asked. No, demanded.

Jameson settled across from her. "New admit." He reached for one of the several coffee cups on his desk. "Could ask you the same thing."

"Forgot to finish a note. Didn't want to leave it for morning."

They were both lying.

If he were a better man, he'd tell her to go home to her soon-to-be husband. Remind her they had to work early tomorrow morning, and he knew she needed a solid eight hours of sleep. But she stared at him with her bright blue eyes, her mouth pressed into a line, the same line on her face the morning before she left him. How hadn't he seen it? Looking back, it was so obvious.

The day that haunted him all these years. She hadn't waited to say goodbye, just fled. He still wondered *why, why, why?*

They shared so much love, so much passion, to just *leave*—it didn't make sense. Even her excuses didn't make sense.

Not unless she'd learned his secrets. Or maybe, she suspected he'd learned hers.

He opened his mouth to say something—what, he wasn't sure. But then he closed it. Because he couldn't say what he wanted. Couldn't ask the questions that lingered in his head, or answer the questions he knew she had. Sometimes, honesty wasn't the best policy. Sometimes, the means to an end meant keeping your mouth shut.

Chloe muttered something about checking her email and fussed with her computer. He didn't move a muscle. Didn't so much as twitch. He shut his eyes and pretended they were somewhere else. Anywhere else. Or maybe somewhere specific —in his home. In the home they once shared. And her breath was the cadence of her sleeping next to him.

He snapped his eyes open. Exhaled slowly, brought himself back to reality. That was over. She was nearly married. If only he knew why she left, what he'd done to make her go. Except, maybe he did know.

But it was in the past. Long enough ago now that he needed to move on. She had. But having her back here, beside him... It was torture. Wonderous torture.

"I don't have your journal," she said, "And I don't appreciate your vaguely threatening messages."

He smiled to himself, because her back was still turned, and she couldn't see. And because he counted the spiral-bound notebooks stacked on his desk. So, she'd come to return it. Good. That's all he wanted.

A sign she would cooperate.

And, he had his notebook back. Some things were precious, irreplaceable.

Maybe it was remembering an earlier time, before things between them became complicated. Or maybe it was relief his notebook was returned. But for some reason he couldn't quite fathom, words escaped him. "Buy you a drink?"

She swiveled in her chair, and he fought not to flinch at the way her face shifted—but it settled on impassivity. Neutral. It wasn't the worst option.

To his surprise, she took a long slow breath and said, "Sure."

THIRTY-TWO

CHLOE

Now

I can't believe I said yes to Jameson. *Drinks* with Jameson, no less. The thing we did when we were, you know, *married.*

I chew my lip and pace the hospital hallway. He muttered something about signing off to his resident, which I almost took as a chance to escape.

But I decided earlier I wouldn't let him screw with me, my life with Elton. That I'll do something to stop him this time, and that means getting close to him. Getting him to trust me. Which given our history may be difficult.

Alcohol is the great social lubricant, though. When Elton and I went on our first "let's hang out," I'll call it, before I had any interest in dating again, alcohol was a big part of it. Margaritas on the beach? Sure. Shot of Kahlúa in our coffee after a morning run? Definitely. And when we graduated to full-on dates, it always started with a beer, a cocktail, a glass of wine.

Elton.

I yank out my phone and fire off a text—*Sorry, sick patient, I'll be stuck here a while*—thank god for patient confidentiality.

Not every nurse takes it seriously, but he does, which means that even though he'll be working this unit tomorrow morning, he won't ask which patient I'm referring to. Lying—again—doesn't feel good.

"So, you're new."

I spin, the voice catching me off guard.

"Oh, sorry, dear. We didn't get a chance to say a proper hello. I'm Cara." A thick hand with bright red nail polish extends my way. The unit secretary with the wide eyes.

"Hi. I'm Chloe."

"Did Dr. Smith make you come back in at this hour?" She raises a brow, and I immediately know her type—she's everyone's mom. I'll bet there are cookies in the break room she personally baked this afternoon.

"I just forgot to do something."

"I see. Well, good to meet you. Glad Dr. Smith got some help. He's needed it, since..." Her voice fades off. The phone rings, and she twists around to answer it, but I swear she was about to say more. I want to ask her what, but a second monitor to her side catches my attention.

Cameras. A live feed. More like a dozen live feeds, patients asleep in beds in each one.

"Cameras in the patient rooms?" I ask.

Jameson's voice comes from behind me. "Yes. It's significantly helped with safety. Fewer patients yanking out lines and tubes, fewer patient falls. The nurse can't be in the room all the time, so it's proved helpful."

"Helped keep us from getting sued, too," Cara chimes in. "We keep a month of footage at a time."

A month.

Maybe I can look up what happened to George and Debra —to any patient who has died. Maybe I have the bird's-eye view I need of Jameson.

"Chloe." Jameson's voice, low and oddly gentle, pulls me

back to the moment. He gestures us down the hall. He's removed his white coat, leaving him in his ever-present black slacks, dress shoes, and button-up. An easy smile graces his face, and he reaches up, presses the elevator down button for us. "Sorry for the wait, had to touch base with Dr. Michaels."

"No problem." I hold my bag a little tighter, fighting a flush of nerves.

He's being too nice. I'm the ex-wife who left him. Who knows his secret. I steal a glance his way, but his face is neutral. Maybe even pleasant.

He's up to something. I can feel it. No one's this nice to their ex.

We get in the elevator. I reach in my pocket, make sure my phone is muted, and tuck it away, thoughts of Elton with it. I have to exist in the present. Have to pay attention and pretend this is a friendly round of drinks with a coworker. Jameson needs to believe that's the reason I said yes, making what I typically would consider a very poor decision.

"You okay?" Jameson holds the elevator door open.

"Fine," I lie.

I step off the elevator, but we're not on the main floor. Gray concrete walls rise up around me. The parking garage. My Lexus sits two rows over.

"I thought we were walking." My heart beats a little faster.

"Oh, it's supposed to rain." Jameson strides to his car, at apparent ease. "I'll drive."

I glance over at my Lexus again. I don't want to lose this chance, nor do I want to get in his car with him. He could take me anywhere, and no one would know. I look up, search the garage for security cameras. Not a single one.

"I feel like a walk. I'll meet you there."

Jameson stands on the driver's side of a BMW X5—the same one he had before. The same one we spent over a year using for road trips, for car camping, for attempting to bring home furniture and books we found along the way. Its familiarity pulls at me in a way that leaves my skin itching. The last time I was in it, we drove to the airport to see Nathan for the last time.

Jameson stares back at me like he's going to argue, tell me how ridiculous that is. After a moment, he nods. "Okay. I'll meet you there. It's called Knock Knock."

"Knock Knock?"

"I'll text you the address. It's not far. Maybe a mile."

I shove my hands in my pocket and hurry toward the parking lot exit. A mile isn't *far*, but it's not short, either. I could go back for the Lexus, but then he'd know I didn't want to get in the car with him, that I don't trust him. Although he is a smart man—he probably figured that out and was too polite to say it. Sometimes, when we were together, I thought he bordered on being a genius—able to understand concepts around medicine and ethics that most people furrowed their brow at.

Now, I know there's a line. That line divides genius from sociopath. And when I picture Jameson, I see him straddling it.

It's the only way he hasn't been caught yet. But before, no one was trying to catch him.

A brisk wind whips through the city street. I look both ways at the road and skip across. Downtown Portland is lit up by artificial gas lamps, and they cast a warm glow over the sidewalk. Trees line either side of the street, swaying now in the breeze. The scent of rain rushes over me.

Any other night, I'd stop and soak it in. I've missed this weather. The Pacific Northwest climate, the abrupt change between a warm summer night and a quick spurt of showers that keep everything green. But my chest is tight, my steps quick, and suddenly the night air feels humid, suffocating.

Fifteen minutes later, I turn a corner and come to an abrupt stop.

Jameson stands there, leaning back against the BMW

parked at the street side. His hands are tucked in his jacket, his head tipped back, looking at the sky, looking like he belongs in the glossy pages of a magazine. When I glance up, clouds shift around the moon, the stars. With the smell of rain, I might call it magical. Then Jameson looks down, gaze locking on me.

The spell is broken.

"There you are," he calls.

I search the stores near where he's parked his BMW. I come up short, seeing nothing even vaguely resembling a bar.

"I don't see it." I beckon at a row of empty shop fronts, including one boarded up with plywood. Two lamps are burned out, the ones closest, leaving us cast in shadows.

"Oh, it's here. Come on."

I hesitate, but he's walking down the sidewalk. I pull my jacket tighter against the breeze and hurry to catch up. This is dumb. Wandering down an empty walkway behind my ex-husband. I keep my distance—enough I can have a running start if I need to. Enough he can't reach out and grab me. But Jameson approaches a blacked-out door and knocks twice.

The door opens, and Jameson slides into the darkness. Of course Jameson can't choose a normal bar. Of course he sends us down an abandoned street to a bar called *Knock Knock*, where you literally have to knock on the damn door—

"Chloe?" Jameson appears through the doorway. "Coming?"

I follow him, hands clenched at my sides. But as soon as I enter, I can breathe again. At least a dozen customers sit at small square tables. The lighting isn't much brighter inside than out, with dim sconces on the wall and candles flickering on the table. A bar up front is backlit in red, turning the bartender into nothing more than a silhouette, grooving along to lo-fi jazz. To the left side are couches and cushy chairs, arranged randomly. A couple relax back in one, sipping what looks like martinis.

"A speakeasy?" I ask. I try to keep a flat expression. To not look impressed. This is the sort of place I would have loved coming with him once upon a time. Would have insisted on coming back to until we'd tried every drink and found our favorite couch to cuddle in. And no doubt, he knows that. Which makes me even more suspicious.

"Call it what you like." Jameson gestures. "Couch? Table?"

"Table."

We find a corner spot, tucked away from others. I again think of Elton, of what this might look like to an outsider. We should have gone to the closest bar to the hospital, a quick drink at the bar, the bartender serving as a chaperone. It wasn't unusual for coworkers to grab a drink together, and Elton probably wouldn't have minded something in that vein. But this is something else entirely.

A young woman approaches, blonde with dark lipstick. She murmurs, "Drinks?" and waits for us to order. The menu is a slender piece of ephemera, a brown shade designed to look old, bold black print reminiscent of something from the early 1900s. Cocktails I've never heard of litter the paper, but I choose familiarity.

"Old fashioned, please."

"Whiskey?" she asks.

"Westward," Jameson answers. "Make it two."

She nods and disappears.

I look at him. "Don't order for me."

A smile plays at his lips. "I didn't. I just specified the whiskey. It's local. You'll like it."

"Same thing."

"You didn't know which bourbon you wanted. I did you a favor."

I don't reply. I'm too busy searching his face again for a sign of why he's being so damn pleasant, if not smug.

"Why are we here?"

His eyebrows go up. "I asked you to drinks. We're coworkers now. That's what coworkers do."

I watch him and wait. After a second or a minute, or maybe five minutes, something changes in his expression. The faux friendliness fades to a blandness, an iciness, that frankly, is closer to the Jameson I know, given the situation.

"I told you we needed to talk," he says.

My stomach twists, remembering the text. Remembering the words he whispered to me. *Till death do we part.*

A paper napkin sits in front of me on the table. My hand curls around it, squeezes it tight. The other shoe has dropped.

"So talk," I say.

THIRTY-THREE

CHLOE

Now

Sitting across from him is like sitting across from a ghost.

Sure, we worked together today. But this is different. The two of us, face-to-face in a dimly lit room. No work phones to interrupt, patients as an excuse to leave. We can't turn our backs to stare at a screen rather than one another.

For the first time, I look unflinchingly at Jameson. The first man I ever fell in love with. The first man I thought my future was with. The man who utterly betrayed me and everyone else who'd ever put their trust in him.

These realizations leave me cold. Or maybe the room is cold —that must be it. I glance around, uncomfortable, gaze catching on a figure in the window who looks as though he's watching us. Or is it a tall woman in a jacket? I can't tell. They turn and stride away—probably looking for a way to get into the damn bar and giving up. All the same, hairs rise at the back of my neck. I swallow, paranoid at being caught out with Jameson.

I wish the bartender would hurry the hell up already. I look over my shoulder, checking if she's coming with our drinks.

Wishing I'd ordered a double, which would actually be *four* shots because an old fashioned comes with two, but that sounds about perfect right now. Something to numb the—well, the everything.

"What do you want?" Jameson asks.

"What do you mean?" I look back toward the window, but the person is gone. I push my chair back slightly, putting more space between us, the intimacy too much.

He waves his hand. "From life. It's been what, three years? You're a different person now. I know what you wanted when we were—" A small, joyless smile. "Together. But that's all changed. You decided to go to grad school. You met a guy. Shit, you bought a house. What's next? A dog? Kids?"

Am I a different person? Not really. I still want what I wanted back then—a partner. Someone who loved me, and who I loved in return. A family. Lucky for me, I found that in Elton.

Our server returns, setting two glasses full of amber bourbon poured over large ice cubes in between us. She leaves without saying a word.

And it's just Jameson and me again.

"I went back to school." I shrug. "I got bored. Travel nursing was fun, but it was the same thing every day—easy patients, because the charge nurse doesn't know you. Doesn't trust you. I want..." I hesitate. "I don't know. To help people."

"That's what every nurse says."

"Probably what every doctor says, too," I reply, then to myself add, *Except in your case you'd be lying.*

Jameson lifts his glass and tips it toward me, offering to toast. Something we used to do. It fractures the moment in my mind—like a mirror shattering, the past and present refusing to come together in a decipherable way. I swallow, and because I want him to believe I'm really here to be his friendly nurse practitioner, raise my glass and clink. Somehow, our fingers brush. Jameson pauses, then pulls his hand back.

I pretend not to notice.

"What else?" he asks. "Kids?"

Our eyes lock, challenge in his, and I swear he somehow knows that Elton and I have agreed to disagree on how soon, on how many. Elton wants a big family, whereas I want to focus on us for a while. In a year or two, when we're ready, I want to have one. And then see where we're at. I once told him quality over quantity, and he'd laughed—he was the youngest of four.

"Maybe." I clasp my drink between my fingers. "What about you?"

His lips twist. "I'm the same as I always was." I must make an expression—a sharp chuckle escapes him. "You don't believe me?"

"Let me get this straight. Three years pass. You assume I've changed, and you haven't?"

He looks down at the glass in his hand, swirls it once, takes a sip.

"Well, yes. After all, I'm doing exactly what I was before. Working. I'm just doing it alone." That same turning up of his lips, but not a smile. "You, however—" He inclines the glass, and my focus goes to the diamond ring on my left hand.

Irritation crawls through me. I gave him a minimal answer, but I gave him one, damn it. I take a drink of my own glass—sweet, strong, burning down my throat, letting me breathe a little easier—and shake my head. I won't let him get to me. Who he says he is doesn't matter. Because I know the truth.

"Are you still helping people die?" I ask. "You know, elsewhere?"

He looks at me, and something's in his gaze, but I can't quite tell what. He fishes a cocktail cherry from his glass and shoves it in his mouth, chewing slowly. I realize he's not going to answer me—not going to admit or deny it. To illegally "helping" people. He already knows I know, so why the hesitation?

"You still like your booze," I say when the silence gets to be too much. "Still dress all in black when you're not in scrubs." I take another drink, courage radiating through my body with the heat of the bourbon. "You still have patients dying every shift."

There, I said it. Put the words out there between us. The boldness I felt seconds ago dissipates. I watch his face for a response, wait for a sharp reply, but he says nothing. Only watches me.

"Not every shift," he says gently.

No denial.

"You're a doctor. Doesn't it bother you?"

"I don't enjoy it." He sits a little straighter and watches me with cautious eyes. "Are you telling me you don't have patients die?"

I did. I do. But I don't answer him.

Jameson clears his throat. "You think you'll stay? Here in Portland?"

There's a weight in his words that makes me pause. Is this a test? He'd warned me not to quit the job.

I give a neutral answer. "We bought a house."

He lifts one shoulder in a half shrug. "You could rent it out. I've known plenty of nurses and providers who got the travel bug and realized they couldn't really stop."

"I don't know."

I hadn't thought of that—of renting the house out. It's Portland, a great neighborhood. We could do that. I could go home and tell Elton I changed my mind. We could pack easy enough —most of it was still in boxes. I could disappear again.

But that would mean I'd never see Jameson again.

A sharp twinge in my chest, visceral pain at the thought, making me squirm in my seat.

No, no, no. It's not pain because I'd never see him again. It's that I'd lose out on putting an end to all this. I stare down in my drink, pushing the thoughts away, thoughts I don't want to examine too closely.

A murmur of voices distracts us momentarily—a group of four rising, collecting coats and bags, moving through the tables toward the door. I bring my attention back to Jameson to find him staring at me.

"What?" I say.

A slight shake of his head. "Nothing." He presses his mouth into a line. "Tell me about Elton."

My face heats, the mention of my fiancé throwing me off. I cross my arms, lean back. "What do you want to know?" I don't want to talk about Elton with him. Elton exists in my new world.

"How'd you meet, when's the wedding. You know. Normal stuff."

I take a breath to collect myself. The table shakes for a second, and I realize Jameson's jiggling his leg, betraying his nerves.

He was afraid to ask. And I don't want to tell. I like separating my old life from my new. Tonight threatens to mix the two, and that's not what I want. It's strange talking with Jameson about Elton, and though I try to summon the words, it's like my body won't let me get them out.

But it shouldn't matter. We're divorced.

I take a breath. "We met in San Diego on an assignment. About six months after I started travel nursing. And at the beginning of the year, he asked me to marry him. I said yes." I say everything plainly, not skewing it with emotion or getting dreamy-eyed like I usually do. It felt like a fairy tale, the way Elton and I came together. And I don't feel like sharing that with Jameson.

A muscle feathers in Jameson's cheek, but he otherwise has no reaction.

"Why did you leave Seattle?" I ask, my tone hot. They are simple getting-to-know-you-again questions, but something underlies them. A thick tension that makes my question feel like tit for tat.

Jameson considers the question. He smooths a hand over the table, and I realize at some point during our conversation he's leaned forward. And so have I. And our hands are mere inches apart. Too close for comfort. Minutes ago I was cold, but now I'm hot, ready to peel my jacket off.

I pull back abruptly.

He notices and gives me a quarter smile. Drains his old fashioned and waves for another. I don't look to see if the server catches his signal, because I'm still trying to understand how we ended up so close to one another.

Our eyes meet, and it's like a physical blow—the moment I realize the pull between us is still there. It's not the thick rope it once was, intertwining our lives on every level. But still, some thin connection, like twine that won't break no matter how hard you wrench it apart. Neither of us drops our gaze. His quarter smile disappears, something else simmering in his eyes, and I know he feels it, too.

I hate that.

Anger lashes through me, and I dig my nails into my palms, wanting to cause myself physical pain.

How dare I.

But of course something's still there. Humans are animals, after all. Pheromones and chemical reactions in our brains. I grind my teeth, angry more at myself than him. He's a killer. Whatever I'm feeling, it's not real.

I clear my throat. "Why Portland?" I repeat the question in a different way.

"Better pay." The lie rolls of his tongue easily.

So that's how this conversation will go. We'll ask one another a question, and the other will give a minimal response. Or outright lie. In other words, we're wasting our time.

I should go home. But when I consider it, I realize I'm not

ready to leave. Not ready to pull away from this table and the intimacy of the bar and go out the door into the cool summer night. That's when I realize something is wrong.

That maybe, it's more than mere chemicals.

Which means I *should* leave.

"I need to go." The words slip from my mouth without thought. I'm about to push my chair back, but the server arrives, fresh drinks in her hands. I stay put long enough for her to set them on the table. Jameson motions for her to wait, pulls out his wallet, hands her cash.

"All paid up," he says. I sit on the edge of my seat, muscles tense, ready to stand up and walk out. "So you can go whenever you want. However—" He gestures at the nearest window without looking. "It is raining quite hard."

"What do you mean it's—" I look, and he's right. The bar's walls have muted it, but water pours from the sky, rivulets of rain running down the dark windows.

"If you don't mind waiting for me to finish—" He touches a fingertip to the fresh old fashioned. "I'm happy to drive you back to the hospital."

I glare at him. I'm aware he can't control the weather— but half an hour ago, it was a warm summer night. And now, when I want nothing more than to leave—this night has not gone at all like I wanted it to; he hasn't answered a single question in a useful way—the rain is coming down in sheets.

"Besides, we could talk more." He nudges the second glass the server set down closer to me. "Would you like a fresh drink?"

I abandon my half-drunk glass, the ice now melted, making it watery, and accept the new one. My chest feels tight, my body rigid with tension.

"What do you want to talk about?" I take another look at the window—still raining.

"Honestly?" His face softens. "I want to know why you left."

"I already told you."

"No, you left a note. You sent me on a wild goose chase for some bourbon three different liquor store owners had never heard of. I assume you called a cab and went to the airport. You bought a ticket and flew home, and I never saw you again. And you did all of this at your most vulnerable, right after Nathan died."

You mean was murdered.

I swallow back the words and squeeze my eyes shut. Yes, I was okay with him helping Nathan die. But Nathan was robbed of the peaceful, dignified death he wanted, he deserved.

His warm hand engulfs mine. My eyes fly open. Jameson leans close, putting our faces inches from one another.

"I wanted to be there for you, Chloe. I was your husband. You should have let me be there for you."

I can't look away. Can't pull back. I'm lost in the bottomless sea that is him, sucked beneath the surface, but I'm okay with it. Somehow, I can breathe in these choppy, murky waters.

And I want more.

THIRTY-FOUR

CHLOE

Now

"I need to go." I'm standing before I realize it. I yank my hand from his and pick up my purse and tighten my jacket around my shoulders.

"It's still raining." Jameson stands, too.

Is he as stunned as I am at what just happened?

Or maybe *appalled* is the right word. Yes, definitely appalled.

My ribs heave, straining as I try to take a normal breath. As the dim bar closes in on me and spins, and I reach out to touch something, anything, to ground myself. To keep the anxiety at bay.

"I don't care about the rain." I turn on my heel, bite my lip, then bite it harder, hoping the pain brings me back to reality.

"Chloe—"

I keep walking, bypassing our server, who watches us, drawn in by the drama. I burst out the door and into the night air, past the overhang until cool rain drips into my hair, my scalp, down the back of my neck. Finally, I inhale, exhale, *breathe*.

"I'll give you a ride."

I didn't hear him step outside. Didn't hear the door slap closed. Was it that quiet, or am I that distracted?

"I'm fine."

"No, you're not." A heavy hand—his heavy hand—rests on my shoulder. "I'm sorry," he says. I don't ask what for. I don't want to know.

But I don't argue when he guides me to the BMW, opens the door, waits for me to get in.

"Come on. I'll take you straight to the hospital."

My feet move of their own accord, and it doesn't occur to me he will do anything other than what he's promised. His hand brushes my back as I step past him and lower myself into the seat, and the moment he shuts the door, our contact broken, something inside me mourns it.

The dark interior is just like his touch—a flashback in time to the best part of my life. Before I realized what he was doing.

The drive takes less than three minutes. I stare out my window the whole time, refusing to look his way.

"I'll see you tomorrow," he says. He stays in the car, letting me get my own door this time, which I'm grateful for.

I lower myself into the Lexus. In the rearview mirror, I watch as he pulls from the lot to head home.

And I realize what an idiot I am. That I'm lucky to be alive.

Lucky he didn't drive me somewhere and kill me.

The squeeze of panic returns. I look at myself in the mirror and try to understand who this woman is. Who I am, to be stupid enough to let myself be drawn back in by his dark eyes, the warmth of his hand on mine, his earnest voice as he told me he'd only wanted to be there for me. And then I'd done the ultimate act—gotten in his damn car, trusting he'd take me where he said he would.

A shudder runs through me.

I got lucky tonight.

And I failed. I am no closer to being free of him than I was a few hours ago when he broke into my home. The only thing I've accomplished is to let him think he's drawn me back into his web, the same way he did before, in Seattle.

And the worst part is, some part of me likes it. Almost yearns for his touch, for another chance to sit across the table and share drinks and conversation.

I shake my head. Start the car. And head home to my fiancé.

THIRTY-FIVE

CHLOE

Now

Elton lies still beneath the covers, the darkness of our room making him a shadow against the shallow light. I stand at the edge of the bed, watching his chest rise and fall. He texted me three times before going to bed.

You okay?

Getting late. Headed to bed soon.

and

Xoxo, wake me up when you get home.

My heart aches to feel his body against mine. To have him whisper to me, "Everything will be okay." To tell him all of it.

I don't wake him up. I shut myself in the bathroom and stare at his texts to remind myself of what I have and how precious that is. I need to keep my shit together.

A text comes through.

Jameson: *Make it home safe?*

I press my palms into my eyes and sigh. Of course he's checking to make sure I got home okay. That's what he did when we were dating, too. Before he pulled me into his bed. Before he whispered, "You should move in," followed by, "Let's elope."

This time, I don't answer. I rinse my face and smooth on moisturizer and hide in the bathroom. I'm wide awake like I went for two coffees instead of two drinks. Elton makes a noise in his sleep, and I crack the door open to peek at him. He's flung one arm over to my side, and his jaw hangs open, a slight snore with each breath.

My body hums with energy. I can't sleep. Can't do what I want and crawl in next to him and feel his skin brush against mine when my body is remembering how Jameson's hand felt on mine. I swallow back shame and slip from the bedroom downstairs. I can't tell which is worse—that my body has a physical memory of his skin on mine or that I lied to Elton. Both feel like betrayal.

Downstairs, I find my laptop. Flip it open. Enter my password and go to a browser. My fingers hesitate over the keys. I've looked him up before. Usually at work, when Elton wasn't around. But it's been a while.

Jameson Smith, MD.

I hit search, but it's the same run-of-the-mill stuff it always has been. Healthcare websites with their supposed ratings. Portland General's website, where his headshot smiles back at me with a brief bio. Even his med school's class paper. I'm not sure what I'm looking for. Anything, I guess, that might be an opening for me to figure out how to catch him in the act. How to prove what I know.

Google is not helpful.

I get to my feet and stretch, raising one hand overhead, leaning this way and that, thinking. Not letting my thoughts stray back to tonight and what an idiot I am. At the stove, I boil water and make a cup of chamomile tea. Coffee sounds better. But eventually I need to sleep. Eventually I need to get over all this and tuck myself in next to Elton.

Mug in hand, I return to the computer and try a different search. I navigate to LinkedIn. And that's when I stop short. To do a proper search I have to log in. But he'll be able to see if I go to his profile. Then again, do I care? I work with him. It wouldn't be abnormal for me to connect with him on the website.

I look around the room, uneasy. The clock on the stove reads 12:33 a.m. I tap my finger on the mouse button, then click. It's easy enough to explain away.

His profile appears, that same headshot all doctors have, in their white jacket, the professional "trust me, I'm a doctor" smile staring back at potential patients. A quick summary of how he's an amazing ICU physician, specializing in critical care. I scroll to the experience section and stop short.

It should have two listings—Seattle and Portland.

But there's a third in between.

My heart beats a little faster, and I reach for my tea, take a scalding sip, then cough it back out, pushing away from the table to grab a napkin. A second later, I'm back at it.

St. Andrews Health, Idaho

Jameson, typical of medical serial killers, had switched hospitals not once, but twice. I click on St. Andrews and navigate around until I learn it's a small community hospital with sixty beds—a tenth the size of Portland General.

A place patients dying would be far more noticeable.

He stayed there for only eight months before coming to Portland.

He didn't mention that tonight. I take a cautious sip of tea and make a face. God, I don't understand why people drink this stuff. I push it away and stare at the computer screen some more. Pick up my phone and consider blasting off a text to Jameson.

But this doesn't change anything.

I already know what he's doing. This is, however, my first inkling of anything resembling proof. Physicians don't change jobs this often, this fast. Not unless they have a reason. Like deaths to hide.

"Chloe?" Elton's voice cuts through the silent kitchen.

I nearly fall out of my chair. I smack the laptop screen down and turn to face him.

"What are you doing still up?" He squints at me, face ragged with sleep.

I force a smile to my face. "Sorry. I got home and wasn't tired."

A faint smile. "So you're updating your LinkedIn profile?"

A flutter of relief. He hadn't seen I was on Jameson's page.

"Well, I figure I got a new job, so..." I grab the mug of tea. "Come on, let's go to bed."

He nods and reaches for my hand. I take it, and his fingers are cool, lacking the warmth of Jameson's hand.

I clasp Elton's hand tighter. Push thoughts of Jameson away. He has no space here in our home. Elton leads me up the stairs. My head swims with the bourbon. With everything I've discovered today.

When Elton pulls me close as we arrive at our bed, I don't say no or beg off. His lips press to mine. His hands intertwine around me, clenching a fist in my hair. We kiss. He backs me up to the edge of the bed, and together, we find our way onto the mattress, never breaking contact.

"I missed you," he murmurs. "No more late nights at work, okay?"

I don't reply, because as a nurse practitioner, I can't promise that. And considering that Jameson's here, that I need proof, it's impossible.

"We'll find time for us." I kiss him back. Run my fingertips over the roughness of his jaw where he needs to shave. He smells so good, and rolling in the silky bed sheets, we're so warm. That familiar feeling of *home* hits me—something I wanted for so long. Something I've found in Elton.

But Jameson enters my mind. And not the bad things. But the way he looked at me in Knock Knock. The way his hand felt hot on mine. The way in that flash of time, I realized I still yearn for him, still feel connected to him.

Elton's hands skim up my shirt. Down the waistband of my scrub pants, releasing the tie, inching them over my hips. Then they're off, and his knee is between my thighs, his hardness pressed against me. Inside, I'm spinning. Want and need mix together as I sit up, capture his mouth with mine, yank his shirt over his head to reveal smooth planes of muscle.

A flicker of guilt.

Because I'm about to fuck my fiancé.

But it's my ex-husband I'm thinking of.

THIRTY-SIX

CHLOE

Now

Morning comes, even without much sleep, and I yank on scrubs and kiss Elton goodbye, telling myself I didn't do anything wrong last night.

In my Lexus, the dark morning takes on blue and purple hues as I make the turn from suburbia toward downtown. We ran out of cream, and my stomach curdles with black coffee swishing in my stomach. Or if I'm being honest, more likely, the memory of last night. The alcohol. The company.

In the hospital, I make a beeline for the cafe. The line is five nurses and two doctors deep, but I file in anyway, the whirr of the grinder, the smell of fresh grounds comforting sensations. A glance at the clock tells me rounds start in seven minutes, but no way am I going upstairs without coffee. Besides, this puts Jameson off a little longer.

Last night returns like a bad dream. I try to shut it out. Try to busy myself reading the menu: drip coffee, pour-over coffee, summer-themed lattes...

But it still happened. We still got drinks and sat across from one another at a candlelit table. But that wasn't the worst of it.

I exhale and grip my bag a little tighter. The line moves slowly, and one of the nurses peels off when her phone rings, summoning her back to her unit.

The worst were his words. That as my husband, he had wanted to be there for me.

"Hey." A too familiar voice yanks me from my thoughts. Sweat breaks out along my skin.

"Jameson."

"Hi." He starts to reach out, like he'll touch me. I look at his hand, then at his face. Those brown eyes stare back at me, wide and serious. He stops, takes a half step back. "I got you a mocha already."

An emotion courses through me I can't quite identify. Instead of saying what I'm thinking—*It's not your place to buy me coffee*—I manage, "I don't drink mochas anymore."

He raises a brow. "No? Didn't you have one yesterday?"

"Americano." I know instantly I will regret my words. That this won't stop him from buying me coffee, but he'll start buying Americanos instead, and I'll regret each and every one and its lack of chocolate.

"Ah." He looks down at his shoes. "You didn't text me back last night."

The emotion changes, writhing into something resembling anger. I raise my chin.

"Of course, I didn't. I went home and got in bed with my fiancé."

"Did you?" He peers at me, and my heart throws a pre-ventricular contraction, aka an extra beat.

"What is that supposed to mean?" He must have seen me on his LinkedIn.

A small smile. "Nothing. Let's get to work."

* * *

As soon as we get upstairs, he hands me a list of patients. "Go see these ones. Let me know if you have any questions." He starts off in the opposite direction.

"Wait." I scramble to find a reason this won't work. If Jameson's hurting his patients, I need a front-row ticket to the show. Not to be relegated to the other side of the unit. "It's only my second day." I hold up the list. "I don't even know where these rooms are."

Jameson considers me a moment. "You've spent years travel nursing. I imagine you can figure it out. Besides, I'll be around. You did a great job yesterday. I think you can work independently today."

And he takes off down the hall without waiting for another word.

I sigh and watch his broad shoulders disappear around the corner. The office is clean, much cleaner than it was yesterday. His stack of notebooks has disappeared, leaving an empty laminate desk behind. He cleaned up. Probably removed anything incriminating. And he has me working on my own today.

It hits me what he's doing—keeping me from finding anything out.

Which means he's onto me. I'm no longer here under whatever pretense he arranged for. Probably, he knew that when he realized I took his notebook. Or maybe the fact I showed back up last night at all. Then what was the point of asking me to drinks? He'd said he wanted to talk...

A shiver of discomfort at how vulnerable I'd made myself. The knowledge he could have done anything to me after I got in his car.

But he didn't.

I shake my head and force myself from the office. I will not buy into the idea I can trust him. That there's anything *real* in the emotion he showed last night. When I reach the secretary's desk, someone new is behind it. I may not be able to *watch* Jameson up close and personal, but maybe I can use those security cameras to see what he's been up to.

"Hi." I stop at the secretary's desk, where I met Cara last night. Her replacement is a man in his twenties, pale, anemic-looking, with a mustache that hasn't quite grown in. His wrists are so skinny I want to suggest checking his calcium levels—not to mention his blood count for the anemia. But he answers phones and answers patient call lights via the intercom, all while watching telemetry monitors on one screen and the video feeds from patient rooms on another. In other words, he's a pro.

"Yes, ma'am?" he says to me, voice thick with a Southern accent, adjusting his glasses, never taking his eyes from the computer monitor.

"Hi, I'm Chloe, the new nurse practitioner."

He looks at me for a split second, long enough to flash me a polite smile. "I know who you are, Ms. Chloe. I'm Peter. How may I help you?" At my hesitation he adds, not impolitely, "I haven't got all day."

I smile for the first time today. "How do the cameras work? Are they always on?"

"Usually. We'll turn them off if the patient is just boarding here until a room opens up in the step-down unit, but it helps us keep them safe." He raises a well-filed nail and taps on the monitor, where an older man has stripped himself half-naked in bed and clearly isn't entirely there. "Then I babysit them."

"And it records?"

He quirks an eyebrow at me. "Why, yes, it does."

"Is there a way to play it back?"

"Mmmhmm." He takes a moment to answer a trilling phone, says, "Hold please," and sets it back down. "Which room?"

"I have a couple different ones I want to look at."

The other eyebrow shoots up. "Why don't you pull up a chair, and I'll let you do your thing."

I pull up the nearest rolling chair, and Peter slides a mouse my way, showing me how to select a room and rewind and fast-forward.

"If it wasn't recording, you'll just skip to when it last was recording in that room." He gives me a look. "I need a coffee. Think you can answer the phones while I go get one?"

"Sure."

"Thanks." And just like that, I'm in control of the whole unit. Give me a patient to code, and I'm good. Give me a phone and a telemetry monitor, and—I curse, realizing the mess I've put myself in. But a patient moves on the screen, pulling my attention back to it. I pull up Room 808, George's, and start rewinding.

But all I see is the patient who's in there now—a woman in her seventies with a no-nonsense bun. I scroll faster, not liking the feeling that I'm invading her privacy. But it only goes back twelve hours before it blanks out.

Crap. Next, I try Debra's, but the room is empty now, and it stayed empty all night after her body was removed.

I go to another room and rewind, and again, it stops twelve hours ago. The nurse said they keep records for a month... maybe from here we can only access a half day back, though. I'll have to ask Peter.

"You a unit secretary now, too?" I look up to see Elton smiling at me with a hint of deviousness. He's in a new pair of scrubs—dark blue—and they bring out his eyes, make him even more handsome.

I smile back. "Just for a few minutes. How's your day?"

My finger hovers over the mouse button, eager to get back to the videos, but I've barely seen Elton other than in bed last night. I was out the door before he even woke up this morning.

"Good. You must be tired after last night." He winks, and a blush works its way to my cheeks.

"I blame you."

Elton laughs and boosts himself over the counter to peck my cheek. "See you tonight?"

I open my mouth to say yes, then I remember Laura's direction we meet at the wine place tonight. "Actually, I'll be a little late."

"Oh." He frowns. "What's up?"

"Just meeting a friend for a drink after work."

"Oh, you made a friend?" He smiles. "Anyone I know?"

It's a fair question—he's been here a month longer than me, and we've only really spent time at the hospital and our house. It's likely he'd know whoever it was. I rack my brain, trying to remember if he would have met Laura in Seattle. Or if he'd realize that Laura and Jameson are siblings.

"Laura," I finally say. "She used to live in Seattle." I watch his expression, waiting for him to realize who she is. But he just smiles again.

"That's great. Well, have fun. I'll see you when you get home."

I exhale and turn back to the monitor right as Peter arrives back at his desk. "How's it going?" he asks. "Find what you need?"

"I could only go back twelve hours."

"Oh yeah." He sips his coffee and scrunches his nose in annoyance. "That's all we keep on-site. Everything else is kept elsewhere." He waves a hand. "Wherever they keep that sort of thing."

Not helpful. I sigh and tap my fingers over the desk, then realize what else I can ask him.

"Hey, did you know Cassandra Valencia? Jameson's last nurse practitioner?"

"Cassie? Yeah, I knew her." He gives me a long look, humor gone from his face. "Why?"

"Do you know why she left? Where she went? Or do you have her number? I need to ask her a couple things. About work."

He tilts his head and sets his coffee down slowly. "I'm not really supposed to talk about it."

Alarm bells ring in my head. She *had* run off. "Oh?" I glance away, trying for mild curiosity.

"The hospital sent out an email and—" Peter frowns. "Sorry, I need to answer this." He grabs at the phone I didn't notice was ringing—wait, was it ringing?—and swivels his chair away from me, effectively ending the conversation.

THIRTY-SEVEN

CHLOE

Now

Once upon a time, Laura was the closest thing I had to a best friend. She took a liking to me immediately, joining in as I rolled my eyes at Jameson's fancy doctor friends and their spouses, what with their perfect manicures (something we as medical providers couldn't imagine having) and thousand-dollar purses (Why? Just why?). She was the sort of person who spoke her mind, who you'd describe as "a good friend to have, but I'd hate to be on her bad side."

And on her bad side, I am.

It's early evening, and I've finally escaped the hospital. The wine bar has dark purple walls, lilac napkins, abstract sketches on the wall in lavender and maroon. It's enough purple to make me puke. I pour myself a glass of water and drink the cold liquid, hoping it calms my nerves. Maybe it's not the purple. Maybe it's the busy day full of Jameson avoiding me, after a late night filled with alcohol and, well, intimacy. Jameson laying his hand on mine. Jameson saying, *I was your husband.* The dark bar, the long looks filled with things that couldn't be said aloud.

A bell jangles at the door, and Laura's tall, lithe form is silhouetted against the outdoor light. Like a superhero. Or maybe, the villain.

"I'm late. Sorry." Her words are cursory, her apology flat. She removes her jacket—odd, for daytime in summer in Portland—and waits for a nearby staff member to hurry over and take it.

"Everything okay?" I pour her a glass of water, which isn't something I'd usually do, but trying to get back in her good graces and all.

"Last second add-on, you know how it goes. You can't say no, but god forbid a patient remembers you have a life outside of work." She sits across from me and hangs her purse on the edge of the chair. "So." She folds her hands, which I can't help but notice *are* manicured, and stares straight at me. "You asked me to drinks. What is it?"

My voice lodges in my throat. I thought she'd at least want to yell at me a little or *something*. Laura always has something to say, so I wasn't expecting this to all fall on me. I search for words and settle on, "I'm sorry I ignored your calls when I left Jameson. I'm sorry I didn't say goodbye. I just... I had to go. And then I needed to be gone."

She raises a brow. "Why?"

I press my lips together, and thankfully, at that moment, the waiter approaches us with long, thin, weighty menus with dozens of wines and wine flights listed. A tiny selection of appetizers is listed on one side.

Laura points at one. "I'll have the dry red flight. Chloe?"

"Um..." I've barely had time to look at the menu, but I choose a flight of white wines.

Before I've had time to gather my thoughts, the waiter takes his leave, leaving my stomach swimming at the scathing gaze Laura redirects my way.

She's waiting for an answer I can't give her.

"I can't talk about it. I'm sorry."

Laura tilts her head. "That's the same damn thing Jameson's been saying since you left. Alternating with *I don't know why.*" Her gaze softens, just a little. "What happened? You two were so happy. So in love."

The dreaminess in her voice hits hard. We *were* so in love. I shut my eyes and imagine that tenuous rope of a connection, the one I felt still there last night. The one that doesn't matter anymore.

"Things changed." I push away the memories.

"Apparently." She presses her cloth napkin into her lap, and a second later, our wine arrives. "Jameson told me to be nice to you. You know that?"

"He told you to—" I grasp the nearest wineglass, but her words make me pause.

"To be nice." She sips her own wine, dark like the blood of someone who doesn't have enough oxygen in their body. I inhale sharply, feeling suffocated myself.

"When?"

"Yesterday."

That gives me pause. He was being nice, too. Too nice. Until today, anyway.

"Well, I hope we can get along again."

Laura doesn't say anything to that—just watches me, like she hasn't decided yet.

"What have you been up to?" I ask. "When did you move to Portland?"

"Last year." She fiddles with the stem of a wineglass. "To be closer to Jameson. But I don't love it. Dating is impossible."

"What do you mean?"

"Everyone's so weird here." She glances around, as if the wine bar is representative of greater Portland. "Everyone has a home brewery or carves statues out of tree stumps or is into joggling." She waves a hand, dismissing the concept.

"Joggling?"

She leans in, and for a second, she's the old Laura, and we're whispering like lifelong friends. "I went on a date with this pharmacist, and he's a competitive... joggler? Is that what you'd call it?"

"But what is it?"

She presses a finger to her temple, as though it gives her a splitting headache just to think of it. "Jogging and juggling at the same time."

I nod slowly. "Okay. That's different."

"The slogan here is *Keep Portland Weird*, but I don't think they really need to try so hard. It just... *is*."

A moment passes, and Laura seems to remember herself—that we're not still besties, that I'm not married to her brother. She pulls back, takes a dainty sip of wine. "So, you're engaged."

"Yes, we..." I hesitate, but I have to be open with her if I want her to be open with me.

"His name is Elton. We met in Seattle. We worked together. Just friends." I give her a look to make it clear I'm being honest. "And I didn't think about him again until..." I think about it. "San Diego? I worked as a travel nurse, and I did an assignment there. We were both on one of the beaches down there, and I recognized him. I didn't know anyone, and he asked if I wanted to go to this party and..." I shrug. "Things just kind of took off."

It hadn't been that simple. After Jameson—after the one person I'd accepted into my life betrayed me—I hadn't wanted to let anyone else in. But Elton had been persistent. And sweet, opening doors and memorizing my favorite foods at restaurants, considering my work schedule when planning his own. And happy to be friends first, which put me at ease. It helped I was intensely lonely. Intensely alone.

"Interesting." She runs a finger over the tip of an empty wineglass. A sadistic glint comes to her eye. "So, how's it going? Working with..." She smiles. "Your ex-husband?"

"It's a little weird." I drop my gaze to the table. "But we're figuring it out." I look at her, realizing what I could ask her. "Hey, do you know what happened with Cassandra? Why she left? Where she went?" I look at Laura again. She's the sort of person who will just tell me the facts—none of the BS like Peter pretending he was too busy to talk about it.

Laura's eyes widen. "You don't know?"

I've just taken a sip of wine, and I swallow it quickly, then lean in. Laura knows, whatever it is. "No one told me."

Laura studies me and picks up one wineglass, then swaps it for another, twisting her lips as if trying to decide which she prefers. "Well... that's strange." She's drawing it out. Teasing me.

I'm no longer able to play at mild curiosity. "What is?"

Laura sighs. "Someone should have mentioned it. Jameson should have mentioned it." Her gaze is still on me, like she's trying to figure something out.

"Well? Are you going to tell me?" I widen my eyes at her.

Laura leans in and lowers her voice. "She was murdered."

It takes me two tries to find words.

"Murdered?"

Laura nods and takes a long pull of wine, like this isn't the first time she's rehashed the story—like for her, it's old hat and not that interesting. That alone catches my attention, and I gaze at her, inspect her face for clues to what she's thinking, feeling.

I stare at her, the world narrowing until she's my only focus. Debra, murdered. Cassandra, murdered. And both of them knew what Jameson was doing.

"Do they know who did it?" I ask.

"Nope. But it happened on the hospital campus in the middle of the night. So either someone who works at the hospital or..." She shrugs. "Maybe someone wandering the street? You know how downtown is after hours."

"How was she killed?"

"Throat slit." She scrunches her nose. "They said it was a small, sharp blade. Like a scalpel—" My heart sinks. A *scalpel?* "Or a small, very sharp knife. It happened in the parking lot. Around three in the morning, they think. So... no one would have been out there." Laura bit her lip and swirled her wine. "It's scary, isn't it? Someone murdered at our hospital."

My wineglass sits heavy in my hand. I carefully set it down, so I don't drop it.

"That's it? No other information?"

She shakes her head. "Whoever did it avoided the security cameras. They think it was someone in the hospital. Something personal, maybe. Apparently, she'd thought someone was following her the week before when she worked night shift—like following her through the hospital. But who knows, right? I mean it could have just been someone going for coffee. Sad, though. She was nice."

I remember the footsteps following me down the hospital hall. The footsteps in my house. The open door. The fact someone was almost certainly there. And the next thing I imagine is Jameson—a scalpel in his hand, slitting the throat of his nurse practitioner who knew too much.

Who had witnessed what he is. Just like I had.

THIRTY-EIGHT

CHLOE

Now

We talk about the ongoing murder investigation—somehow, the hospital cameras hadn't caught the perpetrator at an angle where anything was discernible. She was killed after a particularly long shift and there were no witnesses. Her body wasn't even discovered until the next morning, when the day shift started showing up for work.

"Is Jameson... okay?" I ask. Mentally, I tack on *Did he seem particularly happy the night she died? Pleased with himself? Oh god, is she in his notebook?!*

I take a swallow of wine, fast. When I look up, Laura's examining me. Again. Which maybe isn't that strange. I left her brother. Left her whole family, when all I'd wanted was a family.

"They worked together about six months."

A lull in conversation as I try to sort out my thoughts. As I try to get the picture of him killing Cassandra and Debra out of my head. As I consider he was in my house, and that I might be next, and here I am, drinking wine with his sister. I'm about to get the conversation back on track and ask her why Jameson chose Portland of all places, when she starts talking again.

"I need to get going. But first I have something to say. Something I have to tell you if we're going to work toward any sort of... relationship. Friendship. Working together." She drains her last glass of wine.

"What is it?"

"It killed him. Losing you like that. He hasn't so much as gone on a first date since you left. So just..." She presses her lips together. "Be careful with him, okay? I can't deny that I'm angry with you. But Chloe, I still care about you. And I'm not so sure this is a good idea." She hesitates. "In fact, I'm not convinced he's not still in love with you."

I try to form a response, but nothing quite right comes to mind. I'm not sure what shocks me more: her telling me that she still cares about me or... that he might still be in love with me.

"I'm not here to cause problems," I manage.

Laura sighs. "I know you're not. And he's a big boy. But I'm his sister, and I had to say it." She pauses. "But why, Chloe? Why? What did he do? Or..." She raises a brow. "What did you do?"

I look down at the table. "I didn't cheat on him, if that's what you're asking. I just..." I'd planned to say I woke up and realized I didn't love him. That I wasn't happy, that I had other things I had to go do in my life, and I had to do them by myself. I'd watched a movie once where that was what the woman said to her long-lost love decades later when they happened upon one another again. But now, facing Laura, the words won't come out. She probably wouldn't believe me, anyway. It was obvious, the way we felt about one another. And it's not like I ran off to join the Peace Corps—I'm still a nurse. About to be married again. Back in the Pacific Northwest.

She studies me across the table. It was a mistake coming here. A mistake to talk to her. A mistake to think we could be friends again. She was my sister-in-law who took me in with no questions. Who became my family. But when I left him, I left her. I know she won't believe me if I lie to her.

I can't tell her the truth.

"I'm sorry, Laura. I can't..." I shake my head, rifle through my purse and find cash and set it on the table. "I can't talk about this."

"Wait, Chloe." Her hand lands on mine. Our eyes meet, hers full of compassion, mine, full of tears. It wasn't supposed to be like this. It wasn't supposed to be *hard*. "You can tell me. Whatever it was."

"No," I say. I attempt a smile, but it falls flat. "I really can't."

THIRTY-NINE

JAMESON

Now

Jameson spent the day watching her.

Chloe was up to something. Making friends with the secretary. Scrolling through camera footage. When she made her excuses and left work early—four-forty-five, on the dot—he left his resident in charge and followed her. She stopped at the public bathroom before leaving the hospital, going in wearing her hospital outfit, exiting in jeans and a black tank top, hair out of its bun and down around her shoulders.

She didn't go to her car, but rather paced across the hospital campus until she hit the streets of downtown. Jameson followed at a distance. Thankfully, he didn't have to follow her far—she ducked into the first wine bar she came to, a little cafe with a glass front.

He pulled his phone out and jabbed a quick message.

Half an hour later, he got one in return.

Laura: *She just left.*

He frowned. He hadn't discovered anything following Chloe—hopefully Laura had gotten more.

Jameson: *What did you find out?*

He paced the halls of the hospital, waiting for his phone to buzz. It took too long, but finally she replied.

Laura: *You were right. She's definitely up to something.*

Jameson couldn't be everywhere at once. But between him and his twin sister, who would do just about anything for him, he could be most places.

Thanks, sis, he texted back. *I'm worried. I appreciate your help.*

Thank god he had someone he could trust, no matter what.

FORTY

CHLOE

Now

Cassandra was murdered. The line repeats itself in my head a dozen times as I drive home. Her email echoes, that she felt watched, followed, someone creeping into her *house*. Afraid of *him...* My gaze flicks to the rearview mirror, but no headlights blaze through darkness behind me. No one following me.

At home, I take a shower, then sit down to eat dinner with Elton.

"How was drinks?" He offers an encouraging smile.

"Good." I spear another bite of grilled Brussels sprouts.

"Want to watch a movie after this? Drink wine, snuggle on the couch? Date night in?"

"Sure."

As I watch a movie curled up beside him, I can't keep my eyes on the television. No, it's on those windows—dark and foreboding. Like an open invitation to anyone who wants access to us. I try to wrap my mind around it. Around Jameson, who sat across the table from me, not just doing what I've long suspected he's doing—but murdering women to hide his secret.

I check my phone to find that, for once, Jameson hasn't texted me. He gave me my assignment this morning, then largely ignored me the rest of the day. Putting distance between us after last night. I'm not sure if it's a good sign or a bad one.

I have the weekend off, and Elton and I spend it unpacking. We go through our wedding to-do list, and hit the grocery store in an attempt to learn to cook.

"Fried rice?" Elton asks, holding up a bag of freezer food. "We could make this."

I'm distracted, busy spinning mental circles. I summon a smile for him. "Pretty sure that's only heating food up. Not really cooking it."

He grins, as though caught red-handed. "Bet it would still taste good, though."

We finish shopping and head home, ready to try cooking our first meals together.

On Monday, I go back to work. That week, my second with Jameson, two patients die. One of them makes sense—the other does not.

The third week, Jameson remains distant. He is kind and professional, and it's as though that night at Knock Knock never happened. There are moments when I wonder if I somehow imagined it. Three patients die this week. None of them makes sense. Like Jameson is taunting me. Pushing my buttons. Hoping I say something.

Monday of the fourth week, I get to the hospital and am relieved to see only eight patients are on the unit. Surely, this isn't a pattern. Surely, this doesn't mean we'll see half our patient census die. That would be too obvious.

In the meantime, I've worked back-to-back sixty-hour weeks, drawing questions from Elton like, "Why is Jameson always keeping you so late? I thought you contracted for a forty-hour workweek?" I reassure him it's because I'm new—because

I have a lot to learn. But I feel his gaze on me as I leave for work. As I get home late.

I've looked up every newspaper article there is on Cassandra, but Laura told me everything there is to know.

On Tuesday of week four, arriving to find a small crowd gathered inside a patient room—our first death of the week—my patience snaps. Elton's already hurriedly taking notes from the night nurse he's taking over—he'll be responsible for caring for the deceased's body before it goes to the morgue, then making sure it gets there. Jameson watches from a few feet away, casually leaning in the hall, hands tucked into his white coat.

"Can I talk to you?" I snap.

I walk by him without waiting for an answer. This can't wait. And knowing Jameson and his behavior these last weeks, if I don't talk to him now, he'll disappear, busying himself with caring for a patient.

We make it around the nearest corner, and I stop—no nurses or aides nearby. Just the two of us in an empty hall.

"Hm?" He turns, gives me a polite smile.

"What's your deal?"

"Pardon?" His brows furrow.

"You're being weird. About..." I wave a hand. "About working with me. I thought this was all going to be okay, then we went for drinks and—" I scowl. "You're being difficult. And you have been since that night."

I hope he buys it. With any other physician, I'd be fine with this working relationship. Plenty of independence, no doctor breathing down my neck, doubting and double-checking my every move, or calling me a *nurse* practitioner like it's a dirty word.

An emotion flashes in his eyes—something deep, dark, but then he looks down and back up, and it's changed. All polite and smiles again. Maybe Laura was right. If he really does still have feelings. But damn it, he brought me here. *Why?* And what's more, his feelings don't get to be in the way of me figuring out how he's doing this. How he's killing patients and Debra and Cassandra...

I mean, what if I'm next?

Something occurs to me then.

Maybe that's why he brought me here. Maybe that night at the bar mucked it up. Maybe he has feelings, but initially he brought me here to kill me. Or... I think back to George. Who I consented to be a DNR. My blood runs cold.

Maybe he wants to pin it all on me.

"I'm sorry," he says. "I'm still figuring out how this works. We good?"

"We're good," I lie.

He looks at my hands on my stethoscope, then meets my eyes. "Maybe it would be helpful to spend more time getting to know one another again. As... not husband and wife." He looks away, as though the words are hard to say.

I take a long slow breath, trying to ease my nerves. I expect him to suggest another lunch or drinks, both anticipation and dread building at the thought, thinking of how I'll have to suggest somewhere more public, but instead he says, "I'm having a small gathering at my house tonight. Would you and Elton like to come?"

"Sure." I answer fast, without thinking, without asking Elton. But this is an opportunity. I have to take it.

FORTY-ONE

CHLOE

Now

My first patient of the day is young at fifty-five. He reminds me of a grandfather I have only vague memories of meeting, a thin face, white beard, and kind blue eyes.

"Mr. Gardner, nice to meet you."

"Call me Bruce. You're the doctor?"

"Nurse practitioner." I extend a hand and we chat about his day—*better, now that I'm not having a heart attack*—and what brought him in—*guess I needed a stent.* I do an assessment, and other than the fact he nearly died the day prior, he's in good health.

"I run 5Ks," he says with a proud smile. "With my daughter. When can I get back to doing those?"

"That will be a question for the surgeon. She should be back on Monday to talk to you."

"You look like a runner. My daughter is on the board for the Portland Downtown 5K. Heard of it?"

I was about to leave the room, to go see my next patient, but his earnest gaze draws me back. "I haven't. I'm actually new in town."

"Oh, you're going to love Portland. Here, one sec, I always have a card—" He snatches his wallet off the bedside table and rifles through it. "Here you go. Signup starts next month. It benefits a children's charity." He points to a photo of a little girl. "That's her daughter. My granddaughter. She has cystic fibrosis. That's what the run goes to."

I smile. "I'll check it out. My fiancé likes to run, too."

"Good. That'll keep a couple together. Shared interests like that. My wife isn't a runner, but she comes to all my races. She'll be there, too." He gestures again at the card.

Eventually, I make it out of the room, tucking the card in my pocket. I'll look it up. It's the sort of thing Elton would love to do together. I call Elton as soon as I finish rounding on my patients.

"Let's go see a movie tonight. We can grab dinner, then—"

"We were invited to a dinner party." I try to relax my jaw as my teeth clench.

"Really? That's great. It'll be nice to meet some new people. We can do like... couples dates." His voice teems with enthusiasm. "When is it? What can we bring?"

I hesitate. "Tonight. And I don't think we need to bring anything."

"Well, we have to bring a bottle of wine or flowers or something. I'll walk down to the market. Do you know if they prefer red or white?"

Elton, always wanting to maintain etiquette, make a good impression.

I lean against the wall in the office. "It's actually at Jameson's. He wants to..." I search for the right words. "Meet you." It's not quite perfect, but it's better than *create a nonmarried relationship* or however else I'd describe it.

Elton takes a second to reply. "He's already met me."

"Like get to know you."

"Why?"

His tone makes me pause. It's lost the boyish jovialness he usually talks with and taken on a defensive edge.

"Because we work together, Elton. Because he's... trying."

A pause over the line. I glance back at the office door and hit the lock button, then sift through the stacks and papers on Jameson's desk again, looking for anything new. Maybe I can find an employee file on Cassandra. Maybe—my gaze lands on the notebooks, which have appeared again—maybe she's in one of them. But why would he leave that here, where I might easily find it? Maybe he's baiting me.

I remember a line in a book about serial killers—that they almost *want* to be found out. They don't want to go to jail or be executed, but they do, on some level, want credit for what they're doing. Jameson seems more together than that. More... aware. Intelligent. What I need is indisputable proof. He's slipped through the cracks too many times.

"Elton, you still there?"

"I'm here." He lets out a sigh. "Okay. Let's do it. I just..." His voice trails off. "I'm sorry, babe. I'm not the jealous type. This is hard, though, you know? You spend all week at the hospital with him. And knowing you're spending all this time with your ex-husband. The ex-husband who..."

I pause in my search and sit in the nearest chair, giving Elton all my attention. My hand grips the phone hard, until I realize it aches with it, and switch hands.

"What is it?" I ask.

"He just... he destroyed you, babe. I remember how you two were back when I was a traveler. Inseparable. I was shocked when I saw you in San Diego months later. Without him. Divorced. You were... I don't know what happened. I don't need to know. But whatever happened between you two, it destroyed you. I watched you piece yourself back together over months."

I don't say anything. We've never talked about this.

"You became yourself again, but you were... sad. Angry." A harsh exhalation over the line. "I was afraid to let you know how I felt, because I thought I might lose you as a friend. And I finally did, because I knew I'd regret it if I didn't. And thankfully, it went well. Thankfully, you felt the same way I did. But you were... so scared at first." He pauses, takes what sounds like a steadying breath. "You were terrified to get close to me."

I think back to those early days in San Diego. Walking the beach with Elton, joining in pickup volleyball games. Grabbing margaritas at beachside bars and laughing near the tiki torches late into the night. Wandering through the darkness to the edge of the water, the sand and ocean lapping at our feet. Talking into the wee hours of the night.

"So when I see you with him now—all I can think is that he did something awful. Something that hurt you. And I won't let anyone hurt you, Chloe." His words carry a finality I've never heard him speak with before. The other side of Elton. The side that is my rock.

"I love you," I say. "Thank you for wanting to protect me. But I'm okay."

He sighs. "I know. I know you are. And I'm so impressed with you for that. I don't think most people would be okay. But now..." He pauses. "Now, you're spending all this extra time with him. You're at work every night, late."

I start to speak, then bite back my words, knowing they'll come out defensive.

"What am I supposed to think?" Elton continues. Then he utters a curse, like he hadn't meant to say that.

I take a slow breath. "Elton, I'm working. I'm a new nurse practitioner in a job that doesn't have nine-to-five hours. If there's an opportunity to learn, I have to take advantage of it. I —" I again stop myself, my body tight with annoyance. "If it were any other doctor, would you have a problem with it?"

Silence. Then, "I don't know. Probably not."

"I mean, this is the exact reason we *should* do this tonight. Nothing's going on with Jameson. We're establishing a normal working relationship. Can't you respect that?" Frustration builds as I talk. The last thing I'd do is cheat on Elton, and he should know that.

Elton sighs. "Okay, babe. I'm sorry. I'm trying here."

"Do you want me to cancel?" I ask the question, my gut wrenching at the thought of not going to Jameson's. Not having a chance to search his place.

"No. We can go. Just... it's okay if this job doesn't work out, and I want you to know that. You can get a job elsewhere, or we can sell the house and move or—" He makes a sound of exasperation. "We can wait for the wedding, and get married, and then —do whatever we need to do. I know you don't want that. But I have to say it. It's okay if you change your mind about working with him."

More than anything, I wish I could reach through the phone and hug him and tell him it's all okay. Instead, I tell him I love him. I hang up. And I go back to searching the office. What I want more than anything in this moment is to leave Jameson in the past, so I can move forward with Elton.

FORTY-TWO

JAMESON

Now

Jameson had lied.

There was no gathering at his house planned that evening.

Chloe turned to go into a patient room, and he whipped his phone out to text Laura.

Small dinner party tonight?

As he stared at the three dots indicating she was typing back, Dr. Michaels strode by. He wasn't working with Jameson today, but no matter.

"Dr. Michaels, a word?"

The man flinched but recovered quickly. They'd worked together for some time, but the rumors of *Dr. Death* died hard. Or maybe, they picked back up when he started in Portland and was one of only three local physicians who'd assist with physician-assisted suicide. Or possibly, Dr. Michaels was just skittish.

"Yes?"

"I'm having a small gathering tonight. Would you and your wife like to attend?"

"Oh, I'm not—I'm not married." He offered this, voice almost panicked, as though it was his get-out-of-jail-free card.

"Girlfriend?"

"Yes. She's—"

"Bring her. I'll text you the address. Six o'clock." Jameson gave him a nod and stalked off before he found another excuse. Jameson had said dinner party—which meant at least a handful of people. As he strode down the hall toward his next patient, he called a nearby restaurant. "Hello, is it too late to order catering for this evening? Oh, maybe six or eight people. Salad, bread, main course. Dessert. Sure, I'll hold."

Jameson paced the hall, already thinking of that evening—of her, in his home. It wasn't the home they'd had together, though he still owned that one, in Seattle. He hadn't been able to let it go—let that piece of her, of *them*, go. But his home now resembled their home in Seattle. The same furniture and books and paintings. Hell, he even still had their wedding photo. He'd made excuses to his family for not hosting a big wedding, but it was what she wanted, because other than Nathan, she'd had no one.

Nathan. He hadn't thought of her brother in some time. The memory gave him pause. Made him wonder, but no—no.

A second later, Laura replied.

What can I bring?

Wine, he typed out. *Six o'clock.*

With that arranged, he got back to work. The sooner he was done, the sooner he could go home. The sooner he could go home, the sooner he could make sure the house was ready to receive guests—to receive Chloe. It was a split-second decision. The sort of thing he already regretted, but he couldn't let her slip away. Couldn't let her escape without finding out what she was really up to. And she was definitely up to *something*. And... there was the little fact he was literally pulled toward her. He tried to stay away, but then she spoke to him, and it was like nothing changed. The shy woman grown confident enough to confront him. But he couldn't dwell on that.

He needed to make sure everything was put away where she wouldn't be able to find it.

* * *

Laura arrived first, brandishing half a dozen bottles of wine.

"You didn't say how many people," she said to him, "so I brought plenty." She put the bottles of white in the wine cooler then turned and leaned against the stainless steel counter. Evening sun winked through a broad set of windows. The condo was quite different than the home he'd shared with Chloe—more modern and cold. The furniture they'd bought together looked out of place here—dark wood antiques.

"So," Laura went on, "you're not really the last-second dinner party type. Or the dinner party type, period. What's going on? You meet someone you're trying to impress?"

He raised his eyes to her for the briefest moment, then looked away, snatched up a glass of Scotch he'd been sipping on since he got home an hour prior.

"Shit. It's her, isn't it?"

"Her?" He snorted. "You talk like you two weren't best friends."

"We were. And then..." A ghost of a smile. Everything that came after passed between them in a single glance. "So why the dinner party?"

"She's bringing her fiancé. We're going to make peace or... whatever."

"Is that what you're really doing?"

Jameson shrugged. "She needs to be comfortable with me. Trust me. Otherwise this will never work."

Laura raised an unimpressed brow. Just then, the bell chimed.

Jameson jolted, nearly spilling his drink.

"Shall I get that?" Laura asked, amusement in her tone.

"No. I'll—would you mind opening the wine?" Jameson left his glass on the counter and strode into the foyer. One glance through the frosted glass betrayed it wasn't Chloe's form on his front step—it was someone taller, thinner, who he guessed was Dr. Michaels. The tension knotted tighter in his abdomen, and he opened the door, welcomed them in.

"This is Heather," Dr. Michaels said. "Heather, this is Dr. Smith."

"Jameson, please," he replied, and shook both of their hands. "Dr. Smith is who I am at the hospital. Right this way. My sister is opening some wine."

He'd no sooner turned his back than a knock came at the door—light, tentative. Whoever it was stood directly behind the door, so he couldn't see them. But he'd gotten only a "maybe" from one other colleague, so it was probably Chloe.

Chloe and Elton.

It would be hard to see them together. His guts twisted, thinking of it. He remembered seeing Elton, a nondescript nurse he never paid much mind to—who, in his defense, he'd only worked with for a few months, as far as he could remember. If he'd known then that some random travel nurse would someday become his wife's husband, would he have gotten to know him better?

Or would he have choked the life out of him?

He shook his head. No, he couldn't think like that.

Jameson steeled himself. Whisked away pointless thoughts of the past and opened the door, a smile plastered over his face, ready to meet the man who'd replaced him.

But Chloe stood there alone. Chloe, still in scrubs from the hospital, her hair a bit rumpled, mascara slightly smeared. Utterly perfect. His favorite way to see her. He breathed, because his chest had gone tight, holding his breath.

"Where's Elton?" He waved a hand, ushering her inside.

"He's coming. I got stuck at the hospital, so I came straight from there."

"Oh." He frowned. "What happened? I wouldn't have left if I'd realized—"

"Nothing really happened, just—you know Mr. Gardner in 817? He's so nice. His daughter hosts a 5K, and I noticed some runs of V-tach, so I ducked in to check on him. We got talking." Her cheeks pinked, the first sign of embarrassment he'd seen. Something far more common before.

"That's kind of you." Jameson nodded. "Well, thanks for coming. I know it was kind of last second."

"Happy to." She looked past him, inspecting his house— eyes wandering over the steel and glass, but pausing on the entry table, one they'd found on a road trip to Coeur d'Alene that first summer. They'd had to tie it to the top of the car for the ride back, and nearly lost it driving the mountains. Somehow, she remained expressionless. Something she wouldn't have been capable of before. Like life had thrown her a few more hardballs. His heart hurt, thinking of that. She'd had plenty of hard times before they'd met—he'd decided he'd fix all that. Not let anything else ever touch her again.

Jameson cleared his throat. "Can I grab you some wine? Laura picked up a few bottles."

Chloe nodded after a beat, like she was lost in some memory. "Please."

They retired to the kitchen, which felt full now. Dr. Michaels feigned a smile, seeing Chloe—he hadn't loved the idea of working with a new nurse practitioner.

"Ms. Woods," he started.

Chloe gave him a long look and said, "It's Dr. Woods. I may not be a physician, but I do have my doctorate. Or"—she flashed a mostly kind smile—"you may call me Chloe."

Dr. Michaels, properly chastened, bobbed his head. "Sure. I'm Oliver, and this is Heather."

"Nice to meet you." Chloe accepted a glass of wine from Laura, then set it down and turned to Jameson. "Is there a restroom I could use? I'd like to freshen up."

"Certainly. This way."

Suddenly, they were alone again. He led her down the long hall, past the spare bedroom to the standalone bathroom.

"Here you are." He turned the knob. The room was rarely used, and he kept the door closed most of the time.

"Thank you."

An awkward moment as Jameson tried to move out of the way and Chloe passed, their arms brushing. He wanted to reach out, to touch her, but she was in the bathroom, shutting the door behind her. The click of the lock.

He was being strange. He knew that. He wasn't usually a strange person. But *her,* something about her, always undid him. And as Laura had pointed out before, this wasn't normal. It wasn't normal for your wife to leave you, and a few years later for her to show up working for you. To have to deal with being in her presence when her very absence was still an open wound, when seeing her with her new soon-to-be husband was like plunging a dagger into his heart.

Jameson exhaled. Went back to the kitchen, aware that at any moment Elton would arrive, and he'd need to act as though everything were okay.

FORTY-THREE

CHLOE

Now

Being in his home is harder than I expect. I sit on the edge of the bathtub and breathe. *Breathe, damn it, breathe.* This is an opportunity.

But I hadn't considered that an entirely different place in a different city would look so similar to our home in Seattle. The condo is different—modern and cold-feeling. But everything else is the same. Every piece of furniture a memory of a road trip. The paintings on the walls we bought at art shows together. Hell, even the glass of Scotch he had was part of a set I'd bought for us at an antique shop—an old-school Glencairn glass in his hand, because I'd read somewhere it gave the best whisky-drinking experience, and that seemed to be something Jameson would appreciate.

I squeeze my eyes shut, stand, splash cold water on my face. I wipe away smeared makeup and run my fingers through my hair, then tie it back in a ponytail. Thank god, Elton isn't here yet—that I have a few minutes to adjust. To ease into this. God, this is worse than I expected.

And I need to *focus*. To use my time here to search his home when he's distracted. Maybe, to find evidence he's the one who murdered Cassandra and Debra.

I splash more water on my face, pat it dry with a towel, and turn to leave.

My phone vibrates, and I pull it out to see a message from Elton.

Be there soon. Got stuck in line at the liquor store.

I pocket the phone, open the door, listen down the hall.

Voices in the kitchen. A woman laughing, not Laura, so it must be Heather. Jameson offering to pour more wine. Across the hall from me, a door is cracked open—inside, I can see the edge of the bed. A familiar starched white comforter, one Jameson and I argued about buying. The conversation replays in my head, though it's been years.

It's white. *Every stain will show.*

He'd laughed. *It's okay. We can wash it.*

What if we adopt a cat with black fur?

We'll put a sheet over where the cat sleeps.

I like drinking coffee in bed.

You're an adult, you won't spill your coffee.

Back and forth we'd gone, until we'd ended up laughing so hard it hurt.

In the end, I'd agreed, and we'd gotten the damn thing. I exhale and nudge the door open. Search the room with a glance. It's clean. Too clean, like he doesn't even use the room. But it's his room, I can tell, because a single pair of shoes sits in the corner—a different pair than he had when we were married, but the same brand. Nike running shoes.

I duck out and check the next door. My hands sweat, and I realize I'm trembling. It's one thing to search the shared office at work. It's another to skulk through Jameson's home while he's just down the hall.

But then I think of Nathan, of his eyes closing that final time.

I push the door open.

FORTY-FOUR

JAMESON

Now

She was in his home.

The words pulsed through him as he walked back to the kitchen. As he topped off his glass. As he leaned on the counter and listened politely as Laura and Heather talked about their jobs—Heather, apparently, was a physical therapist, which meant Laura had about a dozen questions about injuries she'd had over the years from tennis. Dr. Michaels listened, brow creased, as though the conversation was deeply interesting. It meant Jameson could stand there, stare at the hall down which Chloe had disappeared, and play through the past in his head over and over, on a loop that always ended in her walking away.

He shook his head, drank more Scotch, pretended to be engaged in the women's conversation. When the knock came at the door, he thought he'd be ready; he thought it would be a good thing for Elton to be here. For him to remember that his Chloe was about to be happily married to someone else, and that outside of work, he had no place in her life.

Instead, dread filled him. He liked having her here—but

Elton? Well, he was tempted to not answer the door. But that wasn't going to work. He set his Scotch down and passed through the foyer.

"Elton. Nice to see you again. Come on in."

Elton, sandy-haired, blue-eyed, offered a friendly smile and held out a bottle of wine. "Picked this up. Thanks for having us over."

Jameson accepted the wine with a murmured thanks. His guts tied themselves in knots, just being in Elton's presence. In imagining Elton's hands on her, Elton beside her in bed, Elton making her breakfast and—

He turned away.

"Chloe is in the restroom, but everyone else is in the kitchen. Can I get you wine? Scotch?"

"Wine is great." Elton strode through ahead of him, greeting Laura with a nod, shaking hands with Heather and Dr. Michaels. Small talk ensued. Jameson busied himself finding a clean glass. Asking "Red or white?" Continuing the song and dance of a polite host.

But his gaze strayed to the hallway over and over.

She was taking a long time.

Maybe avoiding him. Passing time until Elton got here.

"Cheers." Jameson handed Elton the glass of red and held up his own glass.

More inane conversation about work and Portland and hiking and—oh Jesus, he couldn't take it anymore.

"Excuse me." He pretended to wander in the direction of the foyer, but he veered off and walked the length of the hall, halting in front of the restroom, his fingers touching the outside of the door, like somehow he could feel her through the wood paneling.

This wasn't the time. Wasn't the place. And god, what about the secrets they shared? The ways in which they could destroy one another? But he wanted to be near her. Wanted to ask the hard questions. He didn't care that her husband was just down the hall. He needed to know.

"Chloe?" He kept his voice low so it wouldn't carry. He rapped his fingers gently over the restroom door. "Elton is here. But I'd like a word, if you don't mind."

Nothing in response.

He knocked again. "Chloe? Are you okay?"

Silence.

FORTY-FIVE

CHLOE

Now

The spare bedroom is not a bedroom. It's a library. Full of dark wood shelves taller than I am, full of books. A daybed is in the corner, piled high with pillows, like someone might grab a book off the shelf and recline on it, reading all day.

I stand in the middle of the room, taking it all in. Realizing my jaw is practically on the floor.

This is the room Jameson and I talked about building when we bought a house.

We both ferried books around with us everywhere—especially on trips, where we'd snuggle side by side or sit opposite of one another on a couch, our feet and ankles entangled. We'd read into the night, stopping every so often to pour a drink or chat about what we were reading. Sometimes, we'd get two copies and read the same book, together. We dreamed of having a bigger place, a place with a library. Which was well within our means, even then, but the shared dream was more important than the actual act of doing it.

But Jameson did it. Without me.

I turn in a circle and spot a desk we collected in one corner. An old-fashioned writing desk, the rolltop variety, with a matching chair. Even in this place of wonder, I manage to remember why I'm here, and hurry across the room to it. I search the nooks and crannies, pull out the drawers and flip through papers and notebooks. Nothing on patients here—no, he keeps all that at work.

But a folded-up newspaper sits at the top of the bottom drawer, and I pull it out, unfold it, shake it until it lies flat. The date is from two months ago, the ink ever so slightly smudged from handling. I go still when I see what section it is.

Obituaries.

And near the bottom is a familiar photo—the same photo I saw on LinkedIn.

Cassandra Valencia.

I'm about to read it when I notice what else is in the drawer —what had rested just below the obituary.

A knife, but not just any knife—it's thin, like you might filet a fish with it. The handle is small, and it looks handcrafted. Unique. I reach in, lift it up—the blade is thin, sharp, like a razor. Like a *scalpel*.

The newspaper shakes in my hand. This could be the murder weapon.

And a sharp blade is how Cassandra died.

It's at that moment the click of a door sounds behind me, and I let the blade fall back into the drawer. I go utterly still, like maybe he won't see me if I don't move. But I can feel him. Feel his presence, even across the room. Like a fucking magnet, and some part of me wants to look at him. Wants to get close enough to smell him. To touch him.

Even holding the obituary of the woman I think he murdered. I drop it back into the drawer and use my knee to close it. Like maybe he won't notice which drawer I opened. I exhale and turn to face him.

Jameson stands there. "You weren't supposed to find this room."

FORTY-SIX

JAMESON

Now

Jameson wanted to grab her as she stood at his desk, clearly rifling through it.

Yank her to him.

Shake some sense into her. Didn't she see this wouldn't end well? Any of it?

He forced himself to breathe, to take a step back, because she looked trapped—eyes wide, body rigid. Not quite afraid. Not quite at ease. It was a flashback to an earlier time, when she was new at the hospital, when she hadn't yet gained her footing. Her sense of self. Her confidence.

He took her in. That momentary lack of confidence was appealing because it made him want to take her in his arms. To tell her that if she did what he said, it would be okay. She would be okay. He would see to it.

But problematic, too. Because if she didn't...

Well, he didn't want to destroy her. But he didn't see any other way.

FORTY-SEVEN

CHLOE

Now

I meet his eyes. Search their depths for whatever emotion is in his voice.

"You made the room we talked about," I say.

A slow, stoic nod.

"Why?" I ask.

He shakes his head. "Your husband is down the hall. We can continue our talk about the past. But not here. Not now."

I blink, and before I can stop myself, ask, "When? Where?"

Jameson tilts his head at me. His gaze flicks to the now-closed drawer. "Are you sure you want to have that conversation?"

No, not really. But if it gets me closer to the truth, then yes. Absolutely.

He advances a step. "Chloe?"

I take a half step back. Look at him. Say nothing.

"I know what you're doing." His words come out in the quietest whisper. "You need to stop. This won't end well."

He knows what I'm doing.

I stare at him. It's another warning.

A threat.

He takes another step closer, then another, until mere feet exist between us. We could reach out and touch. Take another step and embrace. Or, he might reach out and hurt me. But not with everyone down the hall in the kitchen.

For now, I am safe.

My heart rebounds against my ribs. I don't feel safe.

Not at all.

Because Jameson sees right through me.

"What's going on?" a familiar voice asks.

I jolt. My face heats, my hands tingle. The voice comes from beyond the room, and I glance past Jameson. He's gone still, too. Still in a way I've only seen him go once, that awful day I try my hardest to block out.

"Elton?" I push past Jameson, his words ringing in my ears. The jealousy in his voice flushing me with guilt. We didn't do anything, but Elton doesn't know that. Words escape me.

Jameson and I, alone in this room.

Talking around what I know. What I'm trying to do. What he's willing to do to stop me.

And yet, he warned me.

With Cassandra, he just killed. Slit her throat and let her bleed out on the hospital campus.

With me, he's here. With plenty of other people around.

Begging me to stop.

I grab Elton's hand because I need to be grounded in the moment. Not lost in Jameson's dark, enigmatic gaze, where I can see that maybe I'm not the only one who still cares about the other. Who—

Fuck. Focus.

"What's going on?" Elton accepts my hand in his, but there's a stiffness in his body. The way his gaze roams around the room, rests on Jameson briefly, then to where I'd stood, cornered, before coming to rest on me.

"Jameson was showing me his library." I beckon. "Isn't it amazing?"

Elton eyes me, but takes a step in, inspecting the space. The space that Jameson and I once dreamed of together. Jameson clears his throat. Mutters something about how he created the room and where he got the bookshelves. He's talking to Elton, but his eyes rest on me, and I can feel the heat behind them. The way they probe my soul. How once, he knew me better than anyone else. Maybe, still does.

I drop Elton's hand. Take a step back, out of the room. The two of them turn and stare at me. My past. My future.

"I need a drink," I say.

And I walk away, leaving them both behind me.

Laura's in the kitchen, and despite everything, she greets me with a knowing smile.

"Wine? Or something stronger?" She opens a cabinet door, behind which a full selection of alcohol is stocked.

"Stronger. Please."

"Your usual?"

Her words pierce my heart. They align me with her—with Jameson. When I'm supposed to be with Elton.

"Oh, you know each other?" Dr. Michaels perks up, interested.

"Yeah," I say, searching for something besides *she was my sister-in-law*. "We... used to work together in Seattle."

"Oh, okay." Dr. Michaels nods, like that explains everything.

Laura goes to work preparing an old fashioned.

I thank her, then wander to look out the window. Jameson has a view of downtown Portland and the river. I gaze at it, and behind me, footsteps tell me he and Elton have returned from the library.

The fucking library.

My head spins, thinking of it. Envisioning it. Wondering why the hell he did it.

I suppose it was a shared dream—maybe he'd always wanted to do it, anyway. But I swear I'm the one who told him it's what I wanted. That he agreed, and that suddenly we were talking about someday buying a big house with space for one. I exhale.

I know what you're doing. You need to stop. This won't end well.

I glance back at Laura, who's talking to Heather. Part of me wants to tell her. The other part of me knows better. But she, in theory, is one person I could tell. One person who would understand what happened. Elton meets my gaze across the kitchen, and his face is locked down—purposefully not expressing whatever emotion resides there.

Damn it.

He must think something was going on between Jameson and me. Hell, if I caught Laura and him in a similar position, that's what I'd think. Jameson had me backed into a corner, and I wasn't yelling for help. We were just staring at each other. Like long-lost lovers.

Which we are, kind of.

I glance at the clock on the stove. We haven't even had dinner yet, and I'm already ready to run out of here. To escape and go home. To be in my warm cocoon of a new house and a new life with Elton.

Instead, I have an entire evening ahead of me with my murdering ex-husband who knows I'm onto him.

FORTY-EIGHT

JAMESON

Now

Around the table, people chatted as they ate an arugula salad and sipped at the vegetable soup. Next, he'd bring out the salmon and rice and broccolini and another bottle of wine. Then dessert.

Every course would be slow torture.

He sat at the head of the table. Chloe, opposite him. To her side, Chloe's almost husband, who'd gone from jovial to indifferent, from smiling to merely polite. Elton wouldn't look at her. Wouldn't look at him, either. Which left him Laura, Heather, and Dr. Michaels. He couldn't be sure if they noticed, but he and Chloe did.

When he speared the salad and shoved it in his mouth, he met her gaze across the table. Saw the conflict there. The concern. That he knew? Or that Elton caught them alone in the library?

Jameson couldn't be sure. He couldn't be sure what would happen next, either. He couldn't imagine she'd put up with Elton being anything but a loving husband.

Their eyes met again, and this time, he saw the questions in her gaze.

She truly did want answers. He'd said they could talk more about the past—and he'd meant it. He wanted it more than anything else. But it hadn't occurred to him that maybe she wanted it, too.

Jameson waited until Elton excused himself to the restroom, until Chloe went to the kitchen to pour herself another drink. He murmured to the table he'd be right back with a dessert wine and followed her.

The moment they were alone in the kitchen, he cleared his throat.

She spun, like she hadn't expected him.

"Monday," he murmured. "We can talk Monday. After work."

"Where?"

He hadn't planned that part. He said the first thing that came to him. "The same bar as last time. Six o'clock."

FORTY-NINE

CHLOE

Now

The only thing worse than the rest of the dinner party is walking to our respective vehicles. Elton passes my car, headed to his own, and doesn't so much as turn to look back or wave goodbye. I lean against the Lexus, gazing after him. For once, I'm glad Elton and I didn't drive together. That this loaded, angry, awkward silence won't happen with us side by side.

That simple fact bothers me.

I should *want* to be with my fiancé. I should want moments alone with him after a long day. We should gossip about how the food was good, but Oliver Michaels clearly did not want to be there. How Jameson's condo was over the top for a bachelor. How it was weird that brother and sister both moved to Portland—they were adults, why hadn't Laura stayed in Seattle? By the end of the drive, we should have been laughing and planning our Sunday together. My only day completely off this week.

Instead, it's a relief to tuck myself into the silence of my own car. To drive the path home by myself. Plus, it gives me time to think. We meet in the garage and walk into the kitchen in silence.

The ring of the keys dropping in the bowl by the door makes me jump.

"I'm going to shower." Elton disappears up the stairs before I can say anything. I stare after him, then lower myself into the nearest chair.

I keep seeing the knife in my head, the way the blade glinted in the light. Perfect to slit someone's throat with.

I find my laptop and set up shop at the kitchen counter. First, I search for the obituary I never had time to read. It takes some looking, but I find it and skim the words. There's nothing of note—a brief recap of Cassandra's life helping people, followed by the fact she is survived by a sister and a husband. A listing of where to send donations in lieu of flowers. The typical stuff. All surface-level and completely unhelpful.

I wonder how she found out about Jameson. What he did, how he slipped up. But also, how he killed her without being caught. She'd been on the hospital campus. The hospital was full of cameras, full of other employees, even in the dead of night. It doesn't make sense.

The creak of footsteps on floorboards upstairs reminds me I'm not home alone. I shut the laptop, stare out across the backyard into the darkness.

Someone could be watching me right now.

The sensation of spiders crawling up one leg makes me startle, swipe at my leg.

Jameson could easily park his car, wander through the side yard, get comfy on a rock or behind a tree. And simply watch. Wait.

Like Elton and I are his own personal soap opera. Hell, after the scene in the library, I almost wouldn't blame him.

Elton enters the room, still toweling off his hair.

"We should get curtains or blinds for the back," I say.

He frowns, gives me a look. "Why? No one lives behind us."

I open my mouth, shut it. What is there to say? *Because someone might be watching us?*

I'll sound paranoid. Maybe I *am* paranoid.

"Thanks for coming tonight. I know it was kind of last second."

"Sure." Elton turns toward the television.

I shiver, feeling the chill. I want to go to him. To wrap my arms around him and hug him and reassure him nothing happened.

But something *did* happen. Something I can't tell him about. I hate that. With Jameson, we shared everything—well— at least, I thought we did. Maybe no relationship is perfect. Maybe secrets are normal.

I go upstairs to shower, too, feeling alone for the first time since Elton and I got together.

FIFTY

CHLOE

Now

When I wake, Elton is already out of bed.

Sunshine streams in through the curtains, hitting a pile of boxes in the corner that I resolve to unpack today. I roll out of bed, don joggers and a T-shirt, and wander down the stairs, focused on finding coffee.

But when I arrive downstairs, there's no Elton.

An empty, quiet house. A note, scribbled on a whiteboard he must have unpacked.

Gone on a long run. See you when I see you.

His words scald me, leave me breathless, and I wrap my arms around myself, take a step back as I read them a second time. He's not usually vindictive, but his words are... harsh. Unless I'm reading into them. Unless he meant it with a smiley face on the end, acknowledging he's a slow runner, that a long run might take him a few hours.

I read the note again, then go to the coffee machine.

Empty.

He hadn't even made coffee before he left. Not like him at all. An old fear creeps back in—that he'll decide he's sick of me. I sit with the emotion a moment. I haven't felt this way since we first got together. After my parents died, after Nathan got sick, after Jameson betrayed me, I felt like everyone would leave me. Would disappear, one way or another. And I'd worried about that with Elton, too.

Now, that fear is back, telling me he'll pack his stuff and go. That I'm not worth sticking around for.

My brain takes me through the whole scenario while I stare at the empty coffee pot, heart rate climbing faster, faster, until my phone chiming from upstairs jolts me out of it.

I nearly drop the coffee mug in my hand and race up the stairs to answer it. It's probably Elton—twisted an ankle, calling for help. It wouldn't be the first time it's happened. He can't be mad at me if I come to his rescue.

But when I get to my phone, the message isn't from Elton.

Jameson: *Everything okay?*

I frown. Consider not responding. I try to sort out why he's asking if I'm okay, and then I remember that he witnessed Elton's reaction to the two of us being alone, too. Maybe Elton was easier to read than I thought. Maybe Jameson really is concerned.

Chloe: *Fine, thanks.*

I type it out, hit send, and slump back on the bed. I could just go back to sleep. Let the dream world take over for a while, instead of thinking and worrying and stressing. Instead of considering what life would be like to be alone again, if I've really screwed things up with Elton.

But I hadn't done anything wrong. I'm not telling him the whole truth, but Jameson and I weren't *doing* anything.

Another message from Jameson. *Thanks for coming last night.*

And a second later he adds, *I'm glad we're going to talk.*

I consider how to respond. He's chatty all of a sudden. Then I imagine myself telling Elton how I think Jameson brought me to Portland. How I think he's out to get me, and how in return, I decided to do something about it. How I want to stop him before he interrupts my life with Elton.

Although, in a way, he already has.

Elton would be furious.

Furious I put myself in danger with a man who is a medical serial killer. A freaking murderer.

And furious I didn't trust him with this information. Would that be the final straw? Would he leave me?

Stop thinking this way. We're having a fight. Just a fight.

Another text.

Jameson: *I've been thinking, we should meet at my house. Not the bar. Somewhere private.*

My insides clench at the thought, nerves in overdrive. I don't want to go to his house. Don't want to be alone with him. But if we're going to be honest, to plainly discuss what has happened—god, how much will he tell me? Will this be the evidence I need, finally?—then he's right. We shouldn't be somewhere we can be overheard.

My thoughts shift back to Elton, but it's too late to back out now. I have to finish this. Have to see it through.

Chloe: *Okay. I'll come over after work.*

* * *

I spend the rest of the day unpacking boxes. Sorting through things I put in storage years ago, before I started travel nursing, then brought here when we bought the house. Elton comes home from his run two hours into organizing books in our office but merely says, "Hey," and goes upstairs.

If there was any doubt in my mind that he's mad, it's gone now. I shove another book in its place, then another, and another. Slowly, I alphabetize them, something Elton cares about more than me, but it's an easy concession to make. Eventually, I make my way through all the boxes of books. When I step back to survey the job I've done, it jolts me back to the moment in Jameson's library.

His library that was exactly what we talked about. The shelves we bought for it. The books we gathered over the years we were together. Some of them were probably *my* books, books I didn't take with me when I rushed out of our home.

If he's going to be honest with me tomorrow, I need to record it somehow. To have proof. Maybe there's an app for that on my phone?

I flatten one last box and add it to the stack in the corner, wiping a bead of sweat from my brow. Before I can grab my phone to check, there's a knock at the entryway. I look up, and Elton's there, hair glossy and wet, in fresh clothes, freshly shaven. The scent of soap and deodorant permeates the room.

"Hey," he says.

"Hi." I don't move, waiting for him to guide the conversation.

"I'm sorry about yesterday. I'm just—uncomfortable. About you working with him. And then you didn't have time to come home, and I went to his house, and you were *somewhere*, and then he disappeared, and I got paranoid. So I went looking for you—and he had you—" Elton exhales, runs his fingers through his hair. "It didn't look like nothing, that's all. And I trust you." He meets my eyes. "I do. But it was like you two were having a moment." He licks his lips, crosses his arms, leans against the doorway. "So what was happening, Chloe? I just want you to be honest." He pauses, seems to consider his words. "And if you tell me that it was nothing, then... that's okay. I'll believe you."

My chest aches. The vulnerability in his voice kills me. I want to go to him, wrap my arms around him, bury my head in his shoulder and tell him everything. We've always been open, honest. I decide to stick to the truth as much as I can.

"That room was..." I bite my lip and slide to the ground to lean against the opposite wall. I stare at the wood floor, the details of the grain, the scuff marks that need polishing. I force myself to continue. "That room was a room I wanted to build. The library with the bookshelves and the desk and—it was something we always talked about doing together. So when I saw it, it took my breath away. It was like stepping into the past."

Elton frowns. "His office?"

I look up, his brow wrinkled, trying to understand—but it's clear from that expression he doesn't. Then he glances sideways, at the shelves I've just filled with books.

"Wait, is that why you wanted—" He points at the nearest shelf. "You said you wanted a library, is that why?" His tone grows tense, words coming faster as his voice rises.

"No. I've always wanted a library. It has nothing to do with Jameson. It's just that he built the library he and I always talked about. This is different. This is *ours*." I nod at the books, books we've bought and read together. The desk from IKEA we put together, large enough we can share it. "It's not the same thing."

Elton is anything but placated. He blinks. A muscle bulges in his cheek. He looks down, shakes his head. My stomach plummets, seeing the emotion build in him—frustration, anger. He thinks I wanted a library because it's something I once wanted with Jameson. I open my mouth to say more, to clarify, but shut it because annoyance streaks through me.

It's *normal* to have an office, a library. This room has nothing to do with Jameson's library.

"I gotta go," he mutters, and a second later, the door slams. I consider going after him but decide against it, my jaw stiffening that he keeps presuming the worst.

My phone chimes, and I assume it's him—but it's not. It's Jameson again.

Jameson: *Everything's gonna be okay.*

I read it again, realization dawning—he could be watching me right now. My gaze rises to the window that looks out to the backyard, that vast space full of trees and grass and boulders. If he was watching, Jameson would have witnessed our interaction. Watched as Elton stormed off in a huff. His text might make sense, in that context. I bite my lip hard and move around the edge of the nearest bookshelf, putting me out of the line of sight from the window. My chest aches with tightness, with feeling like there's no escape—from Elton's anger and wrongful suspicion, from Jameson's probing gaze.

The grinding of the garage door opening tears me back to the present. The fact my fiancé thinks I'm stuck on my ex-husband. Which I *am*... but not for the reasons he thinks I am—which isn't fair to him.

I run my hand over my face and wipe away tears. Nothing is going to be okay.

* * *

The rest of my day includes ordering blinds and curtains, cleaning the house, then settling in front of my laptop. I search the online white pages and then social media. But there's no trace of Cassandra's husband or sister.

When Elton eventually comes home, I'm still tapping away

at my computer. I immediately shut the tab I'm on so he doesn't see me looking up information on medical serial killers.

He comes around to where I am, takes one look at the computer, and shakes his head.

"Jesus, Chloe."

"What?" I half turn, both wanting to diffuse the anger in his voice, and annoyed he won't just talk to me.

"You're obsessed," he mutters. I turn back and realize the LinkedIn profile for Jameson is the next tab—the one that popped up when I closed the other one. His photo stares back at me.

"Elton, I can explain—" But Elton has already left the room.

FIFTY-ONE
JAMESON

Now

Chloe reported to work right on time.

Jameson watched from the nurses' station as she strode down the hall, bag over one shoulder, scanning the halls until her gaze came to rest on him. Even now, knowing what he did—what she had planned—he couldn't help the way he felt. The way he wanted to go meet her and walk beside her to their office.

In another life, they would be working just as they were now—but together, still married. He longed for that life. Could almost feel it. Thought about it every night before bed.

A beat later, Elton ducked out of an elevator, coming from the opposite direction—the general employee parking, instead of the provider parking.

Jameson glanced back and forth between the two—her gaze straightforward now, as she hurried to their office.

Elton's face flat, emotionless.

Trouble in paradise, it seemed. He pulled out his phone and sent a message to his sister.

She looks concerned. Nervous. Something off with Elton, too. Maybe see if she'll talk to you? I want to know as much as possible before we do anything else.

Laura wrote back a second later.

Sure.

Jameson wished he could pull her aside now, because now, before she and Elton had a chance to potentially make up, she would be more vulnerable. He might get her to admit the truth. Might influence what she did next.

But a second later, a nurse approached.

"Dr. Smith? Can you come see the patient in room 802? They are asking to speak to the doctor."

He nodded, smiled. "Of course, Mary. Lead the way."

Chloe would have to wait. For now.

FIFTY-TWO

CHLOE

Now

Elton still isn't speaking to me.

He slept on the couch. Left to go to the gym before I was even awake. I drum my fingers over the desk, waiting for the printer to give me the readout of our patient list so I can get started with my day.

He didn't even say hello when we passed one another in the hall.

I exhale. Last night, I'd felt like shit about what happened— of course he was jealous. Of course he thought something was going on. I was spending all my time at work, used our Saturday night to go to a gathering at Jameson's house, where Elton had found us alone in the library where—

Stop.

I sink into my chair. Gather up the printed sheets and separate them into two piles—one for Jameson, one for me. I'd known I'd have to get close to Jameson to fully understand the extent of what he was doing. To get proof.

Not that I had proof.

But I might after tonight.

A knock comes at the door, and I startle, nearly spilling my coffee.

"Chloe? You in there?" Laura's dark hair pools around her shoulders. "Oh, shoot. You already have coffee." She holds out a paper cup. "Well, have a fresh one."

"Thank you." I take it, surprised but grateful. Elton again didn't make coffee at home, which means whatever I poured into my to-go cup is left over from yesterday, the insulated pot keeping it lukewarm.

"You okay?" She settles into Jameson's chair and sips her own coffee.

"Yeah, fine. Why?" I study her, still not understanding this nice act. She's almost... friendly. The last thing she should be with me.

"Well..." She presses her lips together and crosses her legs. "Elton seemed... upset. On Saturday. I just wanted to check on you. I'm sure this is hard on him."

I almost say, "No, he's fine." But it was obvious he wasn't. And once, we were friends. Right now, I could use a friend more than anything.

I still wonder if she might be an ally now, if I tell her everything that's happening. I should at least keep the door open, which means I need to be open with her.

"He is upset," I finally say. "I went into the library by accident, and—did Jameson ever tell you about... that it was what we wanted to do?"

Laura's gaze softens. She brushes a strand of dark hair from her face. "Yes. I knew."

"I couldn't believe it. It was exactly like what we'd talked about, and Jameson came in"—I gulp a breath of air, almost reliving it in the moment—"and then Elton came in." I wipe dampness from my eyes and look at her. "I'm sorry. I know I walked out on you the other day, but I really can't... can't get into it. But just know it hurt me to leave him, too."

Laura considers me. She gives a slow nod.

"Okay, Chloe. I do believe you." She glances at her watch. "I have to go, but lunch? Today?"

I blink back my tears, tears that are either for Jameson or Elton, I'm not sure who. Maybe both. And maybe a little at her kindness when I feel like I have nobody.

"Okay," I mumble. "I'm not sure when I'll be done with rounds, can I text you?"

"Sure. That works." As if on a sudden urge, she leans in and wraps an arm around me for a quick squeeze. "It'll be okay. It really will. Jameson only wants what's best for you."

It's not until she leaves the room that it occurs to me there might be a deeper meaning to what she's said. Jameson wants *what's best for me.* My neck prickles, imagining what that might mean.

Is it possible she's in on our little secret?

If she is, I suspect I know whose side she's taken.

FIFTY-THREE

CHLOE

Now

"Day going okay?" Jameson stops beside me in the hall as I scribble on my folded papers, details that will make it into the patient's chart when I have time to sit down and write out a proper note. He's watching me, a trace of a smile on his lips.

Almost like how it used to be. Working side by side, a hint of flirtation in every interaction. I steel myself against it. Against him. Somewhere on this floor, Elton's taking care of patients. The last thing I need is more ammunition in his belief there's something going on between us.

"Fine. Excuse me." I duck into Mr. Gardner's room.

"Chloe! You're here. Good." Mr. Gardner grins at me from his bed. In the chair beside him is a woman about my own age, slim and fit, with a high ponytail and not a trace of makeup. "This is Lindsay, my daughter. The one who does the race."

I cross the room and hold out my hand. Lindsay takes it, smiling.

"My dad said you're a runner."

I grab the remaining chair and flash them both a smile. "I

run some. I'm not sure I'd call myself a *runner* exactly, but I do enjoy it. Mr. Gardner was telling me about the 5K you put on."

Lindsay's cheeks pink, and she glances sideways at her dad, who's puffed up his chest in pride, grinning back and forth between us.

"He talks a lot." She laughs.

We make small talk for a few minutes before I move in and press my stethoscope to his chest, his back, poke and prod until I'm satisfied he's doing just fine.

"We may be able to discharge you soon." I pull out my paper and go through my notes. "You'll need follow-up care with a cardiologist. She'll be by a little later to touch base with you. Her name is Laura Smith, she's excellent."

We chat a little longer, and I promise Lindsay that Elton and I will sign up for her race. I leave the room with a smile on my face—the first real one I've worn all day. What it must be like to have a father like that. One who loves you. One who's still *alive*. A built-in family, without having to search one out, like I have.

The ICUs are busy, and I have patients in more than one of them. It's nine-thirty before I finish assessments, and nearly noon by the time rounds end. Rounds consist mostly of a group of us trailing from unit to unit, listening as the nurse or resident talks about the patient. Sometimes, we make changes to the plan of care—more often the exact same thing we discussed the day prior is gone over yet again. In theory, it's an important part of care. In practice, it's slow and repetitive and often feels like a waste of time.

"You can go to lunch." Jameson sidles up beside me on our last patient. "I'll finish up."

It occurs to me he's being extra nice. Extra kind. Treating me with kid gloves, like I'm fragile. It's probably because he knows what's coming—that I plan to confront him this evening.

But surely he's too smart to think that a little extra kindness will change anything.

"Thanks." I duck away from the group of people and stride back toward our office, texting Laura as I do. She responds with *Ensalada? I'll grab us a table.* I reply with a thumbs-up. The restaurant is technically off campus, but it's about five steps off campus, and popular among the hospital staff.

It was cool this morning, and I grab my jacket on the way out. I hurry before I can run into Dr. Michaels, wanting to ask a question about a patient, or Elton, who'd no doubt give me a look but continue his silent treatment.

We've never had a real fight—not like this. Sure, we've had disagreements. Yelled once or twice. But nothing that's lasted longer. Nothing where we avoid one another completely. Vulnerability wells up inside me, thinking of it. Thinking of the warmth in the way he usually looks at me, the way he wraps his arms around me and kisses my shoulder just to say hi. And now he can't stand to be in my presence.

Anger follows it. Anger he assumes the worst. That he thinks I would cheat on him.

Laura waits for me in the busy restaurant, two salads already on the table, hunks of bread and glasses of iced tea between them.

"This okay?" She gestures to what appears to be a Cobb salad.

"Perfect." I glance at the line going out the door. "Anything that means not waiting in that line."

Laura laughs. "Exactly."

As we take a moment to add dressing and mix it in, I examine her, thinking through my previous curiosity at her phrasing—if she knows what Jameson's doing. If... A new idea forms, and I nearly drop my fork.

She'd come to Portland with him. What if she was in on it? Helping him, somehow?

Suddenly, I'm not hungry.

Instead, I sip the iced tea and wait for her to ask about Elton, but she doesn't. She chews her salad and remarks on how busy the hospital is. Like last time, acting like everything is as it once was. Maybe this is an opportunity to ask my own questions.

"So, why Portland?"

Laura tilts her head and picks up her hunk of bread. "I don't know. Tired of the Seattle traffic. Not that it's always better here, but it's less—*everywhere* here. Jameson being here. Also, they offered me more money, which is always nice."

I gaze at her, take in her smile. I don't know her tells the way I do with Jameson. I can't tell if she's lying.

"Did you go to Idaho with him, too?"

"Idaho? No thanks."

I wait for her to add more details, but she falls silent, busy with her lunch.

I scour my brain for another question that might get me closer to an answer but come up short. I go for small talk, to keep the conversation flowing.

"I like Portland." I consider our home. Our neighborhood. "It's quieter than Seattle. Than most of the places I've lived. Which I wouldn't have guessed."

"Quieter?" She perks up. "That's because you're living in the suburbs."

"Yeah, maybe." Something pricks at my brain.

How does she know where I live?

I think about feeling watched. I consider her last words to me earlier—that Jameson wants what's best for me. I roll them over in my head as I chew, trying to decide if there was more to it than that. Or if she merely meant, I'm working with Jameson, and my husband has a problem with it, and Jameson wants what's best for me. I opt for honesty—open up to her.

"It makes me mad." I set down my fork.

Laura looks up, eyes wide. "What does?"

"How Elton is being about this."

"Oh."

"I know I've been busy. I know Jameson and I were in the room together. Alone. But does he seriously think that if we were—you know, like, having an affair, that we would be so obvious about it?" I exhale forcefully, pent-up emotion flooding forward. Elton has assumed the worst. Which makes me wonder if our relationship is as rock solid as I thought it was.

"He's barely spoken to me since Saturday," I go on. "He's found every excuse to not be home or around me."

Laura's face creases in concern. She reaches out and presses fingertips to my hand.

"I'm sorry. Is he usually jealous?"

"No. Never." I pick at my food. "But it's always been just the two of us, you know? Travel nursing means you meet a lot of people, but you don't get to know them very well because you're always on the move. So... we spent most of our time together."

"That can be good and bad."

"Yeah. That's true." I turn her words over in my head. She's not wrong. The life Elton and I have been leading these past several years isn't exactly *normal*—most people don't move three or four times a year. We're creating a new normal now. I sigh. "Maybe this is just a little bump in the road. Getting used to things being different. We used to always work the same schedule, too, so we had a ton of time off together. I feel like I've barely seen him." I exhale, a little lighter for having someone to talk to about everything.

"Have you talked to him about any of this?" Laura asks.

"No." I frown, thinking of the moment in the office after I put all the books away. "I've tried to, but he just got upset and left."

"Well, that would help."

"Yeah."

"Maybe tonight?"

"I have plans." I stab a piece of hardboiled egg. "Plans I can't change. But it's not like I haven't made any time for him. We were supposed to spend all day yesterday together, but he was pissed and he took off, and—" I cut myself off. Shake my head. Shove a bite of salad in my mouth because I still have to finish the day at work and I can't do that on an empty stomach.

"I'm sorry, Chloe." Laura sighs and sets her fork down. "Men are the worst. Love them. Hate them. Can't live without them. Sometimes want to kill them." She rolls her eyes, shakes her head, but her words stick.

Sometimes want to kill them.

"Anyway, I have consults, so I have to go in a minute. But I've been wanting to try kayaking on the river soon. Would you want to go with me? Might be a good way to reconnect."

I struggle not to make a face—to show the surprise that leaves me with my fork halfway to my mouth. So nice. Kind. Thoughtful.

Too nice, kind, thoughtful, considering.

She sees my hesitation and laughs. "I promise to not bring up my brother. Just two badass women out in nature."

"Sure. That sounds great. And thank you for listening. Really. I know this is complicated."

"Anytime. You're still like a sister to me." She gives me a one-armed hug and puts the cardboard lid back on her salad to take it with her. "Stay strong. And call if you need anything!"

I watch as she departs, almost missing the days when we really were like sisters. Now, I find her friendliness suspicious. Like Jameson, she's trying too hard to be nice to me.

FIFTY-FOUR

JAMESON

Now

The code blue alarm went off half a second before his phone rang.

"Dr. Smith, code blue in room—"

Jameson didn't wait for the rest of the message. He was already out the door, running toward the ICU. As soon as he hit the hallway, he could hear the alarm blaring from that direction. The only time someone ran in the hospital was when a life was on the line. He sprinted.

"What happened?" Jameson was in the doorway a second later. A visitor, a woman in her early thirties, stood across the room, eyes wide and filled with fear, hands over her mouth as she looked down at the man on the bed.

"Mr. Gardner has a history of—" The nurse rapid-fired the basics as the team moved in perfect harmony—code cart in the room, leads placed on the patient's bare chest, chest board beneath him, compressions started.

Jameson yanked on a pair of nitrile gloves and felt for a

pulse. His eyes focused on the EKG strip, watched the erratic blips of his patient's heart.

"Shit." He uttered the curse without meaning to, and nearly everyone in the room looked up. "Torsades," he said, "magnesium. He needs magnesium." It was a rare heartbeat—something he'd seen only a few times during his career. It could be deadly. It could also, in most cases, be fixed with an infusion of magnesium, which stabilized the cardiac membrane.

The pharmacist yanked open a different drawer of the cart and grabbed one vial, then another, looking for the magnesium.

"Pyxis," she called out, pointing out the door toward the automated medication machine. "Pull mag from the Pyxis. Stat!" She continued going through the drawers, muttering under her breath.

"Continue compressions." He ducked out of the room himself, to make sure someone went in search of the magnesium. A minute later, it was in his hand, and he gave it to the pharmacist.

Laura appeared, and Dr. Michaels, too. He glanced at the clock—the code was going on three minutes now, without recovering a normal sinus rhythm. Not good.

"Torsades de Pointes," he murmured to Laura, who nodded, gaze going to the monitor.

"V-fib," she said in response, and he looked—sure enough, it had transitioned. "Magnesium?"

"Infusing," he replied. "Do we have a pulse at all?"

The nurse with his fingers pressed to the patient's femoral pulse shook his head. "Nothing."

"I assessed him and sent labs half an hour ago. Someone pull them up. See what they look like." Laura pointed at the nearest nurse.

"Sure thing," the nurse said. But a second later he sighed. "Nothing yet."

"Why is she in here?" Laura's gaze flew to the woman, still

staring at her father in terror. Laura approached her. "Lindsay, come on. You can't be in here right now."

"But—"

Chloe appeared in the doorway, face ashen.

"What happened?" She spotted Lindsay. "What the—come this way, Lindsay, come on. Let's see if we can find you some tea and someone to sit with you. No, I don't know if your father will be okay. I'm sorry. We'll do everything we can."

Jameson watched her. Observed how she pulled Mr. Gardner's daughter from the room. He had to wonder how much about Mr. Gardner she knew—she had spent a fair amount of time in the room earlier today. He exchanged a look with Laura, who shrugged.

A heavy weight settled over his shoulders. He sighed, resigned.

Tonight, he would have to end this.

For good.

FIFTY-FIVE

CHLOE

Now

The worst part was not watching compressions, seeing Mr. Gardner's ribs crack beneath the pressure. It was not the moment Jameson took a long look around the room before saying, "Time of death: 1:47 p.m." Nor was it holding Lindsay as her body shook and she repeated over and over, "You said he could go home soon. I just don't understand."

The worst part is finding a free moment to approach Peter, who gives me a sympathetic smile and hands over the mouse and keyboard with a mere, "I'll go grab coffee," knowing I'm about to watch Mr. Gardner die all over again.

I settle into his chair and give the camera monitor my full attention, heart pounding with anticipation and anger. My heart hurts for Mr. Gardner. For his daughter. But I'm here, and I can see who did it—who murdered him.

All the cameras are on—which means I could watch as the nurses bathed Mr. Gardner's body before moving him to the morgue. But I don't want to watch that. Don't want to see the lifeless flesh that once held the animated man who loved his granddaughter and asked everyone to go to his daughter's 5K.

Emotions roil through me as I scroll back through the minutes and hours of footage to twelve hours prior, then put it on a slow fast-forward. Every time someone comes in the room, I stop. Analyze their face. Write down their name if I know who it is, write down a description and their job if I don't. Night shift leaves. The oncoming daytime nurse is Miranda, a kindhearted woman who has been at this job for over a decade. Several other nurses come in throughout the day—answering call lights for Mr. Gardner, delivering fresh water when Miranda was on break. Elton comes in to help him to the bathroom. Dr. Michaels enters to do an assessment before I do, and then I watch my own interaction with the two of them.

After I leave, Miranda is back, along with another nurse I don't know the name of. A young woman who barely looks legal to drive, much less save lives. Then Jameson comes in.

I hit pause. Enlarge the image. Watch it with eagle eyes. A second later—I check the timestamp—fifteen minutes after she left Ensalada, Laura arrives. Jameson is clearly making introductions, and Laura sits at the edge of the bed. After a few minutes of conversation, she does a thorough assessment, from checking his IV lines to listening to his heart to staring at the rhythm on the EKG monitor over his bed. Dr. Michaels comes back in, says something to her. Then Miranda returns. It's a dizzying in and out of people, until finally, they all leave.

Lindsay returns.

And suddenly, I'm again staring at two nurses bathing a body.

I blink. I must have hit fast-forward and missed at least twenty minutes.

I scroll back, then hit play at normal speed, so I don't miss it.

But it happens again.

Lindsay enters and greets the very much alive Mr. Gardner, then his body, pale and gray, being bathed by the nurses.

"Peter?" I look up, but he's still gone. Still off getting coffee.

I frown. This doesn't make sense. Somehow, everything between Lindsay returning and Mr. Gardner dying is just—not here. I check the timestamp of when it begins again, and it's from twenty minutes ago.

I check the whole thing again, and that's when I remember what Peter said—that the cameras could be turned off for periods of time.

And that's when it clicks.

Someone turned off the camera right before Mr. Gardner died. Before they murdered him.

FIFTY-SIX

CHLOE

Now

Six-thirty-eight p.m. Over an hour later than my "normal" hours, though it's hard to define normal in the medical world. Elton will be leaving from his twelve-hour shift soon. I've already told him I'm staying late at the hospital, which is true—and in fact, maybe it's good I'm staying late, because he'll see me still here.

It's a heck of a lot better than him seeing me driving toward Jameson's.

"And the last patient?" Dr. Campbell asks. I look up at her, and she's watching with patient, clear blue eyes.

"He came in for cardiac symptoms, but labs look good. Cardiac cath totally normal." I go over the plan, but my mind wanders—thinking about the words I exchanged with Laura. Mr. Gardner's mysterious death. No one else seemed concerned the camera hadn't caught it. Peter muttered, "Oh, it does that sometimes," and took another drink of his latte.

"What happened to Mr. Gardner?" Dr. Campbell asks, still

jotting notes on the last patient I updated her on. "Was he discharged?"

"He died. Torsades." I look down at the papers in my hand. The X I've drawn through his name, to remind me he's no longer a patient I'm responsible for. "Then V-fib, and we couldn't get him out of it. This afternoon. After lunch."

"Oh, really?" Her face screws up. "He seemed so healthy. Wasn't he supposed to go home tomorrow?"

"Yes. He was."

"What do they think caused it? Did they check his magnesium?"

I nod. "Everything looked normal." It had occurred to me it could have been a random death. It's possible. I've seen it before. But I doubt it. It just doesn't make sense. Especially given his normal lab values. That he seemed healthy. That the cameras were shut off.

Someone did something.

And by someone, I mean Jameson. Or... maybe Laura, who'd just been in to see him. Maybe Laura was somehow involved with it, alongside her brother. She'd said a few odd things, had been on the case. Had *also* been in Portland.

Tonight, I'll confront Jameson. Properly this time. Without the grief at just losing my brother hanging over us. My hands quiver as I fold up my sheet and shove it in my pocket. I'm not looking forward to it. I'm not sure I'll walk out alive. But I've written down an account of everything that's happened to the best of my knowledge and left it where Elton can find it, just in case.

It's gone on too long. Not only are people dying—kind people, like Mr. Gardner—this slow game he and I have been playing is screwing up my relationship with Elton. And he's the whole reason I decided to take on Jameson in the first place. I refuse to let Jameson screw things up for me again.

I'm hoping the way Jameson looked at me, the fact Laura

thinks he still loves me, keeps me safe. Maybe I can convince him to turn himself in. That would show Elton what's really happening, too. Then we would be okay again.

Five minutes later, I stop by the unit and look around for Elton. I spot him helping an older man—stooped and wrinkled with age—ambulate down the hall. He has an arm around his ribs, and holds his right hand, and laughs at something the man says. As usual, caring for the people around him.

"Elton." I give a little wave when he looks up. "I know you're headed home soon. I have a bit more to do, and then I'll be back. Want me to pick something up for a late dinner?"

Elton gives me a long look—filled with conflicted emotions. But I see the flicker of adoration first—before he lets the shields come down.

"Sure," he says. "But I'll pick something up so you don't have to stop on the way home."

"Okay."

He searches my gaze, then looks back at his patient. "Okay," he mutters. He helps the patient to the rail on the wall. "One sec, friend." Elton releases him to ambulate on his own and closes the space between us.

"I'm sorry," he murmurs. "I'm not sure what I'm sorry for, but I am."

I meet his eyes. Hope this isn't the last time we get to fight and make up. His hand clasps mine, and he gives it a squeeze.

"Is there really nothing going on?" he whispers.

"No. There's nothing." I press my forehead against his for a second, very aware we're in a hospital unit and working, but I need this moment with him. The relief is like cool water to this nervous heat that's been building inside me, and I realize how tense I've been these last couple of days.

"Okay." He kisses the top of my head. Squeezes me tight. "I believe you. See you at home."

* * *

The parking garage attaches to the main building via an underground tunnel. The tunnel is brightly lit, and I squint as I stride through it, trying not to think of being followed through a similar tunnel just weeks ago. I can't stop thinking about Elton, relieved we're finally speaking again. About going to confront Jameson. About what role Laura might be playing in his game.

When footsteps sound behind me, I stop and whirl, ready to confront whoever it is. The tunnel behind me is empty. A light flickers off and on, adding to the eerie feeling that something isn't quite right. But it's probably another provider, headed toward their car. Or just the echo of my own footsteps. Of course I'm tense, keyed up. I'm about to go to Jameson's house.

A second later, I'm at the elevators. I press the button and glance back down the hall. Still, no one. In the garage, I pace down the rows of cars toward mine. Day shift has already cleared out, most of them hours ago. Night shift has arrived and reported in. Leaving the garage relatively empty.

I'm a dozen feet from my Lexus when I hear the footsteps again. My heart all but leaps into my throat, and I whirl, faster this time. It wasn't paranoia. I heard them—not an echo of my own, but almost a scuffle, like they tripped or maybe hurried in one direction.

"Sorry," a voice calls out.

I startle and whip around. Dr. Michaels.

"I think I scared you. I apologize." He holds a hand up from two car rows away. "Forgot something, heading back in. You okay?"

I blink. "Fine, thanks. See you tomorrow."

"Sounds good." His form disappears into the elevator bank, and I exhale.

Just Dr. Michaels. No big deal.

But then I see my car—see the rim of the wheel nearly

touching the concrete below, the flattened black rubber of the tire. I hurry over, then gasp. A long slash through the side of it, the rubber splayed open.

It takes my brain a second to process it. To realize what this means.

Someone slashed my tire.

I look up just in time to see Jameson walking toward me.

"What happened?" His words are like his movements—quick, aggressive. I pull away without meaning to, realizing a second too late I'm trapped. I'm between my car and the one next to it, both parked too close to the wall for me to escape that way.

He turns, glances around us—looking to see if we're alone, I think. My body betrays me, trembling. It's not too late to run. I just have to crawl over the front of my car. Or I could scream. Surely, someone is nearby?

I picture Cassandra. I picture her beautiful smile, the caring in her eyes, even as she took a professional headshot. I imagine the knife I found in his desk. Likely, the murder weapon. Is it on him now? I can't see any bulges, but it was a small knife, and he's a tall man. Or maybe, he'll make it look like an accident, as he did with Debra.

"It's the only car with slashed tires." Jameson squats to inspect it.

I take a breath, realize he's not coming at me—not pulling a gun or a knife or reaching for my throat.

A second later, I realize why.

"Come on. I'll give you a ride. Call someone to fix this." He points across the garage. "My car's over here."

Just like that, he's arranged for me to get in his car. To not have a way to get myself home. I look up, but there are no cameras. No one to know where I've gone, why I've left my car here. But I have no other option than to say yes—he'll know I don't trust him if I don't go with him, and he's already got me in a vulnerable position. I have to go with him. Have to play along until the right opportunity presents itself.

At least if Elton comes, it'll look like you're still at the hospital.

"Who would have slashed my tires?" The words come out fast, desperate. I'm stalling, trying to think of another option, but nothing comes to mind.

Jameson crosses his arms, glances down at the tire again. "Well, it's Portland." It is Portland. A city. But still...

A crawling sensation makes me shiver. Makes me cross my arms, too, and want to sprint back to the elevator, take it upstairs, dive into Elton's arms. But I can't do that. I have to sort this out so I can get back to my normal life with Elton.

Almost regretfully, I say, "Okay. Let's go."

FIFTY-SEVEN

CHLOE

Now

I slide into the smooth interior of the car like I've done hundreds of times before. The black leather is soft on my skin. He hits the seat warmers as he starts the engine, something he used to do for me—I was almost always cold.

Now, it makes me clench my fists and look away.

I should be terrified. And I am nervous—but not as scared as I should be. Something about that is deeply disturbing.

When I look over, he's busy on his phone.

"What are you doing?"

"Contacting Triple A. They'll come fix your tire."

I notice he's not using the car's Bluetooth—no, he's holding the phone up to his ear. Who does that these days? Which leads me to assume one thing. He's not really on the phone with anyone. Not calling for help.

"I don't have Triple A."

Jameson waves a hand. "Doesn't matter."

What he means is *I got it*. I exhale. That means he plans on me returning to my car, right? The phone seems to connect, and he murmurs instructions—where my car is, what kind it is, how I need a new tire.

"Hungry?" Jameson sets his phone down, shifts the BMW into gear, and slowly pulls from his parking spot.

"Sure." I'm not, but I haven't eaten since that salad with Laura.

"Okay." He nods, and his gaze flicks my way for a beat. "Pick something up?"

"Sounds good." I remember a second too late that I've promised to join Elton for dinner after this. But that won't be until late.

"Don't be nervous," he says a second later. "It's just me."

I fight back a snort and look away to roll my eyes. Right. Just Jameson Smith, serial killer.

Jameson pulls to a stop sign and looks both ways before pulling into traffic. I take that moment to pick up my phone, swipe to the app I downloaded an hour ago, and press record. It will continue recording in the background until I tell it to stop. It uploads automatically, continuously, to the cloud.

"A lot has changed." I press my hands to my lap to keep from fidgeting.

"That's true." He looks at my hand. "You wanted a diamond ring this time? Or did he just assume?"

"What?" I raise my hand and the slightly less-than-a-carat diamond catches the light. I hide it beneath my other hand. "Does it matter?"

"Yes. A man should know the woman he's asking to marry him well enough to know she doesn't like diamond solitaires."

"Maybe what I want changed."

Jameson's lips curl up at the edges. He checks his blind spot, moves over into the next lane, and exits off the main road to a neighborhood road. We're close to his condo, now. Minutes left to go. My chest is tight, and I have to pay careful attention to my breath to keep it soft, even.

He stops at a small Italian cafe. Through the window, I can see a bar, couples sipping wine and eating soup and salad.

"This okay?"

I nod.

"It'll be a few minutes, so I'll have them deliver when it's ready."

He leaves the car running and steps out. His tall, languid form ducks through the entrance, waving hello to a hostess not over eighteen. She lights up, as many people do—he's an attractive man. What society has deemed *good*.

If only they knew the truth.

He returns to the car, and what feels like a second later, the car dips into underground parking. Another parking garage, this one locked. Jameson enters a passcode and parks in his designated spot. The car comes to a stop. He pulls the key from the ignition, and silence engulfs us.

"Ready?" he asks.

Our eyes meet for a moment, and I'd swear he means something besides talking about the past. I just don't know what. I'm still nervous. Still on the edge of my seat, forcing myself to act a calm I do not feel. But I'm also still not afraid.

I should be afraid.

I take a breath. "Ready."

FIFTY-EIGHT

JAMESON

Now

Jameson was glad for the slashed tires—well, kind of.

He was glad she'd let him come to her rescue. Call someone to fix the tire. Give her a ride.

Maybe it was a sign of things to come. Of them being able to help one another.

He unlocked the front door. The heavy wood swung in, and he beckoned for her to go first. Her scent hit him as she walked by—lavender and mint. Some combination of soap and deodorant and skin. Not exactly the same as before. Not entirely different, either. She looked restless, on edge, entering his home, brushing fingertips over a table they'd picked out together. Not finding a place to sit, not entering the kitchen, where in a few minutes they would share dinner and begin a very difficult conversation.

She just stood there.

Waiting.

"Thank you for joining me tonight." Jameson entered the kitchen. "Wine? Bourbon?"

He thought she'd say no to both, but after a moment she said, "Wine, please."

Jameson selected a bold zinfandel and found two glasses. Uncorked, poured. His phone vibrated, and when he pulled it from his pocket, it was a text from Laura.

Laura: *Sorry for getting back to you late. Been a hell of a day. Things are on the rocks with Elton. He's jealous, suspicious.*

Jameson absorbed the information, attempting to sort it out. Chloe certainly was spending a lot of time at the hospital. More than was necessary. Which was only confirmation of what he suspected. Of what he *knew*.

Maybe there was another answer, though. A different solution. He lifted the glass, offered it to Chloe, who smiled thanks and took it, then backed away to peer out the window at Portland. He watched her, wondering what it would be like for them to be together again.

For her to love him again.

Something loose and rocky inside him solidified. A way forward materialized, and his body felt lighter.

Yes, there was another option.

"So," he said.

"So." She repeated the word but didn't turn to face him.

"What's on your mind?"

Chloe sipped the wine, let the glass twirl in a slow circle. When she finally turned to face him, one lip was pinned between her teeth. Her eyes flashed with something he wasn't expecting: anger.

"What happened with Mr. Gardner today?" She glared at him from behind the thick-rimmed glasses. Gone was the unsure young woman. Here to stay was a calculated, intimidating Chloe. Whatever indecisiveness he thought he'd seen evaporated in that moment. Even her stance turned aggressive as she placed both feet firmly on the ground, set the wineglass on the table, and faced him directly.

"Torsades de Pointes. A fatal heart rhythm," Jameson said without missing a beat. "Didn't you see?" He couldn't help that his tone came out mocking. That he raised a brow and waited for her to offer another solution.

"He seemed healthy. His labs looked normal."

A tiny smile, entirely lacking humor. "Indeed. But as you know, sometimes these things just... *happen.*"

Jameson moved closer, and Chloe took a step back. He edged onto the dining table, perched on the reclaimed wood they'd found together and hired someone to build into what it now was.

The room plunged into silence as they stared at one another.

"I know your secret. I've been watching you." she finally said.

Jameson tilted his head and decided to take the risk. "My secret? Aren't you the one who's been keeping secrets, Chloe?"

"And what about George?"

Jameson's chest contracted at that name. At his long-term patient who'd passed the month prior. "What about him?" He could nearly control himself until she brought George into it.

"What about Cassandra? And Debra?"

Jameson frowned, ignoring the way his heart squeezed, taking in the question, turning it over in his head. A sense of deep betrayal started in the pit of his stomach and wound up into his chest, tightening it. His hands clenched over the edge of the table, the wood groaning in response.

Cassandra. How did she even know about Cassandra? That happened before she arrived in town.

Jameson got to his feet, considering how best to handle this situation. There were so many ways it could go, and given this conversation, he wasn't sure which direction to take it.

"Don't come any closer," Chloe said.

Jameson shook his head and eased toward her.

"I'm sorry, darling. You really haven't left me any other choice."

FIFTY-NINE

CHLOE

Now

Darling.

An endearment, but his eyes flash with pain, frustration. He takes a step toward me. Our wine sits on the table, forgotten. I step back, keeping the space between us. My heart races, my stomach writhes. I look for an escape route, wondering if I'm moments from becoming his next victim.

The only escape is through the hall, and I bolt. My elbow hits a wineglass. It shatters across the tile floor like blood spatter. A sign of what's to come?

It's my chance, and I dart toward the library. Toward the one chance I have to keep myself safe. Shame burns my neck, my face, as I flee—I should have known better. He said he wanted to talk. I believed him. That was my mistake.

I race for the library and close and lock the door behind me. I expect Jameson to be at the door in a second, pounding on it, wrenching at the knob, but he doesn't follow. Doesn't try to force his way in.

My breath comes in short pants, and I realize I'm soaked in a cold sweat from the sudden exertion. I go for the desk. The drawer. The knife.

But it's gone.

SIXTY

JAMESON

Now

Jameson didn't give chase. There was no point. The front door was the only entrance and exit in the apartment, aside from a fire escape. That was behind a locked window within the kitchen. He hated that they had to do this. But maybe, they could find a way. Maybe, if she would just listen to him...

He sighed. Walked down the hall after her. Knocked gently on the door.

"It's okay, Chloe," he murmured. "It's okay."

"It is *not* okay." Her voice raised in pitch, panicked. "It is anything but okay."

"I know everything." Jameson pressed his forehead to the locked door, shut his eyes. "You don't have to hide from me."

"Are you kidding?" Her voice turned shrill. A tone he'd never heard other than the day her brother died. "If you know everything, then you know that I know who you are. What you are. What you've done. And this time, I won't run away, I won't let you get away with it."

Jameson paused.

"What I've done? I know that you will never stop grieving your brother, Chloe. But do you truly think it was better that he continue in pain? When it's come to other patients, you've always wanted them to have the choice in their death. For us to give them that dignity. It's right that we let your brother choose, even when no one else would." His hand curled around the brass doorknob, but it didn't give. She'd locked it.

"Chloe?" Jameson softened his voice, replaying the past in his mind. Everything had begun after Nathan died. "Is that what started all of this?"

Through the door, he heard a sob. A choked, "It's when I knew I was right."

He frowned, her words completely out of context of their conversation. "Right about what?"

"What you are. What you've been doing. Is Laura involved, too?"

"Chloe, that—that doesn't make sense. How many nights did we talk about a person's right to do with their body what they will? Up to and including death, when nothing but pain and misery awaits them, when they will die anyway? Of course I want a dignified death for people. *Of course* I do. And yes, Laura refers patients to me sometimes."

"Right." She snorted. Footsteps shuffled closer. A *bam* as something—her hands? her fists?—slammed against the door. He pulled back, staring at the wood as though he could see through to her. "You want a dignified death for all your patients, don't you?" she hissed.

There it was, again.

"I don't understand," Jameson murmured. "What are you —" He licked his lips. Squeezed his eyes shut. Turned the words over in his mind again and again.

"I found your books," she said. "Kill books. It's horrific. You took an oath—do no harm."

Kill books?

"I saw the knife. Where is it now? On you? Are you going to do to me what you did to Cassandra? And the cameras—you shut the fucking cameras off today."

Jameson's head buzzed.

She thought he was a murderer.

SIXTY-ONE

CHLOE

Now

Jameson is silent on the other side of the door.

"You have nothing to say?" The words slip out of me, scorched with rage. "Did you think no one would notice?"

"Notice what?" His voice lowers a notch. Something else happens, too—some new warmth. Or maybe, an old warmth. I hesitate, hearing it.

"How often your patients die. That you move hospitals so often so one notices. Or people who do notice are just glad you've left, so they don't have to sort it out or think through the fact they suspect a doctor of murdering someone." I pause, wait for his reaction. "One of my earliest memories of knowing you was someone whispering *Dr. Death.* I ignored it. I thought—I thought I knew you."

A beat passes.

Then Jameson says, "I'm not a killer, Chloe."

I'm on edge—thinking about those early days, how I'd so easily set aside the rumors. Thought he was *helping* people when he took those trips. Pushed back when people called him Dr. Death, only seen the good in the man I loved. His words now—straight-up denial—send anger spiraling through me. I almost open the door, almost get face-to-face with him so I can— what? Yell some more?

I'm trapped.

A dangerous man is on the other side of this door.

"I know you enjoyed what you did to Nathan. And when you traveled. I learned all about medical serial killers. How they love the control they have over other people's lives. How they even consider themselves to be giving mercy." A sob jolts from my throat. "You're still a killer, though."

I slide to the floor, my back to the wall. He's not trying to break down the door. Not trying to get in a yelling match with me. Which is typical Jameson—he'd rather approach it calmly. Methodically. I clench my hands, trying to imagine what that means he'll do next. Is he just waiting for the right moment? There's no rush with me trapped in here.

"Can I say something?" he asks.

I give a half laugh, entirely lacking humor. "Sure. Why not."

"I want you to consider a different series of events, Chloe."

I go still, listening.

"Where my wife, who I loved—*love*—more than life itself, disappeared one day. Packed a bag, said goodbye to the life we built together. To me, the man she said she'd love in this life and the next." He lets out a long sigh. "Years later, she comes back.

"In Seattle, I'd been alerted to a high rate of patient deaths and asked to help form a task force to account for it. But I couldn't figure it out. Sometimes these things happen—but sometimes it's a sign of something else. *Someone* else. I started to wonder, but I was sure I was wrong. I was asked to keep an eye out, but I couldn't take being there anymore. Being in the home we built together. I never even got closure." He stops for a moment.

I realize I'm listening intently, hands squeezed together for every word. Inside me, there's some emotion I never once let myself feel—hope.

"I don't know why you left. I never bought what you wrote in that note. If you just woke up one day and decided you hate me, or if you somehow blamed me for your brother's illness. I racked my brain night after night, trying to figure out what it was. I tried to reach out, but you disconnected your phone. Shut down your social media. Went off the edge of the world, it seemed. So I couldn't ask. Couldn't understand what happened." He pauses. "But now I wonder... I wonder if I know."

He exhales audibly. "I moved to Idaho to get the hell out of Seattle. I hated it. I missed the Puget Sound. I left because the state doesn't have a death-with-dignity law. I had patients who were ready to die. Who were in terrible pain and their bodies just wouldn't give up, and they were trapped, bedridden, no quality of life. And I couldn't help them, not all of them, not without attracting attention." He blows out a breath. "I came to Portland when I got a job offer. And things were okay for a while. We had a higher death rate, but we also had sicker patients. Multiple ICUs. But then..." A long pause. "Then you showed up. My nurse practitioner had been murdered in cold blood, which created the job opening. Things started to line up in my head."

"What things?"

"That when you were around, people died. I knew you'd gone to travel nursing. As you said, moving around frequently makes it easy to hide the fact you're killing people."

His words settle in, followed by shock. I gasp.

"Are you accusing me of murder?"

A humorless laugh.

"No, Chloe. I'm not."

I'm about to ask him what he's saying—what he's getting at
—when it hits me.

He thought I was the killer.

And I thought he was the killer.

Which means neither of us is.

SIXTY-TWO

CHLOE

Now

I sit there against the door for what feels like minutes, maybe hours.

Reality like whiplash.

I remember the moment that, together, we'd broken the law, risked our careers, watched as Nathan took his last breath, and at the time, I thought what we were doing was right. Was the best thing for Nathan. Was a kindness. Then the moment I decided he'd killed Nathan out of a desire to extinguish a life—not to give a mercy. The violence of his method. The feeling of being unmoored, having lost both my brother and my trust in my husband. The desire to run—to escape—to never look back at my mistakes.

And now, seeing that I was wrong.

But how was that possible?

I cover my face with my hands like maybe I can hide from it all.

Patients were dying. His travel. The whispers. The drugs I found. The rumor circulating through the nursing staff. And finally, witnessing him force-feeding the lethal dose of medication to Nathan.

The memories pulse through me. The faces of George, and Debra, and Mr. Gardner follow. Especially Mr. Gardner's. And then, Cassandra's.

But how is it possible it's not him?

Or worse, it's not out of the realm of possibility this is an elaborate lie. A ruse to get me to open the door. What if his own words are him spinning a story where he pins it all on me? My heart quickens, thinking through how he could make it look like I'm the guilty one.

"Chloe? Stop overthinking this. Please. Do you know what this means?"

My heart pounds in my ears. My breath comes up short. I have a death grip around my chest, hugging myself.

"What does it mean?" My voice shakes as the words escape my lips.

"Well, two things, I suppose. One—there's another killer. If it's not you, and it's not me, someone else at the hospital is killing our patients. Two—and this is me assuming—it means you never should have ended our marriage."

SIXTY-THREE

CHLOE

Now

Reimagining the past is almost impossible.

Because it's not just reimagining the past. It's erasing the present.

If I never left Jameson, I'd have never worked as a travel nurse. I'd have never stumbled upon Elton in San Diego. We wouldn't have bitched about working night shift and had margaritas at sunrise after said night shift. I never would have let him into my life, my bed. I never would have thought, *He'd make a good husband* or *I'm lonely—maybe I'll give this a shot.* We never would have gotten engaged, planned a wedding. We never would have fallen in love.

And I wouldn't be sitting in Jameson's condo in Portland, a wall between us, as we discuss whether or not the other is a coldblooded killer.

But wait. For all it *can* make sense, it doesn't.

"What about Nathan?"

Jameson clears his throat. There's a thud, which I think

must be him easing to the ground, just like I did. Are we back-to-back through a wall? I picture it in my head, almost like a movie, then shake myself to clear it.

No. This is not some drama where we realize we've been wrong all this time. Everything has changed. *I've* changed. And he has not proven himself innocent; only capable of weaving a story to make himself *seem* innocent.

"Forgive me, Chloe. But can you—can you tell me what you think happened with Nathan? Because I really don't know."

I open my mouth, then shut it. "No. I cannot. You can tell me what happened. And then, maybe, I'll tell you what I think."

What I think.

When did *know* become *think?*

My hands tremble—my whole body is chilled to the core with these revelations. Or shock, maybe. I look up, gaze traversing the room, settling on a flannel blanket strewn across the armchair in the corner. I force myself to my feet, cross the room to nab it, and wrap it around myself. Settled against the wall again, still shaking, I wait for Jameson.

"If you want the whole truth, Nathan was terrified to take the meds that would end his life. He wanted to end the pain and the suffering. He wanted to be in control of when that moment came—hated the idea that he would suffer and lose consciousness, that you would sit at his bedside however long it took, a day, a month. He didn't want you to do that. And he didn't want to be helpless and in pain for that long. He wanted... he wanted to be free."

I shut my eyes. Listen to his voice. Recall the day Nathan told us he wanted us to come visit him. To help him die. We couldn't do it the way Jameson would for someone in Washington, a simple drink that would let a person fall asleep and slowly drift off into whatever came after life and death. But we could be by his side as he overdosed on other meds that would have the same effect. Jameson promised he would calculate how much Nathan needed. Nathan's fear was that he wouldn't die. That he would survive, and maybe be worse off because of it. Hospitalized instead of allowed to die at home. And more than anything, he didn't want to be alone.

"What did you do?"

"I ground the pills up. Put them in juice." Jameson groans in what sounds like regret. Pain. "I never do this, Chloe. Please know that. *Ever.* The key to physician-assisted suicide is that it's assisted. The patient is in complete control at all times. But Nathan begged me to. The day before he died, he begged me to force him to take them. That he was afraid to die, and that he'd chicken out at the last second. Or that because he was having trouble swallowing, that combined with being scared, he wouldn't be able to get them down. He wanted me to force them down. He asked if I could inject something, or—" A harsh exhale. "Basically, he wanted a way to die without having to do it himself. And I couldn't. There was no way I could do that in a way it wouldn't be found out. I couldn't sacrifice our life, even for him. But I promised I'd make sure he took enough to kill him."

Jameson goes quiet for a long moment.

"So I did. He took the first two sips by himself. I'd given him his anxiolytic before that, to help him relax. But he panicked, anyway. So I—" Another breath. "I did what I swore to him I would do."

"You made him take it." I hug the blanket tighter and bury my head between my knees. He did. He forced him to take the meds. But I told Nathan we would help him. I booked the flight for Jameson and me to go. I'm as guilty as he is, even if Jameson is the one who forced it down his throat.

"We showed him a great mercy, Chloe. We gave him the freedom to choose when and how he died."

I swallow back tears.

"I know," I say.

We sit silent until Jameson curses.

"What?" I ask.

"Dinner's here. Let me get the door." His footsteps pad down the hall, away from me. I stare at the doorknob, suddenly thinking how absurd it is we've had this entire conversation with a wall between us.

I find my footing, grab the doorknob, pull myself to my feet. I stare down at it, thinking through his words. The events that happened three years ago. The aftermath. The likelihood Nathan would have asked Jameson to force-feed him the medication.

Nathan was courageous, bold. He'd forgone a college scholarship to become a minor league baseball player, his hopes pinned on making it to the major leagues. That's not how things turned out, but it took guts to make those choices. To believe in himself that much. He also, however, was not a fan of medicine. Of doctors, of pills of any sort. He was terrified of dying, of becoming *nothing*, as he put it, even as he was in terrible pain and just wanted it to stop. I could see the events Jameson described transpiring. See them clear as day. Could hear Nathan begging him to force him to do it, to end it already. It's what he wanted.

If I hadn't seen that, would I have continued ignoring the rumors?

Maybe.

Probably.

Which means Jameson is right. If I believe him—and I think I do—I never should have left. That actually, there was no reason at all to have ended it. That I should still be with him.

A pit of grief opens in my gut. It feels so deep it might swallow me whole. I think of the moments across the table from

Jameson at the bar just a few weeks ago, feeling that heated connection still firmly in place, hating myself for it. Hating him for it. And now, yearning to reach out and grab hold of it. To pull myself back to him.

But I can't. I'm engaged to Elton.

SIXTY-FOUR

JAMESON

Now

Jameson thanked the delivery person, shut the door, and hurried to the dining room, a paper bag clenched in one hand. Outside, the world had grown dark, which meant they'd been talking for some time. Longer than he realized. His insides writhed, wondering how this would turn out. If he'd convince Chloe to emerge from the room, or if she wouldn't leave until he did.

But when Jameson heard the creak of footsteps and turned, she stood mere feet from him. Tears stained her cheeks, and her eyes were red. His instant reaction was to pull her in, embrace her, feel her body against his own and tell her it was all okay— all forgiven. He could understand the things she'd assumed. Hell, he'd lined up the same arguments against her, hadn't he?

"You're not a killer?" Quiet hope filled her voice.

Jameson eased the paper bag onto the table, perched on its edge, crossed his arms, studied her. What did she need to hear in this moment? What would soothe her concerns? What would make her sit across from him and drink wine and eat dinner and for just a moment, they could pretend nothing ever changed? He craved that more than anything.

Jameson quirked a lip. "You're not?"

She shook her head, wisps of hair flying from the bun that had unraveled at the nape of her neck. He reached forward slowly, tucked it behind her ear. She blinked rapidly but didn't flinch. Didn't pull away.

He knew what this meant.

He recalled Laura's text message—trouble in paradise.

Jameson considered what he could do with that knowledge. What he *wanted* to do with that knowledge. The ethics of it poured liquid through his brain, running through the facts, combined with his desires, as well as what the best outcome might look like.

Not the outcome he wanted.

But the *best outcome*, for both of them.

He considered Elton, who was decent looking. Who clearly worked hard and loved her.

But he couldn't shake one thing—Elton was her second choice. The man she'd run to when she thought he might be a danger to her. But knowing that, and now knowing he would never hurt her, didn't that change things?

Decision made, Jameson reached for the abandoned wine bottle.

"With that settled," he murmured, "maybe we could still have dinner?" He let a smile come to his lips. "Catch up properly, without these concerns between us?"

Chloe considered him, eyes flashing with emotions he couldn't define, but somewhere in there, he was pretty sure, was a warmth he hadn't seen in years.

"Okay," she said.

He was in. He could fix this.

* * *

The moment she realized she regretted her choices was clear as day to him—the way her eyes went wide, her jaw heavy. How she looked down, away from him. Her fork dropped to the table. When she finally did move again, it was to take the glass of wine and take a long drink.

When had she started drinking wine, anyway?

"Bourbon?" he suggested.

Again, their eyes locked.

"I have your favorite." Without another word, he crossed the kitchen to the cabinet over the fridge. Retrieved the bottle of bourbon he kept, just in case she ever showed up on his doorstep. He relished that he finally had the opportunity to open it. He wasn't sure he ever would. He poured three fingers for them both, added a single ice cube, and slid hers across the table.

"That obvious?" She took the glass.

"That you needed something stronger? Something good? Yeah." He held his glass up until she raised hers, and they pressed them gently together. "To..." He paused. "What should we drink to?"

Chloe shook her head, didn't meet his eyes. "I don't know. Everything feels so messed up."

He almost said it then—almost made a move. But no. Too soon. *Not yet.* Instead, Jameson lowered his glass and held out a hand. She looked at it, then at him, set her glass down, extended her fingertips, and suddenly, he clasped her hand in his. Small, delicate. Fingertips a little cold, probably from shock.

"Everything will work out the way it's supposed to," he said.

"What does that even mean?"

Jameson pulled his hand away first. Took a sip of bourbon, picked up his fork. Let the intimacy between them lower a notch to give her room to breathe. This would work. *It had to.*

They ate in silence. When he looked up, she'd finished

nearly the entire glass of bourbon, the golden liquid down to the dregs.

"If you didn't kill all those patients, then who did?" The words came sudden, fast, like she'd just thought of it.

Jameson looked up. "I thought at first... that maybe it was just a coincidence."

"What has the death rate been here in Portland?"

Jameson wiped his mouth, pushed his salad plate to one side. He let his eyes wander, thinking. "High," he said. "Not as high as in Seattle, but higher than it probably should be. They thought it was due to poor teaching in the heart failure clinic, but they noticed it was specifically affecting patients in the ICU."

"So someone is killing them."

Jameson nodded, slowly. "I think so, yes."

"And someone killed Cassandra."

His gaze flickered with grief. "Yes."

"I think Debra was killed, too." She told him about the hospital administrator in charge of the task force he was supposed to help with. About Cassandra's email.

"I think Cassandra and Debra are connected. Like they found out who's doing it." Chloe hesitated, like she was afraid to tell him, but pressed forward. "I thought you killed them to silence them."

Jameson blinked. "I hadn't thought about that. But maybe you're right. Maybe someone killed them to protect themselves."

"There's more." Chloe stared down into her glass. "I think whoever it is knows about me. That I know something's happening."

"Why do you think that?" Jameson's voice hardened with concern.

"I swear I've been followed in the hospital. And there was

someone in my house. I thought maybe it was just the wind, but then the door was open. And with my tires being slashed."

Jameson stared at her openmouthed. "You thought I was doing that? Stalking you? Breaking into your home?"

She looked at him. "How could I not? I thought you were killing people. You sent me those threatening texts. I thought you enjoyed killing Nathan. And that maybe you figured out I was onto you. It made sense."

Jameson stood, walked a slow loop around the kitchen, arms crossed, brow furrowed. He stopped to gaze out the window at the city, the river, running her words through his head. She'd thought he'd *hurt* her. That was never his intention. No, he only wanted to... to *help* her, to keep her from hurting herself.

"You're brave," he finally muttered. "And for the record, I wasn't threatening you." He looked over from where he stood at the window. Their eyes met, and a ghost of a smile appeared on her face.

"So you'll help me with this?"

"Of course." Jameson gave her a reassuring smile. "Maybe we should drink to figuring this out. Together. Let me get you a refill, and we'll do exactly that."

SIXTY-FIVE

CHLOE

Now

It's almost hard to *think*. To *breathe*.

The man in front of me is not who I thought he was. I take in the long lines of his body as he opens to-go containers, distributes the main course, pours more bourbon. As he turns, flashes me a quarter smile, almost sheepish, it hits me, becomes real—*we both thought the other person was a killer*.

And it makes sense. I can see how he thought it was me. Especially since I left so abruptly. Went off the radar.

I ended our marriage for the wrong reason.

I shouldn't have ended it at all. The flutter of emails and notarized documents and filing for divorce from far away runs through my head—the headache, heartache it all caused. And it was all because I jumped to conclusions.

I never would have ended things with Jameson had I realized I was wrong. Utterly, completely wrong. Sorrow wells up inside me—for the relationship we lost, but for the tumble of emotions that followed. The hopelessness that filled me. How I wondered if life was even worth living, with my parents and brother gone, believing my husband was a killer. And from what Laura said, from what I've seen, things weren't so different for Jameson—he, too, has led a tortured life these last years.

"I'm sorry." The words tumble from my mouth. "I'm so sorry."

Jameson takes one look at me and sets the food down. A dozen emotions cross his face seemingly at once—pain, relief, hope, back to pain—he steps toward me. Hesitates. Then opens his arms, and I take the half step to enter his grasp. The heat of his body engulfs me. His smell, the same as it ever was, masculine and heady.

Everything is going to be okay.

No, everything won't be.

Because I'm engaged to Elton. And I love Elton. But Jameson—

I peel myself from Jameson's arms. He releases me carefully, and our eyes meet.

"Sorry," I say.

"For what?" He shoves his hands in his jeans pockets and eases back to lean on the counter.

"I ruined us." I blink up at him. "We had the most incredible relationship, and I—I just ran. I assumed the worst about the man I loved, and I disappeared."

Jameson nods, thinks a moment. "I was devastated. Utterly destroyed." He exhales. "But leaving must have been hard, too."

"I was so angry."

A tiny smile curls at his mouth. "I know. I just didn't know why. You made all those accusations, but I thought it was just grief. It makes sense now." A beat passes. "Let's move on to the main course. Maybe everything will make more sense with some real food in our stomachs."

We settle catty-corner to one another at the kitchen table we rescued and refinished together. I run a hand over the dark woodgrain, smoothed for hours with sandpaper. We sat here mere days ago, and I was sure he was a killer. I think through everything I've found these past weeks.

"Why do you have those journals?" I ask. I am relieved, but questions still flow through me. Things that still don't line up or make sense, and I won't be able to relax until I have answers. "The notebooks with the patients who died."

Jameson bows his head, spears a piece of fish on his fork. "To remember them." He frowns. "Death is so final. And so many patients don't have anyone, or only a spouse, who statistically will likely die within a few years of them passing." He shrugs, and I can see the self-consciousness in it. "So I remember them. That way, a piece of them is always alive. Is that strange?"

"A little." I offer him a soft smile. Realize that, actually, that's pretty cool that he does that. That he doesn't let the memory of these people fade away. "What about Cassandra? The knife?"

"Cassandra? I don't know." He takes a bite, chews slowly. "The police haven't found much. They speculated it might have been random. Her purse was taken. But the detective also said the purse might have been taken to make it look random. Supposedly, they're still working on it." Jameson wipes his mouth. "So far as the knife—" He stands, goes across the kitchen, opens a drawer. He removes a small leather pouch, from which he draws the knife. "It's for deboning fish. I went to the Puyallup River for salmon fishing this year. Bought it off a guy who makes them." He offers it up, handing it over handle first. "I use it as a letter opener sometimes. Hence, why it was in my desk."

I accept it, the wooden handle smooth. The leather case stitched with a strong, yellow thread. When I pull the blade out, it's the same one I saw—thin and sharp and yes—he's right. A fishing knife. My face heats, realizing how I'd leapt to conclusions.

George's death plays back in my mind, but I don't even ask him—of course he'd wanted to be there for his patient. Of course he hadn't wanted him to die alone.

I re-sheath the knife, set it on the table.

Jameson watches me, a tenderness in his gaze that opens up something inside me—reminds me of that early yearning after we first met. When he asked me on our first date. When he kissed me and the world faded away. I stopped worrying about everything, especially about being alone. Because I'd found my soulmate.

It was my bad luck I'd divorced him.

SIXTY-SIX

CHLOE

Now

We sit, sipping bourbon, and talk for what feels like a long time.

"Who else could it be?" Jameson is beside me, our elbows not quite touching, hand poised, pen ready to scribble. My eyes are drawn to his forearms, tanned and strong. I want to reach out and grasp his arm. Feel it beneath my hand.

Elton sits in the back of my mind. The wedding we have in a mere month. And I'm here with Jameson. It's late, getting later. My Lexus is still parked in the hospital garage, and Elton is waiting at home. I should at least text him.

"Just a second." I grab my phone and go to the bathroom for privacy.

It's nearly nine o'clock, and I already have a message waiting from him.

Elton: *Headed home soon?*

Staying late, I type out. *I'll be home in a couple hours, I think. So sorry we're missing dinner. Let's do a special dinner out tomorrow night? My treat ;-)*

The last bit is a joke. We combined our finances when we got engaged, so there is no taking turns paying anymore. I hope that cheerfulness will make him more accepting.

He replies a second later with *I understand.*

I perch on the edge of the bathtub, foot tapping over linoleum, waiting for more. The sound echoes in the otherwise quiet room. But nothing more comes. He's not happy about me working late again. Especially given who he thinks I'm working with.

I sigh.

I have to make this better with Elton. I don't want him upset with me. I don't want him thinking I still love Jameson.

Except I do.

That never changed. And he's not a killer. And I haven't married Elton yet.

A chill goes through me, then a rush of heat, of realization.

I could make a different choice.

I tuck my phone away, rinse my hands, stare at myself in the mirror. One glance, and I look away—leave the room—I don't want to see my face right now. Don't want to think about what I have to consider, have to decide. Besides, that's not what's most important right now. Stopping a murderer is. And finally, someone who's been here the whole time, who knows what's happened, who feels passionately about saving lives, can help me with that.

I'm on the edge of the kitchen when a thought makes me halt. Makes me try to grasp onto what, for the briefest nanosecond, I'd had.

Someone who's been here the whole time.

Who else has been here the whole time? Who else could be the killer?

"Jameson," I say.

"Mm?" He looks up from where he's taking notes at the table. His gaze catches mine, and it feels like home.

"Who else has been here the whole time?"

"What do you mean?"

"They were in Seattle. Now they're in Portland."

It hits him at the same time it hits me, dismay shattering his expression.

He says it first. "Laura."

SIXTY-SEVEN

CHLOE

Now

Jameson paces through the kitchen, the dining room. He wanders down the hall, then back, hand brushing up and down his jaw, over the rough shadow of a beard. He combs a hand through his hair.

"I just... it's not possible." He leans on the counter long enough to say, "This is how it was for you, wasn't it? You couldn't believe it, but—"

I press my lips together. "I *didn't* believe it. People called you Dr. Death from the day we met because you did physician-assisted suicide. I never thought much of it. Not until what happened with Nathan."

Jameson expels a harsh breath and collapses into a chair beside me. He drops his face into his hands. "Fuck. Fuck, fuck, fuck. How is it possible? How did I not see it? She's been killing patients—*my* patients."

I reach out a hand, press it to his knee to comfort him. "Let's talk through this. Let's not jump to any conclusions. That clearly hasn't worked well for either of us."

His eyes widen. "Okay. Good idea."

"She was in Seattle and now in Portland, right?"

"Yes." He gives me a nod, playing along.

"Does she have access to all the patients?"

Jameson thinks about it. "Yes, I think so. She sees patients in the ICUs, and that's where my patients are. I wonder—" He blinks. "I wonder if other patients have been dying, too. Med-surg or telemetry. If I just haven't seen it. I wonder if it's all cardiology patients or if she's accessed other specialties or—I don't know. She consults on all sorts of patients."

"Why would she kill them, though?"

Jameson looks like he's about to hop up again, so I snag his hand in mine, pull his attention back to me. "Focus."

He takes a deep breath. "I don't know why she would kill them." He looks at me. "Why did you think I would do it?"

I try to school my features, but he catches my flinch.

"What is it? Tell me. Please." And now he's the one grasping my hand.

"On one of our first dates you told me about your grandmother dying a slow death. How you couldn't help her. I thought you were somehow trying to fix the past." I look down at our intertwined hands. "I know it doesn't make sense, but serial killers don't exactly make sense. Medical serial killers even less. I just... I couldn't understand it any other way. I was *so* mad once I put it all together. Or I thought I did. When I thought you'd taken some sort of twisted pleasure in letting Nathan die." I look up at him now, his dark eyes, boring into me like these are the words he needed to hear all this time. "In my mind, you selfishly were killing people. Which is wrong and psychotic. Evil. But on top of that, you couldn't control yourself, not even for us. And we were everything."

Jameson doesn't speak for a while. When he does, he murmurs, "We were, Chloe. We were everything." Our eyes meet over our hands, grasped tightly together.

And then he leans in and kisses me.

SIXTY-EIGHT

CHLOE

Now

Jameson's mouth on mine is the most normal thing in the world —like coming home and wrapping myself in a soft warm blanket. For half a second, I kiss him back, clutch him tighter, relish the way we fit together.

But reality crashes down—the weight of the ring on my finger, the reminder of Elton, the man I'm marrying.

I break the kiss and shove him away. My body aches at the sudden absence of his mouth, his hands.

It takes me a second to form words. "Don't—don't do that. Please."

Anguish fills his face, brow furrowing, eyes crinkling with pain.

"I'm sorry." Jameson takes a half step back, blinking. Remembering himself, I think. "You're right. I shouldn't have—" His gaze slides back my way. "I apologize."

I can't help my thoughts spinning out of control—wanting to lunge back toward him. Flashbacks to times there was no reason to hesitate, no reason to stop. Before Elton. When Elton was just another nurse.

This is now. Not then. So Jameson isn't the killer, but it looks like Laura could be. Focus on that. That's what matters.

"Laura. We need proof," I say, shifting our attention. "Everything we have is just circumstantial. She happened to be in the same city, she has access, etc. That doesn't mean she did it."

Jameson nods, and I can tell he likes this idea—maybe his sister didn't do it. Maybe it's just a matter of coincidence.

He clears his throat and gets up, starts pacing again. "You're right. So we'll start watching her at work. I'll keep track of the patients she sees." He turns away, walks a slow circle around the room, arms crossed, thinking. My phone buzzes, a reminder my fiancé is at home, waiting. That probably, I should leave. Being here, alone with Jameson, drinking bourbon, it's... dangerous.

I glance back down the hallway, toward the library, where not so long ago we were on opposite ends of the wall. Tonight, when I leave, that one barrier is broken down. But we can't get any closer to one another. Not tonight, not now.

Jameson settles into the chair closest to me and meets my eyes. That pull is still there—the attraction, the magnetism between us.

I need to leave. Not because I'm afraid we'll kiss or have sex. But because being here at all feels like cheating on Elton.

"I should get going. I'll see you in the morning." The door is only thirty feet away. I need to get my bag, go to my car, drive home. I hesitate; hopefully the car service has fixed the tire by now. Otherwise, I'll have to call for a ride.

"You're leaving?"

"It's late. We can talk more tomorrow." I'm on my feet. "Maybe we can get ahold of her phone, her laptop. Maybe she was talking with Debra or asked Cassandra to meet her or—" I come up short, taking in Jameson's pained expression. "I know. I'm sorry. We have to check, though. Hopefully we look into her and find nothing."

"I could just talk to her." Jameson's gaze shifts, goes unfocused. "Maybe if I sat down with her and just *asked*—"

"No."

"Why not?" Jameson looks at me, all big eyes, almost like a little boy. I've never seen him look like this before, and the vulnerability pains me, makes me want to wrap my arms back around him and tell him it'll be okay.

"Because if she doesn't fess up to it, and if she is guilty, she'll know we're onto her. Which means either she'll go after us, or she'll hide what she's doing."

"Or she'll stop." He rubs his chin. "Maybe we don't have to turn her in. Maybe if we talk to her, she'll quit."

I'm still trying to work out what I think, how to respond, when my phone buzzes again.

Elton.

"I have to go."

"I'll drop you off at your car. It's too far to walk this late."

I want to object. The last thing I should do is get in the car with all the memories, next to the man I undeniably still love. Part of me wishes I could stay here, beside him. Sit on the couch and talk into the night and wake up spooned in his arms. It would be so easy to let myself melt back into *us*: Jameson and Chloe. Chloe and Jameson.

But I have to go. And he's right. It's a long walk. The neighborhood isn't so great, and it's late. Not to mention, the slashed tires, the feeling of being watched, followed. It occurs to me if it's Laura—if she's the killer—she's also the one who crept into my house. Who knows I'm trying to figure out who she is.

Which means Laura, who was once like a sister to me, who's

been inviting me for coffee and lunch and kayaking, is actually my enemy. No wonder she's been so kind recently—she wants me to trust her.

SIXTY-NINE

CHLOE

Now

Jameson stops his car behind mine. He unlocks the door, but I sit there, silently. I want to soak it all in—that he's not the killer, that I'm safe with him—for just a second longer. I'm afraid that I'll open the door and leave and somehow this will have all been just a dream.

But I also know I'm headed home to Elton.

Jameson reaches across and opens his hand, palm up. I don't even hesitate, placing my palm against his. He curls his fingers around my hand, and it feels as it used to. Like the whole world revolves around *us*, and we are soulmates. I squeeze my eyes shut to keep them from watering, from tears flowing.

"I should go," I say after a beat. Even though I don't want to. Even though when I look up and meet his eyes, I can tell he doesn't want me to go, either.

But I have to.

I exhale as I walk from his car to my own, chest tight, warm beneath my clothes despite the cool evening. I was wrong, so incredibly wrong. I consider the moment I realized—incorrectly

—that it had to be him. Packing that tiny bag, grabbing my keys, taking off before he could stop me. So sure I'd figured out what the rumors meant, what that moment with Nathan meant.

It hurts to think of the pain I've caused Jameson. The confusion he must have felt when I took off. These years, these lost years between us.

Thanks for having my tire fixed, I type out. A shiny new tire that now sits where the slashed tire did before. I want to send the text to Jameson. To say thank you. Also, because a part of me misses him already.

I also hesitate, because I fear once I open this line of communication, we won't be able to stop. Like recovered addicts, getting a hit for the first time in years, we'll be drawn back.

I can still feel his mouth on mine. His strong arms crushing me to his chest.

I exhale, literally shake myself to come back to the moment. At least for now, I can't do this. Elton's waiting for me.

I slide into the Lexus, lock the doors, start the engine. When I look up, I see a figure—a tall form, at the edge of the garage, watching me, before it disappears beyond the edge of the garage.

I tense. Jameson has already left. It might be a stranger, passing by the hospital parking lot.

It might be Laura.

I shove the car into reverse and back out, hands tight over the steering wheel, almost waiting for someone to jump out at me. But the streets are quiet, and the drive home goes by fast—too fast.

There's no time to sort through my thoughts and feelings, to sort out what I want to do, much less what's *right* to do. It's an impossible situation, like finding out the spouse you thought died in war is actually alive, and meanwhile, you've married his brother.

I hit the button for the garage door opener, and it grumbles to life. The Honda isn't there, and I assume he's parked it on the street, probably so he could chip away at the moving boxes stored in the garage. I ease the SUV in, put the car in park, and steady myself for going inside. For pretending I've been at the hospital this whole time. Guilt sits heavy in my gut—I *kissed* him. Well, he kissed me. And I didn't stop him, not at first.

When I enter the kitchen, the oven clock reads 11:42 p.m. Nearly midnight. My bag goes on the counter, next to what looks like a paper bag that once held takeout. Now, it's empty. Another layer of guilt—I missed having dinner with him, after I said I'd be here. Worse, I'd had dinner with Jameson.

And now, I am keeping yet another secret from Elton—that it wasn't my ex-husband killing those people. That likely, it was his twin sister. Maybe I could tell Elton that part. That we suspect Laura, that...

My thoughts run wild. We don't know for sure it's Laura. We don't know for sure it's not. And I'm not sure of what I'm going to do, either. If I'm ready to marry Elton, after feeling what I did tonight with Jameson. Tapping into that ember that could easily become a flame again. With Elton, it's not so much a fire so much as... I stand in the near darkness of the kitchen, trying to think of what I'd compare our relationship to.

But I can't think of anything. It's not like fire. Never has been. And that's been a relief. Not burning so hot meant we wouldn't burn out. Meant we were safe. Meant I had someone I could trust now and forever. But now, having felt that heat again, I'm not sure anything less is enough.

What a mess this has all become. I pull my shoes off and force myself to climb the stairs. Hopefully, Elton will be asleep. Hopefully, we can save this conversation for tomorrow.

I ease open the bedroom door and tiptoe to the bathroom, where I brush my teeth and rinse my face with water, skipping my usual bedtime routine. After I apply moisturizer and use the toilet, I flick the light back off, open the door, and feel my way to the bed.

That's when I notice something is off. I feel across the bed for Elton—his back or his hip or his shoulder—but he's not there. He's not in bed. I flick the light on, and it casts dim shadows across the bedroom.

Elton is gone.

SEVENTY

CHLOE

Now

A voicemail taunts me from my phone's screen—Elton left it an hour ago, probably when I was kissing Jameson. My phone buzzed repeatedly, but I never looked at it.

My hand trembles, wondering what he had to say. Is he out looking for me? Is he worried or mad? Probably, mad. Then again, what did I expect? How many nights have I been home late, how many dinners have I missed, how much time have I spent with my ex-husband while my fiancé waits alone at home?

I press play and let speakerphone talk to me.

"Chloe, where are you? You were supposed to be home hours ago. You're not answering calls or returning texts. I got worried, and I called the hospital. They said you're not there. But I see that your car is." He heaves a sigh, and a chill runs through me.

He went to the hospital.

I feel for the bed, sit down, hold the phone closer as though I'll miss something if it's not right next to my ear.

"I almost went to his house, but you know what? I'm afraid to. Listen, I just want you to be honest. If you want Jameson, then fine. I mean, I don't want—fuck. I don't want you to want him, but if that's how you feel, fine. I don't know what to do. You're with him all the time. You're lying to me about something. I feel like something's going on, but I don't know what. I don't want to believe you'd have an affair, but what am I supposed to think?" His voice cracks.

A long pause. I think he's hung up, but then he adds, "I thought you wanted this. Me. The house. The wedding." He chokes back a sob. "Listen, I'm... I'm going to a hotel. I can't be in our house alone, wondering where you are. I can't face you if you've been with him. Please let me know you're safe, okay? We can—I guess we can talk tomorrow. But at least text me that you're safe. I love you."

The line clicks.

I gulp air. Realize my breath is coming in short, fast pants. My hands squeeze the phone, and I stab at the dial button, but they're damp with sweat, and the touchscreen doesn't function correctly. *Dial, dial, dial, goddamn it!*

The phone rings, finally, and I sit there, staring at it, waiting for Elton to pick up. Two rings, three...

Finally, "Hello?" His voice is hoarse, like he's been crying. I've only seen him cry once. After he asked me to marry him, and I said yes.

"It's me. I'm home."

Silence. Then, "Were you with him?"

"Elton—" I consider telling him everything. But I can't, not yet. Not until I know who it is for sure. And then, once we have proof, we can take it to the hospital board, and they can investigate. The police will be involved. Elton will understand, because Elton is a nurse, like I am. He'll forgive me.

"I was at his condo, but we weren't—it wasn't like that."

"So you lied." His words come out like wet gravel, dripping

with grief. "You said you were working late, you said you were at the hospital. Your car was at the hospital. What the fuck, Chloe? What kind of game are you playing at? Are you telling the truth *now*? How can I believe anything you've said?"

A gasp tears itself from my throat. I'm not sure if it's a gasp of pain, or the fact he's cursed at me.

"Elton, it's not like that. We're not having an affair, we're—"

A click.

I'm ready to tell him everything. Well, almost everything. To at least tell him we suspect Laura is killing people, and I'll explain that's why I'm spending time with Jameson, and…

But he's hung up. The line is dead.

As I look around my empty home, it hits me that my greatest fear has come true.

I am alone.

SEVENTY-ONE

CHLOE

Now

Morning comes too early, and I make my way to the hospital without speaking a word to anyone.

Jameson texts, and I read it when I'm stopped at a light.

Jameson: *I know I'm being paranoid, but tell me when you're here? I'll meet you in the parking garage and walk you in. Got you a coffee.*

I suck in a breath, hesitate, reply.

Chloe: *I'm two minutes out. See you soon.*

The parking garage is darker than it seemed last night, multiple bulbs burned out. I pull the Lexus forward, keeping watch for Jameson—and Laura—but Elton's voice is on replay in my head. Accusing me of cheating on him. Of lying to him, which, of course, I had. I've been lying to him this whole time.

Even if it was with good intention.

I take the same parking spot I had last night and glance in the mirrors, turn, searching for Jameson.

He's nowhere to be found.

I grab my phone.

Chloe: *I'm here.*

I send the text and wait.

After three minutes, I'm impatient, watching every nook and cranny of the garage for shadows. The tension in my body rises with every minute that passes, and finally, I try calling. It doesn't even ring, going straight to voicemail.

I've never known him to shut off his phone. But reception can be spotty in the hospital. Maybe he's in the basement or in one of the select patient rooms where it seems there's no reception. There is Wi-Fi in the hospital, but maybe he didn't connect his phone or—

God, I need to get a grip. I'm an adult. I don't need an escort from my car to the elevator. All the same, my hand on the door won't quite pull it—won't quite open the door. I can't shake what was presumably Laura's tall figure watching me last night.

At that moment, another nurse practitioner arrives in an SUV. I take the opportunity to get out of my car, wave good morning, follow her onto the elevator. My pulse levels out as I step off the elevator on the third floor, which is also the main floor of the hospital.

Again, I try calling Jameson, but it goes straight to voicemail.

I fight off annoyance. The line for coffee is short, and I get in, order a fresh cup. Even if he did get me one, it'll be cold by now.

Upstairs, the unit buzzes—night nurses finishing their tasks before day shift comes on, residents seeing patients for early rounds so they can report to their attending. I search the unit for

Elton, but he's not here yet, which makes sense. Most day shifters won't be here for another half hour. We need to talk. I can't just sweep aside our relationship. I don't know what I'll tell him. Maybe to trust me? That there's something happening, but I can't explain what, not yet. Or I could tell him my suspicions about Laura. Maybe he could even *help* us.

"Morning," a familiar voice calls out.

I nearly drop my coffee.

"Laura."

She stands in front of me, clipboard under one arm, coffee in the opposite hand, her hair tied back and makeup perfectly done. Her white jacket is freshly starched, and at this early hour, she looks ready and in control of the day.

She looks ready to kill people, I think. *She knows I'm onto her.*

I groan inwardly—here I am, assuming. It's hard not to, adrenaline thrumming through my veins, wondering who else will die today.

She strolls from the direction of the office I share with Jameson—maybe that's why he didn't answer. Maybe he was tied up talking to his sister. I open my mouth to make conversation, to ask if she's just been to see him, but she beats me to it.

"Do you work this weekend? I was thinking we could get in that kayaking trip before the weather turns." She smiles, all lipstick and whitened teeth, like a wolf snarling. It's like I'm seeing her for the first time.

"Sure, that sounds great." *Great for "accidentally" drowning, maybe.* I'll cancel last second if we haven't sent her to prison by then.

"I'll text you." She gives me one last smile and heads down the hall in a rush, before I can ask my own questions.

I check my phone. Still nothing from Jameson.

I round the corner, grab the doorknob for our office, but it doesn't turn. I dig for my keys, trying not to drop my coffee.

When I insert the key and turn, the door doesn't budge. I wrestle with it for a second, jiggling the handle, trying to unlock it a second time, but still, nothing.

Muttering under my breath, I set my bag down, carefully place the coffee cup beside it, trying not to think of the nasty germs on the hospital floor. I turn the knob again, press my shoulder against the door, and heave.

It gives an inch. Just enough for me to see something on the ground, blocking my way. A gasp tears itself from my throat.

A body.

Jameson's body.

SEVENTY-TWO
CHLOE

Now

The crack in the door is just enough for me to squeeze through.

Jameson appears to me in full—eyes closed, mouth gaping open, lying in a puddle of his own blood. My hand flies to my mouth and I gasp out loud. I drop to my knees and try to *think think, think*. I'm a nurse practitioner for god's sake. I can help him.

It occurs to me someone did this to him—and I look up, searching the office in case the offender is still here.

But it's just the two of us.

Laura just walked the other way down the hall.

Jameson lies face down on the linoleum floor. My hand flutters, like a family member, not a nurse. I curse myself. I can freak out later. Not here, not now, not with Jameson hurt. I lay a trembling hand over his back. He doesn't respond when I call, "Jameson? Jameson?" but his chest rises and falls, albeit more slowly than I'd like.

I grab his wrist and a pulse is there. Weak, thready, but present. I exhale, relief leaving me woozy. His dark hair is strewn over his face, obscuring it. I brush it back enough to see the source of the blood—a long cut over his eyebrow and a half inch down his face.

Usually, I'm good in emergencies. Excellent at thinking clearly and making decisions. But it's Jameson, and all I can do is blink down at him and fight to keep my breathing even.

When I first saw his form on the other side of this door, I assumed the worst.

I assumed he was dead.

My best guess is he fell and hit his head. Or, someone hit him, and he went down. Given everything happening, it's almost certainly the latter, but it would be good to know before I call for help.

"Jameson, can you hear me?"

This time a low grunt. His eyelids flutter. I want to squeeze him, bury my head in his neck and tell him it will be okay. He has a head wound, though who knows how bad or if he hit it on the floor when he went down. If he has a subdural hematoma, that would be bad... very bad. Another glance at the door. I need to get him help.

"Did someone do this to you?"

A nod yes, but he winces, like it hurts to move.

"Do you know who it was?"

His lips move, trying to form words. It's silent, but I read the word his lips form: "No."

"Okay. I'll get help." I straddle his legs and shift him enough so I can easily open the door. A nurse's aide walks by, steering an empty wheelchair.

"Hey!"

He turns, hesitant.

"Can you go back to the nurse's station and call a rapid response?" I point at the office. "We have a provider down."

The man nods, stiffly, like he's not sure if it's okay for him to do it, but he goes anyway, and a minute later, a rapid response—

a less emergent type of code—is called over the speakers. It takes another minute for two nurses to arrive, and thirty seconds after that for a provider to come.

It's Laura, of course, all wide-eyed and "What happened to my brother? Who did this?"

Her gaze slides to me, and it's not the friendly, open woman I met in the hall just minutes ago. Her eyes are hard despite her desperate words, and we share a moment of what feels like perfect understanding. I'm not seeing Laura my friend and former sister-in-law. I'm seeing Laura, the murderer.

We share a long look, and it's clear what's in her eyes: *back off, or else.*

I return it.

I'm not backing down now. Especially after she went after Jameson.

But I do know one thing—if she'll go after her own brother in order to keep her secret, she'll go after me, too. Neither of us is safe.

SEVENTY-THREE

CHLOE

Now

I'm at Jameson's bedside when Elton walks in.

Jameson's CT scan showed a small amount of bleeding—"not too concerning," according to the neurologist, but worthy of observation for twenty-four to forty-eight hours.

I sit next to his bed, where he's asleep. Elton's gaze shifts from me to Jameson and back to me again, as if measuring the distance between us.

"What happened?" he asks in a quiet voice. His nurse voice. He strolls closer, crossing his arms, watching the *blip, blip, blip* of the monitor as Jameson's heart beats. Apparently, we're on speaking terms again.

"Someone attacked him."

"Is he okay?"

I search his face for sarcasm, or maybe annoyance, but there's real concern there.

"They're not sure yet. Concussion. Minimal bleeding, observation for a day or two. No work for a week."

Elton gives a stiff nod. "How about you? You okay?"

I want to shrug and say "Yeah, I'm fine." But I'm not fine. After the rush of adrenaline—after getting Jameson help—reality set in. That Laura hurt him, could have killed him. Probably, thought she'd hurt him worse than she did, and that locked in the office, he might die before anyone found him.

Jameson could have died.

I can't think too hard about it. Can't let the way it tightens my chest and twists my heart take over all logical thinking.

I could have lost him mere hours after we found each other again. He could have died before we could speak to one another again. Catch up on these past years. Touched one another, kissed *one another...*

I shake my head, forcing the thoughts away.

I showed up early to work today. I was almost there when the attack happened. Would my presence have kept him safe or would there have been two victims?

Or maybe that's me assuming Laura wanted him dead, considering what happened to Cassandra and Debra. Or maybe —maybe she purposely left him alive. He is her family, after all.

But I'm not. It makes logical sense she'll come to me next because I'm in on the secret. I know someone is a killer, and I'm now convinced that someone is Laura.

Fear and anxiety whirl through me. I try to breathe normally. And this is all layered on top of the reality that my fiancé never came home last night. That he stayed away, suspecting me of betraying him.

An hour ago, I was still angry. Still mad he would assume I was cheating on him, even if I had been at Jameson's the night before.

Now, realizing how close I got to losing Jameson again, this time forever... I'm simply confused. Especially with my fiancé standing here in front of me.

"Let's grab coffee." I step reluctantly from Jameson's bedside. He's on the monitor, inclined at a thirty-degree angle, head bandaged, and he's asleep. He has one of the most experienced nurses on the unit taking care of him, so I know he'll be in good hands. But I can't help but worry that with me not here, something bad might happen.

What if Laura, being his sister, comes for a "visit"? Will she finish what she started?

I can't stay here all day, though. I have to cover the day's work on my own, and what would Elton think? He's already sure I've cheated on him. Finding me at Jameson's bedside certainly didn't help that.

"I heard you found him in your office." Elton holds the door open for me, and we step into the bright lights of the hall. The quiet of Jameson's room shifts to scuffling shoes and the intercom overhead buzzing with pages.

"He was unconscious. Wound on his head."

"He fell?"

"I think someone hit him."

Elton shoots a look my way, hands tucked in his pockets. "Why?"

"Before he lost consciousness again, he said so."

"So he's woken up? That's a good sign."

I sigh. "Yeah, I guess so." We take the stairs down, the silence growing between us with each floor. "I'm worried I'll be next," I finally say.

Elton takes a second to respond. "What? Why?"

I turn to him and make a decision—I have to tell him *something*. At least as much as I can. I'm losing him, one secret at a time.

So I tell him. I leave out the part where I suspected Jameson being the killer to begin with, but detail Cassandra and Debra dying. How Jameson feels like the next target, how I'm likely to be after him. "Providers being picked off," I say.

"But why would anyone be hurting staff to begin with?"

I brace myself for one last lie. "I don't know."

Elton and I come to a stop in the coffee shop line. "It doesn't make sense. They're all so different. Cassandra was killed outside in the middle of the night. Debra was admitted for atrial fibrillation and slipped—she was older and falls are one of the highest causes of death in that age group. And it's possible Jameson was totally delirious when he said someone hit him."

I consider his words. From the outside, it does appear that I'm drawing a connection where there isn't one. But I know the rest of the story. I can feel it in my bones that it's connected. How could it not be? That whatever it is started in Seattle and came to Portland. Laura's eyes, fiery and hard, flash in my mind. I just have to figure out how to prove it. And not die in the process.

The walk back up the stairs with our coffee takes longer. Elton pulls me to a stop on the seventh-floor landing, his hand on my elbow.

"What really happened last night?" He stares into my eyes, gentle and intense at the same time. My fiancé, wanting to know if I still want him. The vulnerability digs deep inside me, makes me catch my breath. The coffee in my hand is suddenly too hot, and I pull away, switch hands, take a breather from gazing into those eyes.

I lean against the wall. Our voices echo ever so slightly in the stairwell. "Jameson and I were trying to figure out who it is that's..." I hesitate, then push through it. I'll stick to the truth as much as I can. "Who's killing people. That's why we've been spending time together."

Elton blinks at me. "But why didn't you tell me? Don't you think that's the sort of thing you should mention to your fiancé? Who works at the hospital no less?"

More silence. Tension, thick in the air. Our eyes meet. For a second, I want to tell him everything. How it *does* make sense, how I suspected Jameson, but now we think it's Laura. But if I tell him all that, then the rest of it will unravel. He accused me of being obsessed with Jameson. He wasn't wrong.

I *can't* tell Elton the whole story.

I told Jameson everything. Every last thing.

But I'm not telling Elton everything to protect *him. To* protect us.

"Chloe?" Elton's voice is hard, challenging.

And I can't tell Elton any more than I already have.

I squeeze my eyes shut. I still love him. I can still see us getting married. I can see our future.

I can see another future, too, though. A future with Jameson.

"I have to go." I start up the stairs and pause. He's my fiancé. We have a wedding coming up. I turn. "Will I see you at home tonight? Can we talk then?"

He sighs. "I just agreed to work until eleven tonight. They're short-staffed."

I press my lips together. "I'll stay up late. Okay?"

He searches my face again. I wish I knew what questions are in his head. What he's thinking, wondering. How can I love him, but at the same time hold him at this distance? What does it mean that with Jameson the truth is so easy, but with Elton it's... not.

"Chloe, I feel like I'm losing you. I love you, and I feel like you're already gone."

"I'll see you tonight," I say. I can't say anything else because I'm not entirely sure he's wrong.

SEVENTY-FOUR

CHLOE

Now

The day crawls by. I check on Jameson every chance I get, and by midafternoon, he's awake, though groggy.

"They think I'll be okay," he says when I enter. "I even get to eat." But what he holds up is hardly food—rather, green gelatin with a white plastic spoon sticking out of it.

The room is dark, the blinds drawn against the brilliant afternoon sun that would otherwise shine through the window. I stand in the doorway, watching him as he adjusts the sheet and blanket, places the gelatin cup on the bedside table, and waves to me to come in.

"Come sit."

I enter but pull up a chair instead of taking the spot beside him on the bed.

"How are you?" My voice comes out in a whisper.

Jameson lays his head back on the pillow. He's raised the head of the bed, so he's upright, and he gazes at me. "Heard you might have saved my life."

"I didn't save your life. Someone would have found you eventually."

"Maybe." He gives me his quarter smile.

"Do you remember what happened?"

"No. No memory since last night. Since I dropped you off at the parking lot." His lips turn up. "But I remember everything before that."

Jameson continues to stare at me. He reaches out a hand for mine, and I give it to him, nervously glancing toward the door. But Elton's working in the cardiac ICU on another floor. Jameson is in the neuro ICU.

"The neurologist said that might happen. She said your memory might be spotty for a while."

"You need to be careful." Jameson squeezes my hand.

"So do you. You're a sitting duck in here."

"Nah. Cameras, remember." He nods at the overhead camera. "It's not on, but I can ask them to turn it on tonight."

"Laura knows to turn them off." I share about Mr. Gardner, the cameras shut off with precise timing around his death. "There's more," I say. "Laura responded to the rapid response fast. Faster than she should have been able to—I watched her walk down the hall. And she looked at me like she... like she knew what we're doing."

Jameson flinches. "My own sister? Trying to kill me?"

"But she didn't. She didn't kill you. She's never failed before, at least not as far as we know, right?"

He sits back and closes his eyes. "Yeah. You're right. I just can't believe it's her."

"She's trying to tell us to stop."

Jameson turns to look at me again. "But we can't."

I meet his eyes. "I know."

* * *

At seven that night, I'm out of duties to fulfill as a nurse practitioner. Actually, I've been done for hours, coming up with extra tasks and doing research at my laptop—namely, on Laura Smith. But she's clean. Even cleaner than Jameson, with a spotless work history, no disciplinary action so far as I can tell, and plenty of hours at a free clinic downtown to help patients manage cardiac medications.

I check on Jameson one last time, sharing that I've found nothing new—but then he's her brother.

"Not surprising," he says. "She never got in trouble as a kid, either. Somehow always found a way to point the finger at me."

He says it with a smile, but his words hit home—she finds a way to blame it on him. And it was all too convenient this time, wasn't it? Jameson does physician-assisted suicide. Given society's morals against it, he looked guilty from the start.

"Grab my laptop from the office. We're connected on social media. Maybe you'll..." He waves a hand. "Notice something I didn't."

"Okay." It's a solid point. I could see that Laura has profiles on Facebook and Instagram, but both are private. With his computer and log-ins, I'll have access.

"You should go home. Dawn's my nurse tonight. I told her no visitors after you leave, and she'll watch the door like a hawk. I'm on a monitor." He points up. "Camera's even turned on. Nothing bad's going to happen."

SEVENTY-FIVE

CHLOE

Now

I walk from Jameson's room to the cardiac ICU. Elton scurries between two rooms, sanitizing his hands at warp speed as he explains something to a resident—Dr. Michaels it looks like—so I wave goodbye without stopping. I spare another thought for Jameson. But he's right. I can't stay here all night. And I can't camp out in his room. I don't know what's happening between Elton and me, but staying would almost certainly ruin any chance of a future for us.

The drive home is rote, the twists and turns of the suburb easy enough. The neighborhood doesn't feel like home, though. These people with their loud children and perfect lawns, and with summer nearing an end, fall decorations already up. We're still unpacking boxes, still trying to turn our house into a home.

For a moment, I long for somewhere easier to care for—a condo, like Jameson has. Maybe I was wrong, thinking this sort of life was for me. I pull into the garage and put my car in park. Probably, all this is best sorted out *after* we've proven Laura is the killer. Once we're safe and our patients are safe. When Elton and I have talked.

But then what?

Elton? Or Jameson?

I can't imagine saying goodbye to either of them.

Inside, I pour myself a bourbon on ice and sink into the couch, Jameson's laptop at the ready. My phone sits nearby, and I text him.

Chloe: *Okay?*

Jameson texts back instantly.

Jameson: *No. They served me more hospital food. I am anything but okay.*

It makes me smile, and I open his laptop, type in the same password that I used years ago, and it gives me access.

I freeze.

Our wedding photo is the background image. Both of us barefoot, Jameson in long slacks and a white T-shirt, his long hair blown back by the breeze. Meanwhile, I'm in the requisite white dress, but something short and beachy.

I can't think about that now. Can't think about *us* or this impending wedding. Not yet.

I open the browser and go to Instagram. Laura's handle is easy to find—it's the same as it was before. And though it's private, Jameson has access. I scroll through photos, a few of her doing doctor-y things, but most of them images of fancy coffees or drinks she has out with friends. A few sunsets.

A trip to Victoria, BC, recently, where she posed with a noble-looking horse. And just below that, photos of a beach. I pull up the post and scroll through several photos, mostly selfies of her with a couple of other doctors who work at the hospital.

The next several posts are more of the same. Nothing interest-ing. Nothing helpful. All tagged as being in Cabo.

I notice the date.

May 15.

She was in Mexico the day Cassandra was killed.

SEVENTY-SIX

CHLOE

Now

It can't be Laura. She couldn't have killed Cassandra while out of the country.

I stare at the screen, sorting out the facts in my head.

No, wait. It can be. Maybe she didn't post these photos *while* she was in Mexico. Maybe she went, then posted them when she got back. The way Laura glared at me—her gaze piercing, *challenging* me—that wasn't normal. That wasn't the look of someone merely worried for her brother.

I snatch up my phone and dial Jameson's cell, hands trembling as I scroll quickly through the rest of her Instagram feed. I pull up Facebook—maybe she posted the photos there in real time. Or even on a different day, proving she posted them after the fact.

But her feed is nearly empty. Birthday wishes from last year and little else. She's not an active user.

The phone rings and rings.

"Come on, Jameson, pick up," I mutter. But he doesn't. Eventually, it rolls to voicemail. I pull my phone away from my ear and glare at the screen, like that will somehow change something. I frown. Jameson had his phone on him when I left. Had texted me minutes ago. Maybe it's silenced. Maybe he has a visitor in the room.

Call me ASAP, I text him.

I take a sip of bourbon and stand up, pace the room, avoid looking at the framed photo of us that Elton must have unpacked and placed on the mantel. One minute ticks by, then two.

No word from Jameson.

I pick up the phone, call again. Voicemail again, but this time, it doesn't ring. It goes straight to his answering message. *You've reached Jameson Smith, please leave—*

He wouldn't have turned his phone off. Maybe the battery died. But that's hard to believe—he has a charger at the hospital. It wouldn't have been hard to ask someone to grab it for him.

I curse. Something feels off.

I try calling once more, then give up. I scroll through my list of contacts and call the hospital directly. Two rings, and thank god, someone answers.

"Neuro ICU," I say. The operator connects me, and it rings through to the unit secretary. I hold my breath, waiting, a scratching over the line as they pick up the phone, silence an alarm, and finally say:

"Neuro ICU, this is Peter."

"Peter." I don't try to hide the relief in my voice that it's someone I know, someone who will help me. "It's Chloe Woods. Can you connect me to Jameson's room?"

"Hi, Chloe. Sure thing, just a sec."

I perch on the edge of the couch, biting my lip, waiting for Jameson's voice to come across the line. I just want to ask him about Laura, about when she was in Mexico, but suddenly it's more than that. Suddenly, the fact his cell phone is going straight to voicemail seems like something more—something bad. A fine sweat breaks out along my neck. A feeling wells up deep inside me.

Something bad has happened.

The words echo through my brain before I can stop them, that same dread and fear as when Nathan died and I realized maybe the worst had happened—maybe Jameson had enjoyed what he'd done.

"Hold on a sec, sweetie, he's not answering. I'll go check in his room. Maybe he's asleep."

My stomach swims. *Not answering?*

Seconds tick by. I wander through the house, phone pressed to my ear, unable to set it down or stop walking. My bag is in the kitchen, next to my keys, and I go wait by them, ready to snatch them up and race back to the hospital.

"Not in there. Maybe he talked a nurse into taking him to the cafeteria? You know how bad the hospital food is."

I waver. He has a point. Jameson *had* talked about how bad the food was. And sometimes reception could be sketchy in the hospital—it's possible he'd hit a dead zone. In normal circumstances, I'd call up Laura and ask her to find him.

But this is anything but normal. Laura can't be trusted. The only other person who could help at the hospital is Elton. Elton, who isn't exactly Jameson's biggest fan right now.

"Okay, thanks." My voice comes out weak, and I disconnect. I'm being paranoid. I'll just wait. I'll give him twenty minutes, then call again.

I settle back on the couch with my drink and click around Laura's social media. She doesn't post often, and the rest of her feed includes well-angled photos of fancy cocktails, selfies with friends, an occasional shot with her family at the holidays. An arm wrapped around her fraternal twin, Jameson. I try to read her expression, what lies behind her eyes, but it's impossible.

At fifteen minutes, I can wait no longer, and dial Jameson's cell again, and again, it goes straight to voicemail. I call Peter, who dutifully checks a second time, only to report, "No one there, sorry."

It's not just the threat of Laura. It's also the fact Jameson has a head injury—and people with head injuries don't always make the best decisions. I stare at the photo over the fireplace, indecisive, then dial once more—this time, I dial Elton.

Two rings, then to voicemail. Like when someone refuses a call. My brow wrinkles as I stare down at the phone and try again. But again, the call is refused. It's entirely possible he's busy with a patient. But this matters—in fact, it could be an emergency. I call the hospital again, but this time ask for the cardiac ICU, where Elton works.

"Cardiac ICU." It's Cara's voice.

"Hi, Cara. It's Chloe. Can you find Elton for me, please? He's not answering his phone and it's important."

"Oh, he's not working on the unit tonight. He volunteered to float."

I open my mouth, shut it. That's strange. Elton rarely volunteers to float—his specialty is cardiac, though he'll occasionally go to the medical ICU, a mix of generally sick patients. It's odd, too, given that he's working a sixteen-hour shift today. Typically, nurses keep the patients they've had all day, because it's a lot more work to pick up new patients and learn about and care for them for four hours than keeping ones you already know. But sometimes, you need a break from tough patients you've had all day. Maybe that's why.

"Oh, okay. Do you know the number for the medical ICU? I don't think I've called down there before. Or can you transfer me?"

Cara takes a moment to answer. "Actually, he's in the neuro ICU tonight."

This time, it's me who takes a beat to respond. "The neuro ICU?"

Elton hates the neuro ICU. He can't stand working with patients who are often confused and combative. "Are you sure?"

"I'm sure. Want me to transfer you?"

"Actually, I'm okay. Thanks. I'll try his cell again."

I hang up the phone and sink into the nearest chair. My mind twists and connects the facts, until suddenly, the pieces of the puzzle fit together in an entirely different way.

There's one other person who was in Seattle and is now in Portland.

One other person who had access to patients throughout the hospital.

One other person who had the opportunity, and maybe, the motive.

And he's working in a unit he despises. A unit Jameson is currently on but missing from.

It's not Laura.

It's Elton.

SEVENTY-SEVEN

CHLOE

Now

It can't be Elton.

I'm connecting dots that don't exist, just like I did before—with Jameson, with Laura.

I reach for the bourbon, then set it down, thinking better of clouding my mind further.

"No, no, no..." I brace my hands against the counter. I don't want it to make sense. It *can't* make sense. But it does. Maybe even more so than it being Laura.

He was in Seattle—even if temporarily—and now is in Portland.

He came ahead of time to start his job, to buy our house, meaning he would have been in town in mid-May, when Cassandra was killed. Debra died on the same unit he was on. He was in George's room the day he died, and as a nurse would have plenty of knowledge and access to the cameras to turn them off and on.

It's all speculation. But something feels off, about Jameson disappearing at the hospital, about Elton volunteering to float to a unit he hates during a sixteen-hour shift.

Keys in my hand, I race for the car. My thoughts race alongside me as I exit the garage and yank the car onto the road, rushing for the hospital. Toward Jameson, toward Elton.

I hope I'm wrong.

SEVENTY-EIGHT

CHLOE

Now

I skip the parking lot altogether and park illegally on the side of the road.

"Ma'am, you can't—" a hospital security guard yells, but I wave a hand, cutting him off.

"I'm a provider, there's an emergency!"

It's not a lie.

I run inside and to the elevator, stabbing at the button half a dozen times. I'm breathless, and it can't move fast enough to get to Jameson's floor. I keep picturing Elton. Imagining him acting so surprised to see me in San Diego—hell, I hadn't even recognized him; we worked together briefly, and only for a short while. He never asked questions about Jameson. Maybe because he knew what happened.

I stab the button again, and finally, *finally*, the doors part, and I shove through.

"Where's Jameson?" I ask Peter, who's on the phone. He blinks up at me through his glasses.

"Pardon?"

"Have you seen him?"

"Hold, please." He covers the mouthpiece of the phone and fixes me with a glare. "Now, Ms. Chloe, what in the world—"

"Never mind." I yank away and go toward Jameson's room. It's empty—the blood pressure cuff hangs there, when it should be around his arm. The pulse oximeter, the little clamp that measures his oxygenation, hangs there, too. Like he stood up and took off. An ICU patient can't just take off—if they're leaving the unit, a nurse has to go with them. Even Jameson, even merely to the cafeteria. I duck out and search for the nurse he had earlier, but when I spot her, she's down the hall with another patient.

"Dawn, where's Jameson?" I call. Heads turn my way. I'm being loud, frantic, in a place where loud and frantic means there's an emergency. Well, there *is*.

"Sorry, we were short-staffed. Elton took him over at seven." She turns back to her patient, helping the elderly man ambulate slowly down the hall.

The hall around me squeezes, contorts for a moment in my vision. Elton should have never taken Jameson—*would* have never taken him on as a patient. First, because he didn't like him. And second, because it was borderline inappropriate—you don't care for someone you personally know, especially someone with the sort of relationship we all have.

The lingering doubt starts to melt away.

I walk back to Peter. "Call Laura Smith. Tell her I need her here ASAP. It's an emergency."

Peter gapes, but he does as asked, and as soon as he's completed the task, I have another request. Half of me wants to not raise the alarm because it might put pressure on Elton to do something if he knows people are looking for him, looking for Jameson.

But I need help. My heart nearly pounds out of my chest, thinking of the possibilities. This hospital is huge, with six-hundred-plus patient beds and a dozen or more outpatient clinic areas. My best bet is to have others looking for them, too.

"I need you to call a code gray for Jameson Smith and Elton Woods." A code gray is putting everyone on the lookout—usually for a lost or confused patient. But technically, Jameson is a patient, and we can't find him.

Peter stares at me. "You've got to be kidding. They *work* here."

"I'm not kidding. Do it. Please. Or go get a coffee, and I'll do it."

Any goodwill I've earned with Peter is burned in that moment—he's scared to call a code gray on staff, a doctor and nurse no less, but he's also not about to turn his job over to me out of fear. Jaw stiff, he reaches for the phone.

"Code gray," he announces into the phone. "Dr. Jameson Smith and nurse Elton Woods. code gray, I repeat—" He repeats the code three times. Meanwhile, I start searching—opening every door to every room, closet, bathroom. When I've completed this unit, I go back toward the cardiac ICU, which Elton would be most familiar with. Somewhere along the way, Peter joins me, and Cara, too. I know security guards will have been dispatched, and Jameson's face is familiar throughout the whole hospital—anyone who's seen him will report back. Hopefully, we find him.

And hopefully, when we do, he's still alive.

SEVENTY-NINE

CHLOE

Now

Thirty minutes pass. I've searched two floors and all the staircases.

I try both their numbers every few minutes, hoping I'll magically hear the ring down the hall and race to the rescue. Peter went to call the police when we put together that no one had seen Jameson in over an hour—and that no one in the cafeteria had seen him, either.

Laura arrives as I come back to the cardiac ICU, almost out of breath from darting around the hospital. Her face is pink with exertion, her chest heaving as she stalks toward me.

"What the hell is going on, Chloe?" That hard look again. "What did you do to him? Where is he?"

Her questions leave me speechless for a moment, but then it hits me—"You think I'm the killer."

She cocks her head to one side, repositions her purse over her shoulder. She doesn't say no.

"I'm not," I say. "I thought Jameson was the killer. And then we thought *you* were the killer."

Her eyes widen. "Wait, what? He said you were—you thought I...?"

I fill her in on what's happened—Jameson and me in his condo, talking through the wall, then adding up the facts of who it could be—how she looked as suspicious as anyone. But then how Jameson disappeared tonight, how Elton did, too. How Elton, now that I thought of it, was as good a suspect as anyone.

"That's why you were glaring at me when I found him on the floor in his office," I say.

She blinks, still taken aback, then spares me a glance as she runs a hand through her dark hair. "That's why *you* were glaring at *me*."

We spend a long moment digesting it all.

"Elton? Your fiancé. You think he's the killer?"

"I think so." That sinking feeling all over again. With Jameson I had been wrong, but the feeling is familiar, regardless —wondering how it was happening right under my nose. How I never saw the signs.

But if it was Elton, there were no signs. He was kind and loving and outgoing. But moving here, he's also been... anxious and jealous. Paranoid something's going on with Jameson.

Jealous.

If he was spying on me, tracking my online computer searches, he'd know I've been watching Jameson. Even after all this time, caught up on my ex-husband. Is it possible...?

"Where could they be?" Laura wonders out loud. "Shoot. What if they're outside? No one's outside at night here. That's why it was so easy for someone to kill Cassandra. I'll go check."

She runs for the nearest staircase. Around us, other staff are searching, but they think they're just looking for a patient who's MIA—they don't realize the truth of it. That we're actually looking for a serial killer and who we suspect is his next victim.

Jameson knows too much.

And Jameson is the man pulling my attention away from Elton.

If ever there was motive, that's it.

Twenty minutes later, we've still made no progress finding them. I'm beginning to wonder if Elton dragged Jameson out of the hospital and into his car—I text Laura, asking her to check the parking lot for the Honda. But thinking of that, I wonder why Jameson wouldn't simply call out for help. Even with a head injury, he was capable of doing that much.

Or, aside from that, where could they have gone where he *couldn't* get help? I can think of only two places. The morgue—among the dead, where there are no staff at night.

Or our office. Our office down a quiet hallway with a door that locks.

EIGHTY

CHLOE

Now

I walk down the quiet hallway alone. I keep my steps soft, so the linoleum won't squeak beneath my soles. The corner is just ahead, and I glance around it before making the turn. The office door is shut tight, but a light is on, shining through the crack at the bottom of the door.

And then, muffled voices.

I press closer to hear, trying to keep my breathing soft, shallow. Inside, my pulse gallops, and all I want to do is burst through the door and demand to know what's going on.

But I think I know.

And that means I must remain silent.

"I think it's clear what I want." Elton's voice, eerily low.

"You want her," Jameson replies, his tone hard. "You wanted her from the beginning."

A soft, sinister laugh. I can tell it's Elton, but it doesn't *sound* like him. It sounds like his evil twin. "And once again, I've gotten her."

"Why did you come here, then? You already had her. Why risk it?"

Elton snorts. "She wanted to come back. Not me. I was happy to continue on traveling, living this new life. But she suggested moving to the Pacific Northwest. Portland." A pause. I press myself even closer to the door, not wanting to miss a word. "I didn't know if she still loved you or if she was angry about what you did to Nathan or... maybe she really did want to move to Portland. I had to find out, though, make sure I really have her heart. Before I marry her."

I fight back a gasp working itself up in my throat.

"She told you about Nathan?" Jameson asks.

"No. But it wasn't hard to work out. You kill people. Her brother was sick. You visited, then her brother was dead. Doesn't take a genius."

Jameson doesn't say anything. I imagine him sitting in his chair, going back and forth with Elton. Or maybe Elton tied him up. Jameson is a strong man, as strong as Elton. He must have *something* on him if Jameson is just sitting there, having this conversation. Also, he's injured. Vulnerable.

"But I needed to know," Elton continues. "Getting the house in Portland was easy. A job for me working as a nurse was easy. But a job for a new nurse practitioner? Not quite so easy. I had to help her out in that respect."

"You killed Cassandra," Jameson says.

"I needed a job opening. One that would put her close to you. So I could know for sure."

My blood goes cold. Elton arranged for the job—the job with Jameson. I should have known it couldn't be a coincidence.

"Turns out, she likes you a lot. Too much. I thought she'd leave the job. But no. She decided to stay. To *work* with you, her ex. That could only mean one thing—that she still loves you." Elton's voice lowers a notch. "People who get in my way have to go. You were in my way before, and it wasn't too hard to convince her of what you were. I take it she found the drugs in your dresser drawers?"

Jameson mutters something indecipherable. A jolt of shock runs through my whole body. *Elton planted the drugs.*

"We aren't so different. You *are* a killer. You just wait for people to be desperate enough they have to ask for help." Elton continues. "Does that make you feel good? Like you're some kind of hero?"

"So you've been killing our patients," Jameson says. "And you were in Seattle, too."

"I help them." Elton clears his throat. "Someone has to."

"And Debra?"

"Debra looked too closely."

I squeeze my eyes shut, barely able to take a breath as realization settles inside me. Elton. *My* Elton, a sweet, kind man who's always gone out of his way to show his love for me, to help others... It was all a façade.

Elton is actually a serial killer.

He arranged for it all—for Jameson and me to split up, and then for us to come back together when he realized I was still thinking of him. *I had to find out though... before I marry her.*

I try to sort out what that means—he wanted to know if I still loved Jameson. Because of what, a Google search or two? The desire to move back to the Pacific Northwest? Who doesn't google their ex occasionally? Or maybe, it was because he set this all up. Set Jameson up to look guilty before, so I'd end things. So I'd be single. Maybe he doubted I'd have chosen him otherwise.

"Well, this has been fun, but it's time for you to go. We'll make it look like an accident. Heroic doctor couldn't set his work aside for a single night. Returned to his office with a bad concussion. Fell, hit his head a second time, but this time... this time, you won't be so lucky."

His words are like an electric shock to my body. I have to stop him—have to save Jameson.

"You think she won't know?" Jameson asks. "Won't figure it out?"

"I think she'll figure something out. Maybe I'll make it look like your sister, or Dr. Michaels. Or maybe she'll think it was you all along, and you tricked her into thinking otherwise. Maybe you couldn't live with yourself. Now there's an idea— maybe you're suicidal. Realizing she's going to marry me in the end. Losing the love of your life once? Tragic. Twice? Most people wouldn't survive that."

I can't wait any longer. I don't have a plan. Have no clue how this will end. But I have to do *something*. I text Laura where we are along with: *911. It's Elton.* That way, even if I fail, they'll know he's been behind it since day one.

My hands shake as I shove the phone in my pocket and stare down at the doorknob. I reach out, twist it—but nothing.

It's locked.

EIGHTY-ONE
CHLOE

Now

A stretch of held breath makes the world go still. I breathe in, out, fish my key from my pocket, insert it, and press on the door once more. It opens, and I fall in, Elton catching me in his arms before I topple over.

The door slams shut. Locks.

And when Elton releases me, I spin, meeting his eyes, except he doesn't look like the caring, loving fiancé who spoke of three children and suggested we get a dog. The laugh lines in his face are taut, serious. His blue eyes no longer oceans to lose myself in, but depths of ice-cold water.

"Oh, hi. I was looking for you both." The words come out before I know what I'm doing—acting. Buying time. "What are you doing in here?" I glance at Jameson. "Shouldn't you be in bed?"

Jameson wears actual clothes instead of a gown, which is likely how he got out of his patient room and down the hall without anyone taking notice. But he looks anything but normal. A cut along one cheek. That same head wound, now open and blood streaming down it. Like Elton hit him again.

"I'm sorry, Chloe." Elton's lips curve into what is supposed to be a smile, but it's more of a sneer. Something about that expression sinks my heart, makes me realize there will be no acting my way out of this situation.

"For what? I told you I'd wait up for you. I don't mind that you're working late."

"He knows," Jameson mutters. "He knows everything." Jameson shifts his weight, leaning against the desk. The way he moves tells me he's been drugged. He almost staggers to stay upright. His eyes are glazed over, and he blinks, trying to stay aware.

"Everything," Elton echoes, too close to my ear, enunciating every sound in the word in a way that makes me shiver. "I know you've been obsessed with Jameson since you left him. And I figured, given that he killed your brother, that was okay. But then you started spending a lot of time with him, darling. Too much time."

I whip around and take a step back, putting space between us.

"I promised your ex-husband if he came quietly, I wouldn't hurt you. I have a feeling that's no longer an option." Elton tilts his head, presses his lips together in faux sorrow. "With our wedding coming up, no less. It will be tragic. Oh, I know." His eyes gleam. "Maybe he killed you—and then himself. Or it could be a Romeo and Juliet thing? You couldn't be together, so you both kill yourselves? Think of the headlines. Mm. No. Too attention-grabbing. Probably better to go with the physician-assisted suicide doc killing his own ex-wife. Still a headline, but less bright and shiny."

His words stun me, leave me wondering how I never saw this side of him—this sadistic, sociopathic side.

Sure, sometimes he seemed too good to be true. But I

figured after Jameson, the universe was finally giving something back to me.

Elton takes half a step forward and reaches a hand out. I look from it to his face, not sure what he wants—but sure I'm about to die if I don't do something. That Jameson will die, too. That the two lives I envisioned earlier—one of them with Elton, one with Jameson—neither will ever happen unless I do something to save myself.

And Elton will keep killing people. People like George and Cassandra and Debra. The cell phone vibrates in my pocket, but Elton doesn't seem to notice. He's too fixated on me.

"What?" I ask.

"Give me your ring."

"My ring?" I hold my hand—the sparkling engagement ring.

"People will assume you were having an affair. You took off your ring while you were alone with Jameson. But when you told him you were going to marry me, well, he got mad. He couldn't stop himself." Elton peers past me at Jameson. "Do you have a kit? Meds to kill someone in here?"

"Controlled substances," Jameson manages. "No. No, I don't."

I know he's telling the truth—the patient themself has to pick up the meds he prescribes. They self-administer, too. Jameson is just there to hold their hand.

"You're lying," Elton growls, shoving by me to wrap a hand around Jameson's throat. Jameson, though bigger, only staggers against his hold. The door is there—I could open it. Could escape. But I'd have to leave Jameson behind. But if we both stay here, we both die.

Before I can reach for it, I hear something—like a key, in the lock. The knob turns slowly.

Elton starts to yank around, to see if I'm doing something, but I rush at him, hit him in the kidney, like I learned in a self-defense class.

"God damn it," he bites out, flinching, but not going down. He turns his attention on me, releasing Jameson who falls to the floor. Those gorgeous blue eyes are anything but attractive now —vicious pools of anger—but he's looking at me as he raises a fist, which means he doesn't see when Laura slips in the door. When she readies a syringe.

When she stabs it into the big muscle in his arm and injects it as fast as she can.

He only realizes what's happening when it's too late. He turns, eyes wide, then falters. Before he can say anything— complain or yell or threaten—he crumples to the ground, unconscious.

EIGHTY-TWO

CHLOE

Now

The next hour is a blur—a rapid response called for Jameson, whose concussion hasn't been made any better by Elton's rough treatment and sedatives. For Elton, who received a huge dose of a paralytic and a sedative via Laura's syringe. "Of course I did it on purpose," she tells the police officer who questions her about it. "He was going to kill my brother. And my sister-in-law, too." Our eyes meet across the conference room we've been herded into, an unspoken communication shared between us. She gives me a tight, but real, smile.

I'm interviewed for hours about what's happened—about what I suspect Elton has done. I leave out everything in the past, only mention I noticed the deaths when I arrived here in Portland. And that Jameson noticed them, too. That together, we were trying to sort out if it was a random spike in deaths, or if there was something more to it.

"I never thought it was Elton, though," I say. And that's the honest-to-god truth.

I was wrong the first time I thought it was my significant other who was a killer.

Unfortunately, I completely missed it the second time around.

I can't help second guessing my ability to see these things—to notice these patterns—but I know from my research medical serial killers are notoriously hard to catch. Sick patients. The idea that we as medical providers should *do no harm*, and our belief that everyone around us feels the same way. We don't want to believe that the nurse across the unit has anything but a person's best interest at heart.

Elton is in jail, with a bail set high enough he won't be getting out anytime soon. Meanwhile, I stay awake every night, mentally combing through each and every travel assignment we went on. Remembering Elton attending codes or telling me after a shift about a patient who had died. The way he talked about it. I hadn't noticed anything at the time—it was normal nurse talk. But now, I wonder if I missed something.

Laura and I get Jameson home two days later. After she leaves, hugging us both and promising to stop by in the morning with fresh bagels, I sit at his bedside. I won't be staying the night. I've already decided that. I do love Jameson—do want to be with him—but it's all too much, too fast.

"Elton set me up to come here," I say. "I can't believe it. He was *testing* me."

Jameson nods from where he reclines on a stack of pillows. His dark eyes soak me in as though I might disappear if he looks away for even a moment.

"He said you were obsessed," Jameson murmurs, "With me."

"I thought you were a killer."

Jameson quirks up a lip. "You were wrong. And I'm so glad."

"Me too." I shift closer, and when he offers a hand, accept it.

We sit in silent reflection for what feels like a long time. It's a little like it used to be, but entirely different. The whole world has changed around us. *We've* changed.

"I have to tell you something," Jameson says in a tone that makes me tense. "Uncertainty, not knowing the truth, has caused all sorts of problems. So I want to be honest."

I look up from our clasped hands and meet his gaze.

"It wasn't all Elton."

EIGHTY-THREE

CHLOE

Now

"What?" I start to pull away, to wrench my hand from his. But his hand tightens over mine, holding me there.

"Not the killing." He shakes his head. "I told you everything about that before we got married. I do help people who don't live in states where physicians are allowed to help them when they choose to die, but that's the extent of it."

"Then what do you mean?" My words come out breathless, fast. Terror takes hold at the idea there's something I missed.

"I just mean..." He lowers his eyes, sighs. "I was watching you. I knew you were travel nursing. I knew where you were most of the time." He glances up. "The world of ICU medicine is pretty small. It wasn't hard. I always knew where you were, Chloe. And I knew you went to school to be a nurse practitioner."

Jameson hesitates, seems to have to force out his next words: "I had nothing to do with Cassandra, but when that job did open up, I pretended to be a recruiter and messaged you about it. And when you did, I told HR to hire you. Only you. Not to bother interviewing anyone else." He swallows, shuts his eyes for a moment, then looks at me. "Part of me did it for selfish reasons. Just because I wanted to see if you were happy. To be around you. And part of me did it because I worried you were killing people. I thought if I got close to you, I could help you. Help you stop before you got caught." He turns away, like he's ashamed. "So it wasn't just Elton. I couldn't have known he killed Cassandra or that he was seeing what you would do. But as much as he pushed you here—I pulled you."

I consider his words. Consider how much I wanted to move to Portland, to get a job here. It was like all three of us were pushing to get me here. Like the universe was conspiring for Jameson and me to end up in the same city again.

I get stuck on one fact, though. "You thought I was the killer and you were going to *help* me?" The thought both enthralls and confounds me.

"Well what else could I do? You were the woman I loved. *Are* the woman I *love*. I couldn't have turned you in. I hoped I could convince you to stop. And if that meant being with Elton, that was fine. But of course, some part of me hoped we'd someday get back together."

All that time, while I was searching for jobs in Portland, I kept getting turned down. And then I landed the perfect job. Because Elton killed Cassandra, because Jameson insisted they hire me. I'm aware I have enough experience to get hired on my own—I'm not concerned about *that*—more confused as to how to feel about all this.

Half of me is utterly charmed that if he thought I was killing people, he'd try to get me to stop instead of turning me in. That he loved me too much to send me to prison. The other half isn't sure how to react to him getting involved in the way he had.

Jameson squeezes my hand, and I look up to take him in—his dark, messy hair. Those brown eyes that I could happily drown in. The face that I've loved nearly since the day I met him.

"So what do you think?" he asks.

I study him, considering my words. But I know what I want. "I think we are a special kind of messed up. But that I wouldn't want my happily ever after with anyone else."

A LETTER FROM JESSICA

Dear Reader,

I want to say a huge thank you for choosing to read *The Good Doctor*. If you would like to keep up to date with my latest releases, please sign up at the following link. Your email address will never be shared, and you can unsubscribe at any time:

www.bookouture.com/jessica-payne

One of the questions I'm constantly asked is this: "Are your books based on real life?"

Well, yes and no.

None of my books are autobiographical. I'm never telling my own story while substituting a new name for the main character. That said, an author's books are made up of a million moments and impressions from their life. Maybe an idea they got while out for a run, or the feeling someone left them with—maybe a total stranger they glimpsed across the room. A relationship might be vaguely similar to one they've witnessed, or even had themselves, or perhaps they read an article they found fascinating and decided to wrap a plot around that idea.

All that said, I feel the need to clarify here, given the content of this book—while working as an RN, I never encountered anyone I thought was a medical serial killer. But I can see how one could easily slip through the cracks. Nurses and doctors encounter death on a daily basis.

The idea for *The Good Doctor* came to me while browsing a book on medical serial killers I got off my local "buy nothing" group. Then Chloe, Jameson, and Elton appeared in my head, as though they were waiting to be discovered, their relationships clear as day. I loved the push and pull between her ex-husband and her fiancé. And I knew who she'd end up with in the end. Maybe not very thriller author-y of me, but even in thrillers, characters and relationships matter the most. I scribbled the idea down in my notebook and didn't think much of it, until one day, it was the next book I wanted to write.

This was a difficult book to write in some ways. It's full of medical stuff, bits and pieces of code blues I attended, some of which ended in a prolonged life, some that ended in death. I also found myself illustrating the relationships between nurses and doctors and how nurse practitioners are sometimes treated.

A dear friend of mine, Annie (or the writing community may know her as Evie), was my residency mentor as I completed my doctorate to become a neonatal nurse practitioner. I knew as I wrote it that she'd love this book—laugh at the same places I did, nod along with the passive-aggressive way some providers treat nurse practitioners. Unfortunately, as I wrote about Nathan's battle with a deadly disease, Annie, a cancer survivor, had a sudden relapse and passed away. She never got to read this book. Never got to text me *Ugh, it's so true!* or leave a comment on the early manuscript like *Actually, I think XYZ is what the doctor might have said here.* I have a feeling she would have liked it, though. Writing about these topics while seeing a friend go through it made it that much more difficult, but hopefully also imbued it with more realness, more humanity. I hope that all came through. And Annie, I miss you.

In conclusion, I would like to speak directly to you, the reader. I appreciate you. I appreciate that you love to read and that you picked up my book of all books. Thank you SO much.

I would love to connect with you—I'm active on Instagram

and Facebook, and have a couple newsletters, too, where I reach out about upcoming book releases, occasionally do giveaways, etc.

https://jessicapayne.net/newsletter

Thanks for joining Chloe, Jameson, and Elton in their book. I have two other twisty thrillers I know you'll love—*Make Me Disappear* and *The Lucky One*—and my next book will be out in 2024!

https://jessicapayne.net

facebook.com/authorjessicapayne

twitter.com/authorjesspayne

instagram.com/jessicapayne.writer

goodreads.com/authorjesspayne

tiktok.com/@authorjesspayne

ACKNOWLEDGMENTS

Thank you to Kimberly Brower, my badass literary agent. From helping me figure out an idea to getting that first draft just right, I'm so grateful we are on this publishing journey together.

Thank you to Joy Kozu. You are insightful and honest, and your input always makes my book better. I appreciate you.

Thank you to my editor Kelsie Marsden. You continue to pull out the most tantalizing threads of my books and help me make them stronger, the book better.

Jess Readett, I'm honored to continue working with you on publicity. Thank you for everything.

Thank you to the entire team at my fab publisher, Bookouture. I know so many people play a hand in my manuscripts becoming books, and I appreciate you all. Special thanks to Mandy, Ian, and John, for the edits and making my book shine.

Thank you also to an incredible cover designer, Eileen Carey. Each one is better than the last. You are so talented, and I appreciate you making my books beautiful.

I've been remiss in properly thanking my audiobook narrators. You all have brought my books to life. Thank you to Amelia Sciandra, who narrated Noelle in *Make Me Disappear*. To Josh Wichard, the voice of Daniel in *Make Me Disappear*, and now, Jameson in *The Good Doctor*. To Jennifer Woodward, who brought Vivian alive in *The Lucky One*. And to Lisa Rost-Welling, the amazing narrator of Chloe in *The Good Doctor*.

My husband, Virgil, who I feel the need to repeat had no idea he was marrying a writer. I know you thought you were marrying an RN, and someday, a nurse practitioner. Things haven't gone as planned, but I think we're both happier for it. Thank you for giving me the space I've needed to take a dream and make it a reality.

Thank you, Emma, for making me feel like a pretty cool author-mom. I'm so impressed with the stories you're already weaving.

To Sara Read, who I've had the great luck of having a parallel journey with. Who would have thought we'd get so lucky as to stumble upon one another and become best writing friends?

To Jaime Lynn Hendricks, fellow thriller author and plot twist extraordinaire. Love you, friend.

To Mary Keliikoa for reading an early version of this book and providing feedback. Thank you also for all of our random check-ins. We all need author friends like you!

With this book, I've had the great pleasure of gaining a new critique partner, Ande Pliego. Ande, I'm so glad to have met you and started working with you. Thank you for helping me make this book better.

To a new writing friend, Tara Goedjen, thank you for your eyes on sections of this book! You helped bring it along to what it is now!

To the Porch Crew, a most excellent group of women who always have my back and cheer me on. I am so grateful for each and every one of you. Mikey, thank you for bringing this amazing community together.

I, of course, must call out #MomsWritersClub. I am still amazed at this community we have formed. Thank you all for being a part of it, for your support, for your friendship. I am so glad we have one another. For anyone reading this, find us over on Twitter! #MomsWritersClub. Everyone is welcome.

To my launch group, filled with family, friends, and even complete strangers who are helping me on this journey, thank you so much for your time, for the fact you keep picking up my books, for spreading the word. You make a huge difference.

I would be remiss without mentioning the powerhouse that is Bookstagram. It is such an amazing community, and I have been so embraced by you all. Thank you for taking the time to read my books, to post and shout about them, to let my covers fill your feed. I appreciate each and every one of you.

I would also like to thank Browsers Bookshop in Olympia, WA, especially Andrea and all the amazing booksellers who work there. Thank you for all your support. Reader, if you are in, near, or traveling through Olympia, Washington, make sure you find time to go by Browsers. It's an absolutely delightful bookstore!

Last, I would like to acknowledge you (yes, you!), the person reading this book right now. Thank you for giving my book your time, your attention, your headspace.

Printed in Great Britain
by Amazon

28025258R00219